Six Inch Nail

OWEN PITT

Copyright © 2019 Owen Pitt

All rights reserved.

ISBN-:978-1-78972-198-0

DEDICATION

My thanks to all the friends, the family and the strangers who have helped me on this journey.

Special thanks to my wife Nicola, (she'd kill me if I didn't mention her first), for her patience and her positive bias.

To Dave Thomson and Elaine Flynn for helping me to edit and correct the schoolboy errors.

To Carol Bennett, who edits for her own husband the Author Paul J Bennett, and who gave me encouragement and advice on how to go about publishing my first book.

And to the countless other people who've encouraged or contributed in any way.
Hopefully you all know who you are.

ACKNOWLEDGMENTS

This is a work of fiction.

Similarities to real people, places, or events are entirely coincidental.

To my good friends across the pond, please note that all spellings and grammar are based on UK English (with a bit of Scots thrown in).

CHAPTER ONE

Four months ago

I was starting to feel annoyed. No. Not quite annoyed just yet, because if I *was* feeling annoyed, my ire would have needed to have been directed at someone, and the truth was that I really had no-one else to blame for how I felt right then, other than myself.

So maybe not quite annoyed, but certainly 'niggled.'

I was niggled by the fact that I really couldn't think about anything other than the events of the previous night, which I guess, given the circumstances, was nothing to be surprised at. There I was, driving to one of the biggest sales meetings I'd ever had, and apart from the obvious need to pay attention to the road, I would have dearly liked to be able to concentrate on practising my sales pitch; but it was not to be.

'MURDERER. MURDERER. MURDERER'

The surface of the road beneath my wheels had been laid in sections and every thirty yards or so they bumped as they thrummed, beating out a rhythmic tattoo,

'MURDERER. MURDERER. MURDERER.' The same accusing words tumbled over and over, intersecting with every train of thought I tried to put in motion.

I supposed that I should have felt sickened by the horrific violence of my actions the previous night. After all, the act of taking another person's life is supposed to leave its mark on you. I *knew* that I ought to have felt guilty about tasering the fuck out of Les before smashing his skull in. But the simple truth was that the only regrets I had that morning were that my actions of the previous night were occupying my thoughts so much that it was threatening to ruin the biggest sales pitch of my life.

I imagine that sounds harsh to most people, but the simple truth is that whilst you can pretend to be someone else, when you peel back the outer layers to reveal your own true personality, you can't escape from who you really are. And there was no getting away from the fact, that in my case, the *real* me was a murdering sociopath.

****

Thirteen months ago I was given the news which brought my world crashing down about me. In truth, my drinking had already gained a momentum which made it difficult to control and with the benefit of hindsight, I had already sunk to an unhealthy depth of introspection and depression. But when those smartly dressed harbingers of doom came knocking it proved to be the proverbial straw which would break the camel's back.

Festering in my own self-pity as I was, it was like breaking the seal on a packet of food which was already out of date. The slow rot which had already begun, suddenly took on a life of its own. To the point where it replaced everything which had gone before, leaving no room for anything other than regret and decay.

I had been sitting in my living room slowly working my way through a bottle of whisky and drunkenly reminiscing over times passed; of memories both good and bad. I needed no television to entertain me that evening as the clarity of the past cut through the fog of the drunken present and I was happy enough to sit in my favourite old armchair with the murmur of a radio in the kitchen softly filtering through, and simply to reminisce. And inevitably, when I contemplated such things, my mind turned back to the root cause of almost every bad decision I'd made in life. My beautiful wife Judy.

CHAPTER TWO

The majority of my childhood days elude memory. Lost amongst the poisoned brain cells from the countless sessions of boozing, or simply vanished in the mists of time. I don't remember my first day at school and I don't remember my last. I have forgotten the names of every teacher that ever taught me and I barely remember the names of any of my classmates.

Except two.

Judy's first day at primary school cuts a clearer memory than my own did. Possibly because I was only five for mine and yet by the time she had hers I was eleven.

A middle aged teacher with an Australian twang had the unenviable task of trying to educate us that day. Whilst her name has long since been forgotten, I remember clearly the cardigan she wore. I remember it because it was bright orange, with a map of Australia printed on the back and, having once pointed out to us on a separate map exactly where she came from, it soon became the perfect target. Every time she turned her back on us a half a dozen of the most unruly kids immediately took the opportunity to try and hit it with our makeshift pea-shooters, using small rolled up balls of paper fired through bic pen casings. Miraculously she never seemed to cotton on. Either that or she just didn't care.

We'd had no idea that someone new was about to join our little class that morning, we'd had no notice. Out of the blue, it seemed, in the middle of our morning lessons and without a word of pre-amble, she was paraded into our classroom and stood before us while the teacher introduced her as Judy Simmons.

Eleven years old and that was her first day of school. Up until that moment, social interaction with kids her own age and the institution of education were completely alien environments to her and she looked nervous and skittish as she stood there with her hands clasped before her. Like a deer about to bolt. She wore a school uniform which had perhaps been purchased that same day from Woolworths; fresh from its packets and with the tell-tale tramline creases running vertically up the front of her blouse.

With scrubbed pink skin but still enigmatically wild-haired and wide-eyed, she brought to mind a child who had been raised by wolves before being thrust into the midst of civilization. Like Tarzan coming home to Greystoke. Every single thing about her exuded an aura of non-conformity.

Prior to that fateful day, she had been home-schooled by her mum, Doree, and probably she would have continued to do so had her father, Nigel, not had the accident which robbed him of the use of his legs.

Before then, he had spent most of each year abroad, doing whatever it was that Marine Geologists usually did, but six months earlier, whilst working in some backwater third world country, he had been run over by a horse and cart, of all things, (there has to be a joke there, but it still manages to evade me after all of these years). In a stroke, Nigel's jet-setting lifestyle changed into a daily drudgery of mind-numbing boredom and inactivity.

The devastating injury was a twist of fate which Nigel never came to terms with. Without the stimulus of work, travel and male bonding, he turned his attention and efforts towards making everyone else's lives a misery, with the hapless Doree being the nearest, the slowest moving and the most convenient target.

The first big change for Judy and her parents was that they had to move from their Edwardian home in the heart of busy Walthamstow into a smaller bungalow on the outskirts. Then came the thankless dreariness of caring for the increasingly obnoxious Nigel who chose to use his disability as a reason to resent everything, and everyone, else. It was no longer feasible for Mother and Daughter to spend their days as they chose and the ever more demanding Nigel made home learning no longer viable or desirable. So Judy had to go to school; home was no longer her sanctuary.

It's a sad story, I suppose, but the simple truth is that Nigel was a mean and cantankerous old sod and if he had never been crippled, they probably wouldn't have moved and I probably never would have met Judy; so as far as I'm concerned: fuck him.

That first day at school was an almighty shock to Judy. At eleven years old, the rest of us were already unknowingly institutionalised, sitting at our allotted desks and wearing the same uniforms, cheerfully submitting to the same routines every morning.

The teacher introduced her to the class and I still remember the collective intake of breath when she told us that up until now, Judy had been 'home-schooled.' To our immature minds, it had seemed the equivalent of having been brought up in a circus. As she stood there with a bewildered look of confusion on her face, it's difficult to say what it was about her that made me feel so utterly bowled over. But whatever the reason, I fell instantly head over heels in love.

In fact, I had fallen so hard that I didn't speak to her for at least another month. The girls and the boys in our school usually sat separately in classes, intermingling only when forced to by teachers. But when Judy first came to us and was introduced as someone who had been homeschooled, everyone, girls and boys, wanted to be her friend, just so they could hear her story.

However, with the passage of time, it soon became clear that Judy was used to being something of a loner and that she was happy to keep it that way. She had been brought up without the company of children her own age and her only previous social interactions had been with her parents. She wasn't interested in the latest fashions or the latest pop groups and if she spoke about music at all, it was of bands we had never heard of. She barely even seemed to have watched television.

Her initial popularity was therefore short-lived and within a matter of weeks, she was left to her to her own devices. At break times she could usually be found in self-imposed solitude, with her head in a book and for my part, it was a solitude which I was ill-equipped to penetrate. Until Bradley stepped in.

Bradley

It seems an inevitable fact of life that in every large group of children, amongst the different backgrounds, personalities, shapes, sizes and colours, there will be at least one bully and ours came in the form of Bradley Thomas. With the benefit of hindsight, and given my own failings, it seems inevitable that Bradley and I would eventually come to blows.

Like most of the bullies I've ever met, he wasn't particularly big and he wasn't particularly strong. Back then, he was a little shorter than me and still had a generous layer of puppy fat still clinging to him. In the modern era he'd probably be regarded as normal in that respect but back in the 1970's he was slightly tubby compared to the rest of us. Despite his less than impressive physical stature he still managed to stand out from the crowd with a shock of metallic ginger hair sprouting out above a heavily freckled face. He also had two older brothers with inflated reputations for violence which was enough to make the rest of the kids wary of crossing him.

He was also in possession of a razor-sharp tongue and a quick wit to match and so, unlike a lot of bullies, he was still popular amongst the majority of his classmates. I say the majority because, of course, every bully needs a victim. The weakest lad in our class was a little chap called Timothy something or other. I don't recall his surname and I don't even remember what he looked like, just the fact that even at such a young age, fate had already marked him out as someone who was destined to spend the rest of his life as a victim.

Like every bully the world over, Bradley had a keen eye for anyone weaker than him, or more importantly for anyone unwilling to defend themselves and so the majority of his attention was concentrated on Timothy, or 'Little Timmy' as he was forever known. Barely a single lesson went by without Bradley finding some way to crack a joke at Little Timmy's expense and it was usually funny enough to have the rest of the class in gales of laughter.

So, for the most part, Bradley's bullying tended to be verbal, although he still wasn't averse to giving Little Timmy, or anyone else smaller than him, a sly dig when he felt like it and playtimes usually entailed Bradley taking every opportunity he had to menace

Little Timmy or anyone else smaller than him. The mere threat of violence was usually sufficient to make them hand over anything that Bradley demanded, from chocolate biscuits to top trumps playing cards.

They say that children can be heartless and it's certainly true of how the rest of us kids reacted. Nobody ever stepped in to stand up for Little Timmy and nobody ever tried to help him. For the most part, Brad was cracking funny jokes and as long as it wasn't at my own expense, that was good enough for me.

I feel that I ought to look back now with a certain sense of shame at how we collectively let Tim be picked on so unremittingly, and certainly, if I was engaged in polite conversation with *normal* people, I would be expressing my personal indignation at such a cruel world. But the truth is, to my mind at least, bullying is a fact of life and always will be. It's a part of the natural order. It doesn't make it right and it's not something I condone, but there's nothing I can do that will ever change it. I know that I *should* feel sorry for the likes of Little Timmy, but the truth is I didn't then and I don't now.

The way I see it, just because someone's bigger and stronger than you doesn't mean to say that you have to become their whipping boy. It's a fact of life that bullies only pick on people who are weaker or those who won't fight back. True, if you fight back hard, you might well lose, but bullies look for someone to dominate, not someone to fight, and so next time they're going to look elsewhere for easier pickings.

And then of course, there's always the final option, which is to just run away.

So I didn't have a great deal of sympathy for little Timothy and I'm not sure how much my classmates had either. We were mostly just glad that it wasn't us who had proved to be the weakest member of the pack. Bravery was something to be learned at a later stage in life; something for the grown-ups to practice.

However, after five years of sharing the same classroom, Bradley hadn't bothered himself with me before and we'd never had any kind of problem with each other. Until Judy arrived that is.

****

The summer break was just around the corner when Bradley and I first came to blows. I often wonder how such a seemingly innocuous little scrap between two boys could still haunt my memories, but I guess that the immediate aftermath and many of the paths we took later in life can all be traced back to that fateful day.

Hanging high in a perfect sky, the midday sun beat down on us without mercy, baking the black tarmacadam playing area with its painted white lined hopscotch areas almost to the point of melting. It was a hot and stifling day in July and in most countries, a hot day such as that would have counted as normal, but in the midst of a London suburb, it was still enough of a rarity to make headline news. The air was so hot that you could taste it as you breathed in; a dry heat carrying the bitter underlying taint of pollen which was bad news for the hay fever sufferers amongst us.

Beyond the softening tarmac surface lay the parched playing fields where almost every child in the school played football or tag, or simply lolled around in groups on the yellowed grass, passing their lunch breaks in whatever fashion they chose.

There were no health and safety bores worrying about sun hats and sun-cream back then. Just a couple of tired dinner ladies and an unlucky teacher loafing about, ready to break up any fights that might occur or to send any broken bones back into the 'office' to be tended to. They were the days when getting sunburnt was your own fault and not someone else's. It was just another one of life's lessons, teaching you to be more careful next time.

Almost the entire school was out there on the field that day; except for Judy and Bradley, and myself. I had popped inside to visit the toilets and as I stepped back out into the blistering heat to re-join my pals on the playing fields, I saw Judy.

By that time, Judy had taken to spending most of her break-times outside the history classroom and that day was no exception as she sat on her usual step clinging to a foot of shade with a well-thumbed book. Sure enough, as I stepped out of the shaded doorway and back into the midday furnace I looked to my right and there she was, away from the other kids playing football and kiss chase, book in hand.

This in itself would not have been a particularly unusual sight, but what set the scene apart that day was that, at first glance, she seemed to be playing a tug of war with Bradley, with her book playing the part of the rope.

Shielding my eyes and squinting against the brightness of the midday sun, I took a step nearer before realising that this was not a game of her own choosing. Her beautiful auburn hair had fallen across her face and fat tears rolled down her cheeks as she cried and pleaded with Bradley for the return of her precious book. But as much as she begged and she pleaded, saying that the book was a present from her mother, it was obvious that Bradley didn't care.

With the rest of the school's kids out on the playing fields and the lunchtime staff with them, we had that blistering corner of the playground to ourselves and there were no other witnesses to the scene being played out before me.

'But it's a book of poetry!' Bradley cried, obviously disgusted that anyone could choose to read such a thing. With a final effort, he tore the book from her grasp and stepped back. Judy leapt to her feet and tried desperately to regain ownership of the book but Bradley held it aloft and out of her reach.

By now she was blubbing uncontrollably and as the dirty tears streaked her stricken face all she kept saying was, 'But it's my mum's. It's my mums'

Her tears and her pleas seemed only to excite Bradley further and, gripping the thin paperback book with both hands, he ripped it cleanly into two halves. Then, with his freckled nose almost touching hers, he screamed into her face, 'What is your Mum, some kind of weirdo FREAK !'

That was a mistake. Had this been an exchange between Bradley and anyone else, I wouldn't have batted an eyelid, but despite having barely spoken a single word to her since she joined our school, as far as I was concerned Judy was *my* girl and as such she was strictly off limits to Bradley fucking Thomas. Or anyone else for that matter.

Without a moment's thought, I balled my fists and strode over to Bradley with three long and purposeful strides. As he turned his head to look at me with a startled expression on his face, I smashed my right fist as hard and as fast as I could into the centre of his face, instinctively swivelling my hips to maximise the force.

I'd given no thought to the outcome of my punch, but the results were more satisfactory than I could ever have hoped for. As my little, bony fist met Bradley's fat, startled face, his head snapped back and instantaneously a gout of blood fountained from his nostrils. Dropping the torn halves of the poetry book to the ground and stepping away from me, Bradley threw his hands up to his face before bringing them away again and looking in disbelieving horror at their crimson coating.

Up until that point in my young life, I had never thrown a punch before, but without understanding how, the connection I made was perfect and the result as spectacular as any eleven-year-old could reasonably expect. In the blink of an eye, Bradley had gone from bullying a crying little girl to having an angry Owen punching him in the head and he seemed completely unable to comprehend what had happened.

For my own part, I stood there equally dumbstruck and hardly able to believe what I'd just done. We eyed each other mutely for what seemed like a frozen age, but was in reality probably only a second or two, before I suddenly became aware of other kids running towards us and someone gleefully chanting out the words that every kid in the school playground loves to hear, 'FIGHT, FIGHT, FIGHT'!

But there would be no fight. Within seconds of landing my epic blow, the bell rang to call us back to lessons and the teachers started to come outside to chivvy us back in. Desperately trying to act as if nothing out of the ordinary had happened, I turned on my heel without another word and headed back to class, dimly aware of Judy picking up the torn halves of her book behind me, still crying softly.

My memory of those brief moments still ring as clear and as true as a bell today but what followed does not. The teachers must have asked Bradley what had happened to him because even the dimmest members of society would have realised that something wasn't quite right when an eleven-year-old boy came back from lunch with a broken nose and a shirt covered in blood. But to his credit, Bradley didn't tell them. And neither did anyone else when the teachers came into class to ask them what had happened and who had seen what.

They must have guessed at the truth though, as a few of my more obvious classmates turned gormlessly to stare in my direction as soon as the teacher asked if anyone had seen Bradley being hit or falling over. But no-one said a word. Against all the odds, it seemed as though I had gotten away with my actions.

At least I'd thought I was in the clear, until three days later when Bradley returned to class, sporting two very black eyes and a look of barely contained rage which made everyone want to steer a path well clear of him. And from the way that he glared at me every time I looked in his direction, it was obvious that there was not going to be any making up to be done.

As soon as there was an absence of teachers, he made it clear to me, and to everyone else listening, that both he and his two older brothers would be seeking revenge at the earliest given opportunity.

I tried to act as cool as any eleven-year-old can in the face of his threats, but the truth was that despite having bloodied Bradley's nose so well only a few days previous, I was more than a little unnerved. But with the benefit of hindsight, I think he announced it in front of my classmates more as a message to them than as a threat to me. I had made him lose face and he desperately needed to try and regain it as soon as possible. The fact that doing so showed that he was too frightened to confront me on his own without the help of his older brothers was obviously lost on him, and sadly to us too at that young age.

Although it's true that I'm no stranger to conflict, I like to think that I'm also not someone who goes out of his way to pick a fight just for the sheer bloody joy of it. I have learnt, however, that the judicious application of violence can not only be extremely satisfying at times but also a highly effective solution to some of the simpler problems which life can throw at you. So, if I'd known then, what I know now, I would have beaten Bradley to a bloody pulp just for voicing the threat.

But I didn't. I was the product of a loving middle-class family and I had no experience of violence beyond the solitary punch that I'd thrown three days earlier. As it was, I was left more than a little nervous by his threats and for the remainder of that term I made sure that I left school either as early or as late as possible to avoid any chance of running into Bradley and his infamous brothers.

Fortunately for me, a little over a week later, the school broke up for the summer holidays and as we were due to start Secondary School the next term, my troubles were well and truly behind me. Or so I'd thought.

CHAPTER THREE

A knock at the door noise pulled me from my reverie and looking down at the glass in my hand, I realised with a start that I had barely touched my whisky. For some reason, this seemed to bother me, almost as though I had forgotten to do an important household chore. I lifted the glass to my lips and drained its contents in one long gulp, grimacing against the acrid taste of the cheap scotch. After setting the empty glass back down on the scarred table beside me I pulled myself slowly to my feet before answering the door to find that no-one was there.

'Bloody kids', I muttered to myself as I peered left and right along the seemingly deserted tree-lined avenue.

'Knock Down Ginger' we used to call it when I was a kid. A simple game which involved knocking on someone's door before scarpering down the road and hiding behind the nearest car or bush so that whoever answered was left as bemused as I was just then.

If you were really daring you might knock on the same door several times in the hope of provoking the householder into some degree of apoplectic rage. All of which was very entertaining to us kids, but it was a bloody nuisance when you were on the receiving end.

It was evening time and darkness had just begun to fall. It was also shaping up to be a particularly blustery autumnal night and I looked out amongst the moving shadows of the tree-lined street. Despite the fact that November was still a couple of weeks away, somewhere in the distance I heard the bang of a firework and as I looked up it fizzled briefly in the night sky for a second or two before disappearing altogether;

I stood there swaying for a full minute, bolstered against the cold by the heat of the whisky in my veins. I wondered whether the knocking might have been a figment of my imagination or if it had perhaps been just a branch against a window. With the sober benefit of hindsight though, the truth is that I probably took so long to drag my sorry backside out of the chair and answer the door and that whoever it was had simply given up and moved on.

Closing the door behind me I drew the curtains and turned the lights on dim before wandering into the kitchen and topping off my tumbler with whisky once more.

With the essentials of my evening to hand once more, I nestled back into the armchair and took up where I had left off before.

****

Two weeks into the school holidays and I was bored. As a family we'd already had our annual week's holiday camping in North Wales, I'd done all my homework and daytime TV was still only a concept of the future.

I also didn't have any real friends to speak of. It wasn't that I didn't get on with other kids, because I did. With the obvious exception of Bradley Thomas I was a pretty popular kid, but at the same time there was no-one who I really wanted to hang about with after school had ended, and as far as I can tell, there was no one who had any great desire to hang out with me either.

That year was shaping up to be a record-breaking summer with long spells of glorious weather and that particular Friday was proving to be no exception. My father was at work and my mother, reluctant to leave me at home to my own devices, had dragged me into town with her on a food shopping expedition. 'Town' consisted of one long high street called Station Road and the supermarket, 'FineFare' which would now be considered to be little more than an 'Express' or 'Metro' shop.

Ours was a house that didn't really do luxuries and without the lure of buying chocolate biscuits or any other kind of treats to tempt me inside the supermarket, I had sullenly declared that I was going wait outside whilst my mother shopped. So, with the sun on my face and the cool glass of the shop window against my back, I loafed about and watched the world go by. In an age before the advent of the huge out-of-town supermarkets with their massive car parks, High

Streets were busy places and there were plenty of people to-ing and froing in capped sleeved T-shirts and RaRa skirts, sporting various degrees of sunburn.

Whilst my mum queued at the checkout with the long line of other stressed mothers and their offspring, I languished happily, no doubt day-dreaming fantasies of Judy. But as I idled the time away, slowly but surely I began to get a feeling that something wasn't quite right in my world. It was a strange feeling and without being sure what it was that was that was bothering me, I cast about for its source.

I looked to my left and was greeted by the awful sight of Bradley Thomas and his two older brothers sitting on a low wall by the parked shopping trolleys, sharing a cigarette. Maybe it was the exact same kind of sixth sense as that which had made me look up at them, or maybe it was just one of life's odd coincidences because, at that same moment, Bradley glanced up from his chattering and looked me straight in the eye.

I was so shocked that my breath caught in my throat and my heart rate felt as though it had rocketed through the gears without the use of a clutch. I held my breath without realising it as time seemed to stand still. Our eyes locked on to each other until finally the spell was broken and I saw him turn and speak urgently to his brothers, raising a finger and pointing it straight at me.

In a movement which could have been choreographed in Bollywood, the brothers looked up at me, paused and then rose to their feet as one. They even stepped off from the same foot in time with each other as they started towards me in a way which left no doubt as to what their intentions were.

A cold web of fear wrapped itself about me, pinning my arms to my sides and my feet to the ground. There was no sudden reckless burst of bravery for me, just a bowel-loosening feeling of terror until finally a rush of adrenaline finally kick-started a 'fight or flight' response. The fear of taking a beating was all consuming and, as far as I was concerned, the only course of action was definitely not 'fight.'

I turned on my heels, about to make a run for it just as my Mother stepped out of the shop in front of me. She had no idea of the drama that had been about to unfold and without a care in the world she put her hand on my shoulder and steered me on towards the next shop on her agenda, all the time uttering banalities about how she had bumped into an old neighbour at the checkouts and how much fatter she was these days. She was clearly completely oblivious to what had just happened, or more to the point, what had just nearly happened.

Still terrified but desperately trying to look as though nothing was wrong, I looked over my shoulder. The Thomas trio had checked their step and were now following at a discreet distance. As soon as he saw me looking back, the biggest and the eldest of the three brothers grinned maliciously, drawing his finger across his throat before pointing at me meaningfully. It was obviously something he'd seen on the TV and as corny as it was, even then, the message was clear enough. If I had been scared before, I was downright petrified by the time I got home with my mother, who was still oblivious to what had happened. The three brothers had followed us all the way back and so they now knew *exactly* where I lived.

For the next three weeks, I barely left the house alone, in fear of the violent revenge they meant to wreak. The first few days weren't quite so bad after I had managed to convince myself that I was being unnecessarily paranoid. This was, after all, middle-class Chingford and not some inner city sink estate that we were living in.

But the next weekend, as I sat in the car with my father, I saw the three brothers loitering at the end of our street, just as they had done outside the supermarket. To the casual observer, they would have appeared to be just three young lads killing time, kicking walls and smoking cigarettes. But of course, I knew the real reason for them being there.

It's hard to overstate how scared I became. I reached a point where I couldn't go to sleep at night without checking under the bed first, just in case they had somehow learned how to sneak into a house which was both occupied and locked without anyone else realising. Like teenage ninjas that weren't turtles. When I got into bed, I'd lay awake, fretting about what they would do to me if they caught me. And when I eventually did drop off, I was often troubled by bad dreams.

I still hadn't told my Mum or Dad about what had happened, or what it was that I was afraid of happening. Probably, I was more than a little ashamed of myself for not being braver about the whole situation. So when my unsuspecting parents sent me out to buy bread or milk from the local shops I had no choice but to leave the house alone and I treated those trips as though they were sorties behind enemy lines. Only after checking the road from the upstairs bedroom window did I sally forth, and when it came to street corners, I made sure to cross over to the other side of the road so that I could see what was coming without running the risk of bumping into them.

Apart from that one time in the dad's car though, I never saw them again. They might have turned up outside the house or at the end of our suburban street again, but if they did, I didn't see them and for the most part, they probably had more interesting things to do with their time. Eventually, with the holidays almost over, I finally came to the conclusion that they had forgotten about me and without even realising it, I began to relax my guard.

The summer holidays were almost over when they finally caught up with me. Despite my paranoid hyperawareness of the previous month or so, there was only so long a lad of my age could keep his concentration intact, and like every other young man on the edge of puberty, my mind was apt to wander, usually with adolescent fantasies of Judy.

I'd been sent that morning to return some books to the library. I'd completed my usual check of the street outside before leaving the house and made sure to keep a keen eye out ahead of me on my way there, but with no sign of the brothers stalking me in the previous month, I was starting to think that they had given up.

After I'd returned the books I left the library empty-handed and started on my way home. The baking sunshine of the previous weeks had finally subsided, culminating in an impressive flood of torrential downpours and leaving behind a more typical excuse for a British summer. Not hot and not cold. Not anything other than a cloudy blandness that was impossible to get excited about either way.

I ambled past a parade of shops in Hatch Lane with my eyes to the front, not really thinking about anything other than whether I'd need to avoid all three brothers the following week when I started my new school. But even if I had been paying more attention I probably wouldn't have seen them as they came out of the sweet shop behind me and the first I knew of their presence was when fat fingers grabbed my shoulders and spun me around.

'This him?' It was the oldest of the brothers asking Brad. I didn't know their names back then but I subsequently learned that oldest was Mick, and he was four years Brad's senior. The other was Rob and was slap bang in the middle; two years older than Brad and two years younger than Mick.

With a handful of my shirt wrapped up in his fist, Mick lifted me onto my toes, leering down into my face so that his freckled nose almost touched mine. Cold fear took an icy grip on me and rendered me incapable of any kind of reaction other than to gawp back up at him in abject terror.

'Yeah. That's the bastard,' Bradley replied, looking as though he was trying to puff himself up in front of his older brothers, perhaps to make up for the fact that I had given him a bloody nose the last time we'd met.

The moment I had been dreading for weeks on end had finally arrived and that fact that I had known it was coming had done nothing to lessen its impact. In a moment of juvenile shame, I felt my bladder momentarily lose control and a patch of warm wetness spread below. It was only a tiny amount, but it felt as though my entire leg had been soaked and I found myself desperately hoping that it would not be noticed.

With the benefit of hindsight it was the least of my worries, but for some reason, I had it in mind that if they knew that I had pissed my pants, it would only serve to make them angrier. I considered running but they had crowded around me by then and my arm was held in an iron grip by Rob so that any real chance for escape had already passed. Mutely, I was herded into the access alleyway which ran behind the parade of shops, resigned to my fate.

The alley was an ideal place to get up to mischief. It was completely devoid of cars and people and un-overlooked by any houses or passing public. Apart from the odd stray cat, some gritty potholes and the heaps of piled up rubbish, there was no-one else to witness what came next.

I still remember the expressions on their faces and I honestly don't think they could have looked much happier if they'd been given a winning lottery ticket. Despite being different ages and sizes, they all shared the same features and it there was no mistaking the fact that they were brothers. They even shared the same shit-eating grins.

We came to a stop behind some large, round, industrial bins and they crowded about me once more, spitting insults into my face; shoving me from one to the other. If any of them felt any guilt over picking on someone smaller than them and with such uneven odds, they didn't show it. They soon formed a rhythm of sorts, with Mick shoving me towards Rob who in turn passed me on to Brad who completed the circle by pushing me back to Mick, each one of them egging the other on with what they planned on doing to me. As I was shoved I was spun so that by the time we'd done two rounds I was just starting to feel a little dizzy.

It was the blow to the back of my head that did it. It was little more than an open-handed cuff really and it didn't hurt in the slightest, but as Rob spun me round to face Brad once more I felt Mick reach out and slap at the back of my head.

Something broke then. Inside me.

I'd spent so long being terrified of what the brothers would do to me that I had never considered what my own actions might be when they finally caught me. Up to that point, all I had thought about was how to avoid them in the first place.

They built their anger and their malice slowly, as they pushed me about in that shitty alleyway, but somehow I knew that the blow which Mick had aimed at the back of my head would be the start of the main event. Like the first crack opening in a dam, it would quickly be followed by others before the final deluge. Mick was the eldest of the three brothers and it's the most natural thing in the world for the young to want to copy the old.

I suddenly found that I was furious with myself for being so lazy and for being so stupid; for getting caught. But taking ownership of my own faults has never been one of my strong points.

So I did then what I've done ever since. I turned my anger around and pointed it at someone else. As Rob shoved towards Bradley I underwent a transformation. I suddenly changed from being a meek victim to a vicious, snarling bastard. Cold fear had given way to even colder rage, and the shock on Bradley's face was plain to see, even before I buried my fist in it. I'd tensed every muscle and every sinew in my little body and had used the momentum of Rob's shove to add force to the blow. It was a savage right cross which immediately sent him flying back into the wheeled bin behind him, with enough force to send it skidding a foot or two.

The sight of his nose erupting in a fountain of blood was deeply satisfying, and unlike the first time I had punched him, there were no feelings of horror or self-doubt to burden me. That last time, in the school playground, the punch I'd thrown had been a subconscious reaction, without any prior thought about what the consequences might be. This time, however, in the blink of an eye, I'd decided what I wanted to do and what I wanted to achieve; and sitting Bradley back down on his arse covered in blood was a pretty good start. If I'd had time to carry on punching him and to spit in his face, I would have gladly done so; but there were two more people I needed to hurt first.

It had never been a fight which I expected to win, but I decided that if I was going to take a beating, I might as well give them a lump or two to remember me by. So, with no time to revel in Bradley's wonderfully exploding nose, I pivoted on the ball of my right foot, spinning left before launching myself headfirst into the face of Rob, who had the decency to look as startled by the sudden change in dynamics as Bradley had. I can't imagine what went through his mind in those broken moments before I put him down, snarling as I did so, I only know that my own head was filled with a savage glee. Like a raging berserker of old going into battle.

There had been no great distance to separate the four of us, so when my dipping forehead punched into Rob's fleshy face with my entire weight behind it, there was enough force to send him sprawling. It was an untidy blow, but no less effective for it, and as he fell back onto the hard ground with the wind driven from his lungs, my own momentum had me floundering for balance on top of him. But whilst he landed hard on his back, amongst the grit and the grime of that alleyway, my own fall had been cushioned from being on top of him. Pushing myself back up, I noted with pleasure that he too was bleeding heavily from his nose, although maybe not quite in the same spectacular fashion as Bradley.

A distant sound of roaring pierced the veil of my consciousness and at first I thought it was the pulsing of blood and adrenaline rushing through my ears before I realised that it was my own cries of anger. I had no idea what it was that I shouted, only that I found myself yelling with rage, adding strength to my attack. I pushed myself up from Rob and made to knee him in the balls as viciously as I could, although somehow I missed. I felt my lips curl back from my teeth as I lost myself in the ecstasy of the moment.

The sheer thrill of the violence I had unleashed set every part of me tingling. In the space of fewer than five seconds, I had gone from being a bully's victim to someone who had taken down two people, leaving them battered and bloodied.

Quickly, I glanced about, hoping to find a bottle or a house brick within reach; anything I could use to keep smashing at his head and his face, but there was nothing there. We were still too close to each other for me to punch him with any force so I pushed myself up again, planning on burying my bloodied fist into his face a couple more times to make sure that he stayed where he was.

White pain exploded through my ribs as I was catapulted to one side. The flaring sharpness felt as though I'd been stabbed and it instantly doused the flames of any further resistance. It was Mick, the oldest of the three brothers, who'd aimed a booted right foot squarely into my ribs with a kick that Jonny Wilkinson would have been proud of.

Moments earlier I'd looked at Rob through tunnel vision, intent on nothing other than battering him senseless, and yet now I could think of nothing beyond the piercing agony searing through my side. I tried to roll away and into a ball but Mick came after me, stepping over the prostrate form of his brother, Rob, and stamping down hard upon my elbows.

From there on, my fight came to a sorry and predictable conclusion. I curled up as best I could in the filth of the alley and did my best to protect my ribs and head whilst the three of them rained down fresh blows upon me. Each one of them was on their feet by then and they used their booted feet to maximum effect, pausing every once in a while as they bent over to pull my hands away from my head so that they could deliver a fresh punch to my face.

I subsequently discovered that I had sustained a couple of broken ribs, but I've no doubt that it was that very first kick was the one which caused them. The beating went on for a hellish eternity. Or at least that's how it felt. Certainly, by the time they had finished they were all panting heavily from the exertions as if it had taken more out of them than it had from me. My ordeal finally ended with Bradley and Mick having to forcibly pull Rob away. If it hadn't been for them I'm sure that he would have carried on methodically stamping on every visible inch of me for as long as it took so that he could exact his revenge for my temerity in actually fighting back.

I must have drifted in and out of consciousness then because it took me a while before I realised that they had finally left me. I lay there a while longer, hoping that someone would come to my aid and pick me up until eventually, I dragged myself to my feet and staggered home; covered in blood and boot prints.

****

'Was it Bradley's brothers that did that?' she asked.

The summer holidays had been long and accompanied by prolonged spells of very un-British hot weather, and the first day back at school was another warm one, albeit overcast and muggy. I say *back* at school, but this was the big step up for my year group. It was our first day at secondary school and a different school meant different classmates, different rules and different teachers. It's a transition which half of all kids at that age seem to look forward to and which the other half dread.

A different school also meant a different journey from home for me and it was one which I trod with a watchful eye, still looking out for potential ambush sites. Whilst the fear of getting beaten up by the Thomas brothers again no longer consumed me (and worryingly it seemed that I would now be at the same school as the older brothers too), it was obviously still a situation that I was determined to avoid if at all possible. Over a week had passed since my beating and whilst the aches and pains were all but forgotten, some of the bruising could still be seen as a dull yellow mask about both eyes.

And so it was that I discovered that my new route now took me right past Judy's house which she had happened to leave just as I was passing. She had stepped out of her front door, spotted me and immediately called out 'Owen!' As I stopped and turned towards her she skipped over to me with an inexplicably wide grin on her face, as if we had been the best of friends forever.

It seemed that she had been busy during the summer holidays and her previously long hippy chick hair had now been cut into a much more modern pageboy style. Beneath the regulation school blazer and blouse, she wore a *very* trendy black RaRa skirt.

To my juvenile eyes, she seemed to have morphed from looking like a dated 1970's throwback to a glamorous 1980's goddess. If I'd been much taken by her before, I was now absolutely smitten.

By contrast, I must have looked as square as any other first termer could possibly look, with my pristine new blazer, new white shirt, new trousers and new shoes. School tie, done up in the correct manner.

'Was it Bradley's brothers that did that?' she repeated, pointing at my colourful face after seeing that the gormless expression on my face was not about to frame any kind of intelligent response.

'Erm,…yes' I replied eventually, feeling thoroughly off balance and completely surprised that she had decided to walk alongside me and chat, 'yes it was.'

'Thanks, by the way. I never did say it before, but thanks for standing up to Bradley for me that day when he tore my book. I told my Mum about it over the holidays and she had a *right* go at me for not saying something before. She's right of course, and I know I should have, but I just felt a bit shy. You know?'

She certainly didn't sound shy now. She was chatting away to me like we were the oldest of friends; and after a nanosecond of contemplation, I decided that I quite liked it.

'Mum says that I should invite you round, you know, to say thanks and all. Do you wanna come?'

I was so surprised at her offer that she could have knocked me over with a feather,

'Erm, when?' I managed to reply.

She nudged me with her elbow as we walked along, sending an unexpected thrill through me. 'Tonight of course, silly. You're not busy, are you? You can have tea with us.'

'I, erm…no… I mean, no, I'm not busy. Tea would be great. I'll have to check with Mum first, but I'm sure she won't mind as long as she knows where I am.'

'Keeps a tight check on you does she?' she said with a teasing twinkle in her eye.

'She does after this.' I said pointing at my yellow eyes, 'she's paranoid it's going to happen again, and if truth be told, I'm still a bit nervous about what's going to happen when they see me next, so I'm trying to keep an eye out. For all I know, we could be walking right past their house.'

'Oh…didn't you know?' she wittered on gaily as we tootled down the road 'They moved last week. To Harlow, I think. We won't have to see them again.'

I couldn't believe my luck. 'How the hell do you know that!?' I had almost shouted.

'My Mum told me. She knows Brad's Mum through Church.'

I'd done my best to try and convince myself that I was no longer going to be bothered by the Thomas brothers and that if they decided to give me another beating, then so be it, but as I heard this momentous news a wave of relief washed over me. A lifting of subliminal stress which I hadn't even realised I'd carried.

'Well that's a shame', I said in as nonplussed a manner as I could muster.

'Eh?'

'I was looking forward to teaching them a lesson again.'

Judy turned to look at me enquiringly and I returned her gaze as coolly as I could muster, until moments later when we both erupted into gales of uncontrollable laughter. The daftness of my throwaway line seeming funnier by the second as our shared laughter grew more and more infectious. It was long minutes later before we managed to stop and catch our breath, neither of us quite sure what had made us slip into such uncontrollable hilarity. From that moment on, it was obvious that when it came to making each other laugh; both Judy and I were on very much the same wavelength.

As the days became weeks, which then became months and so forth, our friendship blossomed and we found that at times we were each able to make the other break into uncontrollable fits of laughter, often with the simplest of comments which to anyone else were nothing sort of banal.

So, whilst to many kids, their first day at Secondary school can be quite terrifying, for me it proved to be something of a high point in my childhood. Not only had I discovered that my brief but deeply concerning conflict with the Thomas brothers was over, but I had also finally got to have a proper conversation with the exotic girl of my dreams. Not only had we walked to school together, but we had also discovered an immediate and natural affinity to each other.

After school that day, I waited by the gates, standing firm amongst the tidal flow of exiting kids, all dressed alike and yet desperately wanting to be identified as individuals amongst their peers. Employing the time honoured tactics of tying their ties in different fashions, sporting trendy or weird haircuts or carrying their books and gym kit in a really cool sports bag.

As I waited patiently, I was relieved and gratified to find that when she exited the school to join the flow, she seemed to be casting about looking for me, and as soon as she set eyes on me her face broke into a broad grin. 'Owen!' she cried out and waved.

'Judy!' I waved and yelled back with the biggest, and no doubt the daftest grin spread across my face. My God, we must have looked like two puppies who had been left locked alone in the house all day.

We immediately fell into step together and, having spent the day in different classes from each other, compared experiences of our first day in our new school; the teachers we now had and our new classmates, both making the other laugh with our impressions and anecdotes.

CHAPTER FOUR

R at-tat-tat. At first, I couldn't work out where the noise had come from. By then I'd been sat in my threadbare armchair for the best part of two hours and my mind was foggy with the effects of whisky and the beginnings of sleep.

Eventually, I realised that the knocking had come from the window, my doorbell having long since ceased to function leaving visitors no choice but to knock. Not that I had many. For a moment I decided that it must be kids, playing knock down ginger again, and I determined to stay where I was, not rising to their bait.

But as I drained the last of the whisky from my glass I realised that the tone and the urgency of the knocks had changed. The first raps had been on my front door but when that had failed to achieve any kind of response, whoever it was had gone for the window option. It was fully dark outside and the curtains were drawn with just the dim light of the standard lamp cocooning me in, but still, it must have been enough for whoever it was outside to be certain that someone was at home.

Deciding that perhaps it wasn't kids this time and that it might even be important, I dragged myself to my feet once more. I staggered slightly before righting myself and stepping into the faded hallway to answer the front door.

I was pretty sure that I knew what had happened before they said a word. This news had been on the cards for longer than I cared to think about and the only real surprise to me perhaps was that it hadn't come sooner. I stood mutely to one side of the front door and dumbly ushered them into the front room, watching them look around the semi-darkness and taking in the mess and the gloom that so aptly reflected the summary of my life.

They stood politely waiting, as I knew they would do until I'd resumed my seat, and when they both finally sat, they took a moment to smooth out the legs of their perfectly ironed police uniforms before they mustered up the courage to tell me that which I already knew. David had died. My son was dead

CHAPTER FIVE

If truth be told David had always been a bit of a Mummy's boy and it was something which had irritated me at times. He was still only nine years old when Judy passed and soon afterwards he became withdrawn and introverted. Despite my best efforts to replace her as the number one parent, he never really connected with me in the same way that he had done with Judy.

We did everything that fathers and sons should do when there's no mother figure to balance the scales of parenthood. We watched TV, kicked a ball around the garden and even did homework together. At the weekends I took him to the cinema or theme parks and in the holidays we went fishing or camping. But although David was my own flesh and blood and I would have gladly laid down my life or killed for him, he was by no means a chip off of the old block and somehow, something never quite clicked between us. If I were to look at the past in a purely dispassionate way, I'd say that as far back as I can remember, David had always been a bit of a strange lad. But when it's your own child your natural reaction is to ignore the cracks and add a little gloss wherever possible.

He didn't much mix with other kids either at an early age and I imagined that, like his mother Judy had, come school playtime, he probably would have sat away from the other kids and alone. His teachers all told me that he was a good kid. Quiet and well behaved. Not the brightest, but not the dumbest either. Slow and steady would probably have been the best way to describe David's early years at school.

But as soon as he hit his `teens, things began to change. Halfway through senior school he fell in with a group of lads who were one or two years older than him. They met up on their pushbikes in the park, after school and at the weekends, just hanging out together. For my own part, I was just happy to see that he had finally made some friends and selfishly, I felt the pressures of parenthood easing from my shoulders.

Even when he started to come home smelling of cigarettes, I wasn't overly concerned, accepting that it was a fairly standard rite of passage for a young man to at least try these things. I assumed that his smoking phase would pass fairly quickly but when it didn't and it became evident that it wasn't just a passing phase, I took him to one side and had a little man to man chat. It didn't seem to make any real difference other than to make him spend some of his pocket money on mints before he came home.

By the age of fifteen, David was truanting regularly and completely out of hand. No matter what sanctions I passed and no matter what I said, he was a complete and utter law unto himself. It soon got to the point that I had no real idea where he was most nights, who he was with or what he was doing. If he came home at night, it was by his choice and his choice alone. By that time his school had made it abundantly clear that they didn't want him attending, being too much of a disruption to the other kids who were gearing up for O' Levels and CSE's, and for his part, he was more than happy enough to oblige them.

Although there were no arrests that I was aware of or policemen bringing him home, I'm convinced that would have been more luck than judgement on his behalf. By the time he was sixteen, he only made it home only a couple of nights a week and by the time he'd reached seventeen, it was only for a few days here and there every month or so. No doubt when he'd been kicked out of a squat somewhere.

I do wonder if he would have turned out differently if Judy had still been alive and usually I decide that, yes, he would have. But I also think that even if he had turned out to be a different personality, it's still just as likely that the end result would have been the same.

I also occasionally find myself wondering if there were things which I could have said or done differently which would have altered the outcome and kept him on the right track, but then I decide that that way lies madness. You can't change who you are and you can't do better than your best. Depression is a backwards looking illness and I try to avoid it as much as I can. Unable to change the past, it's better to look to the future where the possibilities are endless.

Despite what the bleeding heart liberals tell us, I don't believe that there are any hard and fast rules as to the best way to bring up your kids. All you can really do is give them your unconditional love and teach them how to conduct themselves according to the rules of civilised society. The fact that David chose to ignore my love and guidance was on him, not me.

By the time he was eighteen, he had moved down to Brighton, the drugs capital of Southern England. I visited him a couple of times in one hostel or another, trying to talk sense into him and he, in turn, made it home every so often for a day or even a week at a time. By then he was a fully-fledged junkie. I may not have known what drugs he was taking and I never actually saw him taking any drugs, but the dried scabs on his arms and the haunted and emaciated expression were enough to tell me all that I needed to know.

Our brief reunions were not pleasant affairs. Whenever I saw him then, I looked at him with a sense of longing; a longing for the return of my son. As if he was hiding inside a junkie's skin. A Skin which he could suddenly peel off to reveal a normal functioning human being and that all would be right again.

And he just looked at me as a meal ticket. I couldn't refuse him of course, even though I knew that the money he needed to pay off a debt would be a drugs debt, or that the weeks' worth of rent that he told me he needed would be going straight into the pockets of a dealer somewhere. No matter what he had become, he was still my son and I loved him. Right up until the point he died.

I had to go down to Brighton and identify his body. He'd been found in a hostel bedsit with the needle still in him. Apparently, it's not that unusual for junkies to pass out immediately when they inject themselves between their legs so the sight of him lying dead with his pants and trousers around his knees and a needle still dangling from his groin was not enough to shock a Brighton copper into thinking anything other than it was just another junkie overdose.

The Hostel itself was a shapeless concrete block with metal framed windows and a decorative skirting of weeds. Inside, a background aroma of bleach fought a valiant but ultimately futile battle against the pervasive smell of decay and despair. Long corridors decorated in out of date British Rail style pastels gave lie to the fact that the building was little more than a privatised Government institution for the homeless.

As I made my way along those grim and scuffed hallways I passed the scurrying waifs who lived there. Some hurried past with a look of barely concealed fear on their faces, whilst others held expressions of coy longing. No doubt they saw my relatively smart appearance as either a threat or as a potential opportunity.

I had to clear his room, which served only to fuel the depression which threatened to overwhelm my bereavement. It was nothing more than a bare cell with a handful of creased and dirty clothing. There was no money and there were no valuables. It could be that everything of worth had been sold by him before his death and the soiled clothing was all he left the world with, but the policeman told me that it was more likely that both David and the room had been searched and stripped of anything deemed to be of value by the other junkies living in the hostel. The likelihood of this theory being correct was backed up by the fact that the police hadn't even found any drugs.

On my way out, the landlord tried to ask me for two weeks rent which was apparently left owing. I told him to fuck off and threw the bin bag containing David's old clothes at him before walking out to find the nearest pub.

The funeral itself was a sorry affair. Obviously. I had to wait a month or so for the Coroner to complete his enquiries before I could bury him in Chelmsford cemetery The weather that day seemed to complement the occasion as a light drizzle permeated the air, slowly soaking through everything it touched. There were only a handful of people there. He had no family other than me and no real school friends to remember him, having skipped out way before the normal school leaving date.

I hadn't invited them, I hadn't invited anyone, but my old drinking buddy Skip Parsons and my boss Steve Bigham turned up to support me, but I was already so pissed by that time that I barely registered their presence. I was so wrapped up in my own misery that I didn't even bother with a proper wake, but instead invited the handful of people at the graveside to the nearest pub where I proceeded to drown my sorrows and empty my wallet to anyone who'd take a drink from me, whether I knew them or not. I got myself so drunk that day that I don't even remember how it ended, although I have a vague recollection of trying to pick a fight with a complete stranger in the pub and everyone laughing as I tried to swing a punch and fell to the floor instead.

CHAPTER SIX

That miserable day was to set the scene for the next four months of my life. I went straight back to work, having no idea what else to do with myself, and initially, I managed to restrict my binge drinking to an activity which happened at the end of each working day. But whilst I may have been technically sober during those early working weeks, every day dawned with a vicious hangover and it wasn't long before I started popping into pubs at lunchtimes for a hair of the dog, and inevitably, from there on it wasn't long before that medicinal hair of the dog changed from being a quick drink at lunchtime to a regular top up at pubs between every afternoon meeting.

It's not something I'm proud of but I was still driving the length and breadth of the County at that time and God only knows how I managed to avoid having an accident or getting pulled over and breathalysed. It was probably a combination of the lack of coppers actually policing and not fitting the typical profile of an Essex Boy Racer.

I can't tell you at what point it was that I started having a shot of vodka in the mornings to start the day, for the simple reason that I don't remember. I don't remember when and I don't remember why; just the fact that I did. I dragged myself out of bed each morning and stumbled down to the kitchen where I would pour myself a small shot of vodka into a mug and neck it before putting the kettle on. I managed to convince myself that the vodka was actually good for me and that it helped to kick start my day.

I'm not even a great fan of vodka, preferring the harsh taste of a cheap whisky, but I knew enough not to turn up at customer's stinking of scotch first thing. I was drinking so much back then though, that I must have been sweating forty percent proof anyway so I probably wasn't fooling anyone.

I became a regular customer in my local, The Butlers Head, although I did try to move around from one pub to another fairly often to disguise my levels of inebriation. I didn't want some busybody phoning the police and grassing me up for drunk driving. I had no family left to care for and no real friends outside those I propped up the bar with and most of those were, at best, cursory acquaintances. The only people I really cared for, apart from myself, of course, were my long-suffering boss, Steve Bigham, and my two favourite drinking buddies, Skip Parsons and Terry the Campsite.

CHAPTER SEVEN

I don't remember the very first time that I met Campsite Terry or how it was that we were introduced but in all probability, it would have been when we were both drunk and it would almost certainly have been in the Butlers Head being as Terry seemed to be a semi-permanent fixture there. He was known almost universally as either Campsite Terry, or Terry the Campsite, on account of the fact that he had lived on a campsite continuously for nearly two years after his wife had kicked him out of the marital bed and home some twenty years previously. It was only after his death that I discovered that his real name was in fact, Terry Carpenter, which was a little ironic really, considering that he had been a cabinet maker.

Terry was one of those guys that you couldn't help but like. He wasn't loud and he wasn't brash, but if you joined his company he would always welcome you warmly and insist on buying you a drink, no matter how straightened his circumstances might have been.

He was also something of a compulsive gambler and I think that for the most part he probably had a good success rate; certainly, he talked a good book. Mostly he seemed to bet on sports and he seemed to have an encyclopaedic knowledge of most of them, but he was just as happy to have a punt on the result of an election. He never bet on the horses or the dogs, claiming that too many races were fixed and that any study of the odds was worthless.

Although he worked for himself as a cabinet maker, I don't think that he attracted a great deal of business because if he did, he must have started early in the mornings to be finished and in the pub or the bookies by mid-afternoon. He might not have been a gregarious character, but he was certainly an interesting one. He was pretty well read on a wide range of subjects other than sports, from ancient history to current affairs and if you'd gone to a quiz night, you'd have wanted him on your team.

It seems odd now, looking back on how little I knew about his home life, but we were drinking mates only and whilst drinking mates may spend a lot of time shooting the shit, as the Americans say, they tend not to discuss anything much that's too personal or meaningful.

Like all gamblers though, Terry had bad times as well as the good, and sadly for Terry, he wound up paying the ultimate price for his final losing streak.

The first inkling I had of Campsite Terry's run of bad fortune came one Saturday afternoon when I bumped into him in the Butler's Head pub. It was pretty empty that afternoon with a smattering of customers dotted around reading papers or playing pool and a solitary overweight barman polishing glasses. Terry was sat alone at the bar with a newspaper and a half-finished crossword laid out in front of him, although I got the impression that the crossword had long since ceased to occupy his thoughts. A game of rugby was being shown on the television and from his agitated interest in the game; I guessed that he must have had some money riding on it.

It was the middle of the afternoon and I had already swilled a half dozen pints earlier in town that day, as well as my usual vodka breakfast, so I was well on my way to getting fully pisssed. I sat down next to him with my back to the TV so that he could still keep an eye on the game as we chatted idly.

I don't recall who won the match. In fact, I don't even recall who it was between. But I do recall that whatever the result was, it wasn't the one he'd been counting upon.

'NO!!' He leapt to his feet and screamed at the TV, with a look of disbelieving horror writ large across his features.

I spun around in time to see a flying winger in a scarlet jersey score a breakaway try as the rest of the players either celebrated joyously or hung their heads in abject misery. It took me a moment to realise that the clock had just ticked past eighty minutes and that the score had been the final play of the match and one which had dramatically turned the losing side into the winners. I'd seen Terry win bets before, of course. If there's one thing that all gamblers like to do, it's to tell people about their successes, but when it comes to losing bets, Terry was no different to most people and he tended to be a little coy. This time, however, he looked like a man who had lost everything. He stared at the TV with wide eyes and an open mouth, seemingly incapable of any other reaction. I had never seen him react to anything like this before and as the long seconds ticked by, I looked back at him without any idea what say.

'Oh shit' was all he seemed capable of saying as he eventually sat back down and rubbed his hand over his face.

'Terry. Mate. I, erm.., I guess you lost some money on that one then?' I stumbled my words out, feeling as though I'd just witnessed someone being told that their child had died.

'Yeah, you could say that' he said with an air of resignation as he slowly started to come to terms with his loss.

I usually don't care much about other people, but Terry was the closest thing I had to being a real friend and the look on his face was more than I could stand. 'Listen Tel', it's only money. Right? If you need a sub, I'm happy to lend you some cash to tide you over?'

He seemed to consider it for a moment before saying 'Nah. Thanks for the offer Owen, but it's more than just a few quid I need at the mo' and I already owe someone else a bit so the last thing I want to do is to add you to the list'

'You sure?' I asked 'I really don't mind. How much do you need?'

'No, really. Thanks again O, but it's not just a matter of a couple of hundred quid here. It's a fair bit more and I've borrowed it from someone I really shouldn't have.'

He glanced at his watch and seemed to realise that he was late for something, grabbing for the rest of his pint which he necked in three large gulps before setting the glass back down and wiping his mouth with the back of his hand.

'I'd better go' he said, getting to his feet again and offering me his hand to shake. But before I could say or do anything more, the door of the pub swung open and in walked the hulking figure of Les Guscom and another man, braying loudly at something that had obviously been said outside.

Les Guscom was every pub's worst nightmare. A boorish out and out thug who thought he owned the place. Not only that, but he was both an imposing and intimidating specimen of humankind. Six feet six inches tall, by my reckoning and seventeen stone without an inch of fat on him Long swinging arms hung either side of him with ropes of corded muscle standing proud from his forearms. Broad shoulders supported a head the size of a breeze block and with features to match. Deep-set eyes and thick rubbery lips all combined to give him the look of Neanderthal man on crack cocaine. Even more scarily was the fact that none of it looked like the kind of muscle gained in a gym, pumping metal up and down with the benefits of processed proteins and steroids. Every inch and every ounce exuded natural raw power on a freakish scale. The only thing about him which didn't scream Hollywood monster was the fact that for some reason, he always seemed to wear a white plastic wristwatch.

Perhaps it had been a gift from the one person worse than Les to frequent that pub, his mother, Griselda Guscom. Half German, by all accounts, and with a mangled dialect to match, Griselda may not have had Les' imposing physique but there was no doubting where he'd got his looks from. Added to her pug ugly face was a shrill, shrieking voice which made you which made you want to stab your own ears. It was a voice that could empty a pub in minutes. Local rumour had it that Griselda and Les peddled drugs and loan sharked, and from what I'd seen, I had no reason to doubt it.

Fortunately for everyone in the pub that day, Griselda was nowhere to be seen (or heard).

The Butler's Head is not a small pub, but when there are less than half a dozen people in there, it's hard to miss someone. Terry turned his back to Les quickly, but it was already too late. Les had spotted him straight away and homed in like an Exocet missile.

'Well, well' he boomed, 'if it isn't my old friend Terry the Campsite'. He took a grip on Terry's elbow and turned him back to face him. It would have taken a blind man not to see that Terry was shit scared of Les and it didn't take a Sherlock Holmes to work out that this was probably who he owed money to. 'I think you've got something for me. Haven't you?' he said menacingly.

'I,.. erm...I have Les, but I just need a couple more days' said Terry, managing to spread a sickly grin across his face.

'A couple more days is it? I think that maybe you and I had best have a chat about this outside my old chum' and he pulled Terry up from his barstool by the elbow.

'Now hang on a minute' I said, putting out a hand to bar their passage, 'there's no need for this.' I wasn't looking for any trouble. God knows I was already too drunk to have been any use in a fight and I had acted without any conscious forethought whatsoever.

It was like waving a red rag to a bull. 'What the fuck's it got to do with you Owen?' he snarled into my face. It was not a pleasant experience. His shoved his face to within mere inches of mine as he said it and if it wasn't for the fact that I hadn't eaten anything that day I probably would have literally shit myself.

A mumbled 'Nothing Les' was all I could manage. I had said hello to Les before in the past and swapped minor pleasantries the same as anyone else in the pub, and whilst I knew that he had a bit of a reputation, I had never before seen it first-hand. The threat of violence seemed to physically radiate from him and I was under no illusion that if I had said or acted with anything other than my meek acquiescence, it would have ended very badly for me indeed that day.

Grunting with satisfaction, he left my personal space and turned his attention back to Terry, who he then herded out through the back door.

I sat there disgusted with myself whilst Les' mate smirked at me as he bought a drink at the bar. I had allowed myself be cowed and bullied and had let my friend down with barely a whimper of protest. Worst of all was the knowledge that had been a time when I would have stood up and put Les on the floor without even thinking about it. A time which was not even all that long ago. I probably would have regretted it badly afterwards, given the size and the reputation of a guy like Les, but I wouldn't have let the fear of getting hurt stop me from doing what I thought was right.

I hated myself for being a coward but I also knew that there was nothing I could have done to stop Les that wouldn't have involved me being beaten to a bloody pulp. It was scant consolation, to say the least, and my shame deepened by the minute. I finished my pint and took a hasty exit, not even stopping to see if Les or Terry came back in. I spent the rest of the day drinking myself to oblivion. True to form, I don't remember where I went or what I did afterwards, only the vaguest of snapshots of people and conversations.

I was in the depths of an alcoholic depression back then and although I knew it, I made no effort to climb out from my own personal pit of despair. The drunker I got, the more depressed I became, and of course, the more depressed I got, the more I tried to drown my sorrows. When I reached the point where every day finished with me sitting indoors, crying my eyes out with no company other than whisky, the solution I chose was to stay away from home until I'd done my crying elsewhere.

I hadn't made any effort to tidy or decorate my house in years in terms and every picture and photograph laying around brought back memories of better times, serving only to remind me of just how dismal my existence had become. I tried to harden my heart, to convince myself that I hadn't really cared about David and that both he and I were in a better place now that his junkie suffering was over, but try as I might, I failed even at that.

And the more I thought about David, the more I thought back to Judy and the unjust tragedy of losing her at such a young age.

CHAPTER EIGHT

Fourteen years ago

Judy had been suffering from stomach aches and cramps intermittently for some time before her diagnosis but after hearing one of the other mothers down at the school describing her own problems and deciding that they sounded similar, she'd convinced herself that it was irritable bowel syndrome.

One of the things that I had always loved about Judy was that she was something of a stalwart and she rarely complained of any kind of illness or pain, so I was hardly aware that anything might have been wrong with her other than on the odd occasion when she would stop what she was doing and bend over clutching her stomach.

The first time I saw her cramp over I was suitably alarmed and tried to convince her that she ought to see a doctor, but because she showed not the slightest bit of concern herself and brushed each episode away with, 'it's just a little IBS' I decided to trust in her instinct and had no real reason to doubt her. It was also a time when Judy seemed to be modifying her diet from one week to another, stating that certain foods would set off her 'IBS', but still, generally speaking, the cramps were rare. On those odd occasions when I did question her wellbeing, she'd reassure me that if it wasn't IBS then it was just 'women's problems.'

'Women's problems' is a phrase I have heard throughout my life. From relatives, from friends, and from hearing it on the TV; and yet in common with most other men, I suspect, to this day I have no firm concept of what that actually means. Whether or not it is a genuine set of conditions restricted to one or two specific ailments which afflict the female of the species alone, or whether they allude to an entire host of conditions I've never been able to say. The only thing I've ever been certain of is that if a lady tells a man that something relates to 'women's problems,' it means that she does not want to discuss it with him.

So as far as I was concerned, Judy seemed to be in rude health. And then one day she wasn't.

****

I've always been an early riser, even when nursing the most vicious of hangovers, and was usually up and about an hour or so before Judy. That particular Saturday morning was no exception. David was still tucked up in bed. At nine years old he had become a voracious reader and would often lay in until late morning with his nose buried firmly between the pages of his latest book.

I had just boiled the kettle to make a pot of tea and was standing in our cold kitchen, washing away the congealed mess of the take-away curry we'd eaten the night before from sorry looking dishes. Slow footsteps on the staircase caused me to look up as Judy came downstairs in a white nightie and baby blue dressing gown, rubbing her tummy absentmindedly whilst her beautiful auburn hair tangled about her head in disarray.

As I looked over my shoulder and caught sight of her I actually dropped the saucer I was washing, back into the foamy suds, before spitting out a harsh barking laugh.

'I think you might need to reconsider your latest product love', I jested smugly, pulling off a marigold glove as I turned to face her. Ever since we had first connected as childhood friends we had always enjoyed a bit of friendly banter and took every opportunity we had of ribbing of each other when possible.

'Wha.., what are you talking about', she asked me, standing there looking more than just a little early morning dishevelled, but also pretty vacant minded too (we had shared a large bottle of Lambrusco the evening before and it didn't take much for Judy to wind up with a hangover the next day).

Oh, but this was just too funny I decided. 'Have you not looked in the mirror yet'? I asked, grinning broadly.

'Erm, no. Why? What is it?'

'The fake tan. It looks lousy. You look like you've been dyed yellow.'

But as soon as I said it, I was slapped with a wet haddock of truth. As the words left my mouth I knew that there could be no way that the strange yellow colour of her skin was down to the dodgy fake tan I had originally assumed was the cause, and that in actual fact, there was something very wrong about her.

'Fake tan? I haven't used fake tan since last year', she said turning to look in the mirror.

'Oh my!' was about all she could muster as she caught sight of her reflection and put her yellow hand up to touch her yellow face, whilst opening her yellow eyes wide.

Jaundice. Taken from the French word for yellow, 'jaune.' I didn't know it back then but it turns out that it's a classic early warning sign for pancreatic cancer, which in turn turns out has one of the worst survival rates of all of the other cancers put together.

So on that Saturday she was jaundiced and feeling generally 'gripey.' On Monday she had an appointment with our local doctor. On Tuesday she was having tests in hospital and on Wednesday they told us both that she had advanced pancreatic cancer.

Judy and I knew nothing about the disease back then, but we learned quickly enough that the 'advanced' bit of her diagnosis was, in her case, another word for 'incurable'. When something as devastating as terminal illness happens to you, or to your loved ones, you start to take a special kind of interest in it. Judy's death came at a time before the modern era of the internet and my scrambled efforts to research pancreatic cancer consisted of a trip to the library and whatever information I could glean from the doctors we spoke to.

However, with the advent of the internet age and blogging, I've since heard stories of pancreatic cancer victims who managed to hang on for a year or even five before finally passing away. In a way I suppose we had it easy, what with the time left to her, to us, being so short. The speed at which the cancer robbed her of life seemed brutal to me at the time, but with the benefit of hindsight, it was also something of a mercy.

One short month after her diagnosis Judy was as dead as dead gets to be and I was left, not only struggling to come to terms with my own grief, but also struggling to try and work out how to bring up my only child without his mother around to do the myriad of things I hadn't previously realised were going on beneath my nose.

I'll confess that I couldn't have been a great deal support for her in the very early days and was probably more of a burden if anything. I like to think of myself as a practical guy, something of a problem solver, but in this case, I literally had no idea what to do for Judy, for David, or for myself.

Fortunately for me, my father was still alive back then and he was ever a shining example of how an Englishman should conduct himself. The phase 'stiff upper lip' could have been coined with him in mind and he always managed to turn up just when I needed him most. Despite the fact that he was usually reluctant to voice any personal opinions, he seemed to have an uncanny ability to restore calm and order to otherwise stressful situations.

I enjoyed a drink back then, as I always have done I guess, and in the first week of receiving that fateful prognosis, I overindulged in a pathetically vain attempt to dull my senses enough to escape from the reality of my new situation.

By then, we were living in Chelmsford in a 1970s built four-bedroom house. Judy's parents had both passed a few years previously and we'd managed to buy it outright with the proceeds from the sale of their house, Chelmsford being a considerably cheaper place to buy than London was back then. The house was roomy, but pretty tatty on the whole when we first bought it and I had been gradually decorating and updating it room by room in an effort to turn it into a comfortable home. The lounge had not long been finished and we hadn't scrimped when spending money on decorating and furnishing it so that it was a great space to relax in. But sitting there, on our plush leather sofa with a thickly piled carpet beneath my toes and knowing that my wife was on borrowed time with nothing I could do to change it, it felt as though the whole room was mocking me. As if to taunt, *'look at all the effort and money you've put in, and it's all for nothing.'*

It was five days after learning that Judy's time on earth was all but done when my father called round to visit. I had already started tearing into the whisky bottle whilst Judy and David were upstairs and so I'd offered him a drink which he took, as any good drinking buddy would. He never asked how I was, he didn't need to I guess, but nevertheless, without further ado, I selfishly started to unburden myself upon him and voice my feelings of helplessness in a way that I would never have dreamed of doing with anyone else.

Just as I had finished my ramblings of hopelessness and began refilling up my glass, David came down the stairs to see his Granddad. They greeted each other happily and little David sat next to him chatting away and answering the usual questions about how he was getting on at school and who his friends were etc., whilst they both studiously avoided the subject of Judy's health, or rather her lack of it. After another five or ten minutes of childish chatter, David wished his Grandfather goodnight with a big hug and then shook my hand and told me he'd see me in the morning (I'm not sure why but David and I always shook hands formally, but there was never any hugging or kissing for us).

It was an autumn evening and outside night had already fallen as we sat in the lamplight. There was no TV or radio playing low in the background and all we could hear for a moment was David and Judy's muted conversation filtering down the stairs and the steady tick of an antique clock I kept on the mantelpiece.

'Christ', I said, leaning forward and clutching my forehead as soon as David could be heard again upstairs, 'what the hell am I supposed to do with David.'

'Well', said my father after a few moments of silent contemplation, 'he's going to need you now son. And he's going to need you more than you're going to need that whisky.'

So that was that. It was all he ever said on the matter and it was all he ever needed to. It was as close as he ever got to a rebuke of any kind and it was typical of my father, perfect in its timing. I'd always been an obstinate sod and he understood me well enough to know that telling me directly what I should be doing, or more to the point what I should *not* be doing, was just as likely to produce the opposite reaction to the one which was really required. If he'd told me that I was acting like an overgrown child and that it was time to quit the booze and man up, I was a stubborn enough sod to have done exactly the opposite just to prove a point.

We'd carried on drinking a while longer whilst generally avoiding the subject of the future, but the very next morning I woke up in no doubt whatsoever as to what I had to do. There wasn't much left in the bottom of the whisky bottle from the night before but I tipped the inch or so that remained down the sink whilst I boiled the kettle for tea. If there'd been any other alcohol in the house, I'd have poured that away too but in the previous few days I'd managed to polish off any old bottles of wine or cans of beer hanging around the house.

I awoke that morning with a renewed sense of purpose. A sense of purpose, but also a feeling of shame for my self-pitying behaviour and actions of the previous week. Although I was still unsure of exactly *how* to go about it, I resolved to be the best father a son could have and to be the best husband a wife could want for in what little time we had left. Judy accepted her fate with a stoicism I hadn't expected her to have. I guess, she had no real choice. Nothing could change the inevitable. The least I could do, it seemed, was to try to match her bravery, and whilst she confided her sadness and regret to me in not being able to see our only son grow into manhood, I did everything in my power to convince her that David would at least be given the best I had to offer as a father to him.

After my little chat with Dad that evening, I knew that I couldn't be the husband and father I'd promised to be and carry on tearing into alcohol in the same quantities that I had consumed in the previous week. If I'd carried on boozing, it would have gradually edged me into a spiral of maudlin depression. And so I gave it up. I didn't touch another drop of booze for the next two or three years and much to my surprise, it bothered me not one jot. I threw myself into work and made the rest of my time busy either caring for Judy or, after she had passed away, running around after David or helping him with schoolwork.

CHAPTER NINE

After I'd been kicked out of the Royal Marines I drifted one from one job to another, trying to find something that kept me interested and yet still offered the promise of decent money. I did a fair amount of labouring and hod carrying, which was hard graft, but paid me well enough. But despite enjoying the hard graft I knew that I needed to find a job or career which offered more prospects. I answered a small ad in the local paper from a company which sold stationery and after a quick interview the rest, as they say, is history. The starting salary was rubbish, but as with all sales jobs, the promise of fat commissions baited the hook on which I bit. They made it sound so easy, selling paper and pens to businesses, and it was hard to imagine how anyone could fail. Within a month I had learned that the reality was somewhat different.

Before Judy died I had been on the brink of leaving Anglian Press Stationery (or APS as we called them). Much of the job involved cold calling prospects and inevitably, I hadn't been earning anything like the on target earnings, promised at the interview stage. I endured monotonous and soul-destroying hours of telephone cold calling, business after business, methodically working my way through directory after directory, this being an age when the internet was the sole reserve of government agencies and misfit geeks.

The phones at APS office were free to use for these purposes and new recruits were expected to spend at least a couple of hours a day cold calling in an attempt to open new doors. The more established salesman did some of this too, but for the most part, they were kept busy with existing portfolios of decent clients and warm sales leads from prospects who had phoned APS in answer to an advert.

The new-boys were given a token amount of 'cold case', old clients who either ordered minimal quantities from us at irregular intervals or people who had ordered something from us as a one-off at some point in the past. These we visited in attempts to make a face to face contact hoping to convert them into more regular, higher volume customers. Attempts that were all too often in vain.

Much of this was wasted time and mileage; there were no company cars for the new, un-established and unproven sales rep. Let's face it; a self-employed surveyor working from home wasn't going to suddenly start ordering large volumes of paper or stationery just because I had turned up on his doorstep. Occasionally though, these cold contacts became warmer prospects, people who might have used us regularly before changing supplier could sometimes be persuaded back into the fold with the use of heavy discounts. Start-up businesses might become successful and increase their volumes. New services which existing customers hadn't been aware of; that type of thing

In order to make the best use of my time when visiting any of these so-called 'cold cases', I also used to make a point of door-stepping as many other businesses in the surrounding areas as I could. 'Door stepping' was literally walking into shops and office buildings armed with a stationery catalogue and trying to sell my wares and whilst it was also usually a non-productive exercise, every so often it would open up a new customer.

Every new order to a salesman counts as a 'win' and those were the small wins which I enjoyed the most. I knew that most of the other guys did some 'door-stepping' too, but after hours of rejection and failure it became pretty hard to motivate yourself each day and I don't think that any of the others did anywhere near as much as me, so when I returned to the offices with a new order from a door-stepping call, it was always with a small sense of personal pride. But despite my successes relative to the other new starters, having started on such a low basic salary it was difficult to see how I could ever make my money up to a wage that would be decent enough to feed Judy, David and myself and to pay for the roof over our heads.

Finally, after plugging away for seven months I came to the conclusion that life as a salesman was not to be the life for me and I made a decision to look for something else to do with my life, a job with better money and hopefully better prospects too. I was all set to start scouring the local papers to see what other opportunities would afford themselves to me when the bombshell of Judy's cancer was dropped.

When Judy first went into the hospital, I rang Steve Bigham who was the boss and majority owner of APS and explained what had happened and that I needed to take some time off. Two days later, when the doctors had pronounced Judy's death sentence, I made a journey into work to tell them what had happened and to hand in my resignation. After all, Judy and David needed me much more than APS did.

Steve Bigham was like a rock in a stormy sea. If I had to name one man that could match the decency and stoicism of my father it would have been him. He sat me down in his office and offered me a cup of tea, which I gladly accepted. He asked me a few questions about the certainty of the prognosis and also what I had planned for the future, which of course was nothing. Bigham was probably around fifty years old then, twenty years my senior, and as we sat there, sipping tea, he calmly told me that he too had lost his wife to cancer some eight years earlier. Her breast cancer had been a much longer, more drawn-out affair than Judy's promised to be at that time and it had taken her nearly three years of suffering before she finally succumbed. Bigham was a man who I both liked and respected, and sitting there listening to him telling his tale of misery in such a down to earth and matter of fact tone was a strange comfort to me.

Knowing someone else who had been through a situation which was as bad, if not worse than mine, somehow gave me some comfort. I guess that's the reason people form support groups, where the victims of bereavement or trauma gather round to tell each other their stories. A shared experience helps you to feel a little less alone in the world.

Bigham told me that he would continue to pay me for another month and he also said that he didn't expect me to turn up for work but that I might find it a beneficial distraction to do a little each day. There would be no pressure, and I was to work only if I wanted to. He only asked that at the end of the month I come back in either to re-affirm my resignation or to reconsider accordingly. After thanking him for his understanding and his kindness, I left for home thinking never to return.

But Bigham had been right. I did need a distraction, and one week later with a booze-free head and a fresh determination to do the right thing for Judy and David, I started back to work. That first month, whilst Judy shed weight at a rate of a stone a week before she finally wasted away to nothing, I worked for no more than two or three hours a day, but I found that it was a welcome relief to be able to take my mind off of the future, or rather the lack of one for Judy. And bizarrely, perhaps, I made some really lucrative sales during that time. Possibly it was the lack of pressure, the fact that there was nobody expecting me to turn up at work with any fresh orders, or perhaps it was just luck, but for whatever the reason, I managed to hit a rich seam of good fortune during those weeks. Purely by virtue of my unhappy circumstances, I learned that, when it came to sales, trying too hard was often worse than not trying at all. Whilst a lot of people actually quite like to be sold to, they don't like it to be obvious.

After Judy died I found that working as a sales rep was also a job which afforded me enough flexibility to be there for David when he needed me, doing school runs and all of the various taxi runs expected by kids these days. I could call into the office first thing, hit the road and get out seeing as many customers as I could in the space of perhaps four hours, and finish up my day either on the phone or doing paperwork from home.

If Bigham hadn't cut me so much slack back then when I needed it the most, I don't know where I'd be now. One thing's for sure though, I've worked hard to repay him since then and I can safely say now that there's no better salesman than me on the firm.

CHAPTER TEN

Nine months ago

When I look back on the period of my life after David had died and the amount of booze I poured down my neck I sometimes wonder whether the tail was wagging the dog or vice versa. With no parents, no wife and no child left alive and very little in the way of friendships, I needed some kind of reason to carry on.

Anyone who has suffered a close bereavement knows that the emotional trauma also manifests itself physically. It's a feeling of emptiness, an aching in the pit of your stomach, and yet at the same time, it's nothing like a stomach-ache. Without any feelings of hunger, it's as though there is something physically missing from the bottom of your gut.

Trapped in the depths of despair I turned to the bottle to fill the void, knowing full well that drinking a couple of bottles of vodka a day is a slow but certain attempt at self-destruction. But a perverse part of me also thinks that maybe it was what saved me.

Maybe, the drink became the one thing in the world that I had left to care about. *Maybe* the obsession with getting drunk each day was the only thing which stopped me jumping in my car and driving off a cliff. Whatever the reasoning and whatever the rationale, the need to drink as much as was humanly possible each day became all-consuming. At some point, I lost the ability to feel drunk. I knew that I *was* drunk by the way that I bumped into things and from the looks on other people's faces, but the truth was that I felt nothing.

My memories of that period are vague and dreamlike. Whole days went missing and maybe even whole weeks. Somewhere in the midst of my pickled depression Christmas came. And went. For the most part, I have vague recollections of drinking with Skip or Terry, of reversing my car into a tree or of waking up with my face scuffed up and having no idea how it had happened.

I have a vague recollection of an incident one evening when Les Guscom had gotten into a fight. No, that's not right, there was no fight; just Les swinging a huge right hook and flooring some poor devil before stamping up and down on him repeatedly. Two big guys, friends of Les I think, eventually pulled him away from his victim otherwise I think he would have been happy to keep at it until there was nothing left. I have no idea what it was all about and I don't remember feeling sorry for the guy. Just thankful that it wasn't me on the receiving end. The truth was that back then I couldn't have fought my way out of a paper bag.

I spent most nights sitting alone in my car or in my house and crying myself to sleep. It became such a regular end to my day that I don't think I could have slept without it. Eventually, my misery ceased to be about Judy or David and morphed into a full-blown depression. Oh woe is me.

I knew how far I'd fallen, knew how pathetic I'd become and I hated it. I hated myself for being a drunk. I hated myself for letting myself go physically. I hated myself for not going to work and then on the days when I did, for being rubbish at work. I even hated myself for hating myself. If I'd had the guts and been sober enough to make the drive to cliffs I probably would have, but drinking myself to death seemed a much easier option, albeit a lot more longwinded.

And probably, if it hadn't have been for that fateful Friday night, that's exactly what I would have done.

****

I had driven out to the East coast of Essex that day to see some customers and wound up drinking myself stupid in a pub in Harwich. I started my journey home around rush hour but gave up half way when I persuaded myself that stopping off for a pint and a piss was a more sensible option than battling the heavy traffic caused by an accident on the A12. Naturally enough, one pint turned into four and night had fallen by the time I resumed my journey.

I had developed a deep aversion to going home at night, almost to the point of paranoia. The loneliness and emptiness of the dark and silent house served only to amplify the loneliness and emptiness of my own soul and it was becoming something of a habit to find a secluded spot to park up and bawl my eyes out before heading back. I returned home only after reaching a state of inebriation sufficient to guarantee that I could immediately pass out as soon as I got in. Although I spent a massive proportion of my time in pubs back then, often I just wanted to be on my own so that I could wallow in my own misery. Just not in my own home.

That Friday was no exception and I decided to pull into a secluded car park which I had used before to simply sit and nourish my depression with the bottle of vodka I had on standby. The car-park was little more than an area of cleared forest tucked away off the main road. It was used by dog walkers and ramblers during the day, being in a pretty part of Essex, but it was always empty after dark. The area was an exaggerated kidney bean in shape. Once you drove in, you could double back on yourself to the left or to the right and be tucked away out of sight from the other side; and being out of sight suited me just fine.

As I drove in slowly over the broken ground and pulled in tight to the left-hand side my headlights swept the surrounding forest confirming what I'd hoped for, that there was no-one else about. Deep in the left-hand corner I was almost completely hidden by a large bush. I was conscious of the fact that the seclusion of the woods could also be the type of place where young couples might come to make out and also of the fact that in the unlikely event of a police car pulling in to the clearing, if they asked me what I was doing there, I couldn't very well say getting drunk. Better to be as out of sight as possible.

Falling asleep in my car had become such a regular part of my daily routine that I had taken to keeping an old blanket bundled up on the passenger seat for just such a night, but it was surprisingly mild for a February evening and I opened the windows to stop them from misting and, with the radio quietly playing some depressing music, I settled in to my bottle of vodka.

I'm not sure how long I'd been sitting there, it could have been half an hour or it could have been two, but I'm fairly sure that I was starting to nod off when the crunch of tyres on gravel shook me from my stupor. I looked up to see headlights swing into the clearing and turn to the right before being switched off as the car parked. My immediate thoughts were that this was the perfect excuse I needed to put away the rest of the vodka and make my way home. But as I reached for the keys in the ignition, a second set of headlamps swung in and parked up next to the first.

For some reason I can't explain, this threw me into a state of muddled confusion. I wasn't sure now whether to start the car and leave, or to sit it out quietly, banking on them not seeing me tucked away, and wait until they left again. I was well and truly hammered by that time and my addled brain struggled to string together any rational thought process. So when I saw the interior lights click on as the occupants of both cars got out simultaneously I began to wonder if I was hallucinating. I wondered if I was hallucinating, not because there were people getting out of cars in a secluded woodland area in the middle of the night, but rather because the two men who got out shared more than a passing resemblance to Les Guscom and Campsite Terry.

Despite the dark, it was a cloudless night with a three-quarter moon hanging high in the sky and my eyes had had more than enough time to fully adapt, so that whilst the car park and its new occupants may have been lacking in colour, it was otherwise perfectly clear to me.

In the Royal Marines they'd taught us about the basic physiology of the eyeball. The eye itself is made up or rods and cones, with the cones being used for daytime vision and colour perception whilst the rods are what use in the dark. The cones are concentrated in the centre with the rods surrounding them and it's one of the reasons that it is easier to see something in the dark by not staring directly at it, but by looking slightly off to one side and using your peripheral vision. The cones are pretty good at adapting to different levels of daylight, as the pupils expand and contract accordingly, but whilst the rods are much better at seeing in the dark, it takes them much longer to adjust before they can become really effective.

I watched silently as Les cast his eyes about to check that there was no one else in the clearing before stalking over to Terry who held his arms out to his sides with his palms facing forward, seemingly in a gesture of supplication. I wondered how I had managed not to have been seen, but I was pretty well hidden and I guess that having only just turned off their headlights, their eyes hadn't yet had time to adjust enough to let them see as clearly in the dark as I could. With my windows cracked open either side, I could make out their voices, though not their conversation. Fragments of sentences came through a word or two at a time and it was obvious that Terry was pleading with Les about something and that Les was very unhappy.

'…..another week…'

'…already given you….'

'…please Les…'

'…take me for a fucking mug…' By now, Les was shoving Terry in the chest to punctuate each sentence and I watched as Terry stumbled backwards each time until eventually he'd completed a full circuit of his car. The difference in size between the two of them must have been a foot in height and a foot in shoulder width and the difference in build combined with his Neanderthal looking skull and the shadows of the night, served to make Les look like the stuff of nightmares as stalked Terry round his car in a slow escalation of anger and venom.

Had there have been a way that I could have fled the scene without being spotted, I swear I would have left them to it, despite knowing that things were not likely to end well for Terry. My hearing seemed to adapt to the night in the same way that my eyes already had and soon I could hear both of them clearer, although there wasn't much to it beyond Les swearing at Terry and threatening him.

I heard the meaty slap as Les suddenly swung a massive left hook, seemingly in slow motion, the white of his plastic wristwatch serving only to emphasise the blow which connected with the side of Terry's head, lifting him off of his feet before hitting the mud like a sack of dirty washing.

I watched in horror as Les stood over him, still cursing insults onto his barely conscious form as he feebly tried to regain his senses, and I watched as he lifted a size thirteen foot and stomped him back down into the dirt of the clearing.

I was completely off my face with booze but it was one of those curious moments when time seemed to slow and minute details were brought into sharp relief. Memories lie, of course. I know that only too well, but the memory of that scene is as clear today as if it happened last night. I've relived the nightmare so many times since then that it's like watching a video replay. I can even zoom in to certain aspects and see them as clear as I can see my own hands. And of all the things I remember from that evening with the utmost clarity, it was the look of savage glee on Les' face as he began to stomp down on Campsite Terry's head that still haunts me to this day. I even remember the look of brief frustration flitting across his features as one of his stamps failed to make the connection he'd hoped for. I vividly recall the look of happiness return as his kick to Terry's head connected with a level of force that snapped his head back with such force that it may well have broken his neck. I remember the look of grim determination and retarded concentration on his face as he stamped down hard on Terry's head, again, and again, and again…

Worst of is the memory of the sheer ecstasy which spread across his grotesque features as he felt Terry's head split beneath his feet and as he continued to stamp at the blood and the brains spilling across the floor.

Memories.

I had been looking out from an area of darkness, deep in the shade of the trees, but the area in which Les had acted out Terry's final scene was lit by the three-quarter moon and it was as clear to me then as watching a black and white movie, but despite the night, when I recall it now, it appears to me in glorious Technicolor. I've replayed the events so many times now, that it seems as if they went on for over an hour, but in reality, it could have been no more than four or five minutes.

With his bloodlust finally sated, I watched as Les caught his breath and looked about him once more to make sure that he was still alone. Still, he didn't see me sitting in my dark car in the darkened corner and I began to relax as I realised that I had been holding my breath. I had witnessed violence before in my lifetime, Lord knows, I had dished some out in my time too. But never before had I seen anything to match such sadistic savagery as that which I saw in that darkened place. I have met people with a love for violence, for inflicting pain, but I had never before met someone who derived such extreme pleasure from it. For les, it seemed as though it was something akin to a sexual climax. Indeed, when I close my eyes, I can still see him now, standing over Terry's dead body and rubbing his groin through his trousers, before looking around once more and getting back into his car and starting the engine.

I still curse myself sometimes for my cowardice that night as I sat there paralysed with fear, but the truth is that there was nothing I could have done to prevent that gruesome scene from playing out. I was so plastered that if I'd gotten out of my car I probably would have fallen flat on my face before taking more than a step or two.

I thought I'd gotten away with it, thought that I'd managed to keep my presence a secret. Whilst both Terry and Les had looked about them when they first drove into the clearing, neither had been able to see me, tucked away as I was. After the murder, Les had looked around once more, checking again that he was all alone and once again, I had not been seen. But night vision or no night vision, there was no way he could have missed me as he turned his car around in that clearing and lit me up in his headlamps. Like the beam of a lighthouse sweeping out to sea, his headlights came on as he turned about to exit and I watched in horror as they swept the trees and the bushes in a slow and lazy arc, before inevitably washing over me and into the forest beyond. And then they stopped.

I'd like to think that Les had a moment of panic just then. Having believed that he was completely alone and literally getting away with murder, it must have been a metaphorical slap to the face to suddenly realise that someone else had been there to witness his heinous crime. But if it was a moment of panic for Les, it was a moment of sheer terror for me. I should have realised, of course, that I would have been lit up like a Christmas tree the moment either of them turned their cars around to leave, but as drunk as I was, it hadn't occurred to me for even a moment.

I was transfixed, like a rabbit in the headlights. I couldn't have opened the door and run even if I'd wanted to and I sat there helplessly waiting for the next events to unfold. Ahead of me, I could make out Les' car stopped, side on and with the headlights pointing off to my right, but beyond that I was blind. The bright lights shining directly into my eyes as they'd passed me over had robbed me of my night vision and set my rods back to daytime mode.

For a while nothing happened as I sat there rooted to my seat, still clutching the nearly empty bottle of vodka. Les must have been struggling to make a decision about his next move. I hoped against all hope that he would just drive off, but seconds later his headlights went off and the interior light came on as he opened the door and unfolded his hulking frame from the inside of the car and stalked towards me.

By that time, I was a complete and utter gibbering wreck. I can't tell you what I was thinking as he opened the driver door and realised it was me sitting there when the interior light came on. I was so far gone with the booze, that I'm not sure that I was actually thinking anything, just a feeling of pure terror. I suddenly became aware of the fact that I actually had dribble running from the corner of my mouth and I saw his eyes drop to my lap as I wet my pants and farted wetly at the same time.

The presence of a potential witness in that clearing had obviously come as a most unwelcome surprise to him and now that he could see that it was me, someone he knew, albeit only as someone who drank in his local, it must have presented him with a whole host of different variables. He gazed down on me with the flat stare of a killer and took in the nearly empty bottle of vodka, the soiling of my trousers and my evidently petrified and tanked-up state. There is absolutely no doubt in my mind that he must have been considering putting an end to my life too that night, because if I'd been in his shoes it's exactly what I would have done.

But something stayed his hand. Maybe he liked the idea of having a witness. Most of the real thugs I have met in life are actually quite proud of their actions and maybe it boosted his psychopathic ego to have someone who could verify his story and yet still be so frightened that they would never to talk to the police. Who knows? It may even have been the putrid smell of shit that clung to me by that time. Or maybe it was that beating a man to death had robbed him of his appetite for another murder that night. Or maybe he just figured that killing two different people in the same place meant twice the chance of getting caught.

Whatever the reason was, when he finally made his decision, he reached in with a hand the size of a shovel and took a handful of the front of my shirt. Lifting me off my seat so that I knocked my head on the roof of the car, he leaned in and spoke into my face, slowly and deliberately. 'I know exactly where you live Owen' he grinned hungrily at me before finishing 'Longacre Avenue, isn't it?'

He was correct. One hundred percent correct, but how the hell he knew where I lived I still don't know to this day. For some reason, he obviously knew more about me than I did him. 'If you breathe a word of this to anyone, I'm going to take you away and have you cut up into small pieces and then I'm going to make you eat them. You were never here and you haven't seen me. Right?'

I couldn't answer. I couldn't even speak, but he seemed satisfied with my gibbering nod and shoved me back hard into my seat. 'Turn the keys in the ignition then Owen. It's time to go home. We don't want you falling asleep out here, do we now?'

I mutely did as he instructed, and after grinding the clutch and stalling it at the first attempt, I slowly drove off under his watchful gaze.

The journey home is another blank in my memory and in fact, I don't remember anything else of that evening although I knew from the empty bottles I found the next day that I must have poured even more booze down my neck when I got home.

CHAPTER ELEVEN

I awoke the next day feeling exactly like a man who'd polished off a couple of bottles of cheap vodka the day before should do; with a screaming headache and a mouth that tasted like I'd spent the night chewing on Gandhi's flip-flop.

I'd thought at first that I wouldn't be able to sleep, and I guess you could debate whether drinking yourself unconscious constitutes any form of proper sleep, but that's exactly what I did do. I'd probably been out for the best part of eight hours, and despite a vicious hangover, and in addition to the inevitable sense of shame and self-loathing which comes with the knowledge that you've deliberately gone out of your way to get as fucked up as is humanly possible, I found that layered over the top of this all too familiar emotion was an even deeper layer of hatred than that which I'd previously become accustomed to.

Hatred of myself for what I'd become. I hated myself for having become such a coward. It was the self-loathing of a man who had tried to hide while he watched his friend being murdered and had not only been too scared to lift a finger to help him but had actually managed to soil himself in the process. It really doesn't get much lower than that.

Maybe if I'd lived my entire life as a pitiful excuse for a human being it would have been easier, but the fact that I had been an altogether different sort of man not so long ago seemed to compound those feelings. For years I had done my best to be the man who didn't shy away from doing what I felt was right. Granted, my idea of right and wrong didn't always conform to the rest of civilised society, but it was still a moral code of sorts.

Whilst I hadn't usually sought confrontation for confrontation's sake, I hadn't been the type of person to shy away from it either. There was a time when I'd been proud of myself for fighting for my country. I'd been proud that I'd pulled my shit back together for the sake of my son after Judy had died when actually, I'd felt like doing anything but that. And despite my previous assertion that I don't really care about anyone other than close friends and family, deep down there's also a small part of me that hates bullies.

It's true that I have little sympathy for people who choose to live their lives as society's whipping boys. If you're not prepared to stand up for yourself you get what you deserve, as far as I'm concerned.

But even I draw the line when it comes to people picking on children, or to a lesser extent, women. As far as I'm concerned, people who bully women or abuse little kids because they're weaker and incapable of putting up any form or meaningful resistance are just cowards. And if there's one thing I hate, it's cowards. If I had my way they'd all be lined up and shot. Dead.

And yet the reality was that that was exactly what I'd become. I'd pulled up into that darkened car park with the sole aim of getting pissed out of my brains because I didn't have the guts to face up to the bad turn my life had taken. I'd watched as one man beat another to death for the sheer thrill of the violence and I had cowered in my seat, terrified at the prospect of that violence being directed at me.

To have descended into that snivelling wet wreck after all that had gone before in my life gave me more shame than I can possibly describe.

CHAPTER TWELVE

Charlie Patterson

Within twenty minutes of leaving the school gates that first year of Secondary School, Judy and I arrived at her house and I went in to meet her parents, Nigel and Doree. Doree was lovely and Nigel had seemed pleasant enough too, that first day, although more reserved. Judy's earlier invitation to tea was reiterated by Doree and I accepted, with the caveat that I needed to pop back home first to tell my parents.

Home was just a five-minute walk but I was so excited that I ran it in three.

'Mum, Mum, I'm going round a friend's house for tea', I yelled into the house as soon as I'd opened the front door, chucking my school bag into the hallway.

'Wait. What? Which friend? When was this arranged', asked my mother, managing to look thoroughly confused and perplexed at the same time as she emerged from the kitchen wearing an apron and drying a saucepan with a slightly grubby looking dishcloth.

'Judy Phillips. She lives in Beresford Road. Number twenty. Her Mum's making spaghetti' I blurted it out, keen to have our exchange over and done with as soon as possible so that I could rush back to Judy's house.

'Judy Phillips? I haven't heard of her before; have I?' asked my mother, still looking more than a little flustered.

'Yes, she lives around the corner', I repeated rather unnecessarily. 'I'll be back by eight!'

'No you won't Owen', came the deep voice of my father as he emerged from the kitchen, brandishing a tea towel of his own.

'What?' I said, rather gormlessly looking from one to the other. My Dad wasn't normally home until later in the day, and seeing him there then had thrown me off balance. Firstly by his unexpected appearance, and secondly by his apparent refusal to let me visit with a new friend, something that in the past he'd never had a problem with.

I gaped incredulously from one to the other, unable to reconcile the fact that having finally made friends with the girl I had been mooning over for the last few months, my parents now seemed to be determined not to let that friendship progress any further.

'What... what do you mean?' I stammered, 'Why not?' I began to think that I was in trouble over some unknown misdemeanour and wondered whether I had got the wrong end of the stick somewhere along the line. And in a sense I had.

'I have no problems with you going to your friends on any other evening Owen, and I'm glad that you've made a new one. And particularly a girl-friend' he added with a sideways glance and a sly smile at my

Mother 'but just not this evening Owen. I'm afraid that you and I have other plans.'

I looked to Mum for some kind of enlightenment, but she returned my gaze with a slightly embarrassed look upon her face.

'Look it's no big deal', said my father putting his hands out in front of him, face down in a conciliatory gesture before I could say another word. 'You and I are going wrestling this evening. You remember me talking about my old Navy pal, Mudder. Well he runs the wrestling club down at the sports centre and in view of what happened to you a few weeks ago', he gestured vaguely towards the faint bruising still evident around my eyes, 'it's not going to do any harm to learn how to handle yourself a bit better'

So that was that. I had no real say in the matter, it had been decided that I was to take up wrestling, a sport I knew absolutely nothing about beyond the showboating play-actors I had seen on the television, and with such decidedly un-athletic looking figures as Big Daddy and Giant Haystacks being the big names I was used to seeing, I was less than excited at the prospect.

But I was in for something of a surprise.

I dashed back to Judy's house to offer my apologies for not being able to dine with them and assured them that the following evening I would be free to take them up on the offer. Three hours later, after a light tea at home, I had my introduction into the world of martial arts.

Mudder's wrestling club was held on a Monday and Thursday evening at a sports hall in nearby Loughton. If you hadn't already known that there was a sports hall there, you would never have found it, tucked away as it was at the back of a housing estate as if it were ashamed of its own existence. It must have been built back in the 1950s or '60s when the rest of the council estate had been built and then as soon as the estate had been finished, it had been promptly forgotten. It wasn't much to look at from the outside surrounded as it was with overgrown shrubs and a potted tarmac car park.

But once inside, the sports hall was fairly well appointed, and the main hall was the size of eight badminton courts with the usual panoply of conflicting floor markings showing that it was also ready to be used for basketball and football as well as badminton, and of course, wrestling. Upstairs there were squash courts and weights rooms as well as the showers and changing rooms.

As soon as we walked into the hall I saw Mudder holding court at one end and he and my father made a straight line for each other smiling broadly and shaking hands.

Although I had heard both my Mother and Father talking about Mudder in conversations, I knew very little about him. That he was an old friend of my father's and that they had both served in the Navy together was pretty much it back then.

He turned out to be a tough looking Glaswegian with a handsomely battered looking face, shocking blue eyes and a contrasting shock of jet black hair. His rugged good looks would have been perfectly at home on a Hollywood film star were it not for the fact that as soon as he opened his mouth to speak, it became immediately evident that he was missing a full set of dentistry. Only later did I discover that he'd lost four of his teeth whilst wrestling, presumably having been knocked out accidentally by a stray elbow or clash of heads.

Whilst Hollywood could have easily overcome his missing teeth on the silver screen with a set of dentures, one thing which could not have been altered was his voice. It turned out that Mudder was only operating on one vocal cord as a result of yet another wrestling mishap many years before with the result being that anything which came out of his mouth sounded like gravel in a cement mixer. Coupled with this was a thick Glaswegian accent which made him virtually unintelligible to my young ears.

He was extremely well muscled in wholly natural proportions, like the true sportsmen and athletes of those days, long before the casual steroid abuse so common amongst the young these days. There seemed to be not an ounce of fat on him and there was also something about his whole demeanour which exuded an iron aura of unrelenting body and mind.

I was soon to learn that not only were my first impressions largely accurate in this instance but that he was also an uncompromising and cantankerous old sod with a sadistic streak running through him from head to toe.

My father wasted no time in introducing me as the 'troublemaker' he had told him about over the phone, smiling broadly at Mudder as he said this.

'So you're looking to learn how to fight then kid'? he demanded with an intent look whilst crouching down so as to draw level with my eye-line.

However, to state that those were the words that came out of his mouth are to do his voice and his broad Glaswegian accent a complete injustice. What he actually said was more along the lines of 'So, yez looking tae lun hoo tae fight than kid?'

Completely bewildered I looked up at my father, wondering what the hell the scary man from Scotland had just said and what on earth I had done to upset him.

Amused by my obvious confusion, my father knew exactly what he'd said and translated for me, 'He says, "are looking to learn how to fight?"'.

'Erm, yes. Well, no, not really. I'm just here coz Dad said it would be a good thing... For me that is.'

'Och well, we'll soon see aboot that than kid. Ye'll either take to it or you won't. One thing's for sure though, you canna be any worse than your Da.'

Bewildered, I looked to my Father once more for help with translation, but this time he just grinned boyishly at Mudder before saying to me, 'come on Kid, let's help get these mats out.'

The mat area covered the space of two badminton courts and it was quite a task to put the heavy padded mats out at the beginning of the session and to take them back up at the end, so we'd arrived early, along with most of the others to get changed into shorts and T-shirts before helping to put them out.

A little apprehensive, I took the time to study the others who would make up the class. The club was well attended, with perhaps twenty lads of varying ages (there were no girls there), and ten adults participating. Of the adults, I was intrigued to see a mish-mash of body shapes and ages, along with a liberal sprinkling of cauliflowered ears and previously broken noses. They were a far cry from the men I had been used to watching on Saturday afternoon TV.

We started off with a 'warm-up', which was the hardest I'd worked, physically, in my young life up to that point. My father had decided to join in too, although whether for personal gain or to prop me up with moral support I never found out.

I knew that he too, had wrestled many years before, but to my eyes, both he and Mudder were old men now and in my young opinion, I decided that they really shouldn't have been over-exerting themselves.

But with the sweat pouring out of him, my father went through each of the shuttle sprints, the press ups, the burpees and the star jumps and every other sadistic form of exercise which Mudder could think of without a hint of complaint and with very little evidence of any great discomfort.

I had imagined that I would be eased into this wrestling lark gradually, but it seemed that there were no concessions to be had for being the new boy, and certainly no concessions given for being the son of one of the instructor's oldest friends.

The warm-up went on for fully half an hour. I know because I spent much of it looking at the wire mesh covered clock high on the wall and vainly willing the hands to move faster. By the end of that first half hour I was utterly exhausted and looking around me I could see that I wasn't alone.

I also noticed that for the most part, the other lads there seemed to revel in their exhaustion, as if they'd taken some kind of masochistic pleasure from pushing their bodies through such a punishing regime. I wasn't entirely sure that I shared their sentiment in that regard, but when I realised that first part was finally finished I did feel a sense of relief simply to have it over and done with.

But of course, it wasn't finished at all. The warm-up may have been punishing, but I soon learned that any amount of press-ups or squat-thrusts were infinitely less painful than having someone physically pick you up before dumping you flat on your back with a 'cross buttock' or some other arcane-sounding wrestling move.

I was paired up with Charlie Patterson, a lad who was two years my junior and therefore considerably smaller, as you might expect at that age. But the flip side of that particular coin was that he had already been wresting for two years and was actually rather good at it. Better than good in fact.

That first evening of wrestling was to prove to be something of a baptism of fire and I felt the humiliation of every defeat burning in my cheeks as this little guy, two years my junior, took me down or flipped me over, time and time again, driving me into the mat with apparently effortless ease.

Whilst wrestling does not provide the explosive spectacle that a martial art like boxing does, I soon learned that it involves the application of just as much violence, if not more so. Wrestling is a fight. Granted, it's a fight with rules, but it's still a fight and you don't get to take someone off of their feet and drive them into the ground without using plenty of aggression.

Despite the ease with which he seemed to counter my every attempt at attack and the even greater ease with which he managed to take me down to the mat and pin my shoulders, never once did Charlie Patterson even look like gloating at my discomfort, something which I'm sure I would have done back then had the tables been turned. The patience, humility and respect that Charlie Patterson showed me seemed to be being mirrored across the mats by everyone else there that evening.

I knew enough to realise that, as angry and as humiliated as I was at being constantly put on my back by that little squirt time after time, it was important not to show it. In line with other martial arts, wrestling is a form of controlled aggression, and it's important to realise that win or lose, there should be no bad feelings either before or after each bout.

Charlie was the perfect example of how a good sportsman should act. After every painful fall or armlock, he made sure that I wasn't badly hurt.

'Was I OK to carry on? Did I want him to show me what he had done, how I could defend against it next time?'

When Mudder showed the class a new drill or a new hold, Charlie carefully guided me through each movement, trying to make sure that I understood every aspect of what was going on around me. But whilst I knew enough to hide it from him and everyone else, inwardly I seethed. The nicer he was to me, the more determined I was to teach him a lesson he wouldn't forget. Someday.

Charlie's maturity and attitude to life, in general, belied his age. When we were off the mats he would laugh and joke like any other ten year old, but as soon as we were back on, he was all business. Looking around at the other pairs of people fighting each other, it was obvious that they all had the same respect for each other and that although they were all in the business of trying to hurt each other, equally, they were all responsible for not causing any lasting injury to their opponents.

Despite the pain and the feeling and of being generally useless, that evening I became hooked. Hooked on the adrenaline rush of combat. For many people, the attraction was the ethos of a sport steeped in history and mutual respect, but for me, it was all about improving enough to wreak my revenge on Charlie Patterson.

Despite the decent turnout at the club run by Mudder, wrestling was still very much a minority sport, even in those days. It was the era when Bruce Lee and Sylvester Stallone were making eye-catching and thrilling films. Most people were more interested in learning how to perform a roundhouse kick to the head or how to knock someone out with a single punch. They didn't understand that, as spectacular as these fights may have appeared on TV, neither of those moves are viable if someone has already picked you up or dumped you on the floor. They ignored the reality that ninety-nine per cent of real-life fights entail two guys exchanging one or two punches before one of them ends up holding the other in a headlock, or both parties finish up rolling about on the floor.

The failings of these other disciplines of martial arts and the benefits of learning how to grapple were constantly reinforced to me by both my father and Mudder and backed up with stories of their own encounters and scrapes as younger men. Stories which were no doubt embroidered in places and censored in others, as befitted their young audience.

I started going to the wrestling club twice a week, which was as often as it was run. If there had been other clubs available for me to go to on other days, I would have gone to those too, but even back then, when wrestling was more popular on TV and still had a modicum of respect as a 'proper' martial art, wrestling clubs were few and far between.

So twice a week was as much as I could realistically manage, but twice a week at a young age, under the clinical instruction of Mudder and with the fantastically patient guidance of Charlie Patterson was a very good springboard from which to leap.

I was also at an age when puberty had begun to kick in and my testosterone levels had started to rise. Within weeks of that first night on the wrestling mats, my fitness levels blossomed beyond any recognition, as did my carriage and bearing. Twice a week I would compete and fight either with lads who were much older than me, or with Charlie who was far more talented. I became stronger without even realising it, the other lads on the mats were also gaining power so it was a long time before I discerned any real difference.

After two months of slow improvement, Mudder took me to one side and warned me that this would be the case. I think he realised that I was at a point when I was beginning to question my own abilities. He told me, begrudgingly, that whilst it might not have felt like it to me at that time, I was, in fact, making great improvements.

Deep down I knew that he was right, but when everyone else seemed to drop me to the ground or pin me with such little effort, it felt more like flattery than any kind of real assessment.

It was a different story at school, however, where the majority of my young friends either languished doing no sports at all or spent their time chasing an inflatable ball around a playing field.

It gradually dawned upon me that I was starting to be able to do things which most of my friends couldn't. I was still something of a slouch when it came to any activity involving running or sprinting, but when it came to sports requiring strength or fitness, slowly but surely, my star began to shine.

Not long after the start of the school year we completed our first ever cross country run. It was probably only a mile long but was something which was new to us all at that age. Whilst most of my friends alternated between running and walking, I strode on without discomfort. I didn't finish at the front of the class, but fifth place out of thirty was far, far higher than I'd have ever thought to achieve before I'd taken up wrestling.

Football was a game which had never before interested me before as I was, by and large, useless at it, but suddenly I found that I wasn't quite as useless as I'd thought. When most of the other lads had run out of energy and were gasping for breath, I was still going strong. Like a bunny on Duracell.

It's also true, of course, that the more you begin to realise that you are good at something, the more you enjoy doing it. I started to compete in every physical activity the school had to offer. Outside of organised games, I challenged friends, and boys older than me to contests of strength and endurance. Who could do the most press-ups; who could hold heavy books out to the side the longest, even who could hold their breath the longest.

I became so confident that I even picked a couple of fights with kids in the year above me. It was pointless really as I had no real beef with either of them but having gained so much on the wrestling mats, I wanted to put myself to the test in the 'real world.' Both lads regretted not walking away from me. I soon gained a reputation as someone not to be messed with, a reputation which never really left me again for the rest of my school days.

Everyday life soon became one long work-out after another. I never really packed on any muscle mass though, too busy growing upwards I guess, but I was, and have always been, happy with that. I'd rather be the strong guy that looks little than the weak guy that looks big.

The one fly in my personal ointment was Charlie bloody Patterson. No matter how hard I tried, I could never get close to beating him. And the nicer he was to me, the more I hated him (although I was careful not to show it).

CHAPTER THIRTEEN

I gave up the wrestling when I was fifteen or sixteen. It was at a time when I should have been swatting up for exams (not that I made a great deal of effort) and what with that and still being hopelessly in love with Judy I found that I had too many other distractions to keep myself motivated. It was also around that time that Mudder changed jobs and his commitments meant that he rarely managed to attend any more. Without him, the club was never the same.

I didn't really miss it. I'd gotten to be about as good as I was ever going to get and whilst that was still a pretty decent standard, I was never going to pick up any medals at the Olympic games. Neither did I ever get good enough to come close to beating Charlie who, annoyingly, probably *would* be standing on a podium one day, wearing a winner's medal around his neck.

When I quit wrestling I lost all contact with Charlie and it wasn't until I was in my early twenties that I saw him again. I'd stopped at a petrol Station in Epping late one Friday afternoon and as I put the nozzle back in its place and finished screwing the petrol cap back on, I saw a tall, fair-haired lad come out of the shop chatting to a girl.

The girl was dusky skinned and something of a stunner but it was the lad that caught my eye. As he came back to his car he looked up and caught me staring before breaking into a huge and infectious smile.

'Owen! How're you doing mate? I haven't seen you in ages!'

The last time I'd seen Charlie Patterson he had been only fourteen years old but as soon as he opened his mouth there was no doubting who it was. I'm six-foot tall and as a lad I had always towered over Charlie on the mats. But Charlie had grown and he was easily an inch or two taller than me and that, coupled with the fact that he was all lean rippling muscle with a youthful good-looking face, made him look every bit as impressive as Mudder had.

It was no wonder that he had such a good looking girl on his arm.

I greeted him like a long lost friend and such was Charlie's bonhomie and friendly nature that I immediately forgot about all the humiliating falls I'd suffered at his hands. This guy was impossible not to like!

'Where are you off to?' he asked after we'd explained pleasantries and had the briefest of catch-ups.

'Just home mate for now. But I'm popping up the Queen Elizabeth for a few beers later if you fancy it?'

'Love to' he replied 'but I'm just dropping Tracy home and then I've got to get home for an early night'

'Oh?' I said, quizzically.

'Yeah, I'm trialling for the Commonwealth Games squad tomorrow. Up in Birmingham and I'm driving dad's car so I'm going to need to leave around six to make sure I'm fresh.'

The car he'd been driving was an old green Volvo with a GB sticker on the back and so it suddenly made sense to me that it was his Dad's.

'I take it that your Old Man's going up with you, that he'll be driving?'

'No. Mum and Dad are away in Spain this week but he said that it's Ok for me to use it. It's not ideal prep to be driving so far before a competition but I think I'll be OK' he said, with a smile that told me that he had no doubt that it was a competition he would be winning.

We went our separate ways and I spent my evening exactly as predicted. Swilling beer in the Queen Elizabeth pub with a couple of mates, before heading home at closing time.

I was already in my bed before I started thinking back to the chance meeting with Charlie earlier that day.

My mind drifted back to his 'where are you off to' question and I realised then that he'd used it as the perfect excuse to move the conversation onto his own movements and plans. Fair enough, I thought. If I'd been good enough to enter a completion which was a gateway to representing my country at the

Commonwealth Games, I'd probably be bragging about it too.

But the thing about Charlie was that he never did brag. He'd been talking about it because he was excited, not because he wanted to rub my nose in it. I got to thinking about all of the times when he'd gone out of his way *not* to hurt me, when he'd taken the time to make sure that I was all right or that I had understood how a particular movement worked.

And then I got to thinking about all of the times I had resented him for being so nice to me. How I'd actually *hated* him for caring so much and how I'd wanted so much to hurt him but had never been able to.

Then it came to me. In my drunken state it seemed to me that destiny had thrown us together that day, that fate had somehow engineered our meeting. Suddenly I knew that I had to make things right and more to point, that I had to make things right that *very* night.

I threw the bed covers off and quickly got dressed in the clothes I'd been wearing earlier that evening and which I had so carelessly discarded on my bedroom floor. It was 12.45 a.m. and I was still living with my parents at the time and, not wanting to disturb them, I made sure that I did so as quietly as possible before creeping downstairs and going out to my car.

My car was parked out on the road two houses down so I wasn't particularly concerned about the noise of the engine starting waking my parents up, but still, I closed the car door with as soft a clunk as was possible before setting off. I was well over the limit from the several pints of lager I'd drunk in the pub earlier but there was barely another car on the road at that time of night and my only real concern back then was the possibility of being pulled over by a police car.

Fifteen minutes later I was back in Epping.

Back then, Epping was a sleepy town outside of the M25 where nothing much happened and driving through it at that hour was like driving through a ghost town. Nothing open and not a soul in sight.

I wasn't exactly sure what number Charlie lived at, but I remembered the road from a time when my dad had dropped him off many years back. It was a reasonably well to do street, made up of semi-detached houses with garages on the side so that every house had its own driveway. As I turned into it, I cast about left and right looking until my eyes settled upon the object of my search.

Outside number thirteen was an olive green Volvo with a GB sticker on the boot.

There were no lights on inside the house and there were no lights on in any of the neighbouring houses. The pubs had all stopped serving at 11 p.m. and it was a time when there was no television past midnight so that it was rare for people to be up and about in the wee small hours. Nevertheless, I was conscious that I didn't want to wake anyone up and so I parked about fifty metres down the road before getting out and opening and closing the boot as quietly as I could.

The thing about those old cars was that by today's standards they were incredibly easy to steal or to steal from. Any kind of security measure beyond the key you used to get in them was something of an afterthought. So there was no lockable petrol cap on that old Volvo which meant that it was simple enough for me to unscrew the cap and shove the petrol-soaked rags I'd already prepared as far in as I could. I always carried a spare can of petrol in my boot in those days and I splashed the rest of it around liberally, trying to make sure that there were no areas I'd missed.

I was careful not to be too close when it went up and so I set fire to a whole box of matches before tossing it at arm's length. There was no great explosion and no great 'whump', but the car caught alight immediately, radiating a fierce heat and I set off at a run, careful not to look back in case anyone should see my face from their window. As soon as I got into my own car I raced off, not bothering to turn my lights on until I was well clear of the scene of my crime.

I never did find out whether Charlie made it to Birmingham the next day and if he did, how he'd fared. In fact, I never saw or heard of Charlie Patterson ever again.

They say that a leopard never changes its spots and maybe there's some truth in the fact that the underlying nature of most people remains unchanged as they age but personally, I'd like to think that since then I've matured and mellowed.

I'm not proud of what I did that night, it was a pretty cowardly thing to do and if there's one thing I don't like, it's people who are too chicken shit to stand up for themselves.

I'm still a spikey, vengeful old sod, but if I had my time all over again there's no way I'd do that to Charlie again, but the truth was that back then he'd made me feel inferior. He'd pissed me off for years and I whilst I might have taken my time getting around to it, the way I saw things back then, finally I had made things right.

CHAPTER FOURTEEN

Nine months ago
I can be just as vindictive today as I was back then and with a history like that, it was was only a matter of time before I decided to wreak my revenge on Les Guscom for the humiliation he had heaped on me that night. As I sat there at my scarred kitchen table nursing a cup of tea in a 'Best Dad in the World' mug, I knew that it was time to make some radical changes. Things were about to get serious.

Inevitably, I came to the obvious conclusion that self-loathing was an altogether counter-productive emotion and that, *actually*, the real villain of the piece was not myself, but Les Guscom. The truth was that Les Guscom was thus far getting off lightly. In fact, the more I thought about it, he was, of course, getting off scot-free.

I sat there, wrapped in my tired old dressing gown, staring off into space whilst the mug of tea slowly cooled between my cupped hands and I realised that that nasty, vicious, sadistic, and murderous slag, had probably spent the rest of last night getting completely off his face somewhere. Probably boasting to his equally vicious little friends, or even to his vile German mother, of how he'd bludgeoned and killed poor Campsite Terry. And then, the icing on the cake, how he'd terrified me so much that he'd made sure that there would be no witness statements. They'd have all been laughing away as he told them how the biggest loser in town, Owen 'Piss Head' Thomson, had wet his pants, quite literally, when he put the frighteners on him.

The more I thought about it, the angrier I became. From a starting point of grumpy irritability came an anger which I nurtured as it grew. There was no flashpoint of rage or irrationality, just a cold, calculating, quiet fury which ultimately proved to be far more deadly.

I needed to make amends. I had to redress the balance. Obviously. I considered going to the police, after all, it was the natural reaction and course of action for any civilised member of a civilised society. But I wasn't feeling particularly civilised at that time and I was also pretty sure that I knew what the outcome of such an action would have been.

First of all there would have been the embarrassment of having to explain why I was in that car-park in the first place. Then there would have been the shame of telling them of how I'd sat by and watched, without raising a note of protest or a finger of defence. Finally there was the explanation of why I had taken so long to come forward as a witness to consider.

Even if the police did take action, it seemed a reasonable bet that Les would have cleared up by then and disposed of any evidence linking him to the scene that night. He might not be the smartest bloke in the world, but it was odds on that a man who made his money selling drugs would have had a certain level of criminal cunning. I was also pretty sure that he would have been able to find some ne'er do well willing enough to give him an alibi.

So without any forensic evidence, it would have been my word against his. His word against the word of an alcoholic who'd parked up in a darkened carpark with the sole aim of necking a bottle of vodka.

Who knew, maybe they'd even conclude that it was me who'd committed the murder.

Whatever the police decided, I would also have had to contend with the fact that I would then be living on borrowed time. The Guscoms knew who I was and, for some inexplicable reason, Les evidently knew where I lived and they didn't strike me as being the type of family to let these things slip by unanswered. At the time, I didn't feel particularly afraid of dying, I was still too angry, but nevertheless, it was something I wanted to avoid if possible.

So, my self-loathing turned to anger and that anger had slowly turned into a cold fury. A fury which simmered quietly beneath an outwardly calm exterior and which was to give me a clarity of purpose and focus. And the focus of that fury would be Les Guscom.

Revenge. I needed revenge. Revenge for Camp Site Terry. Revenge for the humiliation heaped upon myself and revenge for the countless others that Les must have stomped upon during his time on earth; time that I decided was to be cut short.

I could think of no other sentence worthy of his crime, no sentence more certain and no other form of justice which would satiate my need for revenge. Les Guscom had to die and I was determined that it would be me that made it happen.

I'd always tried to be someone who wouldn't shy away from doing the right thing; or at least what I considered to be the right thing, and it was high time that I regained my self-respect. Granted, my sense of what was right and wrong didn't necessarily coincide with what most other people thought, but as far as I was concerned that was their problem and not mine.

CHAPTER FIFTEEN

Fifteen years ago

Keith Lawson was an Independent Financial Adviser who specialised in setting up investment seminars; seminars which were designed to persuade people that they really needed his services. And judging by the size of the house he lived in and the Range Rovers parked on the gravel driveway, it was something he was quite successful at.

Fortunately for me, and for Anglian Press, it also meant that he managed to get through a fair amount of stationery, as he dished out the personalised brochures and pens sporting his logo, as well as a whole load of other marketing bumph, to the people attending his seminars.

His order volumes were never going to make me rich, but they were steady enough to make it worth my while. Even if they hadn't have been, I always enjoyed his company and it was a pleasure to drop in on him.

I liked Keith because he was interesting to me. Interesting because he was already a very successful salesman (despite being called a Financial 'Advisor' there was no doubting that it was commission based sales practice) and when you admire someone else's talent, it pays to spend time studying it.

Just as hard work needs a little good fortune to turn it into a success, the opposite is also true and since those early days with APS I've worked hard to perfect my sales pitch and the way I say and do things in front of prospective customers. I've read no end of books on the psychology of buying, selling and influencing over the last twenty years in an effort to perfect my sales technique. A lot of those books have been absolute rubbish, but equally, some have been incredibly insightful.

It was Keith Lawson who first got me interested in the psychology of sales. We always met in the study of his Edwardian home which was lined, wall to wall, with books on sales techniques and how to influence behaviour. Realising my obvious interest in these subjects he would often pluck one from a shelf before I left and lend it to me.

It was at one of our regular sales meetings that he told me something I hadn't previously known about him.

'I've been busy with my Open University degree Owen' he replied to my opening questions of how he was and what he'd been up to.

'I didn't know you were doing a degree Keith' I said, settling into a leather, wing-backed armchair. I was genuinely surprised. 'What's it in?'

'Psychology. I'm halfway through my second year' He waved idly towards a section of shelving which I now saw was totally dedicated to Psychology textbooks

'Oh wow! I had no idea! Is it interesting?'

'Well, it is to me!' he smiled, 'I guess you're either a believer or you're not. Overall, it's been good. It's given me a new perspective on quite a few things, although it's true that there are some areas which are less engaging than others. My last academic term was all about child psychology and I struggled a bit with that one'

'Why? Was it more complicated to learn?'

'It's not so much that, Owen, it was more that I just didn't find it interesting. I have no kids of my own and I don't interact with them on a regular basis so it's not an area that really figures in my life. Whereas with *norma*l adult psychology I can see the evidence all about me in everyday life to back up almost all of the case studies and social experiments.'

'Social experiments?' I asked, genuinely interested 'what kind of social experiments?'

He settled back into his own wing backed chair on the other side of his leather-topped desk and took a moment whilst he seemed to consider his reply. The wall behind him was the only one without bookshelves and in their place were certificates and various photographs of him collecting awards so that for a moment I had the impression that I was sitting in a real therapist's office.

'Let's try this one' he said after a moment or two 'I'm going to give you a scenario and I want you to listen carefully and then I'm going to ask you a question about it. OK?'

'OK,' I replied, sitting back and looking forward to hearing something interesting.

'A man called John goes to a funeral. Not the funeral of a family member mind. It's the funeral of another guy who lives in the same road as him. We'll call him Dave and he died in a car accident. Whilst John is at Dave's funeral he meets the girl of his dreams. Someone he's never met before but someone with whom he gets along with immediately and with whom he feels he has a real connection. In fact, so smitten is he, that he falls head over heels in love with her there and then.

John plans to take her number after the funeral to ask her on a date and then, hopefully, to progress things further, but she leaves immediately, and he doesn't see her again. A few days later John kills Dave's brother.'

A short silence followed Keith's little story before I prompted him.

'Go on then…'

'Aren't you going to ask me why he murdered Dave's brother?' he asked.

To me, the answer was obvious. 'Presumably to get to see the girl again. After all, if she was at one funeral, the chances are that she'll be at the other brothers?'

There was silence for a moment as Keith seemed to consider my answer. 'Have you heard the question before?' he asked.

'No' I replied, beginning to feel a little confused, and also a little miffed at the fact that I had no idea what was going on. 'I don't get it..?'

'Owen' he said leaning forwards and opening his hands in a conciliatory gesture, 'please don't take this the wrong way, but that particular question was one which was posed to a number of inmates in American prisons who had been diagnosed as criminals with psychopathic disorders. It was found to be a highly effective indicator of psychopathy'

'In what way?'

'Those that spent a long time thinking about the scenario tended to come up with elaborate backstories as to what might have prompted the chain of events, but those that gave the response which you gave, often seemed to reach their conclusions immediately.'

'So, what is the correct answer?'

'That's just it. There is no correct answer. It's just that the answer which you gave is a strong indicator of psychopathy whereas most other answers aren't.'

Keith seemed a little uncomfortable in telling me this but to me, it was just silly and all I really felt at that time was bemusement.

'Well that's a pretty rubbish test then isn't it?' I joked. 'Unless of course, you think that I have a cellar full of dead bodies at home!'

Keith smiled back at me, perhaps relieved that I hadn't taken issue with his little test.

'A common misconception, Owen, is that all psychopaths are violent when in fact quite the opposite is true. There are probably loads of people you already know who are psychopaths but you would never know it under ordinary circumstances.'

'Well then, what is a psychopath?' I asked, genuinely confused 'what's the definition according to your studies?'

'Bear in mind that I'm only halfway through studying this at the moment so I'm not claiming to be an expert in the field, but broadly speaking, a psychopath is someone who is unable to form any kind of emotional attachments outside of their own interests.'

'Go on…' I prompted as he paused to collect his thoughts, presumably trying to recall his recent studies.

'Psychopaths are usually characterised as lacking in conscience and empathy, or of having any sense of guilt. All of which can manifest themselves in any number of a wide range of anti-social behaviours. Anything, from pathological lying, to impulsiveness, to sexual promiscuity and right the way through to murder. But equally, in normal everyday life, they may display none of those characteristics whatsoever.'

'But if they don't display any of those characteristics, what is it that makes them Psychopaths?'

'The conventions of our modern-day society mean that most of us are bound to react to certain circumstances; often in ways which belie our true nature.

Imagine that you are at work and there is someone there who is incredibly fat. Obese in fact. Let's say that person is called Sandra and you don't particularly like her but you found out yesterday that her mother had just died. Then imagine that Sandra is stuffing her face with a huge cream bun at 10 a.m. in the morning, but unfortunately for her, as she bites into it, most of the cream and jam shoots out of the other end and all down her white blouse and black skirt. What would you do?'

'I don't know. I guess that if she was someone I didn't like, I'd probably feel like laughing at her, but I'm pretty sure that I wouldn't...'

'Exactly' he said, smiling at my answer, 'we're all constrained by what civilised society expects us to do. If you'd laughed at her and told her that it served her right for being so greedy you would have come across as a real bastard. Particularly given the fact that she was in the midst of a recent bereavement.'

'But a psychopath would have laughed at her?' I surmised.

'No. That's just it. A psychopath *might* have laughed at her, but the chances are that he wouldn't. Even a psychopath still knows what's expected of him, or her, in a civilised society. Most of them are careful to project this persona outwards so that you wouldn't know their true nature. They still conform to the rules because, after all, even a psychopath doesn't want to go to prison or to get punched in the face.

The real test is seeing what they'd do if the rules of society were removed. Imagine if you lived somewhere without any law or order, the middle of a war zone might be a good example; Most of us would still abide by the moral standards by which we live by now. Most people would still not steal, they wouldn't go around raping and they wouldn't go around killing people just for the sake of it. But a psychopath would have no such qualms'

'Well I don't think much of your test then if it thinks that I'm a psychopath' I said, slightly indignantly, not necessarily because I felt affronted by the thought but more because I thought that it was expected of me. 'I have a beautiful wife and a son at home. Both of whom I very much love.'

'No, no!' he replied, slightly embarrassed at my feigned disgruntlement 'Firstly, please remember that I'm not a qualified psychologist, in fact, I've only just started reading about this area recently and have a way to go yet before I finish my studies.

Secondly, this particular test is only meant to be an indicator, it's by no means meant to be a diagnosis and thirdly, psychopaths and sociopaths present on a whole multitude of levels and just because someone has one of the acknowledged traits of a psychopath or sociopath, it doesn't necessarily make them one. After all, the fact that an animal has four legs, teeth and a tail doesn't necessarily mean that it's definitely a dog.'

'OK, but what's a sociopath then?'

'Ah, good question!' He seemed genuinely pleased that I'd asked him this question.

'There are different schools of thought on this. As far as I can tell, the term 'psychopath' was coined in the late 1800's but back in the 1930's people switched to using the term 'sociopath' in recognition of the potential harm that they sometimes wreaked upon Society. Then, as more and more people became interested and studied the science, they decided to separate out the terms to describe different categories of people. These days there is a whole multitude of different terminology to distinguish differing and varying degrees of what are all essentially Anti-social Behaviour Disorders. The problem comes when you start to read a text written in a different era or from a contrary school of thought.

One of the most common distinctions that's often used is that psychopaths are congenital, meaning that they are born that way, whereas a sociopath usually becomes emotionally deficient due to traumatic circumstances, like an extremely violent upbringing or exposure to war crimes.

But there's another distinction which I've read in yet another text, and by the way, this is the one I prefer, it's that a true psychopath is unable to form any kind of emotional attachment or empathy with anyone else at all, whereas a *sociopath* is only unable to form an emotional attachment or empathy with anyone outside of his own circle of friends or his family.'

He had me there with his second distinction. As far as I was concerned, he'd described my own personality down to a tee. I couldn't care less if you had killed someone right in front of me so long as I didn't know them. I wouldn't particularly care who they were or what they'd done or how you killed them. Just so long as it wasn't somebody I cared about because then we'd have a problem.

The truth was that the only other thing which really bothered me was when grown men picked on women or children. Two men or two women or even two kids can beat the living daylights out of each other for all I care, but seeing a grown-up smacking a kid or a man hitting a woman always seems to make me angrier than I can rationalise.

So, that was my 'diagnosis.' Granted that it wasn't by a real Psychologist or even by someone who had completed a psychology degree at that time, but whether he was right or he was wrong, his layman's definition of a what a sociopath was; how they cared for no-one outside of their own friends and family, fitted perfectly with the feeling of emptiness I had felt for so much of my life.

CHAPTER SIXTEEN

I wasn't entirely sure how I was going to go about killing Les in those early days, only that I was certain I would do it. Having made my decision, I felt as though a weight had been lifted from my shoulders. I had sunk as low as I was going to in that nasty little episode of my life and things were about to start improving. But first I had to sort myself out.

The day after I'd watched Les kill Terry was a Saturday morning, thank heavens, so there was no need to worry about work. I staggered out of bed and got undressed, having been too drunk to take my clothes off the night before.

I'd like to say that I jumped in the shower, but the truth is that I felt so awful that I stumbled in and wound up sitting down, letting the piping hot water massage my head whilst the steam built around me. I'm not sure how long I sat there for, the plumbing in the house was good enough to provide a seemingly endless supply of hot water, but it must have been more than half an hour. Finally, when my skin had started to look like a prune and continuing to sit became uncomfortable, I got out and scrubbed myself dry with a towel the texture of sandpaper.

It was still less than ten hours since my last drink, and in all likelihood, I was still half pissed from the night before (as well as the constant alcoholic abuse I had inflicted upon my body over the previous three months and more) yet I had a clarity of mind and a sense of purpose which I'd been missing for too long.

I got shaved and dressed and searched the house for alcohol. I hadn't really expected to find any as I had finished the last of my bottle the night before and it seemed unlikely that there would be anything else that had escaped me in the preceding months, but I decided that it would be best to make sure. I found nothing other than a bottle of White Spirits in the garage, which I looked at long and hard before deciding that it wasn't going to do any harm to pour it down the sink. I'd never stooped that low before, but it was better to be safe than sorry.

After that, I unplugged the telly and stuck it in the boot of the car; which was no mean feat considering that it was something of a monstrous antique.

The car was a mess, with mud splattered up the sides and a malodorous atmosphere clinging to the interior, a combination of stale booze and stale body gases. It was enough to make my eyes water and I fought hard to control my gag reflex.

I was starting to see things clearly for the first time in ages and I looked at my car with renewed self-revulsion. Coupled with this was the muddy reminder of last night's shame splattered around the wheel arches. I wondered briefly if there might also have been any blood splatter on the car but decided that, no, I had been too far away for that.

But as soon as decided that I'd been too far away for any traces of blood to be on the car I began to question myself. My memories of the previous night were still slightly muzzy, to say the least, and I had been so tanked up that I knew it was possible that I could have been wrong. Better to be safe than sorry.

For the briefest of moments I reconsidered going to the police again but I had been brought up in an era and a neighbourhood where the one thing you never did was go to the police. It was a stupid rule, if you can call it that, I know. But it's hard to break the habits of childhood and from a selfish perspective, whilst they couldn't now breathalyse me for last night's driving, I still couldn't really justify how it was that I came to be in that dark and secluded car-park on my own. If I told them how wrecked I had been, it would also make me, presumably, an unreliable eyewitness and at the same time. Most importantly, I'd also have to confess my own pathetic cowardice and that wasn't something I wanted to face up to.

I contemplated driving the car to the car wash around the corner but it was time to start taking some long-cuts so I traipsed back into the house and rummaged around for a bucket and sponge and some washing up liquid. Incredibly, I managed to find a quarter bottle of vodka in amongst the cleaning materials beneath the sink. I marvelled at it briefly, having no idea when or how it had arrived at such a destination, before tipping it quickly into the sink.

As I carried the empty bottle and a bucket of warm soapy suds back outside, I dropped the empty into the recycling bin and turned around to see Stiff looking at me with something resembling astonishment on his face. It's probably safe to say that his surprise would have been generated by the fact that I looked set to clean my car rather than the fact that I was chucking yet another empty bottle in the recycling bin.

Stiff's full name was Stifford Rod which was no doubt some kind of ironic humour inflicted on him by his parents. The phrase 'stiff as a rod' seemed to sum him up to a tee and ever since we'd first moved in, he'd simply been 'Stiff' to Judy and me. So when I say that Stiff wore an expression resembling astonishment, in truth, there was barely any discernible reaction at all, just the faintest of nuance in his expression, or lack thereof. In anyone else, it would have gone unnoticed, but with Stiff, it constituted a strong emotional response.

That was the extent of our interaction. I nodded at Stiff and he nodded at me before going back inside to do whatever it is was that Stiff normally did on a Saturday morning. Probably staring at walls I guessed.

The day itself had started dank and grey, but it was also surprisingly warm out. There was no need to wear anything other than shirtsleeves although my body temperature that morning had probably also been raised by alcohol-induced high blood pressure.

I took my time cleaning the car, scrubbing away at the dead flies that had become a part of the paintwork and making sure that I missed not a speck. I was in no rush to be anywhere else or to do anything else and I knew that I had a long day ahead of me to fill.

By that time, I was suffering a full-on assault from my alcoholic alter ego and the mindlessness of cleaning the car was about all I could have managed. Every other thought revolved around drink.

Perhaps it would be easier to put off quitting for another day? Maybe start on Monday when I was at work again? Or maybe I should just try to cut down? Still have a drink but not get so completely pissed? Maybe stick to drinking in pubs perhaps and not drink at home? And besides, surely coming to a dead stop after such a prolonged period of abuse could be dangerous to my health?

But I knew that all those excuses were the lies of an alcoholic, and if there's one thing I've always hated, it's people who lie to themselves. When you start to believe in your own bullshit, you might as well give up.

I see those people all the time. The people who blame being fat on having big bones or bad genes. The ones who would love to get fit, but for a bad knee or shoulder, or elbows, or anything else that springs to mind. The sad losers telling you that they would be rich if it wasn't for the actions of someone else. The ones who plan to start dating, or learning a new language, or decorating or anything else, just as soon as…blah blah blah blah…

So no, I wasn't going to lie to myself, it was time to stop drinking. The alternative was to accept that I was an alcoholic and carry on, but that would have meant that things were never going to get any better than they were there and then, and I wasn't ready to give up just yet.

Whilst I soaped and sponged and scrubbed at the car, I contemplated what to do with the rest of my day. Normally on a Saturday, this wouldn't have been too much of an issue. I'd get the essentials done, putting on a wash and doing my ironing and maybe empty the bins if they looked like they were overflowing (although when you're getting most of your calories from the bottle, it's surprising how little waste you generate). As soon as I'd finished my chores, or more likely during it, I would have gotten the day's drinking activities off to a start. Perhaps I'd have slipped into town to buy some supplies, stopping off at a pub, or two, along the way. If there was rugby or football on the TV, I would have used this as an excuse to while away an hour or so in a pub, watching it.

But I'd decided that today was going to be different and I knew instinctively that I had to find activities to keep me as busy as possible. The Devil makes work for idle hands and I knew instinctively that boredom would sap my resolve faster than anything else. I resolved to buy myself some swimming trunks as soon as I'd been to the dump. I've never been much of a fan of swimming but it was time to start getting back into shape after neglecting my health for so long, and this was something that I needed to take slowly.

Having cleared the car at the dump of its empty bottles and cans, and the ageing television, I headed into town. I parked up at the edge of Moulsham Street and ambled along the pedestrianised precinct and on through to the centre of town. The watery sun had just about managed to break through the slowly thinning cloud cover and it gradually lifted the faces and moods of everyone alike.

I've always enjoyed going into Chelmsford town centre even if there's nothing I need or want to buy. Chelmsford had been pretty much flattened during the last big war and so it has none of the olde-worlde charm of other, more touristy, towns, but whilst it might not have anything to make it a particularly memorable place to visit, it still manages to exude an air of vibrancy. It's a dull place to visit, but a great place to live.

I crossed the humpty backed bridge over the cold and threatening River Can as a busker thrashed away at an acoustic guitar and sang his little heart out with enthusiasm and obvious pleasure. I've always enjoyed a bit of live music. Not so much the big music festivals or concerts, but the guys and gals playing on street corners and hoping to make the big time.

I paused and listened for a minute or two before fishing in my pocket and coming out with a two-pound coin which I dropped into his guitar case, joining an assortment of other denominations. I'm not sure that he even noticed me, so wrapped up was he in his rendition of 'stairway to heaven.'

Moving on, I passed the 'Artisan' market which hogs the centre of town on weekends, funnelling the crowds to either side of the High Street. There's another, 'proper' market, only a couple of hundred yards on in a covered area beneath the multi-storey car-park. But most people from out of town don't know about it. Either that or they'd rather pay over the odds for the same stuff elsewhere.

The 'Artisan' market in the middle of town hosts a multitude of stalls, all of which appear to be doing a roaring trade. Greengrocers, flower sellers and various 'street food' stalls all compete to sell passersby the same goods as those which can be found in the 'proper' market, but at double the price.

And all the while, as I passed through the hawkers and the crowds, a little devil sat on my shoulder constantly nagging at me that it was time to stop off for a quick drink in one of the town's pubs.

On any other day, I would have stopped off at the Nags Head, which was one of those pubs in which time seems to have stood still for the last few decades. Not in a quaint and Olde Worlde way, more like a 1950's working man's pub. There was normally a good core of hardened drinkers like myself who used it as a staging post for the days drinking activities. I would usually stop for one pint and have two or three depending upon who, if anyone, I got chatting to.

From there I'd move on to do whatever shopping I needed to do. I usually liked to have something to buy to justify my trip into town. Shopping completed, usually within a half an hour, I'd move onto the Wetherspoons at the other side of town.

Like a lot of pissheads, I liked to keep moving. I'd travel from pub to pub so that to anyone I met would be given the impression that I was only having a few pints, not a combined total of.... god only knew how many.

But that day would be different. I was starting a new chapter and, as annoying as the voice in my head was, nagging away about how much better it would be if I just slipped off for one drink, I knew that the only way to kill it off permanently was to ignore it. And to keep on ignoring it for a very long period of time. The only problem was, that as the morning wore on, I was starting to feel progressively more hung-over and the only real cure I'd ever known for that was to start drinking again.

But not that day, I decided.

I wandered into Primark and picked out the least lairy pair of swimming shorts I could find and joined the queue to the checkouts. As I stood there waiting to be served I noticed a lady in front of me with a small boy hanging off of her left leg. She seemed to keep looking back over shoulder at me and I wondered vaguely if perhaps she was someone that I knew but didn't recognise. The next time she half turned to look at me, I decided to flash her my most winning smile. To no avail. She hastily looked eyes front again and shuffled on to the checkout which had just become clear.

Ten seconds later and I was up at another till and paying for my purchase. 'Did you find everything you were looking for today Sir?' asked the smiling young lady looking up as she folded my trunks into a bag.

'Why yes. Thank you very much', I responded with another winning smile plastered across my ruddy face. The checkout girl flinched away from me. Not in a big, or even an obvious way. Barely at all actually. But enough for it to register. And suddenly I realised what it was that the other lady had been looking at.

It was the smell. I hadn't realised it before of course, but I must have stunk. I had been busily steeping my body in booze for so long that it must have been leaking out of every pore. I had also polished off the remains of a half bottle of whisky when I'd got in the night before and whisky always seem to carry a more pungent smell the next day (one of the reasons I normally drank vodka during the week was to hide the smell at work).

I suddenly realised how much of a social pariah I had become. Ordinary people I'd never met before didn't want to be around me. Not necessarily because of my drunken nature, but because of the noxious stench I had been giving off. With this realisation came a sudden flurry of memory flashbacks of other complete strangers who'd given me the same curious looks and I realised that this was not an isolated incident. I just hadn't recognised people's reactions for what they really were.

I remember thinking to myself that I must have smelled like some wretched old wino. Only later did I realise that I smelled exactly like what I was at that time: a wretched old wino.

Shamefaced, I quickly paid for the swimming shorts and hurried back to the car. I had originally intended buying some fruit and veg in the indoor market, but the realisation of how offensive my presence was to everyone around me was enough to make me want to hide away. The more I thought about it, the more convinced I was that I could smell it too. Even I didn't want to be near me!

You might think that particular home truth would have gone some way to quelling any further hankerings I had for a drink, but of course, it had the opposite effect. Addictions are masters of deception. On the one hand, they convince us that we need them to celebrate. On the other, they pretend to offer support in times of trouble. You couldn't possibly enjoy a party without them and yet you couldn't wind down and relax without them either. Of course, both stories can't possibly be the truth; it's either an upper or it's a downer: isn't it? Or maybe, just maybe, it's neither. It's whatever particular excuse we need to use at that time to justify having one more cigarette or in my case, one more drink.

Anyway, the urge to dive into the nearest darkened hostelry and drown my sorrows became almost impossible to resist. But resist it I did.

CHAPTER SEVENTEEN

I scurried back to my car and took myself home, clutching my swimming shorts in the paper bag that hadn't cost me five pence. An hour or so later, when I tried on my newly purchased swimwear, I came to the conclusion that my low level of self-esteem had thus far been overrated. I've never been a particularly vain sort of bloke and I rarely bothered to look in the mirror, other than for shaving or to check that my hair was brushed before I left the house. But that day, as I gazed upon my reflection I beheld the visual confirmation of what a complete and utter sack of shit I had become. Gazing back at me was a prematurely ageing, pale, slack, sweating, flabby embarrassment.

Taking stock of my appearance I started to realise how much of a challenge lay ahead of me in my plans to sober up and get back into shape. The skin below my neckline hadn't seen the light of day for a very long time and I had the pallor of something that had fallen into a river and died. The truth was that I had started to let myself go a long, long time previously. Probably at much the same time as I had realised that I was slowly but surely losing my son.

Where once I'd have been out pounding the streets on a five or ten-mile run, or shifting weights and doing press-ups at the end of each working day, I had gradually given it all up as the depression I'd never realised I was suffering from had slowly taken hold.

My muscles had atrophied; had shrivelled and died, although I wasn't carrying a great deal of excess weight. Like so many alcoholics I had lost my appetite and for the most part I usually saw eating as an annoying waste of time and money. Something to be done only when absolutely necessary. I had substituted the calories in food for those in beer. The end result was that my pale skin seemed to hang in drifts, from a skeletal frame which supported little or no muscle, just the sad paunch of my distended belly.

It took a huge mental effort to force myself off to the local swimming baths that day, but force myself I did.

I endured the ticket seller flinching from my alcoholic odour and I endured the mildly disgusted looks of the people who saw me coming out of my changing booth in all my pale and pasty glory. And then I endured the suspicious looks from the protective parents of toddlers; wary of paedophiles when they see any lone male getting in the pool.

I'm not a great swimmer; I don't even particularly like it. I never have. I find it a tedious exercise without reward and look upon it as an evil necessity rather than a pleasurable pastime. I don't know how many lengths I swam. Probably not so many bearing in mind my lousy technique and my even lousier physical condition; but I stuck with it that day for over an hour, knowing that the bleaching effect of the chlorine and the wrinkling effect of the water would make me even more of a macabre sight. But at the same time, I also hoped that the chlorine would at last obliterate the lingering odour of alcohol which had followed me around for so long.

It was late afternoon by the time I got home and by then I carried a raging thirst. Fortunately, in addition to building an even greater desire for drink than that which normally afflicted me during my waking hours, swimming has always had the effect of making me extremely tired and I crashed out for an hour or so, sprawled across the sofa.

I was woken up by my own snoring, with a raging headache, feeling exhausted and ravenously hungry.

I wasn't entirely sure what time the supermarket closed on a Saturday evening, so I decided to head out straight away. I caught a passing glance of myself in the mirror on my way out through the hallway and it wasn't a pretty sight. On one side of my face, I had scarlet lines marking the creases from the cushion where I had slept so heavily. My hair also sprouted out in interesting directions on that side, whilst on the other, it remained neat and ordered.

'Who cares', I shrugged to myself as I walked straight on: 'Obviously, not me' would have been the appropriate response in that instance.

By then, I was beginning to form an idea of what the coming days would bring and how I was going to deal with them. I made sure to stock up on a good quantity of 'proper' food. Food I could cook with. If I was determined to bring myself back to some semblance of the man I had used to be, I was going to need to start eating healthily; although, eating healthily might not have been the right term of phrase. Eating *heartily* is probably a more appropriate description.

I bought foods which I could cook with: Minced beef, chicken breasts, onions, peppers, potatoes, rice, bread, that kind of thing. I chose the staple foods that normal people ate, and I made sure to avoid the snacky foods of the fat and the lazy. There would be no point in kicking the booze, only to become a fat fucker.

I also hit the household goods aisle in a fairly big way, buying up a large selection of cleaning cloths and products and, in a final coup de grace; I picked up three paperback novels for a tenner. All the tools I needed to try and combat any boredom over the next day or so.

I slept barely a wink that night. I contemplated cooking and I tried cleaning but my heart wasn't really in it. I started one of the novels and found it had been written by an American author with a pretty childish story, but I persevered with it anyway.

I paced up and down, tried a few press-ups and generally regretted my rash decision to throw away a perfectly good television earlier that day. I'm not altogether sure what had prompted that particular decision and undoubtedly it was made whilst I'd still been under the influence of the previous night's alcohol consumption. I'd had it in mind that I needed a complete overhaul of my life and to do that I needed to do all of the things that I *hadn't* been doing those last few months. As my recreational time had pretty much consisted of getting pissed and watching TV, those would be my key changes. Maybe, in hindsight it was a good decision, and maybe it wasn't. The jury's still out as far as I'm concerned. Certainly, it didn't do any harm in the long run and I'm sure that I must have been more active as a result of the loss of that particular distraction.

Sunday had dawned in a similar fashion to Saturday. Grey and overcast but once again surprisingly mild. I spent a few hours in the morning hacking away at what I laughingly called a back garden. In reality, it was little more than a patch of wilderness backing on to the house.

A little more clear-headed, although feeling the worse for it, I decided not to use the car that day. Once the recycling bin was full, I piled up the brambles and cuttings in a corner, ready to burn or to transport another day.

Lunchtime came and I cooked a hearty fry up. Sausages, black pudding, eggs, tomato, baked beans and fried bread. It tasted like the food of gods, one of the best meals I'd ever had. I read an article once on the best things to eat or drink when nursing a hangover. Coffee was pretty much the worst thing to have, something to do with the caffeine I think, but a full English breakfast was one of the best; with the cholesterol acting like a sponge to soak up all the excess alcohol.

I had a walk into town a little later, not to buy anything, but just to get out of the house and I felt the same tugging sensation, like a magnetic draw as I passed by the pubs I would have usually stopped at. But I resisted.

Later that day I rustled up a curry before launching an assault on the house with chemicals and cleaning cloths. Sad to say, but it was probably the most productive weekend I'd had in years.

Monday morning dawned early for me, mostly because I'd barely slept a wink the night before. The moment I did wake up, the first thoughts on my mind were of where and when I could have my first drink and instinct told me that if I'd gone to work that day, I would have given in to temptation.

I phoned work and spoke to Sally, the sales force's shared PA. I asked her to cancel my appointments for the rest of the day, telling her, without giving any specifics, that I was too unwell to go in that day. Almost immediately after putting the phone down I regretted my decision and so I rang her straight back, telling her to write the rest of the week off as well. If Steve Bigham was unhappy, I told her, I would take it out of any holiday allowance I had left over.

Bearing in mind that I'd hardly taken a day's holiday in the best part of three years and that the sales force didn't get paid for any holiday days left over at the end of each year, I didn't expect to have too much of a problem with that.

But barely ten minutes after I'd ended the call my phone rang and picking it up I heard the gruff tones of Steve Bigham on the other end.

'Hi Steve' I answered, trying for some unknown reason to sound cheerful.

'What's going on Owen' he said, cutting straight to the point, as ever. 'Sally tells me you're not coming in for the rest of the week and that it's holiday!'

'Yeah, I'm sorry about that' I said rubbing my forehead and trying hard to think straight. 'I er,.. I'm feeling a bit under the weather Steve.'

'Under the weather?'

'Yeah. I'd rather not talk about it at the moment, to be honest Steve, if that's OK with you. I've got some personal shit going on at the moment and I just need a few days to sort it out.'

Bigham had always been a pretty sound bloke and he seemed to know the right time to push and when to back off. He'd known me since before Judy died and, of course, he knew about David's death. He'd have had to have been a blind fool not to have realised how badly I'd fallen as a result.

I could tell he wasn't happy about it, but he instinctively knew that he wasn't going to get a more satisfying answer out of me just then.

'Anything I can do to help?' he asked, after a moment's pause.

'Thanks Steve, but I just need a few days to sort myself out. I'll be back in next Monday. I promise.'

'And', I added as an afterthought, 'I'm gonna get right back on the horse Steve. No more messing about. I'll be top of that sales charts again before you know it.'

'Promise?' he asked.

'Promise' I said, feeling like a ten-year-old boy.

'OK Owen. Hope you feel better soon and call me if you need anything. But I expect to see you next Monday morning. Sales meeting at nine-fifteen, sharp.' With that he hung up, leaving me vacantly staring into space.

By the time Tuesday came along things were starting to get a little tense. The first three days of sobriety had been hard enough work, but by then I could feel my body going into serious withdrawal mode. I'd spent so long drinking myself to sleep, or more perhaps more accurately, semi-consciousness, that my mind had forgotten how to switch onto standby. It didn't matter how tired I was or how desperately important it was that I got a good night's sleep in before the next day, my brain simply wouldn't switch off.

As if that wasn't bad enough, having tried to find sleep again on the Monday night but not managing it until four am, I had woken up, barely an hour later, screaming my lungs out and drenched in sweat.

I'd resisted thinking about it on the Saturday and Sunday, having managed with some success to block it from my thoughts, but unbidden into my sleeping mind had come the violently graphic replay of the brutal slaying of poor old Campsite Terry.

Those awful scenes which had, in reality, played out in the darkness, I now saw in glorious technicolour. I watched every blow in slow motion, saw every wound appear and spread, every nuance of Terry's terrified facial expressions and, with horrific clarity, the ecstatic expression on the face of his sadistic killer. The nightmare was to become a recurring horror, far in excess of anything that I had ever witnessed in real life.

I didn't know it then, but the horror would revisit my dreams every night for a long time to come. For the next few days, and it made no matter whether it was day or night, if I slipped into any kind of slumber beyond that of the briefest of naps, I woke up feeling terrified and sick, and often crying out aloud.

I guess that it may have been a form of PTSD, but not being the type of guy that is ever likely to take himself off to see a shrink, I never had a label for it. My one-off conversation with Keith Lawson all those years ago and his unofficial diagnosis of my sociopathic nature was enough to make me averse to letting anyone else peel back the layers of my personality and peering within.

Whilst I knew that it was true that Keith was by no means qualified and, by his own admission, had only read half of what he needed to on the subject, his uncomfortably accurate description of my deepest feelings and failings had been only too real.

Thankfully my night terrors began to abate after four or five days, but they carried on to a lesser extent for some time afterwards. And so, to ice the cake of alcohol withdrawal, I now had the added bonus of severe sleep deprivation.

I've since read up on the effects of alcohol withdrawal which most serious drinkers experience, and between forty eight and seventy two hours is the period when 'delirium tremens' will kick in, if they're going to at all. According to the internet, delirium tremens is a 'sudden confusion, possibly paired with hallucinations, uncontrollable shaking, increased body temperature and a faster heart rate. All of which can sometimes lead to seizures.'

For seriously heavy drinkers, they recommend a detox from alcohol only under medical supervision, as the severe withdrawal symptoms of going cold turkey can sometimes lead to death.

It's fair to say that the internet analysis described the hell of my next few days pretty accurately. Added to the sleep deprivation, the nightmares and the hot flushes, I developed a banging headache which lasted for a fortnight and which no quantity of tablets could completely cure.

And, for some inexplicable reason, I also began to stink. It wasn't the same stink of alcohol that I must have been exuding for so long but something more pungent and rotten. It's not a problem I'd ever suffered from before, no matter what the climate or the levels of exertion or how much I sweated. But overnight that all changed and no matter how much I showered or how often I changed my clothing, within the hour I'd wind up smelling like the proverbial tram driver's jockstrap.

Perhaps I'd smelled that bad for some time and had simply been too plastered to even notice it, but I suspect that it was more likely to be a consequence of my body making the best of its spare time.

My theory was that my metabolism had been working flat out, for goodness knows how long, just to process the vast quantities of alcohol I had poured down my throat. But now that I'd stopped poisoning myself, suddenly my glands could start to return to doing their day job. Suddenly, they had time to rid my body of all the leftover toxins and alcohol bi-products which had up until then been stored in my glands. But to get rid of them, it had to find an exit route and these found their way out via my urine, my breath and the pores of my skin.

My urine took on the colour of a rich oaky chardonnay and gave off a musty, caustic aroma. I actually began to take pleasure in going to the toilet when my stools went from mush to solids (sad, I know, but there it is) but this pleasure was to be short-lived. Having obtained most of my calories from a bottle for the last six months, I found myself in a state of almost constant hunger. My system, which had been used to digesting a predominantly liquid intake, suddenly had meat, vegetables and fibre to work on. Suffice it to say that the resulting period of intense constipation led to a lot of stomach cramps and an extremely sore backside.

Apart from the obvious physiological changes brought about by my cold turkey, there were also some spectacular flashes of temper resulting from my constant lack of sleep.

One moment I could be sitting in the car, waiting for traffic lights to change, singing happily along to a song on the radio. The next moment I could be literally spitting with rage at the sight of someone turning without using his indicators.

It could be that I'm deluding myself, but I like to think of myself as a man whose default persona is mild-mannered and happy go lucky; or at least that's the face of the man I like to portray in public. There aren't a lot of things or people that *do* bother me, but when they do, I try to be cool calm and collected about it. Better to pretend it doesn't bother you and then get even later has always been my modus operandi.

My sudden and erratic displays of anger were more than a little disconcerting to me but thankfully they still only happened perhaps once a day and they never landed in me in any kind of real trouble.

In the Royal Marines, we were taught how to utilise controlled aggression. Some people mistakenly think that controlling your aggression is about dampening it down, but it in actual fact it's about turning it on; it's about being able to turn yourself from being in a state of rest and contentment into being a raging homicidal maniac in the blink of an eye. About having the ability to turn yourself into a stone cold killer at will; and then, of course, turning it off again when the circumstances dictate.

It felt as though I had developed a faulty switch. A switch which would flip itself into the 'on' position every so often, without any real outside influence and then, thankfully, flick back just moments later, leaving me marvelling at my own ability to 'lose it.'

I called into the supermarket one Saturday morning to pick up a newspaper and some milk. Arriving at the checkout I fished the correct change out of my pocket whilst a young girl I'd never before met swiped my items through. She could have been no more than eighteen years old and wore her hair dyed pink and in bunches.

'Will there be anything else Sir?' she enquired politely.

'No thanks', I replied, 'That's it for today thank you.'

'Not your usual shop then' she grinned up at me.

I felt the switch trip and instantly I saw red. I literally felt my head glow as my face suffused with rage. Whilst there was no way of denying that my 'usual' shop would have involved large amounts of alcohol, I certainly didn't like the fact that someone had picked up on it and I certainly didn't appreciate them teasing me about it. To make things worse, it was from a dyed pink schoolgirl who I'd never met before!

'WHAT THE..!! Who the hell do you think you're talking to!!' I snarled, my face twisted into a mask of rage as I leaned deep into her personal space. The poor girl shrank away from me, looking both horrified and terrified at the same time.

But at the same moment as I shouted down at her I saw the headline blaring out from the newspaper I had just bought and my sudden rage turned to instant shame.

"*Not The Usual Shop*" was the headline splashed across the front cover of the newspaper. I can't even remember what the story was about now; something banal about being served by people in fancy dress I think.

She'd obviously seen the headline too and decided to bounce it off of me as a light-hearted pun. The poor girl had never even seen me before and had no idea of what I normally purchased. | Her eyes welled up with tears as she rolled her chair back in an attempt to put more distance between us and it's not overstating things to say that I was mortified.

'I.. er..' I stammered, having no idea how to explain my sudden Jekyll and Hyde act. But I seemed to have lost the power of coherent speech as well as having lost my marbles. 'Erm…Sorry..' I blurted before scooping up my purchases and practically running out of the store.

I went back to the shop the next day, and the day after that too, hoping to find her working again so that I could apologise properly and maybe even explain what had caused my outburst. I had it in mind that I might buy her some chocolates or flowers by means of an apology, but she wasn't there and to this day I have never seen her since. Something for which she is probably eternally grateful.

Despite my permanent state of exhaustion and the accumulation of those other side-effects, I also began to enjoy a clarity of thought which had long since abandoned me.

When I decided to quit the booze, I'd instinctively known that I would need to occupy both my body and mind, and I'd also known that I'd need to think a little more long-term in order to maintain my discipline. I needed a goal. It wouldn't be enough to say that I wanted to drink nothing for, say, six months, I needed to have a more tangible goal of achieving something, rather than that of simply *not* doing something.

Fortunately for me, I'd already made my decision as to what my goal would be. Fortunate for me perhaps, but unfortunate for Les Guscom. My decision to avenge Campsite Terry and to pay Les back for the humiliation he'd heaped upon me would not be abated by time. The night-time terrors were all I needed to refresh my resolve each morning. But I had to sort myself out first before I could turn my attention to that particular problem.

Within a few days of quitting, I felt a lightness in my step as I immediately lost a couple of kilograms of fluid retention. I began to see a younger looking image in the mirror as my face began to lose its alcoholic puffiness, and I saw the colour returning slowly to my washed out pupils.

Starting to feel fitter really also served to remind me of how far I'd fallen. When your starting point is zilch, it's not so hard to make an improvement.

I started by doing push-ups and going for long walks. At the end of that first week, I started to go jogging. My first few outings were pitiful; I literally couldn't run beyond the end of the road. But I persevered with it. If I couldn't run and had to start walking again I'd do so only until I could catch my breath and then I'd start jogging again. Jog, walk, jog walk. I set myself a target of three miles and in those early day and to begin with, I probably ran less than half a mile in total and walked the rest. After a week of trying to find ways to occupy myself, I was more than ready to go back to work.

CHAPTER EIGHTEEN

One week on

We held a regular sales meeting at APS on the second Monday morning of each month and the second Monday of the month was exactly what my first day back was after the impromptu week long holiday.

I'd woken up early that morning as I had done every other morning for the previous week, but it was the first time I hadn't woken up smothered in a film of my own fear, crying out at the horror of seeing Terry's head being squashed like a melon all over again.

It's hard to put into words the restorative effect of waking up normally. I was still tired, I'd been unable to fall asleep until past midnight and had woken back up before six, but it was the first time I'd had over five hours of uninterrupted slumber since Terry's murder. It took me a moment to work out what was so different that morning, why it was that I hadn't woken up feeling absolutely exhausted. When I realised that I'd managed to have an entire night's sleep without the recurring nightmare, I felt that I'd reached a turning point.

I rolled out of bed and, without even bothering to brush my teeth, I laced up my running shoes and set off for the same three-mile morning constitutional as I had done for the previous week. My legs still ached from the day before, but despite that, I felt so good that I ran for a whole mile before I had to walk for a spell. Not much of an achievement, I know, but for me, on that morning it felt like a major breakthrough.

The day had dawned with a beautiful clear blue sky which served to lift my mood even higher as I completed the three miles of run, walk, run walk before heading home for a shower, a shave and a general shine up. The monthly sales meeting was due to start at nine-fifteen. and I made sure that I arrived there bright and early.

All told there were just six of us sales reps, and I chatted to a couple of the other guys who had already arrived ahead of me. It felt as though the conversation was a little stilted and I guessed that they sensed the a difference in me which they couldn't quite understand. Of course, everyone there would have known about the death of my son and I wondered idly whether in fact all of the conversations since then had been just as stilted, but in my semi-permanent state of intoxication, I just hadn't realised.

At nine fifteen, Steve Bigham appeared and ushered us into the boardroom where we took our usual seats.

APS is still a privately owned enterprise and not being part of a big corporate structure it did things a little different from most other sales organisations. Things had moved on since I began with the firm and the employed sales force was a lot more stable now.

They hadn't had anyone new starting for over a year, but when they did, new joiners were given established territories or portfolios to work. As the Company had built, the job had become more focused on account management than the previous days of cold calling and the desperate search for new clients. Not for them the American model of flogging every last man jack until all they are left with is a quivering wreck of nerves.

In most other sales organisations, sales meetings consist of broadcasting a record of everyone's sales figures for the previous week or month, congratulating the guys at the top whilst subliminally belittling the guys at the bottom. The theory being that all salespeople are highly competitive and will fight tooth and nail to be top of the leaderboard. It's complete rubbish of course. You can't have a sales team where every individual is only happy if they are top of the heap, for the simple reason that there isn't enough room at the top for everyone.

So Bigham didn't bother with any of the pseudo sales psychology. There was a year to date sales graph *outside* of the boardroom for all to see and he figured that this should be enough to motivate those who lagged or those who excelled.

Certainly, that morning, it was enough to give me a solid kick up the arse. For the last ten years, I'd consistently been the top line on his graph, with sales figures which were superior by virtue of my skill at selling to new customers and my hard work in trying to find them. But I looked at them that morning and saw how much I had drifted from the main pack in the last year. It was time to make amends.

Our performances were never mentioned in the meetings and there was no such thing as 'naming and shaming'. If Bigham felt that someone needed praise or scolding, he'd call them into a private meeting behind closed doors. He would never air his laundry in front of others.

The meetings usually began with product news and that morning we had customised ballpoint pens handed out to each of us and details of the pricing, design time and minimum orders were explained. There was a new line in ring binders offered and again samples given out to us as well as two or three other product lines.

As often as not, the samples of new products were little more than an excuse for us to visit existing customers. 'Hey, Mrs Jones. Look at the exciting new range of ring binders we're selling'. Sounds like bullshit, I know, but when it comes to sales, it's often about maintaining your presence.

After our little 'what's new' session, Steve went on to ask each of us in turn to comment on how our month had gone and asked us to share any interesting stories. We might have. One by one we took turns to give some kind of answer as to what has happened in the last month. We spent most of our working days alone, out on the road, and this session was more about team building than anything else. Our answers didn't have to be work related; sometimes these were just funny stories and sometimes personal; one of the guys had been on holiday for three weeks and spent his slot regaling us with his trip to the Bahamas.

All of which helped to make going to work a pleasure, but it also meant that when one of us had a success or a failure story in relation to sales, we could share it with the others so that they could either avoid the pitfall or try to replicate the success.

In times gone past, I've read a hell of a lot of books on sales techniques and NLP and whilst a lot of it was garbage, I'd also found a few gems which had worked for me in the real world. These would be the type of things which I usually shared, the things which had worked for me and the things which hadn't. And because we are all different, I'd sometimes get to hear other guys saying that something which hadn't worked for me, had in actual fact, worked a treat for them.

The meetings would usually break down into good-natured banter until it reached a point where nothing more productive was likely to come of it. At that point, Bigham would call a halt and sum up what had been discussed and agreed where applicable.

The meeting that day was slightly different in that Bigham didn't ask me to stand up in front of the others and I took it to be an ominous sign. Sure enough, when the meeting was called to an end, he asked me to pop into his office for a chat and I began to worry.

The offices of APS were a pretty functional affair, attached to the main warehouse where we stored the vast majority of our goods and had been built barely twenty years ago. They were, for the most part, very plain. Apart from the comm's room, as we called it, (a room where up to eight people manned the phones, taking orders and queries) there was a reception area, a boardroom, and Bigham's office. With the exception of Bigham's office, the entire unit looked as though it had come straight out of an IKEA catalogue.

However, Bigham's office was an altogether different affair. Despite being such a modern building, entering his office felt like going back in time. The lighting changed to a more subdued glow which somehow seemed to still be perfectly adequate for him to work by. Heavy cloth drapes framed the modern windows and a tall yucca plant stood in the corner. A large framed portrait of the Queen hung on the wall behind his desk and every scrap of furniture was antique oak and leather. A deep piled carpet covered the floor.

Bigham's office was his own little fiefdom and you were left with no doubt as to who was in charge when he sat behind his huge leather-topped desk.

'Sit down Owen' he said, motioning to the Captain's chair on the other side of his desk.

I lowered myself opposite him without comment and waited for him to begin. Bigham and I went back a long way and beyond the whole employer/employee relationship, I think it's safe to say that we regarded each other as friends. Which must have made what he wanted to say next difficult.

After a moment or two of silence between us, he cleared his throat and dived in.

'I've had some complaints, Owen. Customers saying that you've either failed to turn up for appointments or that when you've turned up you were smelling of booze'. He paused, like the consummate salesman that he was, giving me time to process the direction he was going in.

'You and I go back a long way Owen and I'd like to think that I've always been fair to you. Cut you slack when you've needed it. I know that David's death must have....'

'It's fine' I said, cutting across him and leaning forwards at the same time to show my sincerity. 'It's fine. I know what I've been like recently and I know how bad I've been messing things up. But I promise you, that I'm over that now. No more. You've cut me more slack than I've any right to ask for and I promise that I'm gonna repay you, Steve. Starting today, starting here and starting now'.

My interjection seemed to have surprised him and he leant back in his leather armchair and took a moment to re-assess. I liked to think that I could read Bigham pretty well and I could almost hear the cogs turning as he looked a little more carefully at my outward appearance and demeanour. He added the numbers together and thankfully came up with four.

'How long?' he asked simply.

'How long since I last had a drink or how long before I repay you?' I asked, forcing a faint smile onto my face in an attempt to lighten his mood.

'Both'

'Ten days and this month' I said. 'I haven't had a drink since the Friday before last and I've got a full diary for this week and next'. It was true; I'd been on the phone to Sally the previous Friday and had her fill my diary with sales appointments.

There was another brief hesitation and then, 'Fine. Don't let me down'.

I could tell that he still wasn't happy and it suddenly dawned on me then that I hadn't realised how far I must have fallen from his grace. Maybe I wasn't as good at reading Bigham as I'd thought. Maybe he'd even been about to fire me. A moment of panic came and fled in the blink of an eye, strengthening my resolve to pay Bigham back for standing by me for so long.

'I won't forget this Steve' I said, 'and I promise you that you won't regret it'.

With our meeting over, I set out to conquer the world of selling stationery.

CHAPTER NINETEEN

Those early weeks of my new found sobriety were a strange mixture of tiredness from a lack of sleep, offset against a new found energy from being alcohol-free.

Every morning I'd wake up early and go for a run, regardless of how much my legs were aching or how bleary-eyed I felt. By the end of the second week, I was running the three-mile route without the need to stop or walk. By the end of the third, it felt as natural and as effortless as walking. I wasn't going to break any records for speed, but that had never been a part of my agenda.

I started to work a little harder on the rest of my body and added sit-ups and press-ups as part of my routine and it wasn't long before I could bash out fifty of each without any great difficulty.

At work, I made a point of visiting every existing customer I had on my patch to let them see the new me and to reassure them that I was still the guy to do business with when it came to buying stationery. Some of these people I'd known for years and had counted as friends, and some of these I could be frank with and apologise for being off the radar for a while, or, for being on their radar but for all the wrong reasons. Many of those long-standing clients knew of the bereavement I had suffered and had understood what I had been through.

I also made an extra effort to try and drum up recommendations wherever possible in order to open up new customers. If I had any time between appointments, I made a point of door-stepping as many businesses as possible.

For the most part, cold calling and turning up unannounced and uninvited on businesses doorsteps was hard graft, with few discernible results, but by the time a month had passed and our next sales meeting came up, I had at least halted the decline in orders which my patch had been suffering. I was also pretty sure that I'd have a good following month as there is usually a bit of a time lag with these things. Just because you've dropped in on a customer and persuaded them to do business with you, doesn't necessarily mean that they need to stock up on paper or printer ink there and then; they'll wait until they are running low before placing an order.

At home, I had a large bookcase in the spare bedroom with an entire row dedicated to sales techniques and with no television in the house to waste my time in front of, I had begun to read a lot, re-visiting this collection first.

For the first time in ages, this new period of clean living and clear thinking allowed me to confront some of my own demons with something approaching sanity. I don't normally hold with the belief that talking about problems will somehow make them go away.

On the contrary, I have always looked upon it as a pretty selfish act, trying to share your own misery with others.

Four weeks later, when it came to my turn at the regular APS sales meeting to comment upon my previous month, I stood up from my chair and took a deep breath before telling the room about my change in fortunes.

But to give them a sense of how much better things were going for me, I first of all needed to let them know how bad things had got. I opened up with frank forthrightness and told them what they already knew. In essence, that I had spent the previous six months or so drinking myself silly.

As I opened up to them, I also began to understand things which the countless hours of solitary self-reflection hadn't previously revealed to me. I realised that much of my grief and despair had been borne from the frustration of being unable to convince David how bad his choices in life were and that my frustration had turned firstly into self-pity, in turn to self-loathing, and inevitably on to self-destruction. I'd moved through this entire cycle of emotions before he'd even died and his death served only to spin the wheel once more as the pattern repeated.

But all that was behind me now. I told them about how I'd been filling my diary and door-stepping in between calls. About the sales tips I had been reminded of in the books I'd read and how some of them had worked and some of them hadn't. I even told them about my efforts to get fit and my early morning running routine. In a bout of verbal diarrhoea, I told them pretty much everything that had been going on in my life for the last few months; with the obvious exceptions of the death of Campsite Terry and my decision to avenge his murder.

Despite the fact that I had known that Bigham would ask me to take my turn in the meeting with a little sales or interesting or amusing anecdote, I hadn't previously given a moment of thought as to what I would say.

I had risen to my feet to give this completely unplanned and uncharacteristic monologue of hubris, without really knowing why I was doing so, or what it was that made me unburden myself that way.

And during the whole course of my bleeding heart confessions, Bigham and the others sat around the table in complete silence, looking up at me with rapt attention. When I eventually took my seat again there was silence. For a moment.

Then Bigham started to clap. It was a surreal moment, looking at me straight in the eye, he started to clap. And then the others followed. Beaming smiles spread across their faces. Those sitting next to me slapped me on the back and I heard what sounded like a cacophony of noise around me, but which was in fact, the sound of the blood rushing to my head. Before I could stop myself, I was in tears; blubbing like a baby, and looking up I could see others around the table crying too. Tears of happiness rolled down our cheeks, and every one of us wore a stupid grin from ear to ear.

I have never before had a more humbling experience. I'd hated myself so much during the months of trying to drink myself to death that I'd lost complete sight of who my friends are and how much people cared for me.

CHAPTER TWENTY

The week before

Living in a house on your own, without any real social life (mine had previously centred solely on going to pubs) and without a television came as something of a shock to the system in its own right. I was doing cold turkey in more than one way.

But it's funny how quickly you can adapt. I started to fill the time by re-reading everything in my neglected bookcase, which held a collection of novels, books on sales techniques, DIY manuals, a dictionary and a selection of old school books which David had either bought or forgotten to return. One by one I read them all, whether I understood them or not. Some of them were entertaining, some dross and some informative.

I also began a long overdue make-over of my house by decorating first the living room and then the spare bedroom.

And I plotted.

Having made the decision to avenge Campsite Terry, and with time on my hands, I gave a lot of thought as to how I might go about it. Slowly and methodically, I worked through my options, making mental lists of the pros and cons for each variation.

I thought about running him over, but then realised that it would be next to impossible to set up. This was a guy who did most of his travelling by van, who probably only crossed a road a couple of times a day. He was unlikely to be so unaware as to get caught out by a car which had pulled out in front of him and even if I did manage to get him this way, there was a high probability of witnesses or CCTV. Whilst I was still determined to achieve my goal, I certainly didn't want to be caught or punished for it.

In the unlikely event that I did find an opportunity for running him down, I would want to do it in a car that could not be traced back to me in any way.

I considered other scenarios whereby I'd jump him in the pub car park and either hit him with something heavy, or stab him. But again, the same problems arose of witnesses, or even worse, associates appearing. Added to this was the suspicion that I wouldn't be able to beat him in a fair fight.

When it comes to a fight the three main factors which decide the outcome are size, skill and aggression and it's as relevant in a street fight as it is in war. Having a bigger army is always going to be an advantage, but if both sides are evenly matched and equipped then the one with the best skill and training will probably edge it. If they are evenly matched in terms of size, equipment and training, then the one with the most aggression is likely to prevail.

Aggression, aggression, aggression. You should never underestimate it. When I think back to the school bullies from my youth, they weren't the biggest or strongest kids; just the nastiest little fuckers around.

Take the British Army. It has a record stretching back centuries of fighting and winning wars against enemies who had superior size and strength. That's because we're basically a nation of well trained, nasty little fuckers.

Les Guscom was six inches taller than me and probably four stone heavier so I certainly wasn't going to compete with him in terms of size; quite the opposite in fact. I'd also seen him lose it in the pub before and I knew that he swung a viciously big punch. From what I'd seen, he looked to be a street-savvy fighter.

For my own part, even though I hadn't set foot on a wrestling mat for some years, I was still fairly confident that I retained enough of the skill set to make me more than a match for anyone my own size and weight. Serving in the Royal Marines had also taught me how to control my aggression and I was certain that I had the willingness to commit the violence needed to kill him, But I'd also witnessed Les beat someone to death and the perverse pleasure it had given him, so I was in no doubt that aggression was something he had in abundance.

On the balance of things I figured we scored about evens for aggression and evens (ish) for ability. But that still left size and there were no two ways about it, I was definitely on the back foot with that one. So could I have beaten him in a fair fight? Perhaps, but there was no way I was going to try and find out.

So how to do it? I decided that to have any realistic chance at all of carrying this through and getting away with it, I was going to need some hard intelligence. I'd heard the rumours about him and his family loan sharking and selling drugs, but the truth was, that at that time, all I really knew was that he often drank in the Butlers Arms and that he sometimes worked as a bricklayer.

I didn't know where he lived or where he spent his days. I didn't even know if he lived alone or with a wife or anyone else. Although I'd heard that he worked as a bricklayer, and despite the fact that he drove a van, I'd never seen him come into the pub covered in cement or caked in dirt so I was a little sceptical as to whether even this was correct. Whilst I knew that he sometimes drank in the Butlers Head, I didn't know if there was any pattern to it; whether he arrived and left at certain times or only on certain days of the week. For all I knew, it may have been completely random.

Where to start then? The only thing I could think of was to stake out the Butlers Head and wait for him to show up. From there, I could start to see if there was any kind of pattern emerging that might help me. Better than that, I could follow him home and see where he lived.

With nothing else to go on, I started my surveillance of the Butlers Head one Monday evening after work. I really didn't want to go into the pub and I also didn't want to raise any suspicions by hanging about for the whole night in the car park, so, after I'd checked the car-park to make sure that there weren't any white vans already there, I drove a hundred yards down the street and parked in a spot which gave me a clear view of the pub's front entrance.

Despite being a large pub, the Butlers Head was tucked away in a quiet residential street. Most of the houses there had been built in the 1920's and had decent sized front gardens, with the consequence being, that most of them had off street parking. It was lucky for me as it meant that I had no trouble finding a space to park up.

It was still daylight when I pulled up and I felt a little conspicuous sitting in a car in an otherwise mostly car-free street, especially as I was doing nothing other than sitting there. A couple of dog walkers gave me curious looks as they passed by and a guy from the other side of the street came out of his house and gave me a long intimidating look before realising that I wasn't going to move and that he had no real option other than to accept it. But he obviously wasn't happy with my being there.

I'd had the foresight to buy myself a sandwich and a bottle of lemonade, but as the clock slowly ticked away at the time, I wished that I'd brought a newspaper or something. The road was quiet enough that I could have done a crossword and just looked up when any traffic came by.

By seven o'clock it had started to get dark and I was feeling a little more confident that by sitting still, I wasn't going to draw any attention to myself. But by then I had other, more pressing issues. It started with needing a wee, a pretty uncomfortable feeling but not so bad that I couldn't resist it. If it had been midnight I would have just hopped out of the car and peed up against one of the trees lining the pavement, but it wasn't. It was early evening, and despite the fact that it was beginning to get dark, there were still plenty of people returning from work or putting their bins out etc and I didn't want to draw any more attention to myself than I had to.

Maybe it was the nerves or maybe the inactivity of trying to sit as still as possible, but shortly afterwards I felt another urge nagging at me. This particular urge was also to go to the toilet only this time it wasn't just to have a wee. Again, I held out for as long as I could, but after another twenty minutes or so I realised that it was time to give up and go home to let nature take its course.

The next evening I decided to have my dinner first and get myself sorted properly before I went out again to perform my surveillance. After a light dinner of pasta and tuna, I set out again and followed the same routine of checking out the car park first before parking up down the street, this time making sure that it was a hundred yards in the other direction.

I was a little on edge because I'd seen a white van in the car park and I wasn't sure if it belonged to Les. I didn't *think* it was his. but as I didn't know what his number-plate was or even what the make of his van was, I couldn't be sure. Those details had never been important to me before. It had been just another white van.

One hour later I saw the same van pull out and leave, and sure enough, it wasn't Les. Despite having half expected this to be the case, I felt a little crushed. I hung on for another couple of hours before calling it a night.

After another long day on Wednesday, I decided to give it a miss altogether. For all I knew, he could have gone on holiday for a fortnight and I decided that there was no point in getting obsessive over it, but that I would stake out the pub as often as it suited me.

I dropped by to carry on my search on Thursday and Friday evenings, again without success, but on Saturday afternoon when I pulled into the pub car park there were no fewer than four white vans.

There was no way I could sit in my car for hours on end in the middle of a Saturday afternoon without looking very odd and so I decided that I needed to man up and go in the pub.

The Butlers Head is a surprisingly big place, given its residential location. With a football match being shown on the TV it was set to be a busy afternoon.

I couldn't see Les anywhere, but I figured he might have been in the toilets so I ordered a lemonade to give me an excuse to hang around for a while. I nodded an occasional greeting at some of the regulars I recognised and tried to look about as much as possible without appearing too conspicuous.

I didn't want to go *into* the toilets, reasoning that if Les was in there, I didn't want to chance a face to face meeting with him. Without having other people around to witness it. I was worried that when we did meet, he'd try and turn the screw on me. I still didn't think I could beat him in a fair fight, but I didn't trust my temper enough not to rise to the bait. I wouldn't have been able to play the same meek pisshead that I'd been the last time he'd seen me.

Across the pub I spotted a familiar face sitting at a table, studying the racing pages and making notes with a bookies pencil. It was none other than Martin Parsons, AKA 'Skip' to most who knew him. Skip was an interesting character. A copper who'd seemingly been in the job since Sir Robert Peel had first licensed his own band of thugs to take control of London's mean streets.

Skip was slightly balding, in his late middle years and sporting a decent sized beer gut. He looked as though he'd spent his whole life living in pubs without having any real home to go to. His black lace-up shoes had probably been purchased in Asda and had evidently never seen a scrap of boot polish. The suit trousers he wore looked clean enough but they had no discernible creases in them at all and he wore a washed out shirt of indeterminable colour, perhaps best described as somewhere between grey and green, open at the collar and with the sleeves half rolled up, and an ancient looking tie hanging at half-mast about his neck.

If you didn't know him, you'd probably have guessed him to be either a Labour politician or a teacher, but I always thought of him as being half Columbo and half Dirty Harry; a scruffy, unkempt, nasty bastard who you'd be wise not to cross.

He didn't look particularly big or fit, or even particularly threatening. But he did look like someone who could care less about sticking a broken glass in your face.

From what I knew of Skip, he was something of a throwback. A throwback to the time when we had a police force, long before it was replaced by our somewhat insipid police *service*. By his own admission, he'd been suspended for assault and corruption on more than one occasion but nothing had ever stuck. Non-stick Skip they'd called him.

He'd started out as an officer in the Met, but at some point, and for some reason, he'd transferred to Essex plod. Perhaps it was a case of escaping from the heat of one internal investigation too many.

Skip was also the closest thing I had to a friend who wasn't just a work colleague or a drinking buddy. He was one of the few people that had turned up at David's funeral, completely uninvited but very welcome all the same. I don't think I'd realised before then what a solid guy he was. I decided to wander over and use his company as cover for a while.

'Hey Skip' I said, sitting adjacent to him so that I could still look up at the footie on the TV. I had no real interest in the game but it would have looked odd to sit opposite Skip and have my back to the screen.

'Owen !' he said, looking up with a genuine smile spreading over his face. 'I haven't seen you in ages. Where've you been hiding? Not found a better class of pub have you?'

'Nah' I replied, gazing up at the TV and trying to look nonchalant. 'I've just been off the booze for a while'

'Oh yeah?' I could feel his questioning gaze upon me. 'Everything alright?'

I looked back at him and it came as a surprise to me to realise that this shabby bag of washed up shite actually cared about me.

'Yeah, it's all fine. I just got to the point where I realised I was taking the piss a bit and decided it was time to take a break for a while'.

'Well, there's no doubt you were kicking the arse out of it. The last couple of times I saw you. You could barely speak. Good job you had the car in the car-park because you were too pissed to walk!' It was an old joke of Skip's but also one which I had no doubt was true.

I'd forgotten the last time I'd seen Skip but it seemed like months and months ago, so I guessed I'd probably bumped into him a couple of times since then and been so drunk that I'd forgotten our meetings entirely; blacked out of any conscious memory.

'Just as well there wasn't any Old Bill around then!' I replied grinning like a schoolboy.

Skip had a knack for making me laugh and we shared the same shit sense of humour, hitting it off without any conscious effort. Right then and right there I felt like ordering up a pint and wasting the afternoon getting plastered with Skip, but of course, that particular option was no longer available.

I spent the best part of an hour and two lemonades with Skip without seeing hide nor hair of Les Guscom. Despite enjoying Skip's company immensely, (I'd had little social contact with anyone outside of work that last month), my mind still wandered as I continued to scour the room for Les, and there is only so long you want to spend in an increasingly noisy pub drinking soft drinks. I said my goodbyes and promised to keep in touch, (neither of us bothering to point out that as we didn't have each other's numbers, this was not particularly likely).

Sunday came and went still without a sighting of Les and I was beginning to wonder if my cunning plan was going to fail at the very first hurdle.

Then Monday. Then Tuesday. Then Wednesday.

I'd been parked up from about seven o'clock on the Wednesday evening, fully expecting to draw another blank, when a white van appeared in the view of my wing mirror. By that time, it was just beginning to turn dark and the streetlights had come on so I could see that it looked like the type of van I remembered Les driving.

Whoever it was, they seemed to be driving extra slowly and I wondered idly if it was a delivery van trying to find a house number, but as he passed I saw that it was a man on a mobile phone, seemingly deep in conversation.

It was Les. He was so intent on whatever he was saying on the phone that it had forced him to drive extra slowly. Fortunately, it also meant that he didn't see me peering up at him from my side window.

Despite the fact that I'd been watching and waiting for him it still came as a complete shock to see him. I had planned for this for long enough that I'd imagined that I would take it in my stride and simply tick it off as being the first part of my plan completed. But as soon as I saw him, my breath caught and my heart rate increased to what must have been an unhealthy pace. I felt my face flush red as I struggled to get a grip and bring my breathing back under control. I also felt a healthy dose of anger at my body for betraying me so. Thank heavens it hadn't happened in the pub in front of him.

So all that remained then was sit it out and wait for him to leave. I didn't care whether it would take ten minutes or four hours. All I had to do was to make sure that I was there, ready to follow him when he left. I was determined to find out where he lived so that I could start the next stage of my surveillance and establish some kind of pattern.

CHAPTER TWENTY-ONE

But just as I was starting to calm down I had another shock. A sharp rap on the passenger window and the leering face of Skip Parsons gave me renewed palpitations.

'God you scared the shit out of me' I said, winding the window down.

'Going to the quiz night?' he grinned.

'The quiz night? What quiz night? Where? When?' I replied gormlessly.

'Tonight. In the Butler's. Isn't that why you're here?'

'Oh yeah. Yes of course. Sorry mate you gave me such a shock that I forgot what I was doing. I was going to pop in and see if it was on but then I had second thoughts. I wasn't sure if I really wanted to spend the whole evening in a pub drinking soft drinks'.

'Well stop thinking about it and come and give me a hand. Linda had said that she was going to join me to make up a team but she's just sent me a text to blow me out. I need a seconder'.

Linda used to be Skip's partner back when they were in the Met together and by all accounts was just as old school as him when it came to modern policing methods. She and I had had a bit of a thing together a couple of yours back but for some reason, which I could never put my finger on, it hadn't really worked out.

'Who else is in the team?' I asked.

'Just you and me kid'

'Oh, OK, sure yes, just give me a second to make a phone call and I'll see you in there.' I didn't need to make a phone call but Skip's sudden appearance and invitation had completely wrong-footed me and I wanted a few minutes to think it through.

I held the silent phone to my ear as Skip walked off to the pub and quickly thought things through. I hadn't wanted to come face to face with Les for fear of letting him know of my plans, but the more I thought about it I decided that this was probably skewed thinking.

Far better to go about my life as normal as possible, and this would indeed have meant bumping into Les from time to time in one pub or another. Besides, the Butler's Head was effectively split into two bars and the quiz night was usually held in the saloon bar whilst Les tended to hang out in the public bar. There was a decent chance that he might not even see me.

My biggest concern was that by sitting with Skip it meant that there was a fair chance that I wouldn't be able to leave when Les did and so I would be unable to follow him home, (or wherever he went to next). But I couldn't think of a good enough excuse to blow Skip out and to continue sitting in a parked car in a darkening street. If Skip then left the pub and saw me still sitting there, after having blown him out earlier, he would start to wonder what the hell was going on and when you're planning on killing someone, it's probably best not to draw attention to yourself beforehand.

Deciding that I didn't really have much of a choice, I locked the car and made my way over to the pub and joined Skip at the bar just in time to stop him ordering me a beer and have it changed to a soft drink.

Les Guscom must have been in the public bar and once again I found it difficult to relax fully while I kept an eye out for him. But as the evening went on and the quiz began in earnest I started to forget my reason for being there. Until an hour later.

The final question of the round before the quiz took a halftime break was 'Who won the FA cup final in 1976?'

'ARSENAL !' came a booming answer.

Shit! It was Les Guscom striding through from the public bar on his way to the toilets out back and laughing to himself drunkenly as if he'd cracked the funniest joke anyone had ever heard.

'Now there goes a nasty fucker if ever you saw one' said Skip quietly.

'He's a killer' I murmured without realising I'd said it. I turned to see Skip looking at me strangely.

'He is' he said, 'but what I'm wondering is how you know that' he asked.

'Well, I *don't* know it. Obviously. I just meant that he looks like one. Doesn't he?'

For once my response had been immediate and to my mind at least, convincing. There was no doubt that Les Guscom looked every inch of what he was. His face had literally become the stuff of nightmares in my case and Hollywood would have had a field day casting him as the Hoxton Creeper in the old Sherlock Holmes movie.

I smiled at Skip but his only response was to stare back at me blankly for a moment longer than I was truly comfortable with.

'Why do you say he's a nasty fucker?' I asked, eager to turn the focus away from me and back to Skip.

'You've seen his Mum?' he asked, to which I nodded.

'Griselda. Some half German bitch who's ugly enough to make Les look handsome. She's the head of a local drugs gang which operates mostly in Witham but has just started locking horns with one of the local firms. We think they're looking to expand their little empire and they've started dealing in Chelmsford.'

Chelmsford is a relatively crime-free suburban area and whilst I knew that there had to be an unsavoury underbelly to the area, I had no idea that there might actually be organised gangs operating there.

'So, do they live in Witham then?' I asked naturally enough.

'Griselda does' he replied, 'but Les lives up on the Melbourne Estate'.

Bingo! The Melbourne Estate was a council estate in North-West Chelmsford, and although it was quite a large area, I felt that as soon as I could identify his van accurately enough, I could drive around the entire area in a reasonably short time and find it. So long as it was parked outside his house.

But Skip wasn't quite finished. Like the gift that just keeps giving, 'Armistice Road' he said, 'do you know it?'

'No' I replied, honestly enough, 'Does he live in in a council house then?'

At that point, Les came back into the bar from the toilets. He saw Skip and I sat together and did a double take. He stopped dead in his tracks before recovering and coming over to us; no doubt wondering what the sole witness to his murder was doing sitting in the same pub with a copper.

'Evening Gents' he said, placing his hammerhead fists on the table and leaning over. 'Enjoying the quiz night?'

A big smile spread across his roughhewn features as he looked first at Skip and then at me. It was the most menacing smile I had ever seen.

'Fuck off Les' said Skip impassively and yet still managing to imply a certain level of threat. 'I'd hate to have to nick you in front of your mates and all'.

I could almost imagine the cogs turning as his primitive brain came to terms with that until, still smiling, he slowly stood up straight again and wished us luck in the quiz before sauntering off next door again. It occurred to me then what a great advantage it was to be a member of the police force and part of the biggest gang in the country. But it also occurred to me that it wasn't just this shield that protected Skip He was also a mean bastard who wasn't the slightest bit concerned about getting into a scrap from which he would probably have come off second best.

I was feeling more than a little unnerved by then.

Did Les think that I was talking to the police about the murder I'd witnessed him committing? I decided that even a retarded gorilla like Les would probably have worked out that it was unlikely. If I had have done, he'd have had his collar felt by now, for sure. No, he knew Skip from drinking in the pub and there was no doubt in my mind that he would have seen the two of us together at some point in the past.

'Fucking wanker' spat Skip. 'Thinks he's the bee's knees around here'.

'Oh yeah?' I said, subconsciously inviting him to open up on the subject.

What followed was a brief history of the Guscom family and the other little gangs' operations in the area and the Essex police force's interest in them. It was gold. Far more than I could ever have hoped to learn from following him or from going to the library.

I learned that Les' Mum, Griselda was the matriarch and the 'brains' of the operation. Apparently, she was as thick as shit but still quite the savvy businesswoman when it came to crime. She had two main enforcers who she always travelled around with. Les was her only son and whilst he didn't need an enforcer of his own, being more than happy to dish out any kickings as and when he saw fit, he often hung about with two other 'medium level' dealers who were equally bad news.

They'd started out back in the day as illegal bookies and money lenders before slowly expanding their business activities into extortion and drugs. It had long been known that they were dealing marijuana and had their fingers in 'low level' crime, but it was only recently suspected that they had moved into the heroin racket and other more serious crimes.

It seemed that Skip's department, the Regional Crime Squad, were generally responsible for gathering this type of intelligence and acting on upon it accordingly, and as such, they had a reasonable amount of free licence as to what was investigated and what wasn't. As a general rule, the more serious the crime, the more likely they were to be called upon to get involved.

With the smoking of marijuana having been effectively de-criminalised, it became something of an hypocrisy to then prosecute those who sold it on a small scale. However, the main players, the ones higher up the food chain who shifted large quantities were generally still deemed to be fair game.

'How come you don't nick him then?' I asked, 'meaning you, as in the Old Bill, not you personally'.

'Ah. The million dollar question!' said Skip, managing to look furtive and at the same time seemingly eager to answer this point.

Having made clear that this was not an 'official' policy and that it would be denied vehemently if I ever repeated it, he then went on to tell me that the trouble was that if you nicked one dealer, another would step into his boots almost immediately. Simply taking one out of the equation usually meant that the next available dealer experienced the corresponding uplift in sales. In fact, it wasn't uncommon, according to Skip, for one dealer to quietly shop another simply so that he could take over his customers.

The reality was, that you could never stop society at large from wanting to take drugs and therefore there would always be a market for it. And if there was a market, there would always be people with enough entrepreneurial spirit and low enough morals to take advantage of it and make some easy money.

In fact, it was felt in some circles that the harder you cracked down on the drugs pushers, the worse you made the situation as ever more vicious and cunning villains stepped in to fill any vacuum left by a spate of arrests. A case in point which was often cited was that the alcohol prohibition in the 1920's and '30s had become the mother of most of America's organised crime families for decades to come.

So it was that the dealers who kept themselves to themselves and didn't stray too far from dealing marijuana, in particular, were given a loose rein. The cops still kept an eye on them, of course, but as long as most of their activities outside of dealing grass was restricted to NHC, it was often just as well to leave them in place rather than risk someone altogether worse stepping into their shoes.

'NHC?' I asked, 'What does NHC mean?'

'*Non Human Crime*' he replied, 'It's what we call it when one junkie stabs another or rips him off in some way. They can do what they like to each other for all I care, but when they start to prey on the general law abiding public or if they get a bit too graphic in public places, then obviously it's time to step in. Otherwise, it's just NHC. Non-Human Crime.'

Skip had given me far more of an insight into the world which Les and his Mother inhabited than I could have otherwise hoped for, and I slowly began to understand the nature of the beast I was hoping to slay.

I made sure, before the evening was done, that I popped out into the car park to clock Les' van. I made a mental note of the number plate and filed it away for future use.

The rest of the evening passed without further incident and we finished a decent second place out of eight teams in the quiz. It seemed that a month without a telly and an eclectic bookcase full of what I'd taken to be largely useless knowledge, had, in fact, had some benefits after all. That and the many hours of listening to Radio 4.

Both of us having enjoyed the evening, I agreed with Skip to meet him there for more of the same the next week and we swapped mobile numbers 'just in case'.

By the time I got home, I was buzzing and found it difficult to sleep that night. I now knew the road where Les lived and it would be only a matter of time before I knew which house. I still had no viable plan as to how I was going to go about finally killing him, but this was a significant step in the right direction as far as I was concerned.

I woke up the next morning with a half-formed plan. As I set off for an early morning run I began to put flesh on its bones. First and foremost, I would find out where he lived. And I would do that by simply driving up and down Armistice Road until I saw the van again. Hopefully, it would be on a driveway. If not, it was reasonable to assume that he would have it parked right outside his house.

Without having seen where he lived or who he might be living with, I thought it unlikely that this would be the scene of the crime to come. I still imagined that it would be more likely to be engineered via some kind of traffic 'accident' or even a workplace mishap if he actually ever did any work.

Whilst I'd always understood that he was a bricklayer, after listening to Skip I was left with the distinct impression that maybe he was a full-time drugs dealer and that his bricklaying days were a thing of the past; either that or just part of a cover story. Whatever the truth, without finding out more about his routines, it was impossible to say. I decided that I needed a way of tracking his van to find out where he went, and when.

I spent a half hour or so looking at tracking devices on e-bay and Google before deciding that I was probably out of my depth when it came to the whole espionage game. I had several concerns which I needed to address before I could make a final decision.

First of all, I worried about whether a tracking device could, in turn, be traced back to me. Looking at the internet, I found that many of them could be attached magnetically to the underside of a vehicle, usually in the wheel arch like you see in the movies. But what if it were discovered? Les might not be the sharpest tool in the box, but even he had to realise that if you were making a living dealing drugs, there was a chance that the police might be keeping tabs on you. I had to assume that Les would suspect they were and check his van from time to time. If that happened, and he found the tracking device, could he then trace it back to me? I assumed not, but you never knew and it wasn't something I wanted to take a chance with.

A bigger concern was the possibility of the police finding out about the tracker. Again, from what Skip had told me, I didn't really think that they were following Les, but *if* they were, maybe they'd have their own tracker which would be compromised by my placing another one there. *Maybe* that would then lead to them finding the tracker I had placed. And *maybe* they could then trace it back to where it had originated and then on to me, having used my credit card to buy it online.

I had too many 'maybes' and the potential pitfalls seemed endless. Although I didn't really think that any of them were likely, the truth was that I didn't know for sure and if I was wrong I certainly didn't want to find out the hard way.

I also didn't know how long the battery would realistically last and more importantly to me, whether they could record a trail for me to follow. I knew that I would be able to see where the van was in real time, but what I really needed was something that would trace its movements over the course of the day so that I could finish work, come home and log in to some kind of app and work out what the pattern of his day had been.

After a couple of hours on the internet, I decided that I needed to speak to a human. I remembered seeing a shop in Chingford called Snake Eyes Security & Surveillance which seemed to have a lot of exciting looking security gadgets in the window. It looked as though it might offer what I needed and so I decided that the next time I was over that way I would call in and see if they could point me in the right direction.

Chingford is a good twenty miles away from Chelmsford and I was pretty sure that there would have been other options closer to home, but I'd decided that it wouldn't hurt to put a little physical distance between myself and the place where I bought an item like this. Besides, I was due to call on a Chingford based client that Friday anyway.

I set my alarm to wake me at 5 a.m. the next day and moved my early morning run time forwards so that I could scope out Armistice Road without being seen. Or if I was seen, at least I would be seen doing something that could be explained away as 'natural'.

I needn't have bothered with the alarm as the next day I woke up at four. Sensing that sleep would not come back to me anytime soon, I pulled on Wednesday's pants and some running shorts before setting off to scope out Armistice Road soon after.

It was still dark but the street lighting was on and so running was not a problem. I have always enjoyed being up and about whilst the rest of the world sleeps. There's something vaguely thrilling about it and yet, at the same time serene.

Of course, if you're not doing anything particularly unusual, there isn't anything really thrilling about it at all, but it has always managed to stir a feeling of anticipation in me as though something unexpected is about to happen at any moment. Maybe it's something I picked up from my time in the Royal Marines, creeping about in the dark on manoeuvres. Or maybe it's something as simple as being up when I wasn't supposed to be as a small child.

The serenity is easier to figure, I guess. With most of the world around you asleep, the silence becomes such that you can hear a dog bark a half a mile away. You notice the sound of distant cars or lorries;

something which doesn't usually register during the day because it becomes part of a constant background noise.

A small thing like a bedroom light being on becomes a point of interest. You start to wonder if the person who lives there has an early morning shift to start somewhere and if so what kind of work they would do to warrant such an early start. Maybe they're going on holiday and have an early flight? Little things, banalities really, but when you are up and about at that time of the morning they take on a new level of interest.

To the North West of Chelmsford lies the large council estate known as the Melbourne Estate, with a solitary tower block in its centre being almost the only high rise building in an otherwise low rise city (one of the best things about living in Chelmsford as far as most people are concerned).

The locals like to call it 'The Bronx' as if to confer an aura of danger and lawlessness upon it, and I guess if you were brought up in Chelmsford, it probably does seem a little bad-ass. But if you've ever lived anywhere that was a genuinely bad neighbourhood, you'd laugh at them. I'd no doubt that Melbourne has the same rotten eggs and scumbag families as anywhere else, (after all let's not forget whose house I was going to check out), but overall it was a safe place to live. Street crime and gang culture were pretty much non-existent, certainly compared the estates of my childhood. There were no boarded up houses and burnt out cars littering the Roads. It was an area that I personally would have felt perfectly safe walking through at any time; day or night.

Armistice Road sat off to the Northern edge of the estate not far where the private housing began and the tarmac roads were better looked after. At around three hundred yards long, Armistice Road seemed to be comprised entirely of semi-detached houses that looked to have been built post-war, probably in the 1950s. They had all originally been built in the same style with the same painted windows and doors no doubt, but Thatcher's right-to-buy scheme would have meant that a high percentage were now in private ownership and those owners had done their best to try to stamp a little individuality on their castles wherever possible.

Quite a few of them had the kerbs lowered and had converted their front gardens into off-street parking areas. Some had small but beautifully manicured lawns to the front with pretty flowers bordering them, whilst one or two had the inevitable pile of builder's material and children's toys hanging around out front.

On both mornings that week, Thursday and Friday, I spotted Les' van straight away and both times it was parked outside what I took to be a two bedroom house. Assuming that it was the address which he lived at (and I'd felt sure that it was) he had a front garden with a low wall to the front and a missing gate.

As I jogged past I saw a wooden front door in need of a lick of varnish with two mortice locks beneath a standard Yale lock. The gate into the back garden looked new enough and also had both a Yale and a mortice lock with a thin strand of barbed wire topping it. I guessed that if you were dealing drugs, you would probably want more than just a basic level of security.

The van was unmarked and un sign-written. At about five years old it looked in decent enough shape not to warrant any unwanted attention from a traffic cop, and yet not so new as to stand out like a sore thumb. A small pile of sand and a couple of empty paint cans adorned the garden and I wondered again whether or not he actually did any real work.

There was no one to be seen anywhere nearby and no lights shone in any of the neighbouring windows so I felt confident that if I came back, armed with some kind of tracking device, I wouldn't have any problems fixing it to the van at that time of the morning.

Friday morning came and I was looking forward to finishing my sales call and progressing my other plans. Fridays were often purely admin days for a lot of the sales reps at APS. They wouldn't schedule any appointments in, instead, using the day to book their diaries out for the following week, make some phone calls and pick up samples and stock from the office. It was all a bit of a doss really.

A short while ago that had been my working pattern too, but now that I had nothing, or no-one to return home to, I was happy to try and make myself that bit busier at work.

I had set up two visits in Chingford that Friday morning and had it in mind that I would be done by sometime around midday when I would take the opportunity to call in at Snake Eyes Security & Surveillance and see if they could help me out.

I left the house just after nine am, avoiding the school run traffic and knowing that I didn't need to rush. Chingford was around a forty-minute drive away and a not altogether unpleasant one. Ten minutes in my mobile rang and I picked it up and checked the screen. I have a hands free kit in the car but I never bother to use it (I know I shouldn't, but let's face it if you're planning a murder, using a phone while driving is of little real significance).

It was Bigham.

'Hello?'

'Owen? Is that you'

'Of course it's me, Steve. Who else would it be?' I wondered idly whether he was finally succumbing to some kind of dementia.

'Sorry, Owen. Of course I know it's you, I'm just having a bit of a senior moment!. What are your movements today?'

'I'm just heading over to Chingford now. I've got a couple of maintenance calls and then I'm gonna sort out my admin'.

'Can you do a call in Harlow at one? I've just taken a call from a guy who'd been on our website asking about our high-end logo pens and I told him we had someone who happened to be in the area today who could drop in on him. He's talking about a decent volume and I'm pretty sure he's serious. You've got some samples with you?'

'Yes, of course Steve' I replied, 'I'm driving at the minute but give me ten minutes and I'll call you back and take down the details'.

What would have been the most natural conversation in the world a year ago suddenly took on a deeper significance. I realised that this was probably the first time in six months that Bigham had given me a new lead. As much as bolstering my already high spirits, it also served as a reminder of how far I had fallen previously and once again I renewed my resolve to do right by him.

And then, just as I was starting to feel like Mr Motivator, a moment of self-doubt threatened to send it all crashing to the ground about me. I recalled the start of the conversation. Bigham had asked if it was me. He had rung, and yet he had asked specifically, "Owen, is that you?" I had initially put it down to a simple moment of absentmindedness. One of those things that we've all encountered at some point or another when we're trying to do too many things at once, but the more I thought about it, the more it sounded like the words of a man who had dialled the wrong number by accident.

The more I mulled it over the more convinced I became that the call had not been intended for me. That he had meant to call one of the other reps to ask them to see the client and had then phoned me by mistake. With this realisation came a short but brutal moment of despair. A feeling of betrayal and that I had been kidding myself about the turnaround in my fortunes. For a long fraught minute, I battled with the black dog that threatened to take me back down into the underworld of self-doubt and depression.

But almost as quickly came the realisation that it didn't matter. It didn't matter one jot. All that really mattered was that I had a chance to demonstrate once more to Bigham that I was back in business. That I was the man he needed to contact when he wanted a deal closed. Most of the other reps would have been either in the office, or 'working from home' on a Friday, but when he'd called through to me, I was already out there, doing my best for A.P.S. I decided that there was no way I was going to be leaving this customer without an order.

This new lead meant that my plans to visit Snake Eyes would have to be put back a little. The morning calls I had were straightforward enough and didn't take long to do, but I had to make sure that I got to Harlow by one and I really didn't want to be late. One o'clock was close to lunchtime for a lot of people and I didn't want to get stuck into my sales patter, only to find that I was limited to ten minutes before whoever I was seeing had to leave for lunch or some other appointment.

To make sure that I was going to be alright on this score, I arrived in Harlow and phoned through to the client at twelve thirty and sounded him out.

'I have it in my schedule to see you at one' I said when I was put through to name Bigham had given me. 'I just wanted to make sure that this was still convenient and that you weren't cutting short lunch or about to go out at that time?'

Had he told me that he was going out at one thirty, I would have brought the appointment forward half an hour, but 'No, no' he assured me. One o'clock was fine and he didn't have any other appointments for the afternoon. Satisfied, I made my farewell and resolved to arrive at one pm exactly.

The client turned out to be a chain of four insurance brokerages and between them, they consumed a decent amount of stationery each day. Without boring you with the details of the sales call, I left with a small order for pens from our high-end logo range and a few other odds and sods. It was too small an order to get excited about, but I had gotten on well with the guy and he'd given me a firm commitment to let me quote the next time he made a larger order which would probably be the following week. It was a small win as far as I was concerned, but instinct told me that it was likely to open up into a valuable client.

Feeling positive I headed back to Chingford and managed to park up outside Snake Eyes Security &

Surveillance at around four pm. I just hoped that it would actually have the advice and the goods that I was looking for.

There wasn't much to look at from the outside of the shop, just a fairly bland display consisting of variations of safes, a CCTV monitor and some boxed up alarm systems. I began to think that I might have been barking up the wrong tree. You couldn't see inside the shop without actually going in and so opening the door, I stepped into an area full of glass cabinets and shelves displaying a veritable smorgasbord of electronic gizmos and paraphernalia.

There was no one there in the shop but the wall behind one of the counters was one long striped mirror of the kind which allows whoever is on the other side to see you clearly, whilst obscuring the sight of them from whoever was in the shop.

When no-one rushed out to see me straight away, I began to peer at the items on display, feeling a little like a kid in a joke shop. The cabinet beneath the main counter seemed to be showing a variety of cameras and recorders; right the way through from fake CCTV cameras to mount outside your house, to miniaturised cameras and voice recorders disguised as USB sticks, pens and even cuddly toys.

The display cabinet to the left held a variety of locks and safes, many of them camouflaged so as to look like a can of beans or an electrical plug socket. Whilst the cabinet to my right held a whole range of electronic looking items whose purpose was completely lost on me.

A man opened a door in the mirrored wall and stepped through.

'OH – MY - GOD!'

I looked up and saw a man wearing thick glasses and a woolly hat. He looked to be of a similar age and height to me with a decent sized paunch preceding him and a dirty ink smudge on his nose. He was looking at me as though I was some kind of film star that had just stepped into his shop, with a half-smile and look of wonderment.

'Owen! It's me. Don't you recognise me?'

It was clear that he knew exactly who I was, but as I racked my brains, for the life of me I had no idea who he was. For a fleeting moment, I wondered whether this was some kind of trick of the trade; that a shop selling spy gadgets would know in advance anyone who walked through their doors.

But then he swept off his thick glasses and woolly hat and threw his arms wide in an expansive gesture that made him instantly recognisable. I felt a huge schoolboy grin erupt across my face and my feet moved towards him of their own accord so that he could wrap me up in a huge bear hug.

He looked nothing like he had the last time I'd seen him, but that was hardly surprising being as over twenty years had passed since then. Older, thicker, heavier, jowlier and balder. But the one thing that almost never changes and is often the biggest tell of all, is body language. As soon as he had opened his arms wide in that expansive gesture with that stupid grin spread across his face, I knew him like I'd have known my own brother.

Bradley. It was Bradley Thomas.

CHAPTER TWENTY-TWO

Twenty-seven years ago

It was during a brief period when Judy had found romance elsewhere and my immature mind was struggling to cope with the loss of our close relationship that, at the tender age of eighteen years old, I joined the Royal Marines. Not from any deep-seated desire to be a soldier or to go to war, but simply because I had no real idea of what I actually wanted to do with my life.

Royal Marines basic training is physically tough, more so than most regiments in the army, but it's the mental toughness demanded which really sets it apart. The ability to think coolly and rationally and more importantly, positively when you're chest deep in the mire and running on gas is a trait which is a source of pride to every Royal Marine that ever served.

The mental and the physical beastings they inflicted on us recruits were way beyond anything we could have imagined prior to joining up. Basic training taught us how to operate effectively when we'd gone beyond our perceived limits of endurance; when minds had started to hallucinate and bodies had started to shut down.

Basic training was like volunteering for torture and promising to laugh about it, because if there's one characteristic that's essential in every British soldier, it's the ability to maintain a sense of humour. Always, always maintain a stupidly positive outlook. One of the worse things a soldier can do, as far as the British Army and the Royal Navy are concerned, is to lose his sense of humour.

I remember my first day like it was yesterday, arriving at Lympstone Station in Devon having been deposited by the short train which plied its trade up and down the single track line. About twelve of us got off of that particular train on a mild September afternoon. None of us knew each other then, but all of us were eying up the others, wondering whether they were recruits like us, or actual real Royal Marines. Some of the lads had short, sharp hairstyles and I guessed that they were already in, not recruits like me, but I was soon to be proven wrong.

We were collected by a Marine Corporal who ticked our names off of his list before herding us aboard a minibus for the short journey to barracks. Once there, we were met by another pinch-faced Corporal who looked as though he'd drawn the short straw and seemed to be pissed off for no real reason other than that he had to deal with us new recruits.

We were lined up outside our accommodation block, with our luggage placed in front of us whilst our names were once again checked off. When that was done, the Corporal laid out the basic ground rules, who was in charge (him) when to speak, (only when spoken to), and the fact that from now on we were the lowest of the low etc. Pretty much everything you would expect as a new recruit.

That done, we jogged over to the administration block to complete some more paperwork; which basically entailed signing our arses over to the military to do with as it wished. It was all a bit surreal and so different from anything I had previously experienced that I didn't feel particularly scared or excited at the time.

Paperwork completed, we were then sent into the next room for a haircut. I call it a haircut, but it was more of a shearing. They gave us a going over with the clippers on a number one setting, leaving us with no more than a millimetre of hair. Everyone went through and some of the lads who had already got pretty sharp haircuts looked a little upset by it, but of course, no-one dared complain.

Back outside and we all looked and began to feel a little like prisoners of war. Looking around me I realised that we had all started to feel a little more nervous at that point. Back to our kit and then we were shown to our rooms, or 'dorms,' and bunks so that we could stash our civvies.

There was one more trainload of recruits due in that day, we were told, and as soon as that came in we would have our full complement. When they had arrived it would be time for us to go and collect uniforms etc, but until then, we were to remain in our rooms.

Each room was divided into twelve bed-spaces, all identical with a metal bed, a chair and a purpose-built unit comprising of drawers, a wardrobe and built-in desk. We were yet to collect the mattresses for our beds.

Most of us were already there in the room I was assigned to and so we stood around chatting quietly and getting to know each other while we waited to be called again by the Corporal for the next stage of our first day.

'OWEN! - OWEN FUCKING THOMSON!' I heard from behind me.

'Yes Corporal!' I shouted and span around to face the voice.

But it wasn't our Corporal. It wasn't any Corporal at all. In fact, it was a lad dressed in civvies, just like the rest of us and sporting a freshly shorn scalp. He stood there, legs apart with his arms held out wide to his sides and a massive shit-eating grin spread across his face.

'I knew it was you. Even from the back! Unbelievable!'

I stood there and gawped. I racked my brains but I really had no idea who he was, despite the fact that he was greeting me like a long-lost relative.

'It's me. Brad! Don't you recognise me? We were at school together'

I was none the wiser. It occurred to me that this might be either some elaborate joke or some kind of strange test set out to recruits on their first day. 'Erm....' Was about all I could manage.

'Don't tell me you've forgotten! Whiteside Primary School. We had a fight over some girl!'

And then the penny dropped. If I had felt stunned before, I was utterly gobsmacked now. Bradley Thomas. My schoolboy nemesis. It was the same person who had beaten the living daylights out of me along with his older brothers and who now seemed to be greeting me as though we were, and always had been, the very best of friends.

'Oh' was about the best I could manage, still expecting this to be some kind of elaborate joke or trial 'Hello Brad. How's it going?'

I had no idea then, but that first day in the Royal Marines was also to be the first day of what was to become a beautiful friendship.

I was suspicious as hell of him at first, of course, but as I got to know him again I came to realise that despite our inauspicious childhood beginnings, Brad had turned into a one of life's genuinely happy-go-lucky souls. There was very little that phased him, and certainly, he wasn't one to ever hold a grudge.

He remembered our schoolboy encounters as well as I did, but from a different perspective of course. The difference was that, as far as he was concerned, the past was the past and there was really no point in dwelling on it. It took me a long time to come around to his way of thinking but come around to it I eventually did. Despite my initial best efforts not to, I came to think of him as my best friend. My decision to forgive and forget was somewhat aided by the fact that, as far as I was concerned, I had come out of our childhood conflicts far better off than Bradley had.

We're all products of our upbringing to varying extents and as I got to know Bradley more I discovered that he'd had a pretty shitty childhood, with his older, psychotic, brother making his life a misery at every opportunity and bullying Bradley far more than Bradley had ever bullied anyone else.

When he'd returned home that fateful day, sporting a black eye, courtesy of yours truly, Paul, the oldest brother had held him down and stubbed cigarettes out on Bradley's legs. It was hardly surprising then that he'd agreed to his older brother's demands that they act out some kind of reprisal.

It turned out that whilst Bradley did develop a love of violence, he never gained a thirst for revenge and as far as he was concerned, however bad yesterday's fight may have been, it tended to have no bearing on the following day's thinking.

Bradley's optimistic outlook on life was infectious and despite my initial misgivings, we came to be the best of friends relying on each other for mutual support when the going got tough.

CHAPTER TWENTY-THREE

A Royal Marine's training is harsh and there are inevitably those who don't make it. During our very first week, we had three lads PVR, (Premature Voluntary Release) themselves from the process.

They were lads who'd thought that what they saw on television was true. Lads who'd thought the US Navy SEALS were a tough lot. I've met a few American so-called special forces in the past I can safely say that, based on what I've seen, very few of those so-called elites would make it through our basic commando training, let alone hold a candle to our real special forces, (I'm talking here about the SBS and SAS).

But I digress; the three lads who PVR'd in the first week would not be the last of our number to fall, with recruits dropping out on a regular basis in the early stages, either from injury, or a lack of mental toughness. Others soon joined them as the natural selection process of survival of the fittest took its toll.

Those that remained evolved into very different men to those that they had been before. Most decent human beings have a natural aversion to the thought of plunging a bayonet into the body of another person, over and over again, and yet that is exactly what we were trained to do. When you're standing face to face with the enemy and both of you are out of rounds, the one who hesitates with the bayonet will be the one in second place.

It was an evolution which came easier to some lads than others. Whilst the army and navy are not made up exclusively of any one social class, they do contain more than their fair share of lads from poorer backgrounds or broken homes. For many of them, the Armed Forces offer something hard to find elsewhere; a chance to succeed regardless of background. It also offers a family, of sorts, for those who have never had one of their own.

The last thing I'd want to do is to smear the good character of our serving men and women, but the truth is that the armed forces also attract a disproportionate number of misfits. In amongst those misfits are the naturally weak and also the naturally strong, a combination of which inevitably leads to an element of bullying.

The Directing Staff knew this as well as the recruits and whilst bullying was never actively condoned, it's fair to say that, for the most part, a blind eye was turned to it. Let's face it, if you can't take being picked on by your roommates, you're not likely to bear up very well when people start lobbing bombs at you. A form of natural selection I guess; survival of the fittest.

But more importantly, they want the recruits to pull together as an effective unit; for the strong to support the weak. When someone is injured or struggling to cope, it falls upon his fellow recruits to help him out as best they can; it's only by working as a team that many of the tasks are possible. United we stand, divided we fall.

So, when one man struggles or drops behind in training, it's not usually him that the staff punishes, it's the entire section or platoon. Not only did it teach us the value of pulling together as a team, but by pissing us all off at the same time, they also managed to strengthen the bonds of fellowship and team spirit, united in our hatred of the staff.

The British Army and the Royal Navy has used this method effectively for hundreds of years to create some of the best fighting units in the world. For centuries we've been churning out soldiers and sailors that were better than anyone else's, it's just a shame that we've also had Generals who were crap.

Sometimes, however, some of the stronger, and less intelligent misfits decide that the easier way round this group discipline is to eliminate the weaker members, to which end, they mete out their own 'justice' by giving the offenders a right good kicking when no-one is looking in the hope that they can 'encourage' them to PVR.

It doesn't make the victims better soldiers but it does, as often as not, lead to them either quitting altogether or picking up injuries which force them to be back-trooped. There may be a twisted logic to their actions, but there's no getting away from the fact that they are usually just a minority group of sadistic bastards.

Our intake was unfortunate enough to have one such group of nasty bastards amongst its number, and even more unlucky to have NCO's, who were either too stupid to see it, or too sadistic to care. We were accommodated in four, twelve-man dorms and in one of these dorms, three of the little bastards ruled the roost. We were eight weeks into a six-month training course and they had already 'sorted' one lad from their own dormitory and one from another, both of whom had subsequently voluntarily withdrawn from the process.

Jones, Jeckyll and Laver were their names and when it came to being nasty fuckers, all three were cut from the same cloth. Jones and Jeckyll were both short, swarthy, Geordies and were similar enough in appearance to pass off as having been related. Laver was around six-foot two, with a gap-toothed grin and what would have been a shock of ginger hair had he been allowed to grow it.

The three of them grouped together wherever possible, but as we were normally split into pairs for most activities, there was inevitably at least one poor sod who had to team up with the odd one.

It was somewhere around the eight-week point that I picked up a flu type virus which was not enough to keep me in bed, but which was enough to make me feel like shit. Coupled with this, I had the severe misfortune of being buddied up with Jeckyll on a five-day exercise, yomping across the sodden moors of Southern Devon. Being buddied up meant that we ran together, we dug together, we ate together and we were generally responsible for the wellbeing and actions of each other throughout the exercise.

If one man's kit wasn't clean, both were responsible. If your camouflage was poor, it was on both of you. If your buddy was struggling on a yomp or a forced march, it was your responsibility to push or to drag him along.

We started out OK on day one. I was feeling a little shabby, but it wasn't a problem to keep up with the rest of the platoon physically, despite being the first day of the exercise. The first day was the day they normally drove the recruits the hardest, so as to set the tone for the rest of the week. If it wasn't tipping with rain, and it's virtually guaranteed to do so at some point on Dartmoor, the directing staff would be certain to have us leopard crawling through a brook or stream to make sure that we were suitably wet and miserable.

Dartmoor National Park is a huge area of moorland decorated with cold granite tors and ancient monuments. It's safe to say that it's wetter, windier and mistier than most other places in England. But what makes a moor a moor is the inability for the soil to drain effectively so that it's impossible to cover any great distance without encountering a myriad of small streams and countless bogs.

The thin heather and grass render it fit for nothing other than grazing sheep. Sheep which seem to spend a huge amount of their time defecating on the landscape and leaving tics in the grass, waiting to attach themselves to poor unsuspecting squaddies.

I have since been back to Dartmoor on a few occasions and the stark beauty of the place never ceases to amaze me. In part, it amazes me because the Royal Marines manage to turn it into such a place of abject suffering for its recruits.

The first day of the exercise consisted at being dropped off in the arse end of nowhere, before yomping on to the next equally remote location, carefully chosen as an area in which it was possible to dig trenches (most of the rest of Dartmoor being too full of granite to enable us to do this properly)

Digging a four-man battle trench took a serious amount of labour. Particularly when the only tool we had to dig it with was a two and a half foot long spade, more suited to a midget. The Directing Staff measured and marked out the dimensions of each trench for us and we cut away the turf in strips from the surrounding area and carefully preserved it before getting on with the main event of excavating the trench itself, throwing the soil to the front and the sides as we went.

The finished trench consisted of underground sleeping areas at each end, big enough for one man and the group's bergens, and a central firing platform wide enough for four men to stand abreast. Once it had been dug out to the required depth and dimensions, we took our previously saved turf strips and re-laid them over the newly exposed soil so as to camouflage the whole area. The end result was a well-constructed earthwork which was raised at the front and sides and offered a perfect platform for firing forwards, or for taking cover from enemy fire to the front.

The overall effect was impressive and when you approached it from the front, and to a lesser extent, from the rear also, you wouldn't have noticed it you were almost right upon it.

But as impressive as it may have been in terms of a defensive structure, it was absolutely no fun at all digging the bloody thing when all we had was a tiny spade each and however much muscle and weight we could bring to bear on it. Also, it may have been a four-man trench, but only two of us could digging at any time; the other pair had to 'stand to' and guard against any possible attack from an enemy.

Several hours later and we were the last section to finish our trench, probably in no small part due to the fact that I wasn't pulling my weight. By that time I was feeling really shitty and the middle of Dartmoor is not the place to be when you're feeling unwell. Most recruits have to work their way through illness or injury though at some point during the long training period and there was no option but to keep at it. The others all knew that they were having to carry me though and Jeckyll, in particular, was moaning like hell.

There's next to little or no rest to be had when you're out on exercise. Some unknown boffin once worked out that you can perform at eighty percent efficiency if you have four hours of sleep a night and the occasional power nap during the day, and that is pretty much what they worked us to over the next few days. As soon as one task finished, another began. If we weren't engaged in some form of tough physical challenge like running around playing at soldiers, then there was always the basic admin of cleaning your kit or cooking your food. Whatever it was, it left us with virtually no downtime. On the rare odd moments when we had nothing to do, say if we'd eaten our food and cleaned up afterwards faster than anticipated, we might snatch a cheeky ten minutes of shuteye, but that was pretty much it during the day.

After the battle of Goose Green in the Falklands war of 1982, the British army decided that all future engagements would be fought at night wherever possible; the upshot of which meant that we spent the majority of each night running around from one location to the next playing soldiers and laying ambushes.

On the second morning of the exercise, we had a kit inspection. Despite the fact that the DS took every opportunity they had to run us through as much shit as they could find, we were still expected to maintain a high level of cleanliness and order.

We couldn't do much about cleaning or pressing the clothes we wore, but everything else like bayonets, cooking and eating equipment, magazines and most importantly firearms, were expected to be cleaned, dried and oiled at every opportunity.

Cleaning rifles meant breaking them down s and cleaning and oiling each individual piece meticulously. To clean inside the barrel, we used a 'pull through', which was a piece of string with a weight on one end and a loop on the other. You passed a small piece of cloth through the loop, dropped the weight down one end of the barrel so that it came out at the other end and then pulled the cloth through it to remove any residue. Once through to clean, and once through again to oil it.

Magazines were just as susceptible to jamming when dirty and those too were dismantled, cleaned and oiled. The slightest bit of dirt or grain of sand risked causing a 'stoppage', rendering your rifle all but useless.

If Boris is bearing down on you with fixed bayonet and yelling Russian obscenities in your face, you want to be sure that when you pull the trigger, he's going to be stopped dead in his tracks. Hopefully in the midst of an impressive spray of blood and guts. What you don't want is a resounding absence of 'bang'.

At the start of these field inspections, we emptied out the contents of our bergens and webbing and laid them out in a prescribed fashion.

The inspections weren't just an excuse to punish us. They served to teach us the harsh realities of surviving in the field. A little leftover in food in a billy might sound innocuous enough but in the middle of nowhere, it meant a potential upset stomach and therefore, a potential man down.

Attention to detail was everything. Ration packs were also inspected as well as the empty wrappers. Nothing could be left behind in the field which could possibly prove to be useful intelligence to an enemy. Everything had to be carried off with us at all times. The theory being, that if we'd all l chucked our teabags away, it might have been possible for an enemy intelligence boffin to gather them up and say, *'Ah ha ! Thirty teabags. Zis means only one platoon of Tommies!'*

They checked to make sure that we had eaten all of our rations. Each pack had been nutritionally prepared to provide 2,500 calories per day and so they checked to make sure that we consumed them all. Personally, I never found that eating every last item was a hardship because I was always so freezing cold and ravenous on exercise.

This wasn't a spur of the moment inspection. We knew that it was coming and had plenty of time to get our kit cleaned and in order. But we also knew that no matter how much time and effort we took, the NCO's would find fault somewhere along the line, whether imaginary or real.

On a damp and misty morning, we stood to attention in a single long line, our kit displayed before us. Each item carefully laid out onto ponchos, which were in turn laid out on the ground before us. We stood rigidly, desperately scanning our kit with a dread of having something out of place.

One by one the NCOs went down the line finding faults, (they could always find fault somewhere). Arriving at mine, Corporal Biggs picked up my rifle and 'broke' it before peering through the barrel to check for cleanness. It's obvious, of course, that the one item of kit beyond anything else that you absolutely must keep clean is your rifle.

Stood rigidly to attention and watching his reactions through my peripheral vision I saw him literally do a double take before looking at me and then looking again through the barrel. I wasn't sure what his beef was going to be because I knew for sure, one hundred percent for sure, that I had cleaned and oiled every last millimetre of that weapon. In fact, I had spent more time cleaning my rifle than any other item of kit before me that day.

And then with growing horror, it dawned on me. I couldn't remember pulling through the barrel! He held the rifle up to my face causing me to flinch before ordering me to look along the inside of the barrel. I turned my head slightly to get the angle right and sure enough, the inside was strewn with debris, tiny grains of grit which were miniscule in reality but which suddenly looked huge as I peered through, knowing full well what the consequences were likely to be.

His apoplectic reaction was entirely predictable given the seriousness of my crime. He seemed to take my slovenly sloppiness as a personal affront and it served to act as a launch-pad to his stratospheric rage. But the consequences of my misdemeanour were not reserved for me alone. In true Royal Marine fashion, the whole platoon was 'beasted' up and down the nearest mountain for the next two hours.

It might seem perverse that everyone else should suffer as much as me, but the truth is that had Jeckyll been a better 'buddy' we would have both checked each other's kit before the inspection to make sure that such a thing didn't happen. But he wasn't and we didn't.

'Beastings' were PT sessions which felt as though they had been specifically designed to make people break, to weed out the weak from the strong, pushing recruits harder and harder until they could physically do no more or until they broke and gave up.

I can't put into words how bad that particular beasting was that day and still do it justice. Every muscle screamed quietly with pain and my lungs felt as though they were literally being torn apart. All I could think about was how much I wanted it to end. Added to the physical torture was the usual psychological anguish of not having any idea when it was going to end.

It finally ended after one of the lads PVR'd. He may have been the only one person to do so, but I'm sure that every other lad there must have gone through exactly the same thought process. So, to add to my personal shame of cocking up so spectacularly at inspection, I now had the added guilt, not only of submitting the rest of my friends to the beasting from hell, but also of being responsible for one of them quitting.

But my personal failings were not entirely finished for the week. The following night we had to lay an ambush which involved yomping through the dark night, across miles of boggy moors, to a pre-planned position where we laid up waiting for the enemy to pass by below us.

The 'enemy' force was comprised of three of the Directing Staff who were set to jog along a predefined route at some time during the early hours of the morning. All we had to do, once we had taken our positions, was to stay quiet and unmoving until they appeared. Once in sight, and at a given signal, we would open up with everything we had, (blank rounds of course).

It wasn't the most complicated of tasks, but for me, fending off my virus, staying awake was proving to be something of a battle. And it proved to be a battle I could not win.

I don't remember dropping off, of course, you never do. I do remember being kicked awake by Jeckyll though, his face a mask of apoplectic fury which was plain to see even in the middle of that black night, despite the fact that it was smothered in camouflage paint.

'Get the fuck up you stupid, useless, fucking, knacker' he spat through gritted teeth, wanting to scream at me but not daring to and looking about with an air of panic mixed into his fury.

I immediately realised what had happened and came to full wakefulness, scrambling to my feet and casting about desperately to see if anyone else had seen me sleeping. I had managed to doze through the entire ambush; with an entire platoon's worth of rifles, light machine guns, thunder-flashes and flares going off all around me. It was a commotion which should have been enough to wake the dead, but which had proved completely and utterly ineffective at rousing me. I found out later that I had actually started snoring just as it all kicked off.

The reason for Jeckyll's panic was obvious. Falling asleep whilst on an exercise like that had to be one of the most heinous crimes a recruit could possibly commit. If any of the NCO's had walked past our position and realised what I'd done, the punishment would have been swift and brutal. And it would not have been reserved for me alone; the entire platoon would have been beasted until we dropped and no doubt made to be even more sleep deprived than we already were.

But fortune smiled upon me that night; I had not been discovered and only Jeckyll had been witness to my awful crime. Jeckyll, however, was not smiling; In fact, he was positively scowling. I had already made everyone's life a misery by failing to clean my rifle properly and with this little episode added into the mix, as far as he was concerned, I was nothing more than an outright liability.

I suffered Jeckyll's brooding silence for the remainder of the week and we spoke to each other only when necessary and then only in short business-like bursts. But the truth was that we had never been friends in the first place. We had got along previously only because we needed to, and as much as I had done my best to hide my dislike of him, it was more than probable that he had done the same to me.

We managed to get through the next few days without any further incidents. Or at least, none that could be pinned at my door, and we returned to barracks on late Friday afternoon. Tired, filthy and just in time for dinner.

All in all, it had been a pretty miserable week, but as the week came to an end and against all odds, I could feel myself recovering from whatever virus it was that had laid me low All in all I decided, it could have been worse.

It was on the Saturday evening when I discovered that there were still one or two more scenes to play out from this little episode.

'You'd better watch your back, Owen'. It was Bradley, come to join me sitting on the edge of my bed as I polished my boots.

'Oh yeah? Why's that then? I asked, expecting him to come out with some kind of corny wisecrack.

'Coz the three ugly sisters are looking to pay you a visit mate, that's why.'

I stopped my polishing for a moment and looked up at him in confusion. 'Who the hell are the three ugly sisters?'

'Jones, Jeckyll and Laver' he replied, smiling smugly at his own cleverness in coming up with such an ingenious collective epithet.

'When?' I asked, immediately grasping his meaning and looking over his shoulder to check that he didn't mean right at that very moment.

'Dunno mate, but I'm guessing tonight. It makes sense, doesn't it? Saturday night. Half the camp is away for the weekend and the other half most likely too drunk or too knackered to stir. Only Corporal Jakes is on duty, and we've got no duties of our own tomorrow to worry about if they stay up for an extra hour or two.'

'Hmmm.' I was more than a little cocksure back in those days and so I wasn't overly worried about what Bradley had just told me. If it came down to a bit of hand to hand combat in an enclosed space which meant that only one or two of them could come at me at a time, I felt pretty confident that I could give them a good hiding. My biggest concern would be if all three of them came at me out in the open; or worse if they came for me whilst I slept. In either case, things could end badly for me.

'Well, I guess I'd better not disappoint them then, had I? Let's just hope it's tonight though so that we can get it over and done with.'

I was so cocksure back then that I was actually looking forward to having a fight with the three of them. The fact that Jeckyll was pissed off with me for what had happened on exercise was fair enough, but the fact that he actually believed that *he* would be dishing out a lesson to *me*, was enough piss me off even more. I decided then that if they didn't come for me that night, I would make a point seeking out Jeckyll to give him a bit of a kicking anyway.

'Don't worry Owen, I've got your back mate. If they do come, they'll have me to contend with too.' From such inauspicious beginnings, Bradley Thomas had fast turned out to be a better mate than I could have asked for and there was no denying that he loved a scrap.

'Listen, I think I'll be OK Brad. As long as I'm awake and on my feet when they come, I reckon I can do the three of them without any bother. My main concern is falling asleep though. If I do, and you think you hear them coming, can you give me a shout?'

Bradley occupied the bed space opposite mine and so he was ideally placed to either wake me up or step in if needed, but the truth was, I wanted the macho kudos of being able to say that I'd taken down all three of them.

Whilst I may have felt pretty smug about my own abilities back then, I wasn't normally someone who liked to brag or give it 'the big 'un', but in a macho environment like the Royal Marines, and with bullies to deal with, it didn't hurt to send out a bit of a statement, 'pour encourage les autres'.

The three ugly sisters' MO had so far been that which had been tried and tested throughout the British army. In fact, as a way of 'sorting out' the weaker recruits, it was already something of a tradition in the marines. Occasionally during broad daylight, but mostly at night after lights out, they would come for their victims wearing army issue shorts, T-shirts and gas masks and fall upon their victims as they lay in bed.

Most of the time, their victims would be just that, victims who would probably spend the rest of their lives, regardless of occupation, being bullied by someone or other. They would lay there mutely, curled into a ball and waiting for the beating to end, hoping that it would not be too severe.

But the Three Ugly Sisters had made a massive error of judgement when they chose me and I was determined to give them something to remember me by as I lay awake that Saturday night after lights out; on top of my bed, wearing PT kit and running shoes.

In the dark silence that enveloped us I sensed that Bradley was laying there tense with excitement too, but eventually, as the time ticked on and no-one came, I heard him snoring lightly. Two hours had passed and nobody had come.

Still tired from the previous week's lack of sleep on exercise, eventually I dropped off. It was during the wee small hours that I was jolted into full wakefulness with a start. I knew immediately, of course, what had woken me up and with the lithe athleticism of youth, I surged to my feet in readiness.

I stood silently in the darkness facing away from my bed-space and adopted the classic wrestler's stance. Hands held out to my front at the ready to take a grip, elbows tucked in tight to my sides and knees flexed with my weight over the balls of my feet. Having been jolted straight from sleeping to waking, my eyes adjusted quickly to the dark and I listened with my mouth open slightly, straining to hear again whatever it was that had woken me.

I heard nothing discernible at first, although some sixth sense told me that the three ugly sisters were already in the room. The corridor outside was permanently lit which meant that after they'd entered as silently as possible, they'd take a minute to check that all was quiet and let their eyes regain their night vision. If they'd had any sense, they would have crept along the lit corridor outside exactly as we were taught to do on night exercise when a flare went up, one eye open and one eye closed. That way, they wouldn't have been completely blind when they moved from the light into darkness.

I heard them then, the soft sound of bodies moving and fingers fumbling with straps and I pictured them nudging each other and putting their gas masks on whilst the rest of the room slept on, oblivious. Little did they know that the ambushers were about to become the ambushed.

I re-assessed my stance and quietly moved my position back ten inches to make sure that I couldn't be seen from around the adjacent wardrobe until the last moment, and then I heard them coming.

The first shadowy figure appeared as if by magic, and if I hadn't been expecting them, the macabre sight which materialised would have held me stood frozen to the spot. The sudden appearance of a man wearing a gas mask in the dark is enough to have an unsettling, if not terrifying effect, on most normal people.

But I was expecting him, and I was ready, and he was the one who froze, taken completely off guard by the sight of me looming large in front of him, having no doubt expected to find me fast asleep in my cot.

I acted fast, having already planned out, in my mind's eye, exactly how my first moves would go down. In the hours that had passed since lights out, I'd had plenty of time to consider what their plan was likely to be and was fully confident of things panning out in my favour. This wasn't some Hollywood action movie and I had no intention of messing around with these guys. I needed to end our little skirmish quickly and decisively and experience had already taught me that there's no better way to end a fight quickly than by dumping someone heavily on their back in your very first move.

Maybe if I'd trained as a boxer, I could have achieved it with a single blow, or perhaps even a flurry of punches, but I've seen enough people seemingly unaffected by being hit in the head to know that it's far from being a certainty.

They call it 'shooting' in wrestling terms.

Dropping slightly on my left knee I took a long step in with my right, planting it squarely between his feet. Bending low I grabbed his right ankle, which was slightly forwards, with my left hand and in one simultaneously fluid movement, I drove forwards with my right shoulder into his groin, lifting his left leg up as high as it would go.

With his hands flailing out towards me he tipped straight back to his rear left corner, landing heavily on his arse before cracking the back of his head on Brad's locker in the bed space opposite.

There was no time to admire my handy work though and without pausing to take stock I regained my balance using a low centre of gravity and turned to face left, where the next gas masked apparition stood silhouetted in the gloom, no doubt thoroughly confused and shocked by what he'd just seen.

We'd been taught that going into battle without a plan was a recipe for failure. Equally, they told us that the chances of the battle going according to *your* plans were extremely unlikely. But at least if you'd started with a plan, you had a starting point from which to adapt your actions accordingly.

And this wasn't supposed to be how it went down as far as he was concerned. I'd accurately predicted that Ugly Sister number one would be easy enough to take down with a leg grab, but I'd assumed that Sister number two would have been a little more aggressive; that he would have come straight in at me. In my mind's eye I'd planned it that rising to my feet from taking down number one, I would shoot my right hand through his legs in a classic 'crotch' movement and, driving up from my thighs, I would have literally picked him up off of his feet and thrown him back at Ugly Sister number three who I anticipated would have been standing behind him.

But Ugly Sister number two had failed to close the gap and he wasn't close enough for me to execute the move I'd planned. There was no time to consider anything other than attack though and I decided to take advantage of his indecision by stepping in fast with my right foot between his, but this time twisting round at the hips so that my feet pointed in the same direction as his.

You can throw an opponent the same height, or taller than you, with a technique called a 'cross-buttock'. It's a move used in most grappling martial arts, albeit using different terminology, but it's not an easy technique to perfect. It requires close proximity and entails facing the same way as your opponent whilst flexing your knees so that your centre of gravity is lower than his, before driving your buttocks low into his groin area and at the same time hooking your arm around his neck or back so that you lock him on to you. From there it's a simple matter of straightening your legs, normally only a matter of inches, and you have him locked onto your back and with his feet off of the ground.

Once he's in the air, he's helpless. He cannot hit you with any real force and he can't push you or pull you. He's ready to be rolled off of your back and driven onto the floor with force and weight. To the uninitiated, it sounds tame, but when it's done properly it's a fight winner in any situation.

But this Ugly Sister must have been either Jones or Jeckyl and was a good six inches shorter than me which meant that dropping my centre of gravity below his would not only be difficult but could also leave me vulnerable to a counter-attack.

It felt to me then as though time slowed down, but in reality it was just my brain speeding up in response to the sudden spike in adrenaline. Realising that the cross-buttock was no longer viable I immediately changed tack.

Throwing my arm around his neck, I stepped in close so that my back was in contact with his front and, in a single fluid movement, I planted my right foot outside of his and twisted hard to my left. Like turning a screw, I twisted left and downwards, at the same time as dropping onto my right knee. Unable to step over my outstretched right foot, he had no option but to fall over it, landing on his back with me on top of him.

Grabbing the front of his gas mask I pulled his head to my left and smashed him hard in the jawline three times with the heel of my right.

There would be no speedy recovery from that and I left him to his own dazed misery so that I could turn my attention onto Ugly Sister number three.

But I was too late.

In what could have passed as a dramatic replay of my childhood scrap behind the shops, I once again felt a burst of pain searing through my ribs as I was kicked over onto my back, landing in the tangle of legs already there. There wasn't a great deal of space down between the lockers and the beds-paces and by now there were three of us sprawling in a tangled heap, in varying levels of pain and consciousness.

A sharp stabbing pain burst through my ribs and hurt so much that I could barely think. For a moment I lost awareness of where I was or what was happening, the gloom of the night only adding to my confusion.

I felt, rather than saw, the figure above me stomp down hard with his plimsoll clad foot. The initial blow missed me completely and landed on the legs of the first Ugly Sister I'd felled, eliciting a dull groan of pain. But the next two stamps connected heavily with my upper arm and shoulder as I tried to roll away and cover myself at the same time.

With Sister number three unhurt and still on his feet while I flapped around on the floor, I realised in a moment of perfect clarity that there was only one way this fight was going to end and, unfortunately for me, it wasn't going to be in my favour.

It was a lesson I shouldn't have needed to learn. I'd been so cocksure of myself that I'd thought I could take on anyone. But whilst I might have been capable of taking on two people my own size, taking on three was asking for a kicking. I 'd been to smug for my own good and had been watching too much television. Even in my stupefied state, I remember thinking this as I curled into a protective ball and prepared myself to take the mother of all beatings.

The next blow came as a meaty thwack but strangely. I didn't even feel it land; almost as though I was somehow disconnected from my own body.

Curled up in the darkness I waited for the next plimsolled foot to land. Seconds ticked by, feeling like whole minutes. But there seemed to have been a pause in proceedings and I began to wonder why my beating had stopped, or indeed *if* it had stopped. A moment later I went from a state of stupefied to one of utter confusion as I felt another body land on top of me.

But this wasn't a part of the attack. It wasn't someone falling onto my chest so that they could continue pummelling me with their fists. This was unmistakably *another* limp body which had joined the party of invalids already on the floor.

Dimly, I became aware of a commotion in the background and I suddenly realised that throughout the attack I had been shouting myself hoarse in an effort to unsettle my attackers as I had launched my offensive. It had been loud enough to wake the rest of the room and more. I looked up and saw harsh light spilling across the floor as the dormitory door was thrown open from the corridor outside.

The brightness stretched into the room and from my prone position cast its light on a sight I'll never forget. I don't think I'd ever seen anyone look so happy with themselves. Bradley Thomas stood opposite me with a shit eating grin which split his face from ear to ear. In a stance which was to become ever more familiar to me, his hands were held out to his sides and a steam iron was gripped in his right.

I realised then why I hadn't felt the last blow land. The 'meaty thwack' I'd registered had been the meaty thwack of Bradley's steam iron hitting the back of a gas-masked head.

'Stand by your beds! Stand by your beds! Stand by your FUCKING beds!'

It was the standard barked command given when any officer or non-commissioned officer entered the room and it meant that we had to immediately cease any and all activities and stand to attention at the end of our respective bed-spaces.

Our reactions were so conditioned, that everyone immediately jumped to attention and I scrambled to my feet in a heartbeat, kicking my plimsolls off and under the bed while Bradley quickly put the iron back down on his desk and assumed the position.

If anyone in the room had managed to sleep through our little scuffle, they were certainly wide awake and on their feet by then.

The main room light clicked on and Corporal Jakes stepped into the room, dressed in civvies and with a look of barely contained apoplectic rage on his face. His eyes were immediately drawn to the groaning tangle of bodies lying on the floor before me wearing gas masks.

He knew the score, of course. Midnight bullying raids had been going on for years and the wearing of gas masks to hide identities was a well-known practice. It was, by and large, considered to be a part of the natural selection process. As long as no-one complained, a blind eye could be turned.

But the wearers of the gas masks were not supposed to be the ones who were laying on the floor in pain. It just didn't fit into the natural order of things. Whilst his eyes took in the scene and conveyed their images to his brain, he struggled to interpret the scene before him. I watched him as closely as I could through peripheral vision. God help the man that dared to make any kind of direct eye contact with him.

He worked his jaw for a moment or two, unable to cobble together any kind of meaningful comment, rant or order, before eventually stepping over to Bradley and spitting into his face, 'What the fuck is going on here Thomas!'

'Dunno Corporal' he replied, standing stock to attention and gazing ahead at absolutely nothing, despite Corporal Jakes' face being mere inches away.

'What the hell do you mean, *'dunno Corporal'*. I think it's pretty fucking obvious that you do know what's going on here when there's three fucking comatose fucking bodies lying at the foot of your FUCKING BED!' He'd started loud and steadily increased the volume with each repetition of the word 'fuck'.

'Corporal. I just woke up and these three lads were all fighting each other. There was no-one else, just these three fighting each other in the dark. Maybe they made a mistake coz they're all wearing gasmasks Corporal.'

I honestly thought that Corporal Jakes was going to have some kind of heart attack there and then. purple with fury, he screamed 'I can see they're all wearing fucking gasmasks, you idiot!'

Spinning on his heel he turned to face me and bellowed. 'THOMSON, what's gone on here.'

Bradley had thrown me a lifeline. If it hadn't have been for his quick thinking I would have been totally flummoxed by this question as well as having been on the wrong end of a good kicking.

'It's like Marine Thomas said, Corporal. I woke up and saw three men in gasmasks having a fight. I think that they all must have knocked each other out at the same time.'

It was a flimsy story, of course, but there was no-one able or willing to contradict us. The Three Ugly sisters were carried off to the medical centre and treated for concussions and a variety of other injuries.

Bradley and I were hauled off to face inquiries. First by the platoon Sergeant, then the Officer Commanding and finally the Regimental Police.

Their questioning went on for the next couple of days in one format or another. They even tried the whole 'good cop bad cop' routine on us. Each one, in turn, made it clear that they didn't believe our flimsy tale, but we stuck to our stories like limpets to a rock and without any kind of proof otherwise, there was not a lot they could do.

The Three Ugly Sisters could have grassed us up of course, but if they'd done that, not only would they have incurred the wrath of the rest of the platoon for being grasses (and they must have known how unpopular they already were), but they also would have had to admit that they had set out in the middle of the night specifically to give me a beating.

Having already heard what mine and Bradley's versions of the events were, they decided that it was in their best interests to play along. The official line was that they had decided to run around wearing gas masks as a dare and had wound up fighting amongst themselves after they started to fall over each other in the darkness of the room.

Everyone knew that it was a cock and bull story but it was a story which minimised the need for further punishments. Not only that, but it also minimised the risk of tarnishing the reputation of the Royal Marines or of any outside enquiries being held into bullying practices.

I still count it as a win, but in truth, if it hadn't been for Bradley, there's no way that it would have been. If Bradley hadn't given me the heads up in the first place, the Three Ugly Sisters would have set about me whilst I was fast asleep and no matter how tough you are, you don't stand much a chance in those circumstances. Then he saved my bacon with his deft and timely application of the steam iron, and lastly, he saved me from the hands of military justice with his quick thinking and his glib lies.

In short, I owed Bradley big time. I'm not a man who finds it easy to forgive, but equally, I've never been someone to forget his debts and I spent the next few years doing everything I could to repay his friendship. I spent four more years serving in the Royal Marines and during that time Bradley and I were virtually inseparable. Whenever we could we ate together, we bunked together, we went on leave together and we fought together. But the minute I found myself back in civvy street, I had Judy back in my life and there was no real room for anyone else.

CHAPTER TWENTY-FOUR

I stood gaping for a moment, unable to summon any kind of reaction. Probably if I'd met Bradley anywhere else that day it would have been fine, but the combination of seeing him for the first time in over twenty years and the fact that it was in a shop I'd chosen specifically so that I wouldn't be recognised, made the whole scene feel like some kind of elaborate set-up.

But Bradley's smile was as big and expansive as ever and quite blatantly genuine. It was the kind of smile which made it impossible not to reciprocate and I stepped forward happily to be swept up into a big man-hug, feeling like a little boy who'd just seen his dad after a long absence.

'Oh my God' was pretty much all I could manage as Bradley squeezed me tight.

'Bradley. Bradley fucking Thomas'. I don't know why I swore, but I had nothing intelligent to say right then.

'You little beauty' he replied with an inexplicable Australian twang, 'where've you been hiding then?'

'Ah. I'm living in Chelmsford mate. I have been for the last twenty years'.

'And what brings you back here, to sunny old Chingford then?'

'Work, Brad. I'm a sales rep. I travel all over'.

'Come to sell me something then have you?' he asked, still smiling.

'Nah. I thought I'd pop in to look for a security camera'

'Well, you've come to the right place old Pal. But first I think we've got some catching up to do. Got time for a brew?'

He took me through to the office which doubled up as a workshop situated at the back of the shop and put the kettle on. With the passage of time, I had forgotten just how much I'd liked Bradley and what good mates we had been, but it was as if no more than a month had passed since we'd last met and I found that chatting to him was as easy as ever.

We had a lot of years to catch up on and he did his best to save me any awkwardness by telling me straight out that he'd heard about my marriage to Judy and that we'd had a son. He also knew that Judy had later died and how sorry he had been to hear it. It was some time after the event that he'd heard about Judy's death and he was sorry he hadn't been able to attend her funeral. But beyond that, in the intervening years, he'd heard nothing of me.

There was no point at all in trying to skirt around my next big episode in my life and I filled him in with the details of David's drug addiction and death as briefly as I politely could, before moving on to tell him how I'd been working at the same job for the last millennia.

Bradley's life story was a damn sight more interesting than mine it seemed. Before I'd been kicked out of 3 Commando Brigade and we'd gone our separate ways, Bradley had already been detached from the Royal Marines to 14 Field Security and Intelligence Company, which was otherwise known as 'The Det.' He'd spent a few years snooping around the streets of Belfast trying to bring down the organised gangsters from both sides of the divide. All of whom claimed to be fighting for freedom or religious reasons, but who in reality sought only the consolidation of their own power and to line their own pockets.

When the relative peace broke out after the Good Friday Agreement, Bradley transferred to the Intelligence Corp and he told me how he'd had a whale of a time creeping around sneaky beaky style and acting like a spy, (his words, not mine).

He didn't go into specifics, of course, and I'm pretty sure that if I'd asked him for any he would have come out with some bullshit along the lines of, 'I could tell you, but then I'd have to kill you' but the long and the short of it was that he'd served his twenty-two years and left the army with a lump sum and modest pension, as was his due. Not bad for a bloke in his forties.

A friend of a friend of a friend had told him about a small home security business that was up for sale. It turned out to be Snake Eyes Security and was based in an area where he'd spent a part of his childhood, so he'd bought it and had been slowly expanding over the past year or so, predominantly via internet sales.

Burglar alarm installations and maintenance were the bread and butter of his business, he told me, but he also had a burgeoning business in internet sales of spyware and gadgetry which was much more fun to be involved with.

Having spent so long in a secretive world which was closed off to most of the rest of us, he had also made some useful connections which he maintained and he took on some occasional private investigations work just to keep his hand in. And some of the *private* jobs, he told me, were ultimately funded from the public purse.

Either Bradley was a Walter Mitty of the highest order, (which I didn't believe for one moment), or the life he had lived since I'd last seen him had become the polar opposite of mine. In short; interesting.

He picked up the strange glasses he'd been wearing when I first saw him and cuffed his nose with the back of his hand.

'I'm just trying these out, for example' he said waving the opened glasses in my direction. 'They're supposed to baffle facial recognition software. See the little marks on the lenses. When you put them on and then bite into this mouthpiece on one side of your mouth, they change the pattern of your features.'

'Eh?' was about the best response I could think of to that.

'Facial recognition software. You must have seen it on the telly. It works by measuring the distances between your eyes, your nose and your lips. It can be incredibly accurate, although you need to have the face in your database in the first place to use it properly. It's what they used to track the movements of the July seventh terrorists before the attack. Once they had one usable image from the CCTV coverage they simply loaded it up and ran all the other CCTV footage available to track them. It's not fool-proof of course, if most of your cameras are pointing downwards and your man wears a baseball cap and never looks up, you have to work a bit harder.'

'So what happens then?' I asked, already fascinated by the subject, 'surely the terrorists ought to know about this too? Or are they not so sophisticated as they make out on the telly?'

'Oh, they can be sophisticated alright. Don't forget the half of these fuckers were taught by the dumb arsed American CIA. They know pretty much most of our tricks and most of their operatives are trained to run counter-surveillance techniques before they set out to meet their maker and his virgins, with a vest full of explosives strapped about them. But the fact remains, that most of these fuckers are retards. They've gotta be in order to believe that what they're doing is gonna give them kudos in the afterlife. Right?'

I nodded. 'Yeah not the sharpest tools in the box, I guess'.

'Damned right. And even if they are clued up, it's not as easy as you might think to never, ever look up. Or even straight ahead; there's plenty of cameras about at lower levels too. There are cameras whirring away everywhere, in places you'd never think of. Every cash machine for example. Plenty of shops and bars have concealed cameras pointing upwards for just that reason too, so they can catch a shot of the next rioter smashing up their shop front'.

'So who are the glasses for?' I asked with a smile, 'You planning on doing some rioting?'

'Nah. To be honest I just saw them and thought I'd order some to try them out. When your selling this kind of tech in general, you need to be able to know what you're talking about and if someone asks me about them, I need to be able to say, 'yes they work' or 'No they don't' You'd be surprised at some of the requests I get.'

'And do they? Work, that is?'

'Well yeah. Surprisingly enough, they do. At least against the kit we sell anyway'

'What? You sell this facial recognition software too?' I asked, unable to contemplate any scenario where it might have a practical use other than one involving the security services for spying or the police for solving crimes.

'We sell a scaled-down version for corporate security. They're normally used to replace keypad entry systems or key fobs. If someone loses their key fob, or someone else sees their keypad combination, it's too easy for them to gain entry if no-one else is watching, so some use fingerprint scanners instead and some, not many but a few, use facial recognition.'

'So could these glasses enable you to gain access to one of those systems then?'

'No, no. The glasses and this mouth corner', he held up a small piece of plastic lying on the desk, 'will only obscure your current facial pattern. They won't imitate someone else's. But people have already found ways around fingerprint technology, in one case recently, just by using a very high-resolution photograph of someone's print. So it seems to me only a matter of time before someone will be able to develop a made to measure facial kit that will work.'

'Wow' I couldn't think of anything else to say so I leant back in my chair, content to cede control the conversation to Bradley and his stories. But my contentment was short lived.

'So, tell me again what you came in here for?' he asked.

I had already stated that it was for a security camera, simply because it was the first thing that had come into my mind when I was still living the shock of seeing him after all those years. But now that I knew that he was likely to have *exactly* what I'd hoped for in terms of expertise and stock, I was reluctant to walk away without obtaining what it was that I'd originally come for.

As a salesman, I can be a charming and fluent speaker at times, but in my case, it comes as the result of many hours of practice, often in front of a mirror. Thinking on my feet or coming up with a witty or clever response has never been a strong point of mine and so I decided to abandon all hope of pulling the wool over Bradley's eyes and tell him at least part of the truth and see where it led me.

'I want to buy a tracking device. One that I can fit to a car' I said on a matter of fact tone.

'Oh yeah? What's it for?'

'Why do you need to know' I asked, trying to make it an inoffensive question.

'Because it depends on what type of tracker you want. Is it just so that you can find out where your car is if someone nicks it? Or is it so that you can see where your Missus goes when you're at work? Or is it to track a parcel delivery? Is it to fit to your own car using the car's battery power? Or is it to be covertly fitted to someone else's vehicle? There's a different type of tracker available for each one of these scenarios.'

'I want something I can fit to someone else's car. Or van actually. I had it in mind that it would be magnetic, like you see people using on the telly. And I want to be able to check at the end of the day, for example, where that van has been so that I could plot it out on a map. Oh yeah, and if it gets found, I need to be sure that it can't be traced back to me.'

A moment's pause followed as Bradley looked at me curiously. 'I can get you that' he replied, 'but do you mind me asking 'what or who it is your tracking?'

'I'd rather not say Bradley if you don't mind. Do you really need to know?'

'No; no. I don't need to know at all. Just curious is all' He waved away my discomfort and was suddenly back to being all smiles, 'It's just that these things are usually the domain of jealous spouses or the security industry and as you seemed to fit into neither of those categories it made me wonder. But your business is your business and I've learned long ago to respect other people's privacy when I'm asked to'.

'Only thing is, we don't hold what you're looking for in stock so it will take a couple of days to get in probably. Here, take a look at this'.

He reached over to a stack of paperwork on one side of the desk and pulled out a glossy brochure, packed cover to cover with all kinds of exciting spyware and showed me a section detailing covert vehicle trackers.

I opted for the one which was easiest to use, with a magnetic attachment and a battery life of up to six days, (depending upon the weather apparently). Some of the models required subscriptions and credits to be able to follow them in real time, but I didn't like the idea that I might be traced back via the subscription payment, so I opted for a dearer model which would allow me to log in to a website and access the data I needed without ever having to reveal who I was. He quoted three working days for delivery for that model and so I paid him a deposit in cash and promised to call back the following Friday.

'Come back around the same time if you like Owen and I'll buy you a pint over the road' he said.

'Sure. Why not?' I replied thinking that now was not the time to explain that I was off the booze.

CHAPTER TWENTY-FIVE

The following week passed without any great changes happening in my life, with the exception of the fact that I joined the gym. I had been considering it for a while by then. Whilst I still enjoyed my early morning runs, I was beginning to get a little bored of doing push-ups and sit-ups. Despite being much fitter and healthier than I had been just a couple of months before; and starting to look pretty trim with it, I still felt as though I was weaker than I wanted to be. I decided that I needed to push some weights up and down and I also felt that a little social interaction couldn't be a bad thing.

Confident that my plans for Les Guscom were well in hand, I no longer needed to spend my evenings searching for him and so I started using the gym after work.

Going to the gym was a new experience for me. They simply hadn't existed in the modern day format when I was a lad, or if they did, there weren't any near me. Back in the eighties, if you wanted to get fit, you either joined a sports club of some description, or you did exactly what I had been doing for the last couple of months; you went running and did some push-ups.

I took advantage of the free session of personal training offer, which was basically an opportunity for a guy with a physique moulded by steroids to try and sell me a course of more personal training. I declined his offer but listened to his tips about using some of the machinery there.

For the first couple of days, I concentrated on pushing and pulling weights up and down, straining muscles and tendons alike. Not wanting to risk doing things by half measures I completely ignored the advice I'd been given and overdid the weights training in spectacular fashion.

Two days after my first session, I found that I couldn't straighten my arms properly as the tendons inside my elbows screamed in protest whenever I tried to do anything other than fold my arms. Coupled with that particular piece of discomfort was the discovery that going downstairs had suddenly become harder than going up them and sitting on the toilet elicited groans of protest from hamstrings feeling fit to snap.

But with the pain came a certain masochistic pleasure; a feeling of achievement, of accomplishment. It was early days, but I knew that it wouldn't take long before I gained muscle mass and strength.

****

The following Friday afternoon found me back at Snake Eyes to see Bradley again and collect my purchase. After checking that I still wanted it, he took it out of its packaging and showed me first how to activate and attach it, and then how to log in online using a code unique to the unit I was purchasing. Once online, I could see a map and timeline of its movements going back over a seven day period.

It was a bland looking piece of kit, which I guess made sense being as it was for covert use, about the size of a matchbox and gunmetal grey. To activate it, I needed to slide off the metal plate at the bottom, which was held on by magnetism, and that uncovered a cheap looking red switch which I then needed to slide to the on position. That done, all I had to do was either attach it to something metal, like the underside of a wheel-arch, or to put the metal plate back on and place it somewhere safe and out of sight.

I paid Bradley the balance in cash and after locking up the shop behind him, we wandered over the road to a pub called the Willingale. I had forgotten that the previous week he'd suggested that we go for a drink, but I was pleased to see him again and glad for the chance to catch up again.

The pub was relatively new, having been converted from an old grocery store a handful of years previously, but it had been tastefully done with wood clad walls and faux roof beams which leant a feeling of homeliness.

I ordered a strong lager for Brad and a weak lager-shandy for me and we took seats in a booth by the back door.

'On the hard stuff Owen?' he said, nodding at my pint having already raised his eyebrows when he heard me order a shandy.

'Well, it is for me. This'll be my first drop of alcohol in nearly two months'

'Oh?'

'Yeah. I got into a bit of a state after David died and I started doing overtime with the bottle. Then a couple of months ago, after a particularly savage session. I woke up and realised it was time to make some changes so I've been pulling my act together ever since'

'Until now' he said, pointedly.

'Until now. I figure now that I've cleaned out my system well enough to enjoy the occasional drink. I never intended to give up permanently, just to rein it in to a sensible level.'

I saw a look of concern on his face.

'Look, Brad, it's one lager shandy. Maybe after I've drunk it, I'll have another. And maybe I won't. This isn't me falling off the wagon. I haven't been craving a drink for the last God knows how long. Granted, I did when I first stopped, but over the last few weeks, it hasn't bothered me at all. I reckon I can have a drink and enjoy it now, without the urge to get completely off my face. I haven't seen you in the best part of twenty years mate, and I don't want to sit here feeling all prissy and nursing a coke. Trust me, this isn't a collapse.'

It was true. I had never intended to give up alcohol completely and permanently. I just wanted to get to the point where I was in control again. I don't subscribe to the theory that if an ex-alcoholic has a single drink, they'll be instantly hooked again. Maybe it is true for some people, but I instinctively knew that it wasn't for me.

Bradley accepted my answer, as I knew he must, and we sat down to do some serious reminiscing, mostly about the scrapes we had gotten into whilst completely off our faces with booze.

It was probably the most enjoyable hour I'd spent in over a year. Years had passed, but we slipped back into the bonds of close friendship without a hitch and it was a bond which brought with it an instinctive understanding. Two pints and an hour or so later, we parted company and agreed to meet up again the following Friday.

I didn't sleep well that night. I'm not sure whether it was the two pints of shandy or the reminiscing brought on from my time with Bradley in the pub, but I suspect that it had more to do with the anticipated thrill of knowing that I would be planting the tracker on Les' van early the next morning. Whatever it was, I didn't get to sleep until close to midnight and I'd already set an alarm for three thirty in the morning.

When the alarm did its duty and blurted it out its electronic bleep at a deafening level that morning, I was sorely tempted to wrench the damned thing from its socket and hurl it against the wall, but I knew that I'd regret it if I delayed my caper for another day.

I pulled on some joggers, making sure to grab the tracker and set off. The weather was a little grim that morning, with a cold bite to the air and a drizzle which seemed as though it had been specifically designed to depress. I say morning, but it was night-time really, pitch black and not even four am.

I have said before that I quite enjoy being about in the middle of the night, but when the weather was like that, there was no real pleasure to be had and I began to wish that I'd taken the car instead of running. But without being entirely sure why, going on foot felt like a safer, more anonymous option than driving.

Armistice Road was little more than a mile away and it didn't take long before I arrived at the end of the road where I stopped and pretended to re-tie a shoelace. I had seen not a solitary car or person on my run over, but I wanted to make sure that absolutely no-one was up and about or looking out of their window. I was wearing black tracksuit trousers and a black long sleeved thermal top so I wasn't exactly standing out if anyone had been looking. On the other hand, I belatedly realised, being dressed head to foot in black clothing did give the appearance of someone who was up to no good.

Here and there were the faint glimmers of hall lights which had no doubt been left on to deter burglars or to comfort children, but from what I could see, it looked as though not a single soul stirred. I walked along the road keeping as vigilant as possible and soon arrived next to Les' van.

I took the tracker out of my pocket and attached it to the underside of the wheel arch and after double checking that it was well and truly out of sight, I walked on to the other end of the road, where I paused and looked back before starting my run back home.

I was back home within a half an hour and feeling mighty pleased with myself. Finally, my hunt could begin in earnest. I would be able to see where Les went and when. I felt sure that a pattern would emerge within a week or two which I could then use to come up with a plan of how, where, and when I was going to kill him.

I had a quick shower and decided that an extra few hours of sleep would not go unappreciated and I slipped back in to bed and fell into a deeply satisfying slumber, not waking up again until gone ten o'clock.

I boiled the kettle for some tea, popped some bread in the toaster and cracked an egg in the frying pan whilst I eagerly waited for my ancient laptop to boot up. The damned thing was so old that it wasn't until I'd finished my breakfast that it finally allowed me to do anything productive.

Sitting at my dining table I opened the web browser and eagerly entered the web address of the tracking company and the long pin number which was unique to the tracker I had bought.

'THIS UNIT HAS NOT BEEN ACTIVATED', came the response popping up on my screen. I must have entered the wrong pin code, I decided and tried again. 'THIS UNIT HAS NOT BEEN ACTIVATED'.

'Bastard' I said out loud. I try not to swear in public, and I don't often talk to myself, but when I do, it's usually because something is frustrating me and I like to make full use of the English vernacular.

'Fucking, Bastard, Poxy, Shit bags' I swore at the screen. 'Of course it's been fucking activated you moronic piece of shit. I fucking stuck it to the van, you c--'

I stopped mid-curse, realising that the moronic piece of shit was, in fact, me, and not my laptop. Sure, I had stuck it to the van. But in my excitement, I had forgotten to turn the bloody thing on! No wonder it said 'THIS UNIT HAS NOT BEEN ACTIVATED', I hadn't flicked the damned red switch.

It felt as though a pin had been used to deflate me. I'd gone from nervous excitement to frustrated rage to dejected disappointment in the space of a minute. Closing the lid of the laptop I stared blindly out through the patio doors and considered my options.

It didn't take me long to realise that there really was only one option available to me. I would have to wait until the following day, the early hours of Sunday morning, when I would go back and turn it on.

Sunday morning came around quickly enough and I managed to detach the tracker, turn it on and reattach it without incident. I made certain that when I got home that I logged on straight away to check it and sure enough it came up straight away, showing the time it had been activated and its exact location on google maps.

I decided to leave the laptop open and switched on so that I could watch it as soon as it started to move.

Sunday proved to be something of a disappointment though. The van didn't move until the middle of the afternoon, and then it went straight to The Globe pub. Having stayed there until six pm, it then went straight back to Armistice Road. I guessed he'd gone to the pub to watch a football match on the big screen.

I'm not sure what I had been expecting, but I had hoped for something a little more enlightening. Still, it was better than nothing I figured.

The week that followed was a little more interesting. On the Monday, when I got back from work and checked online, I could see that he had driven to an address in Witham in the morning and returned home mid-afternoon after stopping at a pub for thirty minutes on the way back. He'd gone back out at six pm and straight to another pub on the other side of town.

I made a note of the routes he'd taken and decided to drive them myself that evening. When I arrived at the place he'd parked at in Witham, I came to the conclusion that he must have been working. In exactly the spot indicated by the tracking software, (accurate to six feet apparently), there was a freshly built garden wall, around three metres long and two feet tall. I wasn't entirely sure, but it seemed to me to be the sort of thing a bricklayer could start in the morning and have done by early afternoon. So, he obviously did do some real work from time to time.

Moving onwards, I called in at the pub he'd used on the way back and used their toilet before having a quick cola and heading off again. There was nothing overtly unusual about the pub; it wasn't particularly low key or high-brow. Just a regular run of the mill chain pub. I tried the other pub where I'd last seen him, but he must have moved on from there too and so I called it a night and headed home.

He'd visited two more pubs that same evening, and over the coming two weeks I was to find that a high percentage of his movements seemed to involve driving from one pub to another. Presumably, he was transacting his drugs deals or money lending or whatever else it was he did in them.

On Tuesday he'd driven to the Beehive pub late morning and stayed there all afternoon before heading home at around seven thirty. Wednesday, he stayed at home all day until the evening, before hitting yet another pub. On Thursday, it seemed he'd done some work again, having called in at a builders merchants first thing before heading off to another address in Witham, not far from the previous one, where I found an almost identical newly laid brick wall to that which I'd found a couple of days previous.

On the Friday he'd driven south of the river to Dartford and stopped at five different addresses. I contemplated driving the route myself, but I wasn't convinced that I would get any benefit so I contented myself with checking them out using google maps street view. Apart from a petrol station where I assumed he'd topped up, they all appeared to be residential addresses.

I pondered the reasons for his journeys heavily before coming to the conclusion that it didn't really matter at this stage. Neither was there a great deal of point in my following up his movements by retracing his routes in my car. All that mattered then was that I kept an accurate log of his movements. I wasn't trying to uncover a crime. I already knew some of what he'd been up to. All I was looking for at that juncture was to establish a pattern which repeated itself. If I could find that, I figured that it stood to reason that I could work out how best to take him down with a minimum of risk to myself.

I bought a week to week diary specifically for the task and meticulously noted the wheres and the whens of Les Guscom's daily life.

Using the tracker to keep a tab on his movements meant that I still had plenty of time to go to the gym, meet Skip for quiz nights and see Bradley on a Friday afternoon for a shandy.

I slipped into a bit of a routine with my early morning runs and the evening checks on Les' movements. Bradley had told me that the batteries in the tracker should last for around six days so I made a point of replacing them every five. Other than that, I didn't really learn anything of much use until the third week. The only pattern I had was that he returned home to sleep, (presumably), every night, but even so, there was no way of knowing whether it would be at eight p.m. or the early hours of the morning.

The only other trip during the first two weeks which had started to look as though it might be a routine, was that his van hadn't moved on either Wednesday and on both Tuesdays, he'd arrived at the Globe at opening time and stayed there until early evening.

But in the third week, I came to realise that none of this mattered.

Our monthly sales meeting had been put back to a Tuesday that month to accommodate Bigham taking a long weekend somewhere. I decided that it made for an ideal day to work my local contacts in the afternoon and to give myself a small respite from clocking up the miles in my car.

The meeting ended at ten thirty and by the time I'd finished faffing around, submitting paperwork and picking up fresh samples etc, it was getting on for midday. As my first call wasn't until two o'clock and was only fifteen minutes away, I decided to pop home and grab a sandwich.

There are a lot of people who seem to be addicted to their mobile phones; people who can't bear to be away from them for any length of time and have an obsession with checking their Facebook accounts every five minutes, no matter where they are and what they are doing. For me, checking up on Les Guscom had become very much like that. I had deliberately chosen not to download the app and have the ability to check the website via a smartphone, but the minute I got through my front door, or the moment I woke up each morning, the very first thing that I did was to check my laptop and see where Les was then and where he'd been.

Sure enough, on that Tuesday by midday he was at the Globe pub again and as I logged it in the diary I'd started keeping I pondered the fact. For the past three weeks his routine had been the same on a Tuesday and although I decided that it was too early to make a definite judgement, it was certainly time to start checking out the possibilities. If he stayed in the Globe all afternoon again and left in the evening, it was reasonable to assume that he would have drunk enough to have his faculties severely affected.

I decided to check out the car-park and see exactly where he left his van. With any luck, he might leave it in a corner un-overlooked by anything else. Maybe I could look at nobbling his brakes or something. Or maybe I could find a spot to hide, ready to ambush him with a baseball bat.

Neither of those options seemed ideal to me, with the one seeming far from certain that it would cause a fatality and the other carrying the risk of going the wrong way and resulting in me being the one taking a beating.

But after so many weeks without much progress, I had to start somewhere and scoping out these options meant that I would at least feel like I was moving my plan forwards.

I made my way to the Globe car-park and sure enough, his van was there, but it was parked pretty much slap bang in the middle and offered no real cover for me to hide or to tamper with it undetected.

If he'd parked up in the far corner it would have been alongside some bushes which looked as though it was an area which would be unlit at night. But this was the middle of the day, and other than Les' van there were only two other vehicles there so it didn't seem likely that he would voluntarily choose to park in the far corner under those circumstances.

There was no point in going into the pub itself, I would have stuck out like a sore thumb at that time of day and so I decided that it was time to put my arse in gear and do some real work.

I had maybe half a dozen calls that afternoon, all within a five-mile radius and all pre-existing clients of APS. Towards the end of the day, as I drove from my final call I stopped for petrol. As I pulled in to the pumps I saw Les come out of the shop with his head down, counting his change, before getting into the passenger side of a black BMW.

I didn't get much of a look at him, but it was more than just a fleeting glimpse and at that moment I knew for certain that I had been barking up the wrong tree by tracking the movements of his van. Gripped by the certainty of how wrong I'd been, I sped home as fast as I could safely go, feeling like a complete fool.

Arriving home, I almost wrenched my front door off of its hinges as I bundled my way inside to the dining room table and lifted the lid on my decrepit laptop.

Sure enough, there was Les' van, parked at the back of the Globe, having not moved an inch since I'd checked it earlier. Despite the fact that I'd been certain that this was what I'd find, the truth of the matter still felt like a punch in the stomach.

I went into the lounge and sat heavily in my armchair and stared at the wall. Following Les' van was clearly not the same as following Les. For all I knew, he had been out and about with the driver of the black BMW since the moment he parked it. Probably selling drugs somewhere I thought.

The more I thought about it the more I realised how inaccurate my records of his movements might have been. The days when he seemed not to have left the house, could just as likely have been days that he had been driven around by someone else.

I could have kicked myself. I'd thought that I'd been so high tech and clever, but following his van was not enough. I needed to find a way of actually following Les himself; of knowing his exact whereabouts at any given time. The trouble was, I couldn't think of any real way of achieving this, given my current skill sets and resources.

I slept badly that night, having lain awake for hours berating myself for being such a dimwit, and once again I woke up in the early hours of the morning drenched in sweat and screaming out in terror.

The recurring nightmares which had been a nightly occurrence in the first two weeks of my recovery from alcoholism had gradually abated and this was the first episode I'd had in over a week. However, it was no less traumatic than the first and when I realised that I wasn't sitting in a car steeped in my own piss and screaming like a baby in fear of a giant-sized Les who had just finished splattering Campsite Terry's brains all over the place, the shame of it came flooding back in an instant.

I felt as though I'd been in a fight and lost. Every muscle in my body ached as I'd unconsciously tensed up in terror. Despite being bathed in a sheen of sweat, I still felt a chill as goose-bumps covered my arms.

As anyone who has suffered from recurring nightmares before can tell you, the fact that they are not real is no real comfort at all. The fact that you are asleep when they come is of little comfort because when they happen, the experience feels a hundred percent genuine and has very real and lasting effects upon you for a long time to come afterwards.

For me the main after effect was exhaustion. Physical exhaustion from the massive hit of adrenaline produced by my body, and emotional exhaustion from the return of my self-loathing, borne out of a disgust of my fear and from having made no effort to save Campsite Terry.

But one positive to come out of this latest attack was a strengthening of my resolve. It re-affirmed my belief that dishing out justice, or perhaps more accurately, retribution, of some kind to Les Guscom was my only real shot at redemption.

I still had no idea how to go about tracking his movements, but I was determined to find a way and the next week or so were a little frustrating as I pondered the problem constantly and racked my brains for a plausible solution.

I even tried to broach the subject in a roundabout way to Bradley when I met with him the following Friday, but without outlining to him the exact nature of my problem, I could only gather my answers in the most generic of terms.

He told me that the most common methods employed by the security services entailed large amounts of manpower, which was something I didn't have. Another option would be to turn his cell phone into a tracking device, but apparently, most smart villains and terrorists were wise to this. And of course, even if he wasn't that savvy, there was no way I could have known how to go about setting it up.

I still kept up my electronic vigil on his van, replacing the batteries on the tracking device every five days, but after another couple of weeks, I was becoming a little despondent about my chances of taking him down in any kind of risk-free and certain method.

It was around about the same time that I decided that my days of sackcloth catharsis had served their purpose and that it was time to bring myself back kicking and screaming into the Twenty First century. To which end, I treated myself to a nice, big LED TV.

I hadn't particularly missed watching TV as a whole, but I did like to see a bit of sport whenever it was on and having watched a game of football or rugby sometimes helped to break the ice with clients as a conversation piece.

Other than sport and the news though, I really wasn't too interested in the rest of it, but it was from watching the news one day that I nearly found a solution to my problem. It was a news item relating to the sad case of a family who had rented out an apartment in Spain which had a faulty boiler. They'd gone to sleep on the first night of their holiday and never woke up again, killed by the asphyxiating consequences of a bunged up flu.

Carbon Monoxide poisoning. They called it a silent killer as you can't see it, smell it, or taste it. If you're awake when it's happening, you might notice a bit of a headache, some dizziness or nausea, but if you are asleep at the time of exposure, the chances are that you would never wake up.

I figured that all I had to do was to block Les' flue while his heating was on and let the build-up of Carbon Monoxide do the rest.

I recalled seeing a caged mesh protecting the flue which protruded from the side of his house at just above head height. I recalled it clearly because I had run past his house countless times in the early hours and seen the gas emissions spewing into the night air as his central heating worked hard to keep him safe and snug on the cold wintry nights.

It would be simple enough, I figured, to cover the flue in expanding foam, the sort of thing that builders used to fill large holes and gaps. It was dead easy to use; all I had to do was to squirt it around the flue and it would expand out to cover a much bigger area which solidifies in minutes.

If I did it just after midnight when the streetlights had gone out and there was barely a soul about, that should still give at least six hours for the 'silent killer' to do the job. I wasn't entirely sure that death by slow suffocation felt like 'justice' as I had envisaged it, but I was pretty certain that it would work.

There were two main reasons to not like this plan though. The first was that Spring had well and truly sprung and we would soon be coming into the summer months leaving his central heating system dormant. Already I realised that it was some time since I had seen the flue emissions from the side of his house pluming into the night sky. With most homes having already turned their central heating either off or down, the chances were that this plan would require me to wait until next winter when the seasonal cold returned. And it was a wait I didn't really want to have.

The other main reason not to like this plan came to me later that same week as I drove past his house one evening. In all the times I had driven up to and past his house and in all the times I had run up to and past his house, I had never once seen him there before. The only evidence I had of him living there was that his van was parked up outside.

But that evening was to prove a first and with it came something of an epiphany. As I cruised past, trying not to turn my head and stare, I caught sight of Les standing at his door with a hearty grin smeared across his face as he said goodbye to an attractive blonde girl who looked to be around thirty years old.

I couldn't risk turning my head to look fully square on at her, but from what I did see, she was quite a looker and was dressed to kill in a short leather skirt, high heels and a low cut blouse.

Who was she? I wondered. She could have been a sister. Could have been a girlfriend. Could have been a prostitute. Maybe even a wife!

The truth was, that for all my amateur attempts at surveillance, I didn't even know if Les lived alone or not. And if he didn't, I certainly didn't want to be the one signing a death warrant for any innocent bystanders in an attempt to gas him in his sleep.

With these fresh questions came the realisation that I needed to find a way of watching his house rather than keeping tabs on his van. Learning the movements of his van hadn't brought forth any significant results in terms of finding a good opportunity to execute him. I had automatically assumed that he could be found at home in bed most nights, but the truth was I really didn't know for sure.

It was time to speak to Bradley again.

CHAPTER TWENTY-SIX

The next Friday afternoon, I made my way over to Chingford again and wandered into Snake Eyes Security at around half past three, making sure that I had enough time to squeeze the advice I needed from Bradley before we went for a quick drink. For the previous three weeks or so I had been turning up between four-thirty and five o'clock, and he had shut up shop pretty much straight away so that we could pop over the road for a couple of drinks and a catch-up. I hadn't warned him that I was coming over earlier that day and he looked surprised to see me, possibly even a little disconcerted.

'Hello Mate' I greeted him, 'I've come to pick your professional brain once more'.

'Oh?' he said, raising his eyebrows questioningly.

On my journey over to Chingford that day I had tried to think of a clever way of getting the advice and the kit I need from Brad without *actually* asking for what I wanted. The trouble was, that after turning this conversation over and over in my own mind I couldn't think of any real way of beating around the bush and still getting what I wanted. I needed to be direct.

'I need to find a way of keeping an eye on someone's house. Some kind of hidden camera I think'.

I watched the cogs turn as he paused, mulling over my request for a moment.

'Come through to the back Owen' he said, lifting the counter before ushering me once again through the door in the one-way mirrored wall. I sat at his desk once more, surrounded by the brochures and dismantled pieces of electronics, whilst Bradley switched the kettle on.

'Tea? White, no sugar, right?'

I nodded back at him and picked up a brochure.

'So tell me about the house. Same as with the tracker you bought. I need some idea of what you're hoping to achieve here. What do you need to see? Front or back? Do you just need to know when there's movement inside the house? Or do you need to know exactly who goes in and who goes out?'

'I want to be able to see exactly who goes in and who goes out' I replied, taking the mug of steaming tea from his proffered hand and nodding my thanks, 'and I need to know what times of day too'.

'Well, that's pretty simple Owen. Most CCTV systems can do that. All you need to do is set the camera up at the right height to make sure you capture their faces and not just the tops of their heads. What sort of budget do you have in mind?'

No, sorry mate' I said, 'I haven't made myself very clear here. I need to watch someone else's house. Not mine. So CCTV isn't really going to be an option'

'OK...' he said slowly, 'and presumably, you're looking for a covert camera of some kind. Do you have somewhere in mind to set this camera up?'

I did, I'd thought about little else for the past few days.

'What I had in mind, and I don't even know if such a thing exists, is some kind of battery powered device, like the Nanny-Cams you see on TV.'

'Yeah, but where are you going to put it?' he asked. 'You can't leave that sort of thing lying around in someone's front garden, can you. Or do you have access to be able to get inside the house and plant it?'

'No' I said. 'I was thinking that it would be something I could leave on the parcel shelf of a car. Park up a car, or a van, outside the house and go from there.'

'Ahhh' he pronounced, smiling broadly and holding a finger up in the air, 'I think I know exactly what you're looking for.' He rummaged around behind him before turning back to me and thumbing his way through another brochure quickly.

'I may have just the thing here. Let me check something out a moment.'

I sat quietly sipping my tea as he discarded the brochure and booted up a battered looking laptop and keyed in a website address.

'Yes! Wait there a sec" he said, before going through another door at the back of the office. I had no idea what lay beyond that door, but he re-appeared moments later holding a small box. It was about the size of a box of tissues and was plain grey with lettering and numbers on the lid. No logos or pictures, just the alphanumeric code.

'I was checking to make sure that this could be run from a twelve-volt battery and I was right; you can' he said, opening the box at one end and pulling out an equally plain looking steel box with a lens on one end and various other ports, presumably for charging.

'There are no instructions, but it's fairly easy to set up. You just need to calibrate it first depending on what distance you're filming from and then point it in the right direction. After that, you connect it up to your computer at the end of the day or just download onto a memory stick. It works on a motion sensor, so it only records when there's movement within the screenshot, (which is why you need to calibrate it first), so it means that when you're playing it back you won't have to sit through hours and hours of recording with nothing happening'.

He seemed to be talking faster and faster and becoming more and more animated as he got into his subject. Bradley was clearly a man who loved his work.

'There's also an option to buy a sim card and pop it in here if you want real-time data, but that can work out pretty expensive and this little beauty's expensive enough as it is'.

'How much is expensive then?' I asked. I had no idea what I was looking at in terms of budget.

'Well, you can't buy these normally. They're supposed to be for government use only. If you know what I mean'. He gave me a theatrical wink, which, coming from him looked odd, to say the least.

'But if you know the right people, it's always a case of where there's a will there's a way. In other words, if anyone ever asks you, you didn't get it from me'.

'No problems Brad, but how much is it?' I asked again.

He paused and seemed to consider the question for a moment. 'They cost me about a couple of hundred quid each and I normally sell them for around six, unofficially of course. But I'll let you have it for cost on one condition.'

'Yes?' I prompted, wondering what was coming next.

'You tell me what you want it for. Who you want it for. And why.'

We sat in silence for what was probably only a few seconds, but which felt like an age, gazing across the desk at each other. Strangely enough, I had considered telling him the truth of my scheme, or at least the bones of it, those past couple of weeks. I'd figured that if he knew what I really wanted, given his background, he could probably give me a solution pretty quickly. And more importantly, there was no-one else in the world I trusted more than Brad to keep a secret.

But now that he had asked me outright, I couldn't bring myself to tell him. I knew that he must have been curious, of course, but I still hadn't expected him to ask me. I didn't have a particularly great social life these days, and other than Skip, Brad was probably my closest friend. Certainly, he was my oldest friend, and I felt pretty sure that I could still trust him with my life if needed.

But did I want to risk him knowing my plan? Did the potential benefit of expert advice outweigh the potential risk of letting someone else in on my misdeeds?

'I'll just pay the six hundred then if that's OK' I'd decided that I didn't want to risk our friendship by putting him on the spot.

'Fair enough' he said without batting an eyelid. 'Let's get it plugged in and I'll show you how it works.'

The camera came with a normal plug-in charger, but Bradley had an adapter, which he threw in for no extra cost, which would allow it to be connected to a car battery and which meant it could be left for prolonged periods without any problem. It also came with a manually adjusted optical zoom and a digital zoom, meaning that you twisted the lens on the front to get the main zoom and focus, but you could also zoom in and out of the picture once it popped up on your computer screen.

We took it through to the front of the shop and set it up to point out of the shop window. The pavement was fairly wide there and I guessed it to be around the same distance as the distance from Les' front door as where I'd envisaged parking the car holding the camera.

With the unit hooked up to a laptop via a USB cable, we could see exactly what the camera was pointing at and what was in focus and what wasn't. We adjusted the lens to focus where we wanted it and Bradley showed me how to upload the memory onto a USB stick as well as how to clear the memory in the unit.

He also showed me how to operate it remotely, if I did choose to do so via a SIM card, but in my mind's eye, I couldn't see that as being a requirement.

'Come on mate. Let's get this packed away and go and have a pint' he said after I'd told him that I didn't have any more questions.

'OK, but I need to hit the cashpoint first' I replied, 'I've got a couple of hundred quid on me now, but I need to draw some more out for you'.

I hadn't anticipated paying anything like the amount which the camera was, but I could see that it was exactly what I needed and with no mortgage and only myself to support, I wasn't exactly short on money back then.

'Fair enough mate, I'll see you over the road in what? Say ten minutes? Give me a chance to clear up and lock up first?'.

'Sure'. Off I went, not sure exactly how much my bank would let me draw out of a machine in one hit.

As it turned out, the most I could have was two-hundred and fifty pounds. I counted what I already had in my pocket and that was a further two-hundred and fifteen but I wanted to keep back fifteen pounds for a pint and 'emergencies'.

First in the pub, I ordered my usual shandy and a Guinness for Brad before taking a seat towards the back. I felt fairly confident that if I explained to him that I only had four-hundred and fifty pounds and that I would drop the other hundred and fifty into him next week, or sooner if needed, that he wouldn't have a problem with letting me take the unit with me there and then.

'I've been thinking' he said after he'd taken his seat and a generous gulp of Guinness, 'Six hundred quid's too much. I'm sorry if I put you on the spot when I asked you what you are up to, and maybe I was a bit out of order. But the truth is, you look like you could do with a little help, and this kind of things my forte'.

'It's Okay, it's Okay' he said holding up his palm towards me to forestall the interruption I was about to make. 'I know it's not going to be anything legit or anything. But if I knew more about what was going on, the chances are I could probably help you is what I really meant to say. But if there's one thing I know, probably more so than most people, it's that there are times when it's just not right to let anyone else know what you're up to. Even if they are your mates.

'So anyway. Here's what I'm going to do Owen, I'm going to let you have the camera for cost. Two hundred quid.'

He held up his hand once more to stop me before I could get my objection past my lips.

'It's fine' he nodded sagely, 'Call it mate's rates. And if you can't help a mate out, then you're not much of a mate are you? I'm going to try and give you some fieldcraft tips too that you might find useful. You might not, but that will be for you to decide'.

He then went on to suggest some do's and don'ts of setting up a concealed camera in a parked car, some of which I'd already worked out, but some of which I hadn't.

Firstly, the car itself had to fit in with its immediate surroundings. You didn't park a battered Skoda in Bayswater, and you didn't park a Porsche in a council estate. It was fine to have a bit of an old banger, but it still had to look like it was being used. If it looked like it had been abandoned, the local oiks would break into it in double quick time.

Keep it clean, (but not gleaming). Move it as regularly as is practical to do, even if you only change which way round the car is facing. A good idea was to leave a copy of the previous day's newspaper on the passenger seat if possible. That way, any nosey parkers ought to be satisfied that it hadn't just been abandoned to rust.

The dilemma was whether to tax the vehicle or not. If, whatever it was that you were up to was legit, you should absolutely make sure that it had up to date road tax. The last thing you wanted to happen was for your surveillance vehicle to get towed away. But if you were up to no good, you had to balance the possibility of someone linking the car to your plan against the possibility of having the car towed away for not being registered or taxed.

He knew his stuff did Bradley, of that there was no doubt. He even covered the positioning the camera to make sure that it didn't face the sun at any time of the day so as to avoid any glare.

And finally, he said to me, 'Look. Owen, I know you don't want me knowing your business, and that's absolutely fine. But we went through some things back in the day that nobody else here', he gestured widely about the pub, 'has any idea about. If you ever do want or need my help, don't be afraid to ask. I can't guarantee that I will be able to, but I can guarantee that I won't tell another living soul.'

We'd finished our second pints by then and that was normally the time for us to part company, so we stood up together and shrugged our jackets on.

I nearly said it then; nearly came clean about my plans to kill Les. For some inexplicable reason, I suddenly found myself having to fight an overwhelming urge to open myself up to Brad and tell him everything. Maybe it was his generosity in letting me have the camera at cost, or maybe it was because I had the utmost faith in his confidence. Or maybe it was just that I felt that I had to tell *someone*.

He'd been such a good friend to me and the urge became too strong for me to say nothing at all, so that I suddenly found myself saying, 'I'm planning on robbing someone. Don't ask me who and don't ask me why though please. Just trust me that it's something that has to be done. Or at least it does as far as I'm concerned.'

A slow smile spread across Bradley's face as he relinquished our handshake and it was my turn to be caught off guard.

'Excellent!' he said. 'There's nothing like a bit of mischief to let you know you're still alive! Just be careful how you go about it and we'll say no more on it. Unless you need to, of course.'

I'm not sure what kind of response I'd expected from him, but I sure as hell know it wasn't that. He looked positively overjoyed to hear what I was up to. The fact that it involved outright criminality seemed to have made his day.

Looking back, I'm pretty sure that if I'd told him the truth, that I was planning a murder, he would have had the exact same reaction. They say that birds of a feather flock together, and it was one of the reasons I valued his friendship so much.

CHAPTER TWENTY-SEVEN

I played around with the camera as much as possible when I got home, but before I could do anything useful with it I needed a car and I decided to buy one for cash without registering it in my name.

There were always plenty of cars parked up on the verges of roads with For Sale signs in the windows, often in the same regular spots, and I figured that the people selling them were probably the kind of people who lived in the cash economy and who weren't so keen on declaring their transactions and profits. I had already decided that this was the route I was going to take, and I'd bought myself a pay as you go SIM card in readiness.

Saturday morning came and I set off early doors to trawl the streets looking for something suitable.

I had a thousand pounds in cash which I'd withdrawn earlier in the week for exactly this purpose. I didn't really care how reliable the car would be, just so long as it started and could drive a few miles up the road without breaking down or falling to bits. More important, was whether or not the seller would be happy to let me buy it without giving him any ID.

Sure enough, there were plenty of cars parked in the usual places, by the Miami roundabout and on the verges of the A414, all with home-made For Sale signs sellotaped in their windshields. All of them had price tags of under a thousand pounds and with mobile numbers for contacts.

But it occurred to me that buying from someone in my hometown of Chelmsford might not be the smartest move. Not when I wanted anonymity. So I drove to Harlow, which was about forty minutes North on the A414.

I reasoned to myself that Harlow was an area with more than its fair share of ne'er do wells (sorry Harlow), and sure enough, after driving around for the best part of an hour, I had a handwritten list of half a dozen numbers to try. But then I realised then that I still wasn't being smart. If I bought the car in Harlow, it would mean leaving my own car there and trying to find someone to give me a lift back.

Romford. I could get a train to Romford. Feeling that the day was slipping away from me with nothing to show for it, I put my foot down and motored over to Romford as fast as common sense would allow. I was starting to get annoyed with myself.

Finally, I found what I had been looking for. It was an eight-year-old Ford Focus with an unhealthy amount of miles on the clock and an asking price of £750. After a quick phone call from my pay-as-you-go phone, I did the deal with an Asian guy who was more interested in taking my cash than seeing my documents. I handed over a false name and address and the full amount in cash and drove off there and then.

The car itself was a silver hatchback and at first glance, looked to be in reasonable nick. There were no big dents or scratches that stood out and the tyres had a reasonable amount of wear left in them. Apart from an old Disney Mickey Mouse sticker the size of my hand being cemented so firmly onto the boot that it was impossible to remove, there was nothing remarkable about it at all.

The giveaway to the real amount of miles it had covered was more evident when you got in the car. It obviously hadn't been kept in a garage as the plastic interior looked to have been well bleached by the sun, so much so that I wondered if it had lived part of its life in another, hotter, country.

The cloth seats were clean enough, but they too seemed to have endured an unnatural amount of fading and as sunk my weight into the driver's side I could feel the springs beneath.

I didn't want to go far, just far enough away from where I'd bought the car, so I left it in a side street a mile from the train station and walked back to my own car. The day was pretty much done by the time I got back to Chelmsford and so I waited until Sunday morning before taking the train to Romford to pick up my brand new, second hand car.

CHAPTER TWENTY-EIGHT

By Monday morning I was up and running. As soon as I'd got back with the car on Sunday, I set about making it fit for purpose. I cleaned the rear window inside and out, making sure that my new camera would have a clear view. I dumped an old Hi-Vis waistcoat that I'd had in the garage on the back seat, and on the parcel shelf I scattered an empty coke can, a local newspaper and an old sweatshirt.

I placed the camera in a tissue box I'd already prepared, with a hole cut in one end for the lens and the back cut away to enable me to access the USB drive, which I'd be removing and replacing on a regular basis, so that I could study the footage in the comfort and safety of my own home, without fear of interruption.

I made sure that I placed the adapted tissue box in a way which would look innocent enough, but which would also give me the camera angle I needed. I'd had to experiment with this quite a bit, but eventually, I settled on placing it on top of an A to Z road atlas to give it enough height to see out of the window and I finished by placing a newspaper on top.

My piece de resistance, as far as I was concerned, was that after quite a bit of trial and error, I had taped a pencil to the top of the tissue box which I could use like the iron sights on a rifle, so that when I looked directly along it, I could see exactly where the camera would be pointing before covering it over with the newspaper.

The tissue box and pencil sight worked really well and I felt particularly pleased with myself because it had been all my own idea and not Bradley's.

The only negative thing to happen while I completed my preparations on the front driveway was when Stiff came out and gave me one of his non-committal nods. Inwardly, I cursed myself for my stupidity for having parked the car on my own front drive, especially after all the lengths I'd gone to ensure my anonymity whilst purchasing it. But I reasoned that it was a million to one shot that anyone would ever associate the car with my crime to be, and it was a million to one shot that if Stiff was ever questioned that he'd remember the number plate.

I left home in the small hours of Monday morning, driving in my tracksuit so that after I'd parked the car and positioned the camera I could jog home, which I did without drama.

I spent the rest of that day in a frisson of excitement and had difficulty trying to concentrate on doing any real work. I knew that it was counterproductive but there was nothing I could do to dampen the nervous energy coursing through me. I would just have to wait until the following morning.

I set out just after three the next morning. I'd planned on running over to Les', but despite the onset of early summer, it was a particularly cold and moonless night. There was also no street lighting for most of the journey and I didn't fancy the idea of tripping over and breaking a leg in the pitch black night, so I took the Volvo and parked up around the corner.

I had been a little concerned about the logistics of switching over the USB drives without being noticed, but as it turned out I needn't have worried.

I hung about at the end of Armistice Road for a minute or two, making sure that no-one was up and about, before I walked straight over to the Ford Focus, unlocked and climbed into the back seat. The interior light came on as soon as I opened the door and after I'd quickly turned it off, I set it so that it would stay off the next time I got in.

I dropped a well-thumbed copy of the previous day's tabloid on to the passenger seat and waited a moment for my eyes to adjust to the added gloom of the interior, making sure that there was still no-one out there watching. In the end, I had to use the light from my mobile phone to see what I was doing, it was so dark, but it was literally as simple as pulling one memory stick out of the back of the tissue box and putting another one in before covering it over again.

Despite the fact that it still wasn't even 4a.m., I couldn't wait to see what was on it and as soon as I'd got home and made a cup of tea, I plugged the memory drive straight into my laptop.

Looking back, I'm not sure what expectations I had, but the clarity of the footage it revealed was startlingly good. The positioning had been spot on and I had a view which encompassed an area spanning from just before Les' front gate right, up to his front door, and by playing around a little, I found that I could zoom in so that something the size of a playing card could fill the whole screen. The zoom and the resolution were so good that I began to understand why the camera had demanded such a high price tag and why it was not something readily available in the High Street.

But if the quality was great, the quantity was less so. It was motion activated and so only filmed when there was movement detected within screenshot. The problem was, that having parked the car on the other side of the Road to Les' house, every time a vehicle passed the camera kicked in and carried on filming, not ending until thirty seconds after it sensed there was no longer any movement.

The result was a lot of footage of vehicles suddenly appearing and disappearing on the screen, followed by nothing. The footage went from night-time to full daylight in the blink of an eye and picked up the school run just before nine.

A giggle of school girls were closely followed by a gaggle of housewives who stopped for a natter right outside Les' house.

Yummy Mummies was certainly not a phrase you would use to describe these three ladies. They looked to me like the type of women whose only aspirations in life was to have the right number of children so that they could maximise their welfare benefits. All three were fat, unwashed and dressed in a depressing uniformity of leggings and shapeless tops. Sadly, I had to sit through ten minutes of that unedifying sight before they moved on.

Then the camera clicked on at ten thirty in the morning, and it took me a long time to work out why. At first, I could see nothing and I wondered if perhaps a fly or a bird had flown by close to the lens and disappeared before the camera could capture it. I looked about for a dog or a cat skulking around, but could see nothing. It was the first episode I'd had of the camera filming with seemingly no motion in front of it and I replayed it several times before I realised what had happened.

Les must have had a lay-in that morning, or for all I knew, perhaps he did so every morning. But what I did finally work out, was that it had been him drawing back the curtains that had kick-started the camera rolling. It hadn't been immediately obvious because he had nets hanging down below the fan lights so that only the top eight inches or so of the curtains were visible.

It hadn't occurred to me that the motion sensor on the camera might also be able to detect movements *inside* the house, and once again, I reminded myself to thank Bradley for letting me have such a high calibre piece of kit.

All in all, it took me about an hour to go through twenty-four hours of filming and there wasn't a huge amount to show for it.

After drawing his curtains at 10.30 a.m. he had left his house on foot ten minutes later, before returning with a pint of milk and a packet of cigarettes. He seemed to spend the rest of the day indoors and didn't leave again until 5 p.m. when he climbed into his van and headed out before returning again at about 10.30 p.m. I guessed that he'd been to a pub again, but as I'd removed the tracker from his van the last time the batteries had eventually run out, I had no sure way of knowing, although, looking back at the log I had kept previously, there wasn't a great deal of doubt in my mind. I considered putting the tracker back in situe for a while before deciding that, at this time, it wasn't needed and that the potential risk of reattaching and monitoring it outweighed any likely benefits.

So, there was nothing earth-shatteringly interesting to come out of my first twenty-four hours of surveillance, but the truth was that I had always anticipated it being a drawn-out process and I'd never expected to come up with an instant solution to my plans.

Over the next few weeks or so I developed something of a routine. After the excitement and anticipation of the first week, I switched from changing the USB memory drive every day to every two days, reasoning that doing so halved the risks of something going wrong compared to doing it daily. Also, the disturbed sleep patterns from my night-time activities had started to take a bit of a toll.

Depending on the weather, I sometimes drove, or sometimes ran over to Armistice Road, always with a copy of the previous day's newspaper which I left prominently on the passenger seat so that no-one would think the car had been dumped.

I moved parking spots just as often, sometimes leaving it in the same spot after I'd driven around the corner and turned back so that it faced the opposite direction. Sometimes moving it only ten or fifteen yards up or down the road.

I knew from my conversations with Brad that this was an important part of the routine in order to stop anyone from reporting the car as abandoned to the police. But it was also a pain in the arse. Every time I moved it, I had to re-sight the camera using the pencil sight. Most of the time this worked perfectly fine, but once or twice I wound up with only half a screen of usable information.

Three weeks later I changed tack again.

CHAPTER TWENTY-NINE

Skip Parsons had taken to picking me up in his car on the way to the Butlers Head quiz nights, and as a man whose formative years existed in the 1970's and the eighties, he never seemed to have any qualms when it came to the thorny subject of drinking and driving.

In fact, despite managing to tuck away a decent volume of beer in any one sitting, he rarely gave the impression of being remotely drunk. I guess that coupled with being a copper meant that he probably didn't have a great deal to worry about when it came to getting pinched for drunk-driving.

That particular Wednesday I had completely lost track of the time as I found myself absorbed in checking the latest three days of footage which I'd recovered that afternoon. After three weeks of tracking the van, followed by five weeks of camera surveillance, I had collected enough data from both the tracker and now the camera to feel confident that Les would be out for the duration on Wednesdays, and so I felt comfortable enough to drive the car home to switch memory sticks before returning to park it back in Armistice Road during the daytime.

I figured that it looked less suspicious doing this in broad daylight than it did doing it at four in the morning. Coupled with the fact that my initial enthusiasm for the project had dulled at the edges, I had begun to really dislike getting up so early.

For the previous fortnight, I had restricted myself to two switches a week, one on Wednesday afternoon and another in the early hours of Sunday. The advantage of having less chance of being noticed was counterbalanced by the fact that the fresh newspapers and the repositioning of the car were less frequent and so raised the risk of a nosy neighbour complaining to the police about it.

The other slight downside was that there was sometimes a serious amount of film footage to go through before I could update my log.

So, there I was, deeply engrossed in watching and logging of movements around Les' home when the doorbell went. Without giving it a second thought I stood up from my kitchen table and went to answer the door. Answering the door was something of a subconscious act that afternoon as my mind was still focused on the pattern which I had started to see emerge in Les' movements, and as I pulled the door open to find Skip standing there, I was caught completely off guard.

'Come on mate, shake a leg' he said, looking down at my slippered feet. 'We've got quizzes to win and beers to drink!'

I had really lost track of time that day and still feeling caught off guard, I moved to one side and invited him in before suddenly realising what I had left running on the laptop which was sat on the dining room table. And sure enough, it drew him straight over, like a hound to the hare.

'What's this?' he asked leering over at the images on the screen.

I pushed ahead and leaning in front of him closed it down quickly whilst trying to hide my feeling of rising panic. 'Erm, nothing. I was just looking at some properties on some Estate Agency sites. I was toying with the idea of moving.'

It was a pretty lame excuse, I knew, and the camera angle of Le's house had not looked like anything I'd ever seen before on Rightmove but I literally had no idea of what else I could possibly have said at that time.

Skip eyed me curiously for a moment. I somehow knew that he wasn't convinced, but bless his heart, he was too good a friend to call me out on it.

'I see your neighbours on the move too' he said. 'Is that anything to do with it?'

'What?' I asked, genuinely confused now. 'Wo's moving?'

'Next door' he said pointing over in the direction of Stiff's side. 'I was toying with the idea of moving myself and I see that your neighbour has his house up for sale too.'

I made my excuses that I needed to run upstairs to quickly change and managed to park the conversation without further discussion. But the fact that Stiff was putting his house up for sale was news to me, which in itself would not have made any difference, but being as it *was* news to me, I then had to make a point of going online later to check it out.

And when I did check it out, I got something of a shock.

The picture they'd taken of Stiff's house was a very flattering one. They'd obviously made a point of moving his car off of the drive before taking the shot and they must have stood on the other side of the road to get the whole house and the driveway in. But they had taken a shot which included a healthy proportion of the neighbouring houses and much to my dismay, there on the driveway of my house could be seen, as clear as daylight, a six year old Ford Focus with a Mickey Mouse sticker on the boot and a tissue box in amongst some other clutter on the parcel shelf.

I zoomed in and I zoomed out, desperately hoping that by doing so it would change the evidence that was there for all to see.

It only showed half of the width of the car, but the first four characters of the number plate were as clear as day and I was fairly sure that the chances of there being another Ford Focus with a number plate beginning the same would be remote, at best.

'Shit! Shit!' I cursed out loud. I thought that they had to blank out the number or pixelate that type of thing! But still, I was hardly in a position to go and complain. The last thing I wanted to do was to draw any further kind of attention to myself or my situation.

I stressed over the situation for a day or two before realising that there was nothing I could do to change it. In itself, it shouldn't really matter at all as the car was only there to be used as a hide for my surveillance set up. With that being the case, it could only be relevant if someone had noted the presence of the car and reported it as suspicious to the police when they conducted their investigations.

The more I thought about it, the more I decided that chances of that happening were remote, and as the car wasn't registered in my name or otherwise traceable back to me, outside of a half a photograph of it in an estate agent's window, the chances then became minuscule. And even then, my connection to a car that was parked near his house was hardly concrete evidence of anything further.

But I had hoped to plan the perfect murder, and in order to do that, I didn't want to leave behind any kind of connection to the murder, the man or the location, however tenuous.

After careful consideration, I decided to torch the car and destroy any physical evidence linking me to it. But not yet. Not until I had finished using it. In the meantime, I would no longer park it outside my house for the brief periods on Wednesdays when I switched out the memory stick full of footage, but I would park it around the corner. Disposing of the car before I had finished with it and before I had even committed any kind of crime felt like an unnecessary overreaction to something which would probably never become a factor anyway

CHAPTER THIRTY

As with the tracker I had fitted, I kept a written log of all Les' movements in and out of the house. After six weeks, I worked out that whilst most of his movements were erratic and for the most part without a pattern, there were one or two constants which had started to emerge.

First of all, he seemed to spend Wednesdays out on the Road and didn't return home until much later at night. I didn't know what he was up to of course, but in my mind, I had decided that he was out buying and selling drugs, or maybe extorting money from some poor bastard.

Secondly, there was the Tuesday night Pizza. Every week since I'd started my vigil, he had arrived home on Tuesdays, from wherever he had been, at around eight p.m., and every time his return home was followed by a pizza delivery some thirty minutes later.

After four long months of trying to come up with a workable plan to kill Les, the seeds of a plan began to germinate as I parked up a short distance from his house one Tuesday evening and waited until I saw his van coming.

My long surveillance had also taught me that, for some reason, Les only ever seemed to turn into

Armistice Road from the Swiss Avenue end and as soon as I saw him turning into the road, I drove off in the opposite direction so that there was no chance of him seeing me.

Ten minutes later I phoned Domino's.

I have always been a decent mimic of people and accents and I reckoned I could pull off a passable enough impression of Les over the phone.

'Domino's Pizza. How may I help you?'

'Hello? It's Les Guscom here, 71 Armistice Road. I just phoned through an order for delivery?' I said in a deep voice dripping with stupidity.

'Yes sir' said the girl's voice on the other end of the line, 'a sixteen-inch meat feast. Deep pan'.

'Am I too late to cancel it? Only I've got to go out'

'One moment please' I could hear her voice in the background, presumably asking her manager or cook before she came back on the line. 'No problems sir I can cancel that now for you.'

'Actually no' I contradicted, 'carry on with it. I've just had a text from my mate so I'm not going out now after all. Half an hour yeah?'

She confirmed that the order would be going ahead as usual and we hung up. I felt confident that Les would never know about my little conversation, working on the assumption that the delivery driver only collected and delivered and would almost certainly not be the girl I had spoken to on the phone.

Fifteen minutes later, after I'd settled back indoors I rang and ordered a pizza of my own to be delivered. This time using my own voice.

It duly arrived thirty minutes later, delivered by a lad on a scooter wearing a white crash helmet. No real mysteries there I decided. But short of delivering a poisoned or exploding pizza, I still wasn't entirely sure how I could use this insight to my advantage.

I thought back fleetingly to my one-time idea of blocking the flu to his central heating boiler as it had also became apparent that he did live alone, although on a Friday or Saturday night he sometimes came home with a female who would either stay the entire night or just for an hour or two.

The identities of the girls varied and I wondered whether they might be prostitutes, but there was nothing that I could see that marked them out as such, not that I had any personal experience with how they worked.

He would also occasionally have men call for him, business associates I assumed, but while he often left with them, they were never invited into the house and were invariably left to stand waiting on the doorstep whilst he grabbed a coat or whatever else it was he needed.

Sometimes he'd go to work, maybe once or twice a week I'd see him loading tools in or out of his van and on a couple of occasions, he set off with another builder in his van.

CHAPTER THIRTY-ONE

It was late in July and over two months after I had started my nefarious vigil when two things happened which brought my plans to a head.

The first was a meeting I had with Skip Parsons for our usual Wednesday evening pub quiz. I had moved away from drinking shandy by that point and once again began to enjoy the feeling of getting tipsy with a few pints of the hard stuff. I wasn't particularly concerned about setting off on the slippery slope to alcoholic dependence again. Other than those Wednesdays and my Friday afternoon meetings with Bradley, reminiscing as old soldiers do, I didn't drink on any other days.

Unusually, on that particular evening the quiz had been called off at the last minute and so we sat there drinking beer and generally chewing the fat in comfortable companionship. We were half an hour into our soiree when an all too familiar shrieking voice cut through the crowded pub.

'Uh oh. Someone's in trouble' said Skip, as we both looked up in the direction of the door.

It was Griselda. Les' mother. With a face that looked like a bulldog licking piss from a stinging nettle and a voice like fingernails on a chalkboard, she came in shrieking at Les in her strange accent of half German tones.

As a child our family had owned a foul-tempered and scruffy mongrel named Zed who to this day has to have been the ugliest dogs I've ever seen, and there was something about the lovely Griselda which immediately put me in mind of him; to the extent that I immediately started to think of her as 'The Mongrel' rather than as Griselda Guscom.

Flanked by two heavies standing vigil at the door, she launched a verbal assault on her son in a fit of rage. As loud as she was, I couldn't really tell what she was saying but I'm fairly sure that at least part of it was in German.

As meek and sheepish as Les looked beneath her verbal barrage, the moment she left, less than two minutes after her awful entrance, he looked more menacing than ever as he scanned the pub with his Neanderthal jaw jutting forwards and daring anyone to look at him directly.

As with a lot of thugs, I'm pretty sure that he used violence to cover his embarrassment and there was no doubt that he harboured a deep desire to hit something or someone right then. An electric air of suppressed rage positively radiated from him.

But no-one was stupid enough *not* to realise this, and ten minutes later Les left without having sated his thirst for violence.

'Looks like trouble in paradise' I said to Skip in a low voice.

'Yeah. We think he's killed a guy in Baddow who owed them money and it seems the Wicked Witch is less than impressed.'

My ears pricked with interest. 'When was this?' I asked, thinking back to poor old Campsite Terry.

'A couple of days ago. A bar owner who borrowed money from them; if the rumours doing the rounds are anything to go by.'

He swung his head to me suddenly, a look of deadly seriousness on his face, 'But you didn't hear that. Right? I could get sacked for saying things like that out loud.' This wasn't the first time that Skip had been less than discrete after a pint or two.

'Skip, it's me you're talking to mate' I said, smiling and spreading my hands out in an open book gesture. 'Did you ever hear me telling you anyone else's secrets? I'm not some bar-room gossip you've just bumped into. Anything you tell me is just between you and I. Now come on mate; dish the dirt!'

He looked around us to make sure that he couldn't be overheard before he leant in again. 'It seems that Mummy Griselda sent Les round to put the frighteners on someone who was reluctant to pay them what they thought was owed. At the moment we're not sure if it was a genuine loan or some kind of extortion, but whatever it was, Les got a little over excited about the whole thing and wound up beating the guy to death'

'Like Terry the Campsite' I said nodding.

As soon as I said it I realised that I had made a schoolboy error. I actually think that my heart may have stopped for a beat at that moment. Certainly, it felt as though someone had punched me in the chest.

But I kept a poker face as Skip swung his eyes up from the beer mat he had been steadily picking to pieces and locked his gaze upon me without saying a word.

'What?' I asked, lifting my eyebrows in mock surprise.

'What do you know about Terry's murder?' he asked. All business now.

'Only what you told me mate. That he had been beaten to death and you suspected Les. Or one of his gang.'

It was a blatant lie of course, but I delivered it well enough. Or so I thought.

'But I never told you that we thought it was Les' he said. 'In fact, we've only just started to think that way in these last couple of weeks.'

The intensity of his gaze upon me was a little like looking at the sun, but I gamely smiled back at him as if it were the most natural thing in the world.

'Well if *you* didn't tell me, how else would I know what you suspected? I can't remember when exactly, but I'm sure you told me sat here not so long ago. Maybe *someone* had a few more than they realised that night.'

You don't get to spend as long in sales as I had without learning the ability to lie glibly when called upon, and luckily for me, I'd been with Skip when he'd had a couple of heavy sessions in the previous few weeks, so it seemed as though he'd fallen for it. Not that he was happy about it though.

'Jesus' he said, shaking his head 'I must be starting to lose it. Listen, don't ever breathe a word of this to anyone else will you, but Guscom and his family have really cranked up their activities lately. They seem to have suddenly developed delusions of grandeur and they're trying to come over all Mafiosi on us.'

'How so?' I asked.

'Beatings and most probably murders too. We're hearing stories of a couple of low-level dealers being kidnapped and tortured. Whereas before it was mostly just cannabis they were dealing, they're moving into much heavier shit now, even heroin, and whenever that happens, more money means more violence. We even found a strangled prostitute last week with her tits cut off. We have a suspicion that her death was also linked to the Guscoms somehow'

None of this information really changed anything other than my planned timescale.

I was already intent on ending Les' life, but now I decided that sooner would be better than later, for everyone's sake; except Les' of course. I had spent enough time and gathered enough information to formulate my plan and now it was time to put it into action. Which was made even more possible by the discovery I had made the day before.

CHAPTER THIRTY-TWO

I had steadily been working my way through the house for the previous six months, re-decorating it room by room. It started as a form of occupational therapy when I first gave up the booze. I had needed something to keep me busy and something to focus on, but as I moved on from one room to the next, I'd been so pleased with the results that I carried on, long after my alcoholic cravings had ceased.

But the one room I had avoided so far had been David's old bedroom.

The past can be painful place to visit and ever since David's death I had studiously tried to avoid thinking too much about him, and as part of that process, after stripping his bed bare, I had simply closed the door to his old bedroom and left it. Like closing a book after the final chapter.

But I was stronger now. Not just physically, but mentally too, and it was time to face some old demons.

I pushed open the door to David's room and watched as the dust motes swirled in the sunlight streaming in through the window. Aside from stripping the bedding, his room had been untouched since the day of his death and had been a no-go area for some years before that. Whilst it wasn't particularly untidy, it sure as hell warranted a good dusting.

I opened the window to let in some fresh air and sat on the edge of his bed, looking around at the scattered memories of his childhood. The walls were covered with Batman wallpaper and the curtains with Superman logos. It was still the décor of an eight-year-old boy, but he'd never complained about it as he got older, never asked me to change it.

An IKEA wardrobe stood forlornly in the corner with one door hanging slightly off its hinges and a variety of stickers attached. Plastic soldiers and cars stood sentinel on the dusty window sill.

Tearing off a black bin bag from the roll I had brought with me, I picked up the toys from his window sill, one by one, and threw them in. By the time I'd cleared those and the games and toys resting on the top of his wardrobe, I was already on to my second bag.

I contemplated taking some of the stuff to the charity shop, but it was all junk really. If he'd had any electronic games or anything remotely valuable, it would have been sold years before to feed his drug habit.

Slowly and methodically, I cleared the contents of the wardrobe and the rest of the room, putting to one side only a couple of old school photo's as keepsakes.

I carried the rubbish bags downstairs and loaded them into the back of the car ready to take to the dump and then, with an electric screwdriver and a hammer, I went back to his room and set about dismantling the wardrobe.

A Volvo estate is pretty big and the ideal car for a salesman to use when carrying around samples and supplies. Having filled it with David's old junk and the remnants of his now dismantled wardrobe, I figured that I still had enough room to squeeze in the single mattress. I traipsed back upstairs and paused for a moment to take in the shell of his room. Darker patches of wallpaper showed where they had remained hidden from sunlight and previously undisturbed cobwebs shifted gently in the breeze coming in through the opened window.

I reached down and wrestled the mattress of his single bed into an upright position, ready to carry downstairs, when something between the exposed slats of the bed caught my eye. No; not between the slats, beneath.

I'd already checked under the bed and cleared it of anything that had been there, but as I looked closer I could now see that there was a wooden box, nestled into the far corner, which had eluded my earlier attentions. I pulled it out and set it on the floor before me whilst I sat back on the edge of the bed to examine it.

It was the size of two shoeboxes stood one on top of the other and looked to be homemade, like the type of thing we used to make in woodwork classes at school, un-varnished and unadorned.

I lifted the lid and discovered a child's treasure trove of memories.

The only thing was, none of them were David's. There was a pocket diary containing some basic entries such as 'Mum's birthday' and 'meeting with Karen', none of which tallied with any dates or people in our little family.

There were black and white photographs of unknown people and some colour ones too. But the colour photos did at least hint at the owner's identity. About a dozen in total, they seemed to chart the formative years of a blond-haired boy who I surmised from the names written on the back of two of them, was probably called James.

The oldest photo seemed to show, in faded colour, 'James' and another lad, possibly a brother, dressed in Arsenal shirts and shorts and grinning broadly at the camera. I figured them to be around ten years old.

The next photo showed him a few years later, I guessed at fourteen or fifteen years old, in a school uniform and holding up a trophy of some sort whilst looking at the camera with a serious expression. From there on, it seemed that James' days of smiling were over and the remainder of the snaps went from those of a serious looking little to chap, to those of a glum-looking young man.

As I flicked through them I came across a photograph of James and my son, David, in a bar somewhere holding aloft bottles of beer. It was as though they'd had their picture taken under protest though as neither of them looked to be enjoying themselves. David's hair was short in the picture and I figured that had to mean that it had been taken around three years before. Flipping the photo over I saw that someone had written in a shaky hand '*James and David – Nancy's Bar*'.

There were other pictures, but that was the only one in which I recognised anyone. The most recent looking one appeared to be of 'James' and a sickly looking girl, sat arm in arm on a bench by the seaside, staring intently at whoever had taken the photo.

There was something in the shot that resonated within me and it took a long minute or two of contemplation before I recognised it.

It was the girl who gave it away to me first. She was dressed smartly enough and looked to be washed, but the prominent cheekbones and the bony wrists hinted at a body that was undernourished. And then, when I looked again at the eyes, I realised what was missing. Her. There was nothing in those baleful eyes other than the thousand yards stare, telling you that although the lights were on, there really wasn't anyone at home.

I had seen that look before when I had travelled down to Brighton to clear what had remained of David's belongings. Thin, haunted individuals, scurrying about the hostel's corridors or standing slightly hunched over from the stomach cramps which gnawed at heroin-addicted bodies. As if they had been scraped out from the inside, bit by bit destroying any previous personas until all that remained was the outer husk of a body, desperately trying to cling on to life by fuelling itself with more and more heroin.

I looked again at the picture of James and saw the same thing.

Realising that this was not likely to bring forth any happy memories, I sighed inwardly and continued to look through the box. Beneath the photographs there were some postcards and a half a dozen letters, mostly from James' mother, begging him to come home and start afresh.

Beneath the letters lay an assortment of odds and sods which I assumed had held some kind of sentimental value to their original owner. Certainly, they seemed to have no monetary value. A couple of old toy cars, a copy of the Beano, some throwaway lighters, a pocket dictionary with 'James' written on the front cover and a ten-year-old magazine about yachts.

It was a curious and eclectic collection of random items which I guessed were all that remained of an addict's childhood dreams.

I paused to wonder how my son had come to be in possession of these items which had clearly belonged to someone else, before deciding that the most obvious and the most likely explanation was that the mysterious 'James', had come to lose these items in exactly the same way that David had come to lose all of his.

I figured that James had probably overdosed and been found in the same circumstances as David. Who knew; maybe even in exactly the same Hostel. As soon as his body had been found, he'd been stripped bare of all and any worldly possessions he'd had remaining by the other inmates.

It pained me to think of David as one of those scavenging addicts, but I wasn't going to lie to myself and pretend that it was anything other than the truth, however unpalatable it might have been.

I reached in to take out the magazine which I had thought was at the bottom of the box and as I did so, I found that it was folded about something.

As soon as I saw it, I guessed what it was. I'm not sure how because I don't recall ever having seen one in real life before, but perhaps I'd seen them in the movies some time.

At around the size and shape of a box of cooks matches, it was made from black plastic and had two copper probes, each about an inch long poking out from one end.

On the face of it, there was some lettering which was too faded to make out and a lightning flash emblem that wasn't. On the long edge there was a spring loaded switch and, without even pausing to consider my actions, I held it at arm's length and turned it on.

Nothing.

I had turned my head to one side in anticipation, but looking back at it, I could see that the sum total of my pressing the switch forwards was exactly, nothing.

I had been pretty sure that what I held in my hand was a taser, or hand held stun gun, and that pushing the switch would have resulted in a sharp crackle of electricity but now I wasn't so sure. Maybe it was just some kind of tool which an electrician might use. Or maybe it was a stun gun but a broken one. Or maybe it *was* working, but silently, without any tell-tale signs of arcing electricity.

There was nothing else for it, I simply had to find out. I'd immediately recognised that this could be the breakthrough in my planning which I'd been searching for, but frustratingly, I couldn't even tell if the damned thing was what I thought it was. And if it was, whether it even worked.

I decided that there really was only one way to find out and so I carried it into my bedroom and sat on the edge of the double bed. I wasn't entirely sure what I expected it to do, but if it made me fall over, I wanted to make sure that I had a soft landing.

Holding it in my right hand, I pushed the copper probes against the inside of my left arm and once more pushed the switch forwards.

Nothing.

A small part of me was relieved. I hadn't relished the thought of zapping myself with a stun gun. After all, they weren't designed to be pain free.

But for the most part, I was severely disappointed. I had allowed myself to get carried away with the thought that it had been a working stun gun and that it would be the perfect tool for taking down a big ugly bastard like Les Guscom; to the point that I felt my mission was all but done. But now that it had proven to be broken, or not to be what I had thought it was, it felt as though I'd actually taken a step backwards in my planning.

I trudged back into David's old room and started to throw these last items into a bin bag when I suddenly realised that there was one last item in the box which I had failed to notice. I looked at it for a moment incredulously. Incredulous at my own stupidity. I fished the stun gun back out of the bin bag and took a closer look.

It was so obvious really that I'm still not sure how I managed to miss it. There in the base of the unit was a small round hole. And there in the very bottom of the box was the charger that plugged into it.

I took the charger and the stun-gun back into my bedroom and plugged them in. After a couple of seconds pause, a dull red LED light blinked on next to the switch and so I decided to leave it be whilst I went back to finish clearing David's room.

CHAPTER THIRTY-THREE

I've always found that dropping a load of household rubbish at the dump brings about a certain sense of wellbeing. A feeling of accomplishment and achievement which is totally undeserved. As if finally throwing away something which you should have chucked out years ago represented good household management. But it is what it is and I returned home from the council-owned dump feeling pleased with myself and at the same time excited to see if there had been any change in the stungun's status.

Sure enough, when I went upstairs to check, the dull red light had turned into a slowly blinking dull green light.

With a feeling of nervous anticipation, I unplugged it and sat back down on my bed, holding it aloft before me. Strange, but I remember thinking that it seemed heavier, as if soaking up electricity had given it an extra weight. Convinced of my impending success, I once again held it at arm's length and pushed the sprung switch forwards.

My God! I nearly shat myself! Such was the crack of electrical charge that rendered the air before me that I could actually smell it burning and in a split second of panic I literally threw the unit away from me and cowered backwards.

The moment I let go of it, the switch slid back and the current ceased as the stun-gun hit the carpeted floor. During my time in the Royal Marines, I'd fired rifles and lobbed grenades, but I had never, ever, experienced something as physically shocking as that stun gun the first time I fired it up. I'd been apprehensive, of course, but I was still totally unprepared for the sheer violence of the thing as it discharged god alone knows how many units of pure and convulsive energy.

I picked it up and fired it up once more, marvelling at the ferocity of its force. Just holding it there, alone in my bedroom, seemed to fill me with a feeling of immense power. Like some kind of Norse God with control of the elements, and in particular, lightning.

I had only charged it for a couple of hours, but it didn't seem to wane in power as again and again, I clicked it on and off until finally, it began to lose the ability to grip me with awe.

I was certain that what I held in my hand was the ability to tilt the scales to such an extent that I would have no problem dealing with someone as big as Les Guscom when the time came. But I had to know for sure. What if I was mistaken and although it looked mighty impressive, it proved to be no more than a major irritant, serving only to make him more pissed off.

I needed to find out if this thing really was powerful enough to take him out of the game completely, and the only way I could think of doing so, short of zapping some poor unsuspecting stranger, was to use it on myself.

Once again, I sat on the edge of my double bed and tried to prepare myself mentally for what I suspected was coming next. Holding it in my right hand I pushed the copper probes against the inside of my left arm and once again pushed the switch forwards.

What happened next is not a hundred per cent certain, but rather a version of events I have contrived based upon a fragmented memory.

I remember the blue flash of electricity lighting up the smooth and hairless skin of my inner arm, followed by the loud sound of rushing water and the howl of an animal in the distance as the lights went out.

I felt the coil of an invisible elasticated rope wrap itself about me and constrict my entire body, my confused brain panicking as I fought for breath.

And then I came to. Although I'd never fully lost consciousness, I had lost all sense of where I was or what I was doing for those brief agonising moments. I lay on my back and looked up at the bedroom ceiling feeling more completely and utterly exhausted than I can ever remember before.

I've since read up a bit more on the effects of massive electric shocks and that of being hit by a Taser or a stun-gun, and it seems that when the electricity zaps straight into the muscle fibres, it highjacks the central nervous system. This causes the muscles to contract violently and uncontrollably and it is this temporary paralysis which causes people to fall over, stiff and rigid.

I realised later that the sound of the wild animal must have been me, an involuntary outburst caused by the constriction of chest and lungs. I have never read of anyone else experiencing the sound of rushing water, but I hadn't pissed myself so I think it must have been just the sound of blood rushing to my head.

A slow appreciation of my surroundings washed over me and I found myself staring at the ceiling, with hands held out like claws and my legs sticking out over the edge of the bed, feet held off of the floor.

It took a conscious effort to relax each part of my body, muscle by muscle and limb by limb. When I finally found myself in a position to sit back up again, I felt as though I'd been run over by a truck.

Wow!

If I'd had any doubts before as to the effectiveness of my newly discovered toy, they had just vanished in spectacular fashion. That night I ordered Pizza.

CHAPTER THIRTY-FOUR

I decided that the next Tuesday would be the day when I finally gave Les Guscom what he deserved and in my mind, I came to think of it as 'G Day'.

I sat quietly in the second-hand car I'd bought specifically for this purpose. Waiting. A nervous wreck of fear and anticipation. I've never jumped out of a plane, attached to a parachute or off of a bridge, bungee jumping, but I imagined that the feeling before the jump must have been quite similar.

Every imaginable precaution had been taken and I housed no real expectation of failure, and yet the knowledge that if things *did* go wrong, it would mean the end of my life was what made it so thrilling. Let's face it, if a roller coaster didn't *feel* dangerous, no-one would bother to go on it.

It was early evening and I was parked alongside some fencing at the end of Les' road so that there was no chance of anyone seeing me from their living room window. I already knew which end he normally came from when he returned home and I knew that every Tuesday night for the last six weeks had been a pizza night so I was feeling pretty confident that I had at least this part of the plan right.

The clock ticked by and I glanced down into the passenger side foot-well at the motorcycle helmet waiting patiently for its call to arms. I went through my preparations once more in my head, trying to see if I had omitted anything vital from my planning, but again, I was feeling confident that I hadn't.

I'd picked up the Ford Focus from its usual spot on the previous Sunday and, ignoring my previous discipline, had parked it on the driveway of my house, ready to take me on to its final mission on the Tuesday.

In the weeks before, I had bought some cheap and therefore disposable clothes for cash as I travelled about the County and I planned on burning them, and the car, before the night was out. On my feet, I wore a pair of cheap trainers that I had never worn before, with socks to match. I was anxious not to leave any possible trace of DNA that could conceivably track back to me and I had changed into these socks and trainers in the car as well as the awful puffa jacket I had bought in Primark. Beneath my outer clothes, I wore thermal leggings and a long sleeved base layer, working on the theory that being skin tight, they would stop me from shedding any tell-tale hairs.

The night before I had rubbed my fingertips and palms against fine sandpaper and I also had some disposable decorator's gloves to put on when the time came, so I didn't feel that there was any danger of leaving any prints at the crime scene.

I had fully charged the stun-gun that afternoon and test fired it before I left the house and I resisted the urge to flick the switch once more. Just to double, double check.

On the passenger seat was the pizza box needed to complete my charade and I had cut away a section at the bottom and the back so that I could conceal the hand holding the stun gun, until the moment when I needed to use it. The disguise wasn't perfect, of course, they usually delivered pizzas with a kind of thermal bag around them to keep them warm, but I felt confident enough that I wouldn't arouse suspicion without one.

I had meticulously cleaned, with baby wipes, the stun gun and the disposable cell phone with the pay as you go SIM card so that, even though I had no intention of leaving them at the scene of the crime, there would still be no fingerprints to match up if things went awry.

The motorcycle helmet felt like a weak link though. It was an old one which I'd had hidden away in the loft from a period many, many years ago when I had owned a scooter for a brief time. It was a full faced helmet, black with a red stripe running through the centre and fairly distinctive in its own way. I'd toyed with the idea of buying a new one, but decided that as I planned on torching it along with everything else that night, it shouldn't be a factor.

The crash helmet was an essential part of the disguise. It was a tight fit so that it squashed my cheeks forwards like a hamster and it ought to be enough to prevent anyone, including Les Guscom, from recognising me. In addition to helping to disguise my features, it would also be a great way to prevent someone from smashing me in the teeth, although I really didn't expect that to be an issue.

I'd expected him to arrive home around seven thirty that evening and he drove past me at a quarter to eight.

The next part was slightly tricky in that I didn't know for sure how long it would be before he phoned Domino's to have his pizza delivered. Despite disliking them, I had ordered three pizzas myself in the previous week. All of them in the evening and all of them took twenty five to thirty minutes to be delivered. From my video surveillance of the previous months, I knew that the pizzas Les ordered always arrived around thirty to thirty five minutes after he arrived home and using this data, I made the assumption that he normally phoned his order within five or ten minutes of arriving home.

This was a potential stumbling block. Although I had successfully tried my dummy run of phoning through and pretending to be Les, there was no guarantee that it would work again. There was no guarantee that he hadn't ordered the pizza an hour ago, to be delivered for eight o'clock. No guarantee that he didn't have the shits that evening and had decided to forgo his guilty pleasure. There were no guarantees of anything and so I was just going to have to give it my best shot, and if it didn't work, think of something else.

I waited ten minutes before firing up the burner phone.

'Domino's Pizza. How may I help you?'

'Hello? It's Les Guscom, 71 Armistice Road. I just rung you to order for delivery?' I said, once more doing a passable enough impression of his gruff tones.

'What was the order sir?' she asked efficiently.

I hadn't expected this question at all and it threatened to derail me before I'd even begun, but suddenly, out of nowhere, I remembered the girl's voice from my previous call, all those weeks ago. '*Yes sir*' she had said back then, 'a *sixteen-inch meat feast. Deep pan*'

'A meat feast' I blustered 'I've only just phoned it through'

'Oh yes. Sorry sir. I think you spoke to my colleague. How can I help you?'

I managed to cancel the order and sat back feeling pleased with my ingenuity and at the same time half of me wishing that I'd failed.

At ten past eight, I put on the crash helmet and got out of the car. Zipping up the puffa jacket, I walked around to the passenger side and brought out the empty pizza box with the stun-gun held in my right hand beneath and inside it, whilst holding the box level and steady with my left.

I'd rehearsed my next actions over and over in my head and walked briskly across to Les' house, without pausing and pressed his doorbell. I placed my left foot on the doorstep in anticipation, ready to drive off from my right so that I could barge my way in at the moment he opened the door. I wanted what followed to take place behind a front door which was closed and not in view of any potential witnesses.

What I hadn't counted on, though, was Les opening the door at almost the same moment as I pressed the bell. I had imagined myself having a few moments to compose myself for the explosion of violence I knew must follow. The sudden opening of the door and the sight of the huge figure of Les Guscom looming over startled me so much that I nearly turned and fled. I felt like an adolescent playing knock-down-ginger and being caught red-handed.

My startled look must have registered with Les enough to make his spidey senses tingle because as I stepped in towards him, sweeping my right hand out from under the empty pizza box and sparking it into action, he stepped back and caught my wrist in his left hand, wrapping it up in a grip of iron.

At the same time, he grabbed the front of my crash helmet by the chin guard and hauled me into his hallway, so that I stumbled and fell amongst a mess of work tools discarded at the foot of the stairs.

My God but he was fast!

It's tempting to think that the big guys are going to be slow, and maybe it's true of some of the steroid-pumped bodybuilders, but with people that are naturally huge, it's total rubbish. They're as fast and as nimble as anyone else. Maybe even quicker. I'd hoped that the element of surprise would be enough to buy me a second or two which was all I'd need to bring the stun gun into play and finish him off.

But Les was clearly one of life's natural fighters and deep in the middle of a scrap was when he came into his own. It's probably true that he'd only ever fought guys that were smaller than him before, but when you're a man of his stature, there are not that many people left to fight who are your own size or bigger.

The stun gun arced into life once more but such was his grip on my wrist that I couldn't bring it to bear and being flat on my back while he remained standing left me no real chance to do so. A look of alarm flashed across his face as he registered the threat as it sparked and crackled brightly between us and he clamped his other hand around the same wrist to keep it away. As the air charred and burned between us with each high voltage discharge, it was as though a third presence had joined us in that cluttered hallway.

Still standing over me, he began to stamp down on my right shoulder in a bid to make me drop it, but he had taken his boots off when he got home and his stockinged feet lacked the impact he needed.

I made to grab at his left leg and knee with my left hand, by this time having no real idea what I was going to do to try and fight my way out of this and in answer, he dropped his weight heavily onto his right knee on my chest.

'Ooooph' the air was forced from lungs and my ribs screamed in protest as I momentarily lost control of my body and the stun gun fell heavily from my useless fingers.

I'm not sure that Les had even realised that I'd dropped my one and only advantage as he kept a tight hold on my right wrist with his left and punched me hard in the chest a couple of times with fists like bricks, before deciding that it was really my face that he wanted to hit and, grabbing the chin-guard on the full-faced helmet, he tried to wrench it off.

By that point, I was well and truly flapping.

The helmet, which I had envisaged being so useful in a close quarter fight, was now proving to be a complete hindrance. As he yanked the helmet this way and that in a bid to loosen it, my head had no option but to mirror the movements and it's virtually impossible to mount any kind of co-ordinated action when you don't have control of your own nerve centre.

He managed to work the helmet half way up and off of my head, and by that time I was willing him to succeed. I was also totally blind by then as the half on and half off helmet smothered my vision.

He still had my right wrist clamped tight and I had given up trying to hurt him with my weaker left arm as any blows which I might have landed with it would have felt like those of an eight-year-old girl.

We had landed in his narrow hallway which was cluttered with the tools of his trade and blindly I scrabbled about the floor beside me, searching for a weapon or something I could use to try and even the odds slightly. At the same time, I tried my best to twist my head to aid him in ripping the helmet off so that I could at least see my fate coming.

As I flapped about, I felt my hand close around the rubber grip of a handle, but whatever it was, it seemed to be jammed beneath a canvas bag. I changed grip and tugged hard until it came free. Although I still couldn't see, from the feel and the weight of it, I knew that I held a hammer.

I think that Les must have seen it at the same time because I felt his weight suddenly shift as he began to push himself upwards. Blindly I swung, as hard as I could, and I felt with satisfaction the arc of my newly found weapon halted by the thick bone of Les' head.

I don't know what part of the head I hit him in but I'm guessing that it must have been the temple and I felt him collapse heavily about me as his lights were abruptly distinguished. I felt so weakened by then and so heavy was he that it felt as though a horse had collapsed on me. I tried to swing the hammer again but missed, before realising that it would have been pointless even if it had connected, as Les was well and truly out of the game.

I managed to roll myself out from under him with no great trouble and frantically pulled the crash helmet from my head, finally restoring my vision. I was greeted by the sight of Les, laying on his back, mouth agape and with his eyes rolled back into his skull. His skin had begun to pale already and I was sure then that I had managed to kill him with that single blow.

But I was still flapping and there was no way I was going to take another chance with this big bastard so, kneeling astride his chest, I smashed him in the head with the hammer once more for good measure. There was no reaction at all, which served only to convince me that my first instinct had been correct and that I had finally achieved that which I had set out to accomplish all those months ago. The blind terror that I had experienced only moments before changed quickly then into a blind rage as adrenaline coursed through my body and brain, desperately seeking an outlet. I smashed his head with the hammer again. And again. And again. Until finally I felt the thick fabric of his skull give way beneath and I stopped to catch my breath.

I had probably hit him a half a dozen times, but none of them had been to his face and the sight of his slack, yet brutish features staring blankly back at me, sheathed in blood, is not a memory I like to hold dear.

I knew that he was dead, knew that I had succeeded in smashing his skull in, but somehow it didn't feel as though it was enough. It didn't feel a dramatic enough ending to his shitty existence.

The contents of a tool bag were strewn about us and without really thinking about what I was doing, I plucked up a long nail from the carpeted floor, placed it slap bang in the middle of his forehead and drove it home with a final blow of the hammer.

With that final blow, all of the fear and all of the pent-up fury I'd harboured for so long instantly drained away and I knelt there for a moment longer, utterly exhausted. Driving that nail into his brain had felt symbolic, although it didn't register at the time what it was that made it so. Only later did I realise that I had finally avenged Campsite Terry. Terry Carpenter.

I looked at the hammer, still held in my surgically gloved hands, covered in blood, and noted a splash of white paint along the shaft. I contemplated taking it with me when I left, to dispose of the murder weapon, but I soon realised that this would have been pointless. I hadn't brought it with me and there was nothing to tie it back to me as the gloves would have prevented any fingerprints or DNA being left on it.

I took a moment to take stock of the situation before noticing that the front door was shut. Thankfully, one of us must have kicked it closed by accident in the first moments of our struggle and I became aware then of how silent it was in the house.

Incredibly it seemed, despite the bloody mess I had made of Les' head, there was very little of it splashed onto me other than my right hand, which was sheathed in blood. I carefully peeled the surgical glove off and turned it inside out before popping it into my pocket. I would have to be careful not to touch anything as I left, but it was better than walking back down the street looking like an axe murderer.

I was tempted to have a good look around the house, but they say that curiosity killed the cat and so I settled for sticking my head around the doorway to the lounge. It was perhaps a pointless risk, but the pile of banknotes stacked on the coffee table made it well worthwhile as far as I was concerned. I quickly scooped them up and shoved them in my pockets and took a moment more to look around.

In contrast to the messy hall, cluttered with workman's tools, the lounge looked spotlessly tidy, with dried flower arrangements and pictures of bare-chested men on the walls. If I hadn't known better I would have guessed that it was the home of a young woman.

The cash was an unexpected bonus and although I was tempted to explore further, I decided that it was best not to try my luck any further than I already had and so I picked up the crash helmet and jammed it back on my head. The pizza box lay battered and crumpled by the front door and I picked it up along with the taser which I placed back inside before making my exit.

Outside the street was as deserted as it had been when I arrived and I resisted the temptation not to run like crazy back to the waiting car.

Little did I know then that my brutal slaying of Les Guscom would have far, far wider reaching consequences than I could ever have imagined.

CHAPTER THIRTY-FIVE

The next day found me driving my Volvo halfway across the country for one of the biggest sales pitches of my life.

I had waited until after midnight before dumping the unregistered Focus in the same clearing as the one where Les had met up with Campsite Terry before beating him to death. I wondered whether I was tempting fate with the irony of the location, but reasoned that if it was a secluded enough location to murder someone, then it ought to be a secluded enough place to burn a car.

I had already bought a can of petrol for the purpose and having changed out of every item of clothing that I'd worn in Les' house, including the distinctive crash helmet, and dumped it on to the driver's seat, I doused the lot and threw a match in.

Before setting out the previous evening I had made sure that the tank was full and, after taking the petrol cap off I jammed in a petrol soaked rag in the hope that this too would ignite.

Although I had set fire to poor old Charlie Patterson's motor all those years ago I had not hung around to see the results and for all I knew it might have failed to burn anything other than the paintwork. I hadn't even known whether his car was petrol or diesel. I was therefore not entirely sure of what to expect if the tank did ignite and I was a little nervous of being caught up in an explosion of sorts; and so having previously removed my surveillance kit, I soaked the boot and set fire to that in the hope that it would spread to the tank after I had left.

It crossed my mind that I might end up burning down half the forest and that it really wasn't a nice thing to do to a local beauty spot, but when you'd just killed a man in cold blood, a little bit of eco-vandalism seemed fairly benign by comparison.

The clearing was about three miles from my home and I decided that the best thing to do was to walk home wearing dark clothing, ducking out of view at the first sight of any headlamps, until I reached built up Chelmsford once more and could blend in as someone making their way home after a late night out.

After I'd lit the car up, I quickly jogged away, my back to the brightness of the fierce blaze which grew rapidly so that it seemed to light up the entire night sky. Hurrying home as fast as I could I listened out for the 'whump' of an explosion, but none came. I expected to hear the sirens of a fire engine at some point on my journey back, but again, there was nothing.

Halfway home, a light drizzle began for which I was grateful as it meant that I had an excuse to wear my hood up, further disguising me from identification.

When I reached home, I switched the water heater on and took a long hot shower, scrubbing vigorously at my skin and nails in an eager effort to sanitise anything remotely evidential as soon as I could.

By that time, my head was all over the place and thoughts scrambled for purchase as competing emotions swam steadily in and out of favour. On the one hand, I pulsed with elation at the adrenaline rush caused by fighting for my life. And not only surviving the fight but winning it too.

But it's not easy to override the moral conditioning of our society and I also knew that what I had done was just not right. Not really anyway. And this particular feeling came as something of a surprise to me.

For years I had convinced myself that I really didn't give a shit about anyone other than myself, close friends and family. Ever since Keith Lawson had offered his own personal definition of a sociopath, I had decided that it fitted my own persona down to a tee and I had allowed it to shape my emotions accordingly. After Judy had died, and then again after David's overdose, I figured that not caring about other people would help to make me stronger again. If I didn't care about other people then they couldn't affect my own emotional well-being. It was a state of mind which I'd worked hard to cultivate until it become self-fulfilling.

But maybe I'm not as much of a bastard as I'd like to think I am.

It's true that I have a vicious temper at times and it's also true that I really don't care whether the people I *don't* like, live or die; so maybe I am a little less empathetic than *normal* people. Certainly, if you pissed me off sufficiently I would have no qualms about sticking a knife in your neck.

But the whole not caring about anyone else at all, in any way, shape or form, has been a bit of a front; something to make me seem tougher than I really am, I guess.

I mulled through my introspection as I scrubbed at my skin before finally deciding that, no, I didn't care that I'd killed Les; what I really cared about was the possibility of getting caught.

I was fairly sure that I'd covered my tracks completely, but I fretted whether or not I had overlooked some vital piece of evidence which might lead a murder investigation back to me. The only things I had retained from that evening were the concealed camera which I'd promised to return to Bradley, the cash I had picked up from the coffee table and the handheld stun gun.

I counted the cash out which totalled just short of four thousand pounds, but worrying that this could potentially link me back to Les' murder, I wrapped it up with the stun gun, (I'm still not sure what made me keep it), and hid it in the loft beneath a layer of insulation fibre.

****

I never understood why it is that in films that the murderers always returned to the scenes of their crimes, but sure enough, the following morning I felt myself drawn to the clearing where I'd burned the evidence of the previous night.

In part, I had worried that the fire might have been extinguished before it had fully destroyed any trace of evidence; that maybe the fire brigade had arrived too early, or that the drizzle had been heavy enough to foil my plans.

But I needn't have worried. I drove into the clearing and the acrid smell of burned plastic and rubber hung thickly in the air as I looked upon the wrecked shell of a melted car.

The fire had done its work better than I could have hoped for and there was very little left that wasn't metal. The plastic bumpers and panelling had all gone and the windows had shattered with the heat. Inside, the dashboard was a melted mess and all that was left of the seats were charred and rusting springs. There was no sign at all of the crash helmet or the bag of discarded clothes other than the fact that the area where I'd left them seemed to be even blacker than the rest; no doubt a result of all the extra petrol they'd been soaked in.

I was also glad to see that although the ground about the car was blackened and burned, none of the surrounding trees or bushes had been affected. Like I said; I'm not a complete bastard.

Satisfied, I wheeled about and began my long journey to Birmingham.

CHAPTER THIRTY-SIX

Beneath a bulletproof sky, long lines of early morning traffic snaked through the heart of the Essex countryside. A watery light lifted the veil from a rural Essex landscape and the urban traffic flow slicing through its centre. A thin layer of ankle-deep mist clung stubbornly to the newly ploughed fields on either side of the road, which had itself been swept clear by the moving traffic.

Thousands of drivers and passengers, making their way to their dreary jobs, under a dreary sky, and through a dreary landscape.

But there was nothing dreary or remotely drowsy about my state of mind that morning, despite the fact that I had barely slept a wink the night before. The previous two nights hadn't been much better either as I'd tossed and turned in anticipation of the attack I'd planned. My dry and gritty eyeballs felt as though they'd been dusted with flour, but the residual adrenaline still coursed through my veins from the previous night's exertions and completely screwed any attempt at calm or rational thinking, and I sat there twitching with nerves in the long line of early morning traffic.

The fact that I really couldn't think about anything other than the events of the previous night was starting to really get on my nerves though. I was driving to one of the biggest sales pitches of my life, and apart from the obvious need to pay attention to the road, I wanted to think about what I needed to say.

My journey that morning would take me to Birmingham to see Toby Stiles, the Director and owner of STILCO Insurance services. Hopefully to turn him into the number one customer for yours truly and Anglian Press Stationery Ltd.

Coincidentally, STILCO had recently swallowed up the small chain of insurance brokers in Harlow, which Bigham had asked me to drop in on the same day as my first visit to Snake Eyes Security and Bradley Thomas.

STILCO was one of the biggest privately owned insurance intermediaries in the country, and they competed in an industry which, no matter how hard they tried to run a paperless empire, inevitably ended up using more and more.

The reason for this anomaly was simple enough: Lawyers. These days we live in such a litigious society that every Tom, Dick and degenerate Harry sits waiting to jump on the next bandwagon and claim that they were mis-sold their home insurance, their life assurance, their accident cover, even their pet insurance if given half a chance.

With the promise of a free payday to be had, these otherwise upright pillars of modern society conveniently forget the fraudulent claim they made on their house insurance fifteen years previously and immediately start gobbing off to anyone who'll listen to them about what a bunch of unscrupulous thieves the entire finance industry is.

Key to the whole monetary merry-go-round are the lawyers and companies offering to pursue your spurious claim on a 'No Win No Fee' basis.

For the likes of Toby Stiles and his industry peers, there are two main forms of defence. The first is to hire his own lawyers. And not any old lawyers, but the best that money can buy. The pinstriped London based lawyers on thousands of pounds an hour who are far too gifted to be working on a 'No Win No Fee' basis. Their main purpose is to ensure that the company never puts itself in a position where it will be called to account in the first place.

For STILCO the second form of defence is part and parcel of the first. Everything is put in writing. Everything. In every single medium available.

Every contract, every invoice, every request, every policy document is printed, delivered and stored in physical, as well as electronic form. Emails are sent containing copies of every communication followed by hard copies of exactly the same information. Texts are sent to the customers telling them to expect these documents. Every telephone conversation is recorded and transcribed onto paper before being emailed, posted and stored.

In short, the customer can never say that they didn't receive what they were supposed to receive. It might not be environmentally friendly, but as long as the Company treats its clients fairly and in accordance with the letter of the myriad of changing rules, regulations and laws applicable, it should stand up to any scrutiny it needs to.

The upshot of this is that STILCO uses a lot of paper; shitloads in fact. And not only the paper for copying and printing but also envelopes, files, labels, clips, folders, etc., etc., etc. The whole stationery kitbag.

I'd met with Toby a couple of times before and I had a pretty good idea about his volume of stationary usage. If I could get the order to supply the entire Company, it would boost APS's sales volume by twenty-five percent, thus making yours truly the Alpha dog's bollocks.

In the space of three months, I had already gone back to being the second highest selling Account Manager in the company and it was only a matter of time before I gained the top spot again. I'd promised Bigham that he wouldn't regret standing by me when I first started to clean my act up and I was damned sure that I was going to make good on my promise.

No matter how good a salesman I was though, or how experienced I was, there was no getting away from the fact that driving to Birmingham less than twelve hours after hammering a six-inch nail into Les' head, was not ideal preparation for a sales call of that magnitude.

****

Incredibly, my trip was a success. Fortunately, I had met and spoken with Toby on previous occasions so I didn't need to make too much small talk and, without the need for ad-lib, I soon settled into the patter of my tried and tested sales pitch.

I didn't secure the stationary rights for the entire group, but I did secure them for the whole of East Anglia. Being a new supplier for STILCO this would be on a trial basis and in a trial area to ensure that we could deliver on my extravagant promises of great service and great prices.

I had talked this through with Bigham previously, and this deal was exactly what we'd hoped for, as expanding our logistical support into Cambridgeshire and Norfolk would come with its own costs and in order to justify this, we needed to expand our customer base further, something which couldn't happen overnight. In short, this was just the beginning of our expansion plans at APS.

I left the offices of STILCO trying hard to suppress the grin which threatened to consume my face and the spring in my step which was just shy of skipping.

But, by the time I got back into my car a sudden wave of exhaustion had swept over me and I realised that there was no way I'd be able to drive back to Chelmsford without falling asleep at the wheel.

Bigham had been as excited as I was at the prospect of expanding our customer base beyond

Essex and I had promised to phone him as soon as I left Toby Stiles, which I did as soon as I got back into the car. But I also told him not to expect to see me the following morning as I was going to find a local hotel and stay overnight. Bigham was so excited that I could have told him that I was off to California for a week and he wouldn't have minded.

I booked into a Holiday Inn about half a mile from STILCO's offices without even asking what the room rate was and went straight to bed despite the fact that it was only two-thirty in the afternoon.

I fell asleep almost immediately as the exhaustion which had been building for the past few days finally overtook me, but by five o'clock I was fully awake again, managing to feel simultaneously refreshed and dog tired. The two hours of slumber had not been enough to catch up on the lost hours of sleep of the previous few days, but was enough to take the edge off of my feeling of total exhaustion.

I continued to lay there for a while, trying hard to empty my mind and go back to sleep, but the events of the last couple of days made it impossible.

On the one hand, I still had the anxiety which gnawed at the edges on my consciousness, wondering if I might have left behind some vital piece of evidence which would lead the cops back to me. On the other hand, there was still a thrill and excitement skittering through me whenever I re-lived the grim, hand to hand, fight for life with Les in the scatted mess of his hallway floor.

I tried to think about the future instead, but that meant thinking through the possibilities and problems of servicing STILCO as well as opening up new channels of business in geographical areas previously ignored by APS.

No rest for the wicked.

I lay on my back for a while looking up at the LED light blinking softly on and off in the smoke alarm, and contemplated getting back in my car and heading home, but if I was going to do that it would mean starting the journey at the worst possible time of day as the rush hour traffic began to snowball on the main road outside the hotel.

Eventually, I made a decision.

Killing Les had been a good thing, and a job well done deserved a celebration of sorts. I had seen a big Tesco sited two hundred yards away on the other side of the dual carriageway and so I walked down and bought some cheap underwear and toiletries for the following morning. After that, I sat alone in the hotel bar and started to get drunk.

Three pints of lager and a couple of whisky chasers later I suddenly realised that I had barely eaten a thing in the previous days and instantly I became ravenously hungry. I booked into the hotel restaurant and as I'd decided that this was to be a celebration of sorts, I ordered the biggest and most expensive steak they had on the menu and the dearest bottle of red wine they had to offer.

I've never been a connoisseur of wine and it didn't taste all that great to me so I probably should have saved my money, but that night I slept like a baby.

CHAPTER THIRTY-SEVEN

My minor commercial success proved to be a great distraction over the next few weeks as it meant covering a lot of miles, making sure that I made as much face to face contact as possible with the extra offices and shops that we would now be covering.

Distracting as it was though, it was impossible to turn my mind fully away from the events of that fateful night which I had started to think of as 'G Day' (Guscom Day). I still felt a frisson of excitement when I recalled twatting him round the head with the hammer, feeling his weight fall away from me, and I was still convinced that I had done a good thing, that I had saved the world at large from future wrongdoings.

But there was also a sense of anti-climax. For the best part of six months, my every waking thought had revolved around planning Les' execution, but now that I had finally achieved my aim, I felt as though there was something missing again from my life.

It seems, though, that sometimes six inches is just not enough. I had thought that driving a nail through Les' brain would be the end of my journey, as well as his, but I would soon discover that it was just the beginning.

It was three weeks later before I next saw Skip

Parsons and we went to the Butler's Head quiz night. By then, my nerves had finally settled to an extent that I felt confident there would be no repercussions to come, and that I had gotten away with Les' murder scot-free.

After nodding politely to some of the other quiz night regulars we settled into a cosy booth off to the side of the half-full pub, whilst the quiz master tested his microphone and prepared his question sheets.

'Where've you been hiding the last couple of weeks then' I asked as I sat opposite him and watched him wipe away a beer froth moustache with the back of his hand.

'Don't ask' he said, rolling his eyes. 'Work's gone crazy again lately. In fact, the whole world seems to have gone crazy. Murders, beatings, rapes, you name it, and for some godforsaken reason it's all landed on my plate these last couple of weeks'.

My ears immediately pricked up at the mention of 'murders' of course. Despite combing every inch of the local papers and tuning in to local news radio at every opportunity, there had been no mention of Les' grisly demise.

'Oh' I asked, trying to adopt an air of nonchalance, 'I haven't seen anything in the papers. Who's murdering who then?'

'It's not in the papers because mostly it's NHC's, 'Non Human Crimes' and we don't usually waste too much time when one junkie wants to top another, or if it's gang-related stuff and it doesn't spill out into *civilised* society.'

He'd told me before about what they called 'Non-Human Crimes' and I made an effort not to wince as I thought back to how my son had ended his days.

'But there's a limit' he continued 'and at the moment the sheer volume of shit going on makes it impossible to brush under the carpet. Drugs dealers in some kind of turf war, we think. Our old friends the Guscoms in particular'.

'Oh? Why's that then?'

'We're not entirely sure who started what, but it seems that somebody did a number on Les Guscom and now Mummy and her crew are lashing out at anyone and everyone who might have been involved. Could be a straight out turf war, or it might be some kind of tit for tat grudge thing going on. We're waiting on a bit more info from our snitches at the moment to try and make more sense of it.'

'So, who do you think killed Les then?' I asked, purposely gazing off at the quizmaster.

'Oh, he's not dead. He's just in hospital.'

I lost any semblance of control over my actions then as I felt myself gape and slowly to turn my head to look at Skip incredulously. A wave of sick fear settled into my gut.

'What do you mean, not dead? He must be dead.' I nearly said, '*You don't get to have a six-inch nail driven slap bang into the middle of your head and to not be dead*'. I nearly said it, but I didn't.

But with the benefit of hindsight, even if I had said it, I don't think that it would have made much difference. The damage had already been done.

Skip sat there for a moment without a word upon his lips, watching me and calculating with that methodical policeman's brain of his. I'm sure that he knew then. He knew that I was privy to something more than I had let on and he sat there in silence, watching me closely and, with a technique which he had probably honed over decades of policing, silently offered me the opportunity to say something more in the hope that I'd trip over my own words.

But like a Mexican stand-off, I knew that he knew and I wasn't about to give him anything more than I already had and so I simply gazed back at him, trying my best to look both innocent and quizzical at the same time.

Eventually, he broke the peace. 'Why must he be dead Owen? There's something you're not telling me, isn't there? What do you know?'

I spread my hands out in front of me and offered him what must have been a very sickly smile. 'Why would I know anything Skip? You told me that there had been murders and that somebody had done a number on Les Guscom. Call me old fashioned if you will, but I just added the two together and made four.'

It was a good enough answer to halt any further questions at that time, but it wasn't a good enough answer to give the lie to my reactions. They had said far more than the actual words could ever have done and we passed the rest of the evening as uneasy companions, coming second from last in the quiz.

Despite the atmosphere and despite Skip's misgivings, he still went on to inform me that Les had been admitted into a hospital, badly beaten and with a six-inch nail driven through his skull. I'm not entirely sure why he shared these details with me but I suspect he may have been fishing for some further reaction.

It turned out that a six-inch nail was not, after all, a certain way to kill someone, but in Les' case, it had been enough to make it touch and go for some time and had caused enough brain damage to turn him into a gibbering idiot. Luckily for me, that gibbering idiot was also totally incapable of helping the police, or anyone else for that matter, with their enquiries.

Fortunate for me but unfortunate for a lot of other people, because dear old mummy, Griselda Guscom, had by that time reached the not unreasonable conclusion that the attempted murder of her son had probably been perpetrated either by a rival gang of dealers, or someone trying to avoid paying their debts.

The nail in the centre of his forehead had been interpreted as someone trying to send a message, a warning of some kind, and she had decided to react accordingly and decisively. The result of that had been two reported kidnappings, (although once the tortured and badly beaten victims had been released they were unwilling to assist the police with their enquiries) two stabbings and one fatal shooting, as well as a suspected arson attack on a corner shop.

The one thing which all of these crimes had in common was that in none of the cases could the police gain direct testimony from any of the victims, although uncorroborated eyewitness accounts and the word on the street from snitches, all pointed the finger of blame firmly in the direction of Griselda and her crew.

That night I sat at home after returning from the pub and pondered this new information. It's fair to say that Skip's revelation that evening had taken the wind out of my sails somewhat. As stressful as the last few weeks had been, they had also afforded me a sense of well-being; of a job well done.

It had taken balls and determination to go through with my original plan and there had been plenty of times when I began to question my motivation and my resolve, but I had driven those thoughts from my mind as quickly as they had arrived, in the midst of what had become something of an obsession.

It had taken a prolonged period of mental strength and, after I had finally succeeded in killing Les, or at least when I'd *thought* that I'd killed him, I had given myself a metaphorical, congratulatory pat on the back and allowed myself to relax once more.

All for nothing.

As disappointed as I was though, for the most part, I fretted.

I fretted over the extent of the brain damage which Les had suffered. Skip had told me that he was severely brain damaged and in no fit state to make any kind of identification of his assailant, but what I didn't know, and hadn't dared to probe Skip over that evening, was what the prognosis was. Whether this was a permanent state of affairs or whether there was the possibility of some kind of recovery.

If Les did recover sufficiently to point the finger of blame in my direction, it seemed that, from what Skip had told me, the police would be the least of my concerns. That if Griselda found out, I could expect an untimely and very unpleasant ending to my time on earth.

There was only one thing for it I decided. I had to go back and finish the job I'd already started; which was a pain in the arse really because it would mean starting all over again from the beginning, with the surveillance and everything else which went with it.

It occurred to me then that I was no further forward than I had been four months ago. I didn't know whether or not he was still in the hospital, or if not, whether he was still living in the same house as before; and if so, whether he now lived with a carer or someone else. Christ on a stick, for all I knew he might have fully recovered from his brain injury yesterday!

There was no time to lose, I decided, I needed to pick up where I left off and to go back to keeping an eye on his house until I knew more. I set an alarm for four o'clock the next morning and tried to get some sleep.

CHAPTER THIRTY-EIGHT

My legs felt heavy and sluggish the next morning as I pulled my tracksuit trousers on and set off once more for a jogging recce to Armistice Road.

We were halfway through August by then and it would be another couple of hours before sunrise so I took my time and slowed to a walk halfway there. It may have been August but in true British style, a heavy drizzle misted the air and soon left me feeling depressed and bedraggled. In the early morning gloom, I struggled to find the motivation to go through this all over again.

I finally made it to Armistice Road and jogged past Les' house without pausing, but from the absence of lights and his otherwise ever-present van, and the fact that the curtains had been left drawn, it seemed obvious to me that he wasn't home and probably hadn't been for some time.

On my way back home I took the time to try and think through my options as pragmatically as I possible.

First of all, I decided that running past Les' house at some ungodly hour was a complete waste of time. Back at the beginning of this whole sorry affair, I had chosen to run, partly because I was doing my best to get fit again after kicking the booze, and partly because I was concerned about traffic cameras recording my number plate in the vicinity.

I had chosen to do it so early in the mornings to mitigate the risk of a nosey neighbour spotting me while I was fitting a tracking device or downloading camera footage, as well as negating the likelihood of Les seeing me near his home.

But none of that mattered any more. I no longer had the camera and if Les was too brain damaged to identify his assailant, it wouldn't matter even if I bumped into him face to face. I might just as well have driven past his house at a normal time of day to check if there was anything worth seeing.

I had a strong suspicion that I would be wasting my time but I decided to start driving by his house a couple of times each day to see if anything useful could be learned, at least until I next had a chance to try and winkle out some more information from Skip Parsons.

Later that morning I rang Skip on his mobile phone and asked him if he had any plans for Saturday. When he told me he didn't, I asked him if he fancied an afternoon at Great Leighs race track, explaining that a grateful customer of mine had presented me with two tickets to the afternoon meeting as a gift. He readily accepted and after arranging our meet times I hung up the phone and went online to buy the tickets.

Saturday came and Saturday went with both of us coming away from the track more or less even; which I counted as being a good result.

I'd hoped to grill Skip for more information on Les' status but the opportunity never presented itself, so I chanced my arm and suggested that we meet for a pint the next day to watch a football match in the Globe.

It wasn't that unusual for us to bump into each other in the pub when a football match was on but we didn't usually arrange to meet in advance. If he found it odd that I suddenly wanted to see him three times in a single week, after having not seen each other for three weeks or more beforehand, he didn't comment on it.

I decided to try and meet Skip every Wednesday for Quiz Night and on a Saturday or Sunday too, working on the theory that you should keep your friends close, but your enemies closer. Not that Skip was someone I'd have ever classed as my enemy, he had become too much of a good friend for that, but there was no getting away from the fact that he had the power to put me in prison; maybe not for murder any more, but definitely for attempting it.

I planned on using our meetings and considerable volumes of alcohol to probe him gently for any fresh intelligence on the Guscom family, or for updates on the investigation into the *attempted* murder of Les.

That Sunday afternoon we sat side by side on high stools in the pub, watching two teams of overpaid prima donnas rolling about a football pitch and play acting, instead of getting on with the business of trying to score goals against each other.

All in all, it was a piss poor excuse for entertainment which was a shame because, although neither of us had any allegiances to either side, it had looked on paper as though it would be a good game.

'How's my favourite crime family doing lately then?' I asked as nonchalantly as possible during a lull in conversation.

A pause followed and I looked sideways to see Skip looking pensively at me before answering my seemingly innocent question.

'Since you're so interested, *Owen*, I think that the SOCA boys have hit a bit of an impasse. Mind you, half of those kids are straight out of college with barely a toe in the real world, let alone any experience of real police work so it's no wonder they're so fucking dumb'

'SOCA?' I asked, not really all that sure what he was saying.

'Serious and Organised Crime Agency' he said, his voice dripping with disdain. 'It seems that the Guscom family have got big enough and busy enough to finally pop up on their radar, which means that the reins to any current investigations into their activities have effectively been passed over. Lucky old sods.'

'What's lucky about it?' I asked. I had assumed that he meant that it was SOCA who were the lucky ones. But I was wrong.

'Because for the most part SOCA don't know their arses from their elbows. Turns out they've had surveillance on Les' house for the last three months. *Three* bloody months and not only have they still not worked out who tried to kill him in his own home, but it was two whole weeks after he got discharged from hospital before they realised that he wasn't living back in his old house!'

Skip's voice had gradually gained volume as he spoke and this whole subject seemed to be bothering him in a way that I couldn't quite understand. After taking two large gulps of beer he angrily wiped at his mouth with the back of his hand before continuing on; 'and even if they do get some concrete evidence on the Guscoms (bearing in mind that every fucker seems too scared to testify against them at the moment) the chances are that they'll let them walk anyway.'

'Why?' I almost cried out, more than a little dismayed at what Skip was telling me.

'Because after dear old SOCA, comes the dear old National Criminal Intelligence Service and their idea of policing is to let everyone carry on as they are so long as they're all snitching on each other. Fuck the public and fuck the victims of crime. So long as they know who's offing who in the criminal underworld, for the most part, they're happy to sit back and watch.'

Skip wasn't quite shouting at that point and whilst he still wasn't loud enough for anyone else to listen in on our conversation, what with the noise from the football on TV in the background and all, he was just loud enough for one or two heads to turn at his use of the word 'fuck'.

We were only on our third pints but Skip seemed suddenly to be the worse for wear. Deliberately lowering my voice in the hope that he would take the hint and drop his too, I asked 'So the surveillance on Les' house didn't see anything? Or it did, but it just couldn't identify them?'

'Buggered if I know mate, I haven't had access whatever tapes there are yet. All I know is that they haven't got a suspect.'

There wasn't anything more that Skip could add that day. It seemed that whilst the chances were that he personally would eventually get to see any evidence SOCA gathered, it would only be after they'd vetted it and if they deemed it suitable to share. They needed to make sure that there was no-one inside the police feeding the Guscoms information.

There was no doubting that talking about the Guscoms had really got to Skip. I couldn't quite work out why that was, but the truth was that I had bigger worries of my own to worry about back then.

Only a week before I had been congratulating myself on being oh so clever, but stupid sod that I was, I hadn't even managed to make sure that Les was dead. I'd previously been pretty sure that most of my efforts to cover my tracks had been overly cautious and that they were, for the most part, unnecessary but the news that my whole damned adventure had probably been filmed made me glad I hadn't tried to cut any corners.

As far as I could tell though, there was still nothing to link me to his attack. Although the execution had turned out to be a complete balls-up, I had been meticulous with my planning and I remained certain that there was no physical evidence linking me to the scene. There were no prints, I had shed no blood, my face had been covered by the crash helmet and the unregistered car was now nothing more than a burned out wreck in the middle of the woods.

My main concern was whether Les would recover his faculties sufficient to point the finger of blame in my direction. Skip told me that Les had suffered enough brain damage to turn him into a gibbering idiot but that was hardly what you'd call a medical diagnosis and I had no real idea what the true prognosis was.

And, if he did become capable of identifying me. I wasn't sure who to be more afraid of; the police or Les' mum.

Barely a week before I had been congratulating myself on being some kind of master criminal but now, no matter how much I racked my brains, I had no answers to my problem.

Maybe prison was the answer, I mused. Not for me of course, but for Les and Griselda. Maybe there was some kind of way in which I could frame or incriminate them sufficient enough to warrant a long spell inside. But almost as quickly as the thought occurred to me I realised that this was extremely unlikely.

If what Skip had told me was true, the police had already been after the Guscoms for a long time and even with their resources, they had been either unable or unwilling to make anything stick.

Eventually I came to the conclusion that there was no option other than to sit tight and hope that Les remained a vegetable. There was no way that the Griselda and her heavies could link what had happened back to me without Les recovering enough to tell them who had attacked him.

I resolved to try not to think about it too much, realising that there was nothing to be gained by worrying about it, particularly as I couldn't affect the outcome. But I also resolved to continue grooming Skip for as much information as I could squeeze out of him. With particular reference to the wellbeing of one Les Guscom.

CHAPTER THIRTY-NINE

I gained no fresh insights from my next few meetings with Skip, other than to confirm that, as far as the police could ascertain, Les was unable to communicate properly outside of a few unintelligible grunts. He was up on his feet and able to walk about unaided but was otherwise unable to function normally. Like a monstrously overgrown one-year-old child was how Skip described him. I asked again whether they thought he'd ever recover but according to Skip, the prognosis was not good.

With the slow passage of time, and the snippets of information gleaned from Skip, I should have found myself re-assured, yet somehow, the uncertainty of Les' future started to eat away at me.

For the most part, I worried about being caught by the police, What had started as nagging self-doubt slowly but surely grew to a state of barely suppressed paranoia, to the extent that I found myself constantly checking my rear-view mirror whilst driving and checking parked cars close to my home for signs of surveillance.

I knew that I was being daft but I couldn't help myself. After all, why would the police bother following me if they had any evidence linking me to the crime? Surely, they would just knock on my front door and come right out with it.

But, irrational as I knew it was, I couldn't shake the feeling that, at any moment, I was about to have my collar felt.

****

It was the best part of a month after I'd *not* killed Les before I next saw Griselda.

I'd arranged to meet Skip in the Globe one Saturday afternoon, ostensibly to watch one of the autumn rugby internationals over a pint or two, but also to hopefully give me another chance to confirm that Les hadn't made some kind of miraculous recovery.

After a pretty mediocre sort of summer it seemed that winter was itching to sink her claws in as soon as possible and not only was it blowing a gale, but it was also unseasonably cold for the time of year so the warmth of the pub that day should have felt more than just a little welcoming as I walked in.

But there was something *off* about the whole ambience which struck me as soon as I walked through the doors. It didn't take more than a moment or two before I realised what it was, or rather *who* it was that strained the atmosphere.

On the far side of the pub stood one of Griselda's goons keeping a menacing eye on the rest of the pub's customers, while Griselda seemed to have commandeered a table to herself in the corner.

Whilst it wasn't completely unheard of, it was still fairly unusual for Griselda to visit the Globe and I had only ever seen a few times before in previous years. Once more I was struck by just how pug ugly she was. It wasn't just the piggy eyes and upturned freckly nose that did it; there was something about her body shape and language, her whole demeanour, which was somehow repellent. I'd only seen her a handful of times before, but this was the first time I had seen her without Les and also the first time I seen her and not heard the awful screech of her voice cutting through the air.

But even stranger than that, it was the first time I'd ever seen her talking to Skip Parsons. They sat opposite one another across a small round table, devoid of any drinks, with their heads almost touching as they discussed something in earnest.

It took me another moment then to realise that they weren't *discussing* anything, because a discussion is a two-way communication and their little conflab was very much a one-sided affair. They both had their heads slightly bowed over the table but Skip's head was the lower of the two and with Griselda's an inch or two above, as though she was talking down to him and either giving some kind of instruction or admonishing him.

I couldn't quite work out what I was seeing because Skip was always such a confident and laid back kind of guy. I'd never seen him take any shit from anyone, not even Les; and yet here he seemed to be looking very sheepish indeed. I made to take a step towards them but even though I was on the other side of the pub, Skip seemed to pick up on my intent and glanced up at me quickly before giving the faintest shake of his head, silently asking me to stay away.

At the time I was more curious than concerned. It crossed my mind that I had witnessed a similar type of situation between Les Guscom and Campsite Terry a month or so before his murder, but Skip Parsons was a totally different kettle of fish and I couldn't see him getting into the same kind of trouble. Especially given the fact that he was police.

I assumed that Skip had seen her come into the pub and decided that it was as good a time as any to ask her to assist him with his enquiries. But judging by the body language I was seeing, Griselda had decided that no, now was *not* a good time for her to assist him with his enquiries.

Not knowing how long they were likely to be I bought myself a lager and settled down at the only table left free to watch the French hopefully get stuffed by Scotland on the big TV screen.

The pub was doing a steady trade that afternoon, but nowhere near as much as it would have done if England had been playing; which was fine by me as it meant I could relax and enjoy the game without the noise of the usual loudmouths who turned up wearing

England jerseys stretched tight over beer bellies, and who didn't understand the game.

There were still one or two in there cheering on the French on the basis that they 'hated' the Scots, but I managed to filter them out. I'm all for cheering on your own team, whoever they are, but I've never subscribed to the small minded thinking that if you support England, you must, therefore, want Scotland, Wales and Ireland to lose all of their games. I'm English first, but British second.

As much as I enjoy a good game of football, I'll always prefer an exciting game of rugby and this was proving to be just such a game, with the scoreline see-sawing wildly from one side to the other as both teams seemed to be equally gifted with ball in hand, and yet both woefully poor in defence.

I was nearing the end of my first pint and the scoreboard was starting to make it look more like a cricket match when Skip appeared at my side with a pint of bitter for himself and a fresh pint of stella for me.

'Alright mate?' I greeted him.

'Not really Owen. Everything's seems to have gone to shit at the moment'

He did look a little forlorn just then and his usual 'normal devil may care' attitude seemed to have gone on the missing list. He usually maintained a relaxed attitude, regardless of anything else that might be going on in the world, but that afternoon he looked as though his strings had been cut as his shoulders slumped forwards and his face seemed to have lost its elasticity.

'Care to share? I asked, slightly concerned about the new look Skip.

I knew that Skip lived alone and perhaps he was looking for a shoulder to cry on that day because he leapt straight in with the whole 'woe is me act'. It's a characteristic which is a permanent state of affairs for some people, but for Skip Parsons it was completely out of character.

'I'm getting hassle from work, hassle from the neighbours, hassle from the cat and now hassle from the Guscoms'

'The cat?' I asked, somewhat taken aback, 'you're getting hassle from a cat?'

'Yeah, fucking thing's got dementia or something, coz it keeps shitting everywhere. Eleven years I've had it now and it's always gone outside for a crap. It's got a cat flap in the back door to come and go as it pleases. Never once has it ever crapped anywhere in the house before two weeks ago, but now it doesn't want to go anywhere else'

I'd never owned a cat myself and up until thirty seconds before I'd never known that Skip had one. 'Perhaps it's scared to go outside' I suggested, slightly bemused.

'Oh no, quite the reverse,. It spends all night and half the day outside but recently it seems to have decided to come in just to use the house as a toilet. It walks in, struts about a bit and then takes a piss or a shit wherever it chooses. I seem to spend half my time cleaning up after the bloody thing recently and I've got a sneaking suspicion that it's pissed in my wardrobe.'

With that, he lifted his sleeve up to his nose and took a good long sniff before proffering it to me to smell. I declined the offer with a smile and asked him 'so what are you going to do?'

'I've still not decided. The way I see it, I can either let things carry on as they are and put up with it, but I really don't see that happening. Or I could just block up the cat flap and disown the little bugger, but that seems a bit of a cowardly way out to me.'

'Try the vets?' I suggested.

'Nah, it's only a cat and it's had a good innings so far, so I think maybe it's time to call time on it and drown it.'

'Drown it?' I asked, genuinely shocked.

'Yeah, drown it in the bath. It's what my dad did to our old cat when I was a kid after it got knocked down by a car, but that was to put it out of its misery. In this case, it will be putting the cat out of *my* misery but then again, I can't have the little bastard strutting around thinking he's the boss now can I?'

I wasn't entirely sure whether Skip was kidding me on or not, he certainly wasn't smiling. I never found out for sure but I suspect that he genuinely *was* thinking about drowning his cat just to show it who was boss.

I should have been shocked I guess, but the truth is I've made friends with some seriously fucked up people in the past and it seemed that Skip was no exception.

'And what about the neighbours? Why are they hassling you?' I'd had enough of the strange cat conversation and although I desperately wanted to ask him about the Guscoms, I decided to beat about the bush a little first so as not to seem too interested.

'The neighbours are always hassling me, so nothing new there really. A few years ago I shagged the woman next door and somehow her husband found out and ever since then he does everything he can just to annoy me'.

I nearly spat my beer out when he said that, and, once again, I wondered whether he was kidding me, but once again, I suspected he wasn't.

'You shagged the woman next door and now you find it strange that her husband's giving you a hard time?' I asked incredulously.

'I guess when you put it like that it does sound a bit odd' he said, smiling now. 'but I just wish that he'd either come right out with it and square up to me, or put it to bed and pretend it never happened. He should stop pussy footing around and be a man instead of blocking my car in at every opportunity or throwing rubbish on my drive when I'm not there.'

Any other time I would have spent the entire afternoon quizzing him about the neighbour he'd shagged and joking about it; but of course, I was more interested in hearing what his meeting with Griselda had been about.

'Jesus Christ, Skip. You do make like to make life difficult for yourself sometimes. What about the Guscoms then?'

In an instant, the smile fell away from his face as he became serious once more.

'Ah yes. The Guscoms. Your favourite subject I believe Owen' If he saw the brief look of shock pass over my face he chose not to comment on it.

'The delightful Griselda and her crew have kidnapped, beaten, or tortured just about every other local villain she can think of in her efforts to find out who smashed Les' skull in. If her victims were all as evil as her I wouldn't mind too much but some of them are just kids. Kids who thought they'd have a go at being all gangster by peddling a bit of dope, but suddenly find themselves trussed up in the back of a van and threatened with having body parts cut off. In fact, to my knowledge, at least two of them have had a finger cut off and god alone knows how many others have been beaten senseless or worse. I suppose in some ways it could be a good thing; it might deter a few of the wannabes from pursuing a life of crime, but sadly, for the most part, it just strengthens her reputation and her hold over local crime.'

'And still no evidence to arrest her?' I asked.

'No, she's a crafty old bastard and for the most part, she leaves others to do her dirty work. That coupled with the fact that everyone else is too terrified of her to talk to us makes it next to impossible.'

'But surely you could offer them some kind of police protection?' I countered.

Skip glanced over his shoulder again to make sure that we weren't being overheard before leaning in.

'Listen Owen, there's more than one bent copper on the force and more than one in Griselda's pocket. You didn't hear it from me but the chances are that if someone *did* start to talk to the cops, they'd either disappear or have a swift change of heart before any kind of protection was even considered, let alone offered. I hadn't realised it until recently, but the Guscom empire has managed to expand quite a lot in the last few years and Griselda's involved with some very serious players indeed. Hence the Serious and Organised Crime Agency's interest.'

'So how come you were questioning Griselda then?' I asked 'I thought you told me that you weren't allowed to investigate and that it was down to SOCA now?'

'That wasn't me interrogating Griselda, Owen. That was Griselda quizzing me. She's running out of people to hurt and is starting to think that we coppers know more than we're letting on, so she's trying to squeeze information from anywhere else she can think of.

'And I'll tell you this for nothing Owen' he said looking at me more earnestly than I'd ever seen him look before, 'whoever it was that fucked up Les Guscom needs to go back and do the same to Griselda. SOCA has more information than they're letting on at the moment but it's only a matter of time before it gets passed down to Griselda.'

It felt like a warning at the time, like Skip somehow knew that I was the one who had tried to kill Les and that he was now urging me to do the same to Griselda; but I realised that it was just the paranoia talking.

Up until then, for the most part I'd worried about being caught by the police, and only slightly concerned about Griselda finding out, working on the assumption that the police had the resources whilst Griselda only had the ability to threaten and hurt people. And the people she'd threaten would have no idea who I was, let alone what my involvement had been. But now I began to realise that perhaps I had underestimated her influence. Certainly, it sounded as though Skip was concerned by it. Even more worrying was the fact that he thought that SOCA would soon be able to identify Les' attacker...

I still had my doubts whether Skip was correct on that score as I'd been over the events of that night time and time again. Every time I assured myself that I'd left no fingerprints and that all that any surveillance cameras could possibly show was a man in a motorcycle helmet and a car that had never been associated with me and which was now a burnt out shell.

But the seeds of doubt had been planted some weeks before and all Skip had really done that day was to ramp up my own anxiety.

I tried to kid myself that I wasn't bothered and that, *que sera sera*, whatever would be, would be, but deep down I knew that I was kidding myself.

I left the pub that afternoon more sober than I'd intended and yet still unable to recall who'd won the game of rugby. Despite the fact that I'd started out enjoying it so much.

As I walked out of the doors and zipped up my jacket against the cold, I couldn't help but look around me to check that there was no-one waiting for me or watching. The walk home was twenty minutes. Despite the fact that it was still a Sunday afternoon and broad daylight, I felt as though something sinister was waiting for me around each corner. I knew it was ridiculous, I knew that it was all in my head, but even so, I stopped twice to pretend I was tying a shoelace, just to check that no-one was following me. I must have been watching too much television that week.

CHAPTER FORTY

The next couple of weeks were not good times.

The events of the past were catching up with me fast and I once again found myself waking up each night bathed in sweat and screaming in terror or horror as a gruesome variety of nightmares came back to haunt me. Every one of them based on the murder of Campsite Terry, or my attempted murder of Les.

Was it PTSD? I'll never know for sure because the one thing I definitely wasn't going to do was to submit myself to a shrink and so I suffered in silence, as I had to by necessity.

The lack of decent sleep soon began to take its toll on my overall wellbeing and served only to fuel my feelings of paranoia and persecution. If it hadn't have been for the fact that I was terrified of being caught by the police, or by Griselda unawares, I would have immersed myself right back into the bottom of a bottle. And if I hadn't had a job which forced me to leave the house and travel the county, I might well have become something of a recluse.

In a pathetic replay of my childhood fear of the Thomas brothers, I found myself starting to check the road outside from gaps in the curtains before each time I left the house. At times I imagined that I could see someone waiting and watching, but then they would leave their van or their car and walk into someone's house.

Driving became an exercise during which I became more intent on watching the road behind me than the road in front. Occasionally, if I thought a car had been behind me for too long I would take an unintended turning into a shopping precinct or a carpark, just to see if they followed. My whole life became a modern day parody of Shakespeare's Macbeth, where the lead character slowly but surely descends into a pit of insanity, haunted by the ghosts of his past.

Two weeks after my last meeting with Skip things finally came to a head as I knew they must.

My super vigilance had finally given me the result which I had been looking for. The results might not have been correct but sometimes that doesn't matter. If you spend enough time looking for something that isn't there, the chances are that you'll find something else that fits.

For the last week, I had been convinced that a silver saloon car, not unlike the unregistered Ford Focus I had bought, was following me from a distance, with sometimes one, and sometimes two, burly looking individuals inside it.

Added to the sinister threat of the car following me was the presence of a heavily tattooed man at the end of my road first thing in the morning for the last four days in a row. He didn't seem to be doing anything other than sitting in his van and smoking each day when I left the house.

But finally knowing that I was correct in my suspicions that I was being watched didn't really do anything to resolve my situation. Eventually, I came to the realisation that there was nothing else for it but to man up and confront the situation head on.

I had been woken up in the early hours of that morning by a particularly nasty nightmare which involved being sodomised by Les Guscom whilst Campsite Terry stood before me with half of his brains dribbling out of a hole in his head. And if that wasn't enough it also had Terry trying to hold a nail against my own forehead so that he could smash it into my skull with the paint splashed hammer he held in his other hand.

I'm not sure if it was my cries of anguish or the thrashing of my head from side to side which finally saved me from the nightmare but whatever it was, I was mighty relieved to escape its clutches.

Sleep is supposed to be restorative, a chance for the body and mind to take a rest and rejuvenate, but for me that week, it was more like one long workout after another, without the pleasure of any accompanying endorphin release.

The lack of sleep and the physical exhaustion served to put me in a particularly foul mood that day, so my decision to have it out with the tattooed idiot watching my house became somewhat inevitable. I was spoiling for a fight and I aimed to sort things out once and for all.

If it was the police keeping tabs on me. I could confront them and try to force them into showing their hand. I imagined a sheepish look of embarrassment on the van driver's face as I asked him what the fuck he was doing. At least if I knew what it was that made them suspect me, I might have a chance of burying any evidence or throwing them off my trail.

And if it was Griselda's goons, well, better to chance my luck against one of them in broad daylight than to wait for them to come at me whilst I lay asleep in bed. The mood I was in that day, it wouldn't have mattered if there had been two of them; I was still more than ready to get stuck in.

I left my house under a deep blue sky which was in complete contrast to my mood, and looked over to see the same van parked in the same spot with the same driver sitting in it; staring. The van was a good seventy yards away, and although I couldn't make out the driver's features from that distance, I was sure that it was the same guy as the previous mornings.

I strode purposely over, half expecting him to see me coming and to turn the key in the ignition and drive off. But he just sat there and appeared to be staring straight ahead as though he hadn't even seen me, although the tinted glasses he wore prevented me from seeing his eyes.

I was ten paces away from him and still, he hadn't looked directly at me. As if by ignoring me he might hope that I wouldn't notice him and leave him alone. Like when you're a kid and you think that by not looking at someone or something it's going to keep you from harm.

This pathetic little bit of play-acting served only to enrage me further and I stepped up to the passenger side and yanked open the door before yelling 'WHAT THE FUCK ARE YOU LOOKING AT THEN?'

I probably should have stopped for a moment and taken a look inside before I did so, because if I had then I would have seen the headphones in his ears and the tablet propped up on his dashboard playing an episode of Game of Thrones.

But I didn't and I did, which must have given the poor sod the shock of his life and certainly, it was enough to make him spill the cup of tea from the thermos he'd been holding into his lap. He jumped back into the driver's side door trying in vain to put some distance between himself and the maniac who had just 'crept up on him and given him the shock of his life.

There's an industrial estate near my house that employs a lot of shift workers and as the spot he was parked up in was alongside a row of fencing, probably he'd chosen it as a spot to get away from wherever it was he was working and to have a tea break, or maybe he was waiting for someone else to show up so that they could both leave in one vehicle. Whatever it was that he was up to, it clearly wasn't spying on me and as soon as I realised it I instantly went from red spitting rage to meek contrition.

I must have said sorry a dozen times without being able to offer any kind of real explanation as to why I'd invaded the peace of his morning tea but his English seemed to be poor and so I'm not convinced that if I'd concocted any reasonable excuse that he would have understood me anyway. In the end, he just seemed happy to see me leave and sure enough, as soon as I did start walking back to my house I heard him start the engine and drive away.

I went back indoors and made myself a cup of tea to try and collect my thoughts before setting out again.

One of the benefits of being a sales rep for APS was that I usually had control of my own diary and although I had arranged to meet a number of different customers that day, I hadn't specified timings so there was no particular urgency as to what time I set out. If I had paperwork to catch up on, I could always do it from home that evening and it was ten o'clock before I set out again, having done my best to get my head back in the game over a cup of tea and a bacon sandwich.

I probably shouldn't have bothered though as I went through the familiar cycle of deep embarrassment and possibly shame, which slowly but surely turned itself into a feeling of being angry with myself, and then inevitably, into pointing my anger and resentment at the outside world in general.

****

Two hours later and I was arriving in Maldon feeling even more irate that I had when I left the house. The reason for my intense irritation was that I had become more certain than ever that I was being followed once again by the silver saloon, which had sat about four cars behind me for the previous half an hour.

It was hanging too far back for me to make out the occupants in any detail, but by continuously checking the rearview mirror, I could see that there were at least two people sitting up front, and from the look of them, burly looking characters.

In truth, I only had fleeting glimpses of their silhouettes through the windscreen as we moved along, but in my mind's eye I built up a conviction that they were two black guys. Something to do with the hair. The glimpsed silhouettes suggested two broad-shouldered guys sporting full sets of Rastafarian dreadlocks.

I'd first clocked them about five cars behind as we left the Army and Navy roundabout in Chelmsford, and although I wasn't immediately concerned, I resolved to keep an eye on them; just in case.

At first, as we left Chelmsford on the A114 where the short stretch of dual carriageway lends itself to overtaking, they dropped back and as I pulled off half a mile later onto the A414, I lost sight of them altogether.

But the A414 is a long stretch of road which winds itself from Chelmsford, through Danbury and into Maldon, with very little in the way of an opportunity to overtake and within five minutes I realised that I hadn't lost them at all. They still there, maintaining station, four or five cars back.

In vain I waited for them to take a turning to the left or to the right into one of the smaller villages on either side of the route. With each additional minute, I my stress levels rose.

Finally, we hit the roundabout which signalled the outskirts of Maldon and instead of turning left towards the main town centre, which was my actual destination, I deliberately turned right towards the promenade and sports centre where there was much less housing and relatively little traffic.

The majority of cars behind me did what I'd expected them to do which was to take the turning left and I told myself that I had been fretting over nothing and that the detour I had taken was a waste of time and petrol. But then as I watched behind me in the rear-view mirror I saw the silver saloon slowly come round the round-about and turn right, a hundred yards behind me.

They obviously had no remit to catch up with me as they appeared to be driving at the regulation thirty miles per hour on a stretch of road where any normal person would immediately be doing forty or more.

In the school holidays or on the weekends there would have been more traffic heading to the promenade but on that windy Wednesday morning there were no pedestrians and no other cars in front or behind, so it seemed that we had that quarter-mile stretch of the road all to ourselves.

I made up my mind in an instant, although the simmering anger I had nurtured for the last fifteen minutes left me little other choice. I dropped my speed down to a crawl and waited for them to catch up before pulling suddenly across the road so that they had to either stop or make a dramatic U-turn.

I fired up my rage to maximum, knowing that I would need all the help I could get against two opponents and as they pulled to a gentle halt twenty yards back I threw open my car door and burst out onto the road, sprinting as fast as I could towards their car.

I've suffered a few embarrassing moments in my time but there are very few which compare to what happened next. It's fair to say that all rational thought had fled by that time, and as sad and as shameful as it is to admit, I even ran towards them with one hand behind me, tucked into my belt as though I had a gun tucked back there which I was about to draw.

I definitely watch too much TV. I look back now and realise how pathetic I was, but at the time I was convinced that I was going up against two six-foot Rastafarians who may or may not have been armed.

On the plus side, at least I didn't go as far as I had done earlier that morning and yank their door open before realising my mistake.

Credit to them and their faith though, the two nuns sitting in the front of that car simply smiled up serenely at me when I uttered my apology and mumbled something about mistaken identity.

The benefit of hindsight is a wonderful thing of course and when I think back to that morning, I realise that my own burgeoning paranoia would have had me seeing threats wherever I looked, regardless. The fact is that probably every tenth car on the road that morning was a silver saloon of one description or another, and the outlines cast by two nuns in full habits, whilst being far from being an everyday sight, should not have been enough to set off the alarm bells in any normal and sane person's mind.

I may not believe in any kind of god, but the sight of those two Sisters of Mercy that day was enough to bring me crashing back down into the real world and realise what a delusional and neurotic wreck I had become. My cure was instantaneous.

CHAPTER FORTY-ONE

The following morning I left the gym after a heart-thumpingly strenuous session of circuit training and walked out into the blustery autumn morning, cherry red in the face from my exertions.

It was Thursday and I had taken the end of the week off of work simply to use up some of my holiday entitlement. I hadn't had an actual going away holiday in years, and rarely did I use anything like the five weeks entitlement I had. To be honest, I never felt the need for one, although I'd certainly swung the lead enough after David's death to have evened the score up as far as work was concerned.

The circuit training on its own would have been enough to put my middle-aged bones through a vigorous stress test, but I had woken up that morning feeling inexplicably full of vim and decided to run to the gym and lift some weights before the class had even started.

Although I'd already exercised as much as I might do on any other day, I still felt fresh enough to do the class when it began. But halfway through, I realised that I'd seriously overrated my fitness and as the strength and wind drained from my body, so did any semblance of enjoyment.

But I managed to struggle through to the bitter end, although I felt my stumbling efforts draw some arrogant glances from a few of the mummies who obviously still considered themselves 'yummy' until finally the hour-long class reached its conclusion, slowly and painfully, amidst the steady whump of loud disco music.

The majority of people doing those daytime classes tended to be female and whilst many of the ladies might chat and have a coffee together afterwards, I've always found the gym to be a fairly anti-social environment for us menfolk, and I showered and changed in my own little bubble, swapping only a weary nod of the head with the receptionists on my way out.

I still felt good, of course, as I always do at the end of vigorous exercise, but I also felt spent and the small daysack containing my sweat-stained gym kit was already starting to feel like a burden as I exited the main doors.

In the weeks running up to that day, as my paranoia ran on at full tilt, I had been much more heedful of my surroundings, imagining secret policemen and hidden cameras at every turn. What had begun as a vague suspicion soon became an obsession until I reached the point where I couldn't leave the house or exit a building without taking a good, long and hard look at my surroundings first.

I realise now, of course, that my paranoia had been misplaced in part. There were no secret policemen and there were no hidden cameras; and just as well really, because if there had have been, there would have been nothing more likely to confirm any suspicions that something was amiss than the way I had acted during that time.

My outrageous reactions to the van driver and the nuns of the previous day had made me realise that even if I was being watched, I wasn't about to do anything that would incriminate me anyway. If the police were watching me, they couldn't have had anything on me beyond their basic suspicion. And if they didn't have enough to arrest me then, they certainly wouldn't have gained anything from watching me go about my mundane days of work and weekends.

Perhaps it was that realisation which added a spring to my step when I'd left my house that morning, inspiring me to run to the gym instead of driving and to train so much harder than usual.

But the earlier spring to my step had definitely gone by the time I left, and maybe it was my exhaustion, or maybe it was the gusting wind in my face that kept my head down that morning, taking little notice of my surroundings. As I hunched into the stiff breeze, my only thoughts were of getting home and finding something to eat.

Whatever the reason, be it carelessness, tiredness or walking into the wind, it prevented me from registering the man in the blue van with a sliding door looking my way and talking urgently into a mobile phone.

I guess the fact that I can recollect it now means that I must have noticed it in a peripheral or subliminal manner, but at the time it didn't register in any way that mattered.

The van, which had been parked across from the short private road on which the gym was sited, started its engine and pulled slowly away from the kerb and as I reached the end of the road, the sound of the side door sliding open was what finally caused me to look up and take note of what was happening.

Everything happened at speed then as a bald-headed muscle mountain suddenly appeared in front of me, having previously been stood around the corner, just out of my line of sight. As I looked up at him barrelling towards me, I realised straight away that something wasn't right, but a second or two of confusion halted me dead in my tracks and robbed me of any chance to react. I suddenly knew, beyond any doubt, that something very unpleasant was going on.

I found myself enveloped in a bear hug as another pair of heavily tattooed arms wrapped themselves about me from behind and lifted me off of my feet. Only then did my survival instincts finally begin to kick in.

The time for flight had well and truly passed and the only true option remaining was to fight, but as I swung my head backwards in an effort to connect with the head of the tattooed guy behind me, the baldy headed guy swung a twenty stone punch into my stomach and I collapsed like a sack of shit into decorated arms.

I felt like a drowning man. A tidal wave of panic consumed me as I was bundled towards the inside of the van and I started to struggle once more; albeit feebly as I struggled to catch my breath. But my efforts were worthless and I was literally thrown into the back by the bald guy with his tattooed accomplish clambering in on top and punching me hard in the face before muttering something unintelligible.

The door immediately slammed shut and the engine roared into life as the van jerked forwards and I struggled with everything I had to try and shift Tattoos from atop me and make an escape.

The van lurched noisily forwards and around a corner with Tattoos still on his knees, straddling my chest and aiming punches at my face in a bid to stop me from struggling. Desperately I thrashed my head from side to side, causing most of his blows to miss, and I did my best to ignore the ones which didn't.

In the midst of our frantic scuffle, I managed to free my left arm and wrap it around his right which was holding a fistful of my jacket as he tried to pin my shoulder. Sensing that I was trying to gain an advantage somehow, he sat up on my chest and began to pull away.

If he'd ever done any kind of wrestling or grappling type of martial art, he would have known that it was precisely the wrong kind of thing to do in that situation, but fortunately for me, it seemed that he hadn't.

As he pulled away from me, his right arm straightened and he inadvertently trapped his hand under my armpit. With my left wrapped around his upper arm I linked up with my right and yanked him into a vicious arm lock.

I watched the agony flare across his face and he cried out in pain as tendons tore in the joint of his elbow. He did his best to lean over me again and close the gap in to relieve the pressure, but I now that I had my lock on I wasn't going to give it up easily and I hauled away for all I was worth.

The benefit of hindsight is a wonderful thing and if I'd had the time to think it through, I probably would have been better off letting him go at that point. If I had, the chances are that he would have rolled away from me just to nurse his torn and injured joint and I would have had at least a chance to make good my escape.

But I didn't have time to think, and I didn't let him go, and he couldn't roll away.

Robbed of the opportunity of flight himself, he too had no option left but to fight and he punched me hard again in the face, maybe two or three times, but knowing that I was literally fighting for my life, there was no way I was about to relinquish the arm-lock and I thrashed my head from side to side once more in an effort to dodge the blows.

Over the loud rumbling complaints of the van's engine, I heard the sound of other voices shouting, as well as heavy objects sliding around in the back as the noisy van lurched back and forth whilst we struggled on.

It was a moment or two before I realised that he'd stopped punching at my head and was scrabbling about on the floor with his left hand. I swung my head to the right and looked on in horror, as in choreographed slow motion, a claw hammer slid across the floor of the van and into his groping hand.

It was a terrible moment of déjà vu coupled with an almost unbelievable incidence of ironic justice as I recognised the splash of white paint on the shaft which identified it as the very same hammer which I had used to attack Les all those months before. There was nothing I could do, other than look away, as he swept it up from the floor of the van and in one continuous movement swung it hard at my head.

I lost consciousness then. I'm not sure how long for, maybe seconds and maybe minutes, but I was definitely out and when I came to the van was still moving with Tattoos still astride my chest, only now he was zipping my wrists together with a cable tie, rather than punching me. I became aware of the other voices once more and it seemed that Tattoos was talking to Baldy in another language. I don't speak any other languages other than a little schoolboy French, but it sounded to me like something Eastern European and it was much later before I found out that they were indeed from Russia.

But although I could hear their voices, even if had understood the language, I don't think I could have understood them then as everything sounded as my head was submerged in the bath; dull and echoing.

There was another noise cutting through and punctuating their guttural exchange, a shrill, piercing noise which was vaguely familiar. It was a noise I'd heard before, but it took me time before I realised that it was actually someone's voice. It was a rather unpleasant surprise to realise that it was the less than harmonious tones of the less than delightful Griselda Guscom; and true to form she was shrieking away at the top of her voice.

Without being able to see her my mind conjured up the mental image of her as my drooling childhood pet, Zed, sporting a shock of curly hair and I was struck with the certain knowledge that this would be an image to haunt my future nightmares. That is; if there actually was a future ahead of me.

'You fucking Russian idiot' she screamed, 'If he's fucking dead, he's no fucking use to us is he!'

'His not dead. His eyes are open' said Tattoos in a thick Russian accent, gesturing down towards my face.

It came as a bit of a shock for me to realise that he was right and that my eyes were, in fact, open. It was a peculiar sensation and not a pleasant one either. It was as if I existed in a kind of waking dream, able to hear what was said, albeit in a rather strange and echoing fashion, and able to see what was in front of my eyes, but only as a hazy image.

With a growing dread, I realised that I was completely incapable of any movement, or reflex, with any part of my body which, as I came to understand, was stopping me from even adjusting the focus of my vision. For a moment I wondered if this was what death felt like, before deciding that the vicious blow to my head must have caused me to suffer from some kind of temporary 'locked in syndrome'.

'I can see his fucking eyes are open, you fucking moron' Griselda screeched in her strange mongrel accent, 'but he doesn't look like he's going to be answering any of our fucking questions any fucking time soon does it!'

A moment of panic hit me as I became suddenly aware of the fact that I couldn't breathe. My tongue had fallen back in my mouth and blocked my airway. I managed to choke a little, so it became apparent that I must have been capable of some movement, albeit a totally involuntary one.

Tattoos must have realised it at the same time and he rolled me over roughly onto my front allowing me to breathe once more. If I'd had any doubts at all as to what a bad state I was in then, they vanished instantly as Tattoos cut away the cable tie he'd used to bind my wrists only minutes before. He obviously didn't think that there was any chance of me being a threat once more.

We continued our bumpy journey for what felt like an eternity, with me drooling onto the grubby floor and Tattoos constantly checking on me as he continued to argue with Griselda and Baldy the whole journey.

My head felt as though it was splitting in two, with my brain trying to force a passage through the gap, which I guess would only seem normal after being walloped with a hammer. But added to this screaming agony, came a fresh, and in its own way far more uncomfortable feeling.

At first, I thought that when I'd been rolled over onto the hard floor by Tattoos, he must have lain me on a hard object which was forcing itself into my right eye. It was as though someone had jammed his thumb into the socket and was constantly working it over; and a thumb with a particularly long nail at that.

But through the fog of my stupefied thoughts, I slowly realised that although it was my right eye that hurt so much, it was the left side of my face which was in contact with the floor. I wasn't sure what caused it, but as Tattoos kept checking on my status, I became dimly aware that he too must have seen something amiss.

Both eyeballs also seemed to be locked into position, so that although I could see that which lay before me well enough, any form of peripheral vision was completely lost. Every once in a while, Tattoos' face would appear in front of mine as he continuously checked and checked again to make sure that I was still alive, and he seemed particularly attentive to my right eye.

The grumbling van continued to jostle its way onwards with the constant background noise of foreign accents bickering away. stopping every so often as we stopped at junctions.

I may have lain there immobile and completely unresponsive, but every bump and every jolt served to pile on fresh and unique feelings of pain to some part or other of my body.

CHAPTER FORTY-TWO

I lost all track of time on that journey, but finally we came to a halt and as everyone piled out, the sliding door was opened and the wooden door of a dilapidated stone and brick built house swam into my vision.

The flaking door had no window to it but a spyhole was set into the centre. The blistered and cracked paintwork was an ancient yellow but the three keyholes set into it looked much newer and suggested more recent use.

As they pulled me up, ready to heave me out of the van, Griselda grabbed my chin and her ugly bulldog face swam into view in front of me so that I had no option but to watch as her eyes roamed over my face.

'He don't look too fucking good, does he?' she shrieked, and once more I heard her berating her thugs about how they had better not have killed me otherwise, how were they going to find out what they wanted to know?

Two of them held me up and dragged me over the threshold, the toes of my trainers scraping and scuffing the floor for the entire journey. My drooping head aimed my eyes at the bare and dusty floorboards passing beneath me until we arrived at another flaking door which they opened inwards. Beyond that ominous door was a short wooden landing, ending in some creaking stairs leading down into a gloomy cellar.

A solitary bulb hung from the ceiling and it shed its light on an uncared for and drab looking space. From my vantage point at the top of the stairs, I saw that the cellar was a decent size and had a table and two chairs in its centre. A filthy mattress was pushed up against the far wall and there were other unidentified items of detritus scattered around. Worryingly, in addition to the mattress, I could see what looked to be an iron ring set into the wall and a handful of cable ties scattered over the table and floor, some of which looked to have been previously used and cut open.

On one of the chairs sat an ominous looking pair of pliers and a ball-pein hammer, both looking stained with something which my overactive imagination immediately decided was dried blood. I arrived at the uncomfortable conclusion that I wouldn't be leaving the cellar any time soon.

I was hoisted over a broad shoulder, amidst grunts and muttered curses, into a fireman's lift and carried down into that pit of despair like the dead weight that I was. They dumped me heavily on the table and prodded me about, not bothering to restrain me in any way. It was obvious to them that I wasn't going anywhere.

Strangely at that point, I started to feel a little more lucid, although still incapable of any independent movement. Whilst I was still unable to move my eyeballs, I managed to focus them and regain a little peripheral vision. Noises and voices lost the dull echoing timbre they'd had earlier and I was able to hear and discern most of what was said. What caused my marginal improvement in faculties, I couldn't say, but I suspect that it had something to do with the back of my head hitting the table hard when I was dumped without ceremony onto its stained and pitted surface.

'You think he's going to die?' It was the bald guy slapping my face and looking for a reaction.

'Shit! I hope not. Griselda gonna go mad if he don't talk' said Tattoos.

They were speaking in English to each other but their accents were thick with Eastern European vowels.

'Maybe Doctor will know what to do. After all, he know how to treat stabs and shoots'

'I hope so. Who you think he work for anyway? He don't look like Greek'

'He don't look like anyone' replied Baldy, peering in at my face once more, 'He look like fucking accountant to me'.

I could hear Tattoos snort with laughter at this, but he was out of my line of sight by then. A strange mixture of emotions weaved their web about me then. I was terrified that this would be the end for me and that I had slipped into some kind of comatose state from which I would never recover. They had mentioned a 'Doctor', but I really didn't expect that, whoever this turned out to be, he would be a doctor in the sense of someone you went to when you had the measles.

Like most people, I guess, I had wondered at times when and how death would take me; hoping to go out in some kind of heroic blaze of glory but suspecting that an alcoholic heart attack was more likely. What I hadn't considered was that I would slip silently away, without a chance of any last words or actions, in a grubby cellar, god knows where, and with my body disposed of in a way that no-one would ever find it.

It struck me then that not only would no-one care, but also barely anyone would even notice if I exited this world that day. It was an uncomfortable truth and I decided not to dwell on it for fear of giving up there and then.

But as scared as I was of not recovering from my head injury, I also knew that it was the only reason I wasn't being worked over with the hammer and pliers at that time. The minute I was able to respond to their questions, there was no doubt in my mind that fresh horrors would be rained down upon me.

Griselda and her shitheads had been turning the town upside down in a bid to find out who it was that had tried to kill Les, and they had obviously come to the conclusion that it was me. What it was that had given me away or how they found out, I had no idea; but clearly they had, and with no obvious motive to my actions they had reached the conclusion that I must have been a part of, or hired by, some rival gang and naturally enough they now wanted to know who it was that had put me up to it. They must have been as keen to find this out as they were to exact their sadistic revenge, but my catatonic state was robbing them of either opportunity.

Perhaps ten minutes passed, perhaps thirty. I lay on the hard table in my own little world of misery, the pain in my head and in my eye intensifying slowly so that it blocked out all other thoughts.

A vehicle pulled up outside and I heard the wheels crunch to a halt on gravel, doors opening and shutting and the murmur of voices. A tiny flame of hope sparked within me with the realisation that there could be virtually no sound proofing there, and I decided that if I did finally manage to regain the power of speech, I would scream for help as loudly as I possibly could.

But that was a big 'if'.

I heard the outer door to the building open and shut, and slow footsteps on the wooden floor above. Tattoos and Baldy stood up and moved towards the stairs as I heard the door above us opened and a fresh voice calling out, 'One of yous come and keep an eye out of the front will you? We don't want any unwelcome visitors'

This voice was Scottish and nasal, Glaswegian I think, and without being able to see its owner, I imagined it belonging to someone resembling a weasel and I immediately added his nickname to those of Baldy and Tattoos.

It was Baldy who went up the stairs, his heavy weight making them creak with every step. 'Hello Les, hello Doc. You think you can fix him?'

'How the fuck should I know? I haven't even looked at him yet! Go on, wait out front and make sure we're not disturbed'.

I thought I'd heard him wrong when I heard Baldy say 'Hello Les', but the creak of the stairs told me that there were definitely two people coming down and if I could have panicked then, I would have.

And then I heard Griselda. Maybe it was her that had gone to collect the Doc, aka, Weasel, and Les, but she certainly hadn't been down in the cellar earlier. Now I heard her barking out nonsensical orders and insults once more as she followed them down the stairs.

'Take a look Les' she shrieked, 'is that the fucker what attacked you?' She grabbed a handful of my hair and turned my head so that I was treated to the horrific sight of Les Guscom looking down at me and grinning from ear to ear.

My heart sank as I realised that he was nodding vigorously, but just as quickly I realised that his expression and head movements were the results of the severe brain damage he'd suffered rather than those of affirmation. It was the first time I'd seen him since I'd driven that nail into his forehead in the hallway of his own home, and I was shocked by his appearance.

The point where the nail had been driven home was pretty much healed up with just a small patch of red skin to mark its entry, but his hair was cut short and a network of scars crisscrossed the side of his head where the hospital had patched up his battered skull from my frenzied attack. His injuries must have also caused him to lose a couple of stone and the fact that he had been all lean and corded muscle beforehand meant that he now looked gaunt and malnourished.

'For fuck's sake' said Griselda, clearly exasperated, 'I might as well talk to meself!'

I had my first sight of the Weasel then as he bent down to look into my eyes. The face matched his voice with its sharp nose and chin and a pair of squinty eyes looked out from behind wire-rimmed spectacles. There was something about him that seemed familiar and it was a moment or two before I realised what it was.

He reminded me of David, my dead son. Not that they looked alike in their facial features or the colour of their hair; more it was the way that the Weasel held himself, slightly hunched, and that they both shared the same, slightly haunted look, which inhabits the eyes of heroin addicts. And when he pulled his lips back in concentration, I was treated to the sight of a crooked row of teeth that were brown with rot and decay and were no doubt the cause of his truly awful bad breath, which was foul enough to be weaponised.

The Weasel took my chin in his hand and turned my head this way and that, clicking his fingers in front of my eyes as he looked for some kind of reaction.

'Jesus. He's no exactly a pretty boy, is he? What'd you fucking hit him with, a hammer!?'

'Yes' said Tattoos, completely deadpan.

A pause as the Weasel realised that he was being serious and then with another 'Jeez', he went back to his examination of my scalp.

'Well? Can you get him to talk?' Griselda was not a patient woman.

'He needs a hospital'

'I know he fucking needs a hospital, I'm not a fucking idiot!' she exclaimed, 'But he's not going to go to the hospital is he? I don't care if he dies. I just need him to tell me who hired him'.

'I've seen this before' said Weasel. 'Back in Bosnia. One of our guys got hit by a lump of rock in an explosion and it caused a compression'.

'You mean a concussion, don't you?' she interrupted.

'No. I mean a compression. It's an internal bleed on the brain. It's what kills boxers. The bleeding has nowhere to leak out of the skull and compresses the brain until finally, you die. See his eye here; how it's sticking out of his head like it's about to burst?'

He turned my head to face Griselda and waved a finger uncomfortably close to my eyeball.

'That's the fluid in his skull looking to find a way out. Looks like it's been coming out of his ears too.'

'So what you gonna do?' Griselda was nothing if not persistent.

The Weasel was silent for a moment as if considering. 'In Bosnia, we took him to a makeshift medical tent and they drilled a hole in his head'

'They did what?' she was shrieking again.

'I think they call it trepanning, or something. They drilled a hole in the side of his head and all of the shit and fluid came squirting out'.

'Did it work?'

'I don't know. I saw them do it and he was alive when they finished but then I had to go so I don't know how well he recovered afterwards. He wasn't in my company, I think he was para's or something..'

More silence as everyone contemplated what was being suggested. Not least of all me.

'Do it' she said.

'I can't promise it's gonnae work' said the Doc turning to her, obviously getting in his caveat nice and early.

'If he's going to die anyway, we may as well give it a go. What do you need?'

They sat Les in one of the wooden chairs to the side of me, still grinning and nodding idiotically and sent Tattoos off to fetch the necessary tools for the Doc to perform my brain surgery, Heath Robinson style. Ten minutes later and they were all set.

Understandably, perhaps, they were all a little excited by what was about to happen and they chatted and quipped as I heard them moving about me. For my own part, I was actually starting to look forward to it also. I'd reconciled myself to the fact that I wasn't going to be admitted to any kind of medical facility and the prospect of further paralysis followed by a slow and painful death was not one to be relished. Even if I managed some form of recovery and the alternative was being beaten or tortured to death, it at least offered a *possibility* of escape or reprieve, and therefore some glimmer of hope.

The pain in my head by then had reached epic proportions, and my eye felt as though it was about to pop itself out and roll across the table. In fact, if it had have done so, I probably would have been grateful for the drop in pressure.

I was laid in the recovery position and Weasel shaved a patch of hair from the side of my head, just behind my right temple using a dry safety razor. They had discussed restraining me, but being as unresponsive as I was, they had decided that there was little need for anything other than Tattoos to hold my head as the Weasel performed the makeshift operation.

Les remained sitting on his wooden chair, grinning and nodding. Griselda hovered about, clearly relishing the thought of seeing someone have a hole drilled into his skull while Baldy lurked at the top of the stairs, not wanting to be left out.

I saw a modelling knife being lifted from the table in front of me and I felt a prick to my scalp and the wetness of blood as he cut into it. I'd heard the Weasel talk about sterilising the blade and the drill bit earlier, but he had been slapped down by Griselda who had pointed out that it really didn't matter whether or not I wound up with an infection, as I was unlikely to live long enough for it to set in.

He'd also asked for a hand drill for safety's sake but was told that there wasn't one to be had and that an electric one would have to do. He would just have to make sure he didn't slip. I watched the bloodied modelling knife put back down on the table before me and felt a squirt of water wash over my head. The drill was picked up and I heard it whine into action above me as Griselda moved closer to get a better view of the proceedings.

Even though I was unable to move and unable to take in my surroundings other than that which lay straight ahead of me, I could feel the tension in the air and the nervous excitement which had been building amongst the gruesome spectators.

The drill must have had some kind of gearing or speed setting and I heard it slow to a steady drone as Weasel tested it. A moment later I felt a pressure as he settled an elbow onto my neck in an effort to steady his aim. Tattoos was still cupping his hands around my head, front and back, but without making any real difference to the proceedings.

'Oh my fucking God!' I heard him mutter and I felt the drill bit finally bite into my cranium.

It was the strangest of feelings. To say that it was uncomfortable would be to understate it, but there was no real pain to it either. A little like going to the dentist and having a tooth drilled. So long as the dentist has done his job and anaesthetised your mouth properly, all you really feel is the grinding vibrations. Deeply unpleasant, but most of the actual pain is a figment of your imagination.

I had imagined that my skull would have taken a bit of effort to go through, imagined it to be like drilling through a piece of hard oak, with wisps of smoke curling and rising as the pressure was applied. But the reality was that he was drilling into soft living bone and it must be a lot softer than I had imagined as it took only a second or two to complete its task.

The effects were both immediate and colourful as I watched a spray of watery blood bespatter Griselda's face and chest as she leapt back in a futile effort to avoid the fallout. It must have been like popping a massive boil and as the contents erupted outwards in spectacular fashion, all around me I heard a collective swearing and cursing as people belatedly tried to jump back and avoid it.

The effect on my own physical being was no less immediate or dramatic and the feeling of the debilitating and lethal pressure vanishing was sheer ecstasy.

It may have been my imagination, of course, but I swear that I actually felt my right eyeball sinking back into my skull, settling back into the socket where it belonged. A blaring background noise which I hadn't even realised was there previously, departed and it seemed as though my hearing was suddenly sharper than it had ever been before.

I tried to lift my hand up to feel the back of my head, but despite the relief from the easing of my mental and physical pain, I still couldn't move my body. Couldn't even bat an eyelid, let alone lift a finger. Fresh waves of panic and despair washed over me then as I once again contemplated a life of living in a vegetative state, to be wheeled around by carers who wouldn't care. The deadly irony of the fact that I was unlikely to be leaving that cellar in anything other than a piece of rolled up carpet or a rubbish sack was completely lost on me at that time.

But the truth is, that the fact that I still couldn't move was the factor which probably saved my life.

After they had all finished jumping up and down, swearing and trying to wipe brain fluids from their faces, they each gathered around to peer at my head and face, commenting on the mess and the fact that my eyeball had retracted into a normal position.

'Well? Can he talk now?' demanded Griselda.

'How the fuck should I know?' replied Weasel in his Scottish whine. 'Can you talk?' he asked me stupidly, leering into at my face.

They all seemed to hold their breath and stare at me for a few seconds as if miraculously I was going to be able to sit up, request a cup of tea and start having a civilised chat with them, but of course, I was still completely and utterly locked in.

Finally, Griselda lost her patience. 'Give him a slap will you. Let's see if that makes a difference.'

Tattoos was only too happy to oblige and I watched in paralysed fear as he stepped around and pointed a meaty fist at my face.

'No! Don't be stupid!' said Weasel, stepping between us and pushing Tattoos out of the way. 'If I remember rightly, he's in this state because some idiot hit him round the head with a hammer. I don't think that hitting him round the head again is likely to make thing better somehow. Do you?'

'How do we know he's not faking it' demanded Griselda.

'Look' And I watched in horror as the Weasel picked up the pair of pliers and then felt him clamp them onto an inch of meat on the fleshy part under my arm before vigorously tugging and pulling at it.

Indescribable agony flared through every inch of my body as time seemed to stand on its head and what passed as seconds, felt like an entire night of misery to me. I literally felt as though my brain somersaulted as it tried to reel away from the agony inflicted.

I couldn't believe that such a simple act could have such a devastating effect. Thankfully, I have no idea how painful waterboarding or having your fingernails pulled is, but the pain caused by that those pliers on my arm was beyond anything I could have imagined. If I could have moved or spoken at that time, I would have been blubbering like a baby and telling them anything they wanted to hear.

But I couldn't. I still couldn't move a muscle and to their eyes, it must have seemed as though I was impervious to the agony they caused.

'Let's give him an hour' suggested Weasel. 'It could be that this is the best he's gonnae get, or it might just be that it's gonnae take time for him to recover. You saw how much shit had built up and came squirting out once we put a hole in his head. Releasing that pressure has to have made some difference, right?'

Griselda paused to consider before looking at her watch and issuing her verdict. 'OK, we'll give it an hour. But if there's no difference, we'll have to get rid of him'

They left me there in my own mess, my bladder having emptied itself some time previously. Nobody had bothered to clean up in any way, presumably in anticipation of creating even more mess, either when I came to or when they decided to 'dispose' of me.

Griselda, Baldy and Tattoos left the cellar to potter around upstairs, doing God only knew what. I was left alone with the Weasel, Les, and a broken body which felt as though it belonged to someone else. Or at least it would have done had it not been for the constant firing of traumatised pain receptors.

As the time ticked slowly away, my brain adjusted to the realisation that my body was incapable of doing a single thing to help itself. The pain gradually dulled into the background of my thoughts and I started to take stock of my surroundings.

Les still sat in one corner, dressed in jeans and a polo shirt, which looked too big for him now, and still wearing the stupid white, plastic, wristwatch. He was flicking through a children's comic, now and then nodding at the pictures, while the Weasel sat in the other chair, playing with his smartphone and occasionally looking up at me. Presumably to make sure that I didn't miraculously spring to life before him.

Apart from the dull thuds of people moving about upstairs and the low murmur of their voices, the silence was complete. Although I'd heard the vehicle pull up earlier, there had been no sound of any other vehicles or traffic and I slowly formed the opinion that we must have been somewhere remote.

It hadn't been a commercial building which they'd dragged me into and I guessed at an old farmhouse of some description. Somewhere far enough away from prying eyes and prying ears that they could strap a body to a chair and torture it to their hearts' content without fear of interruption.

As a silence settled around me I heard an unseen clock slowly ticking away the seconds. The side of my head was still wet and although there was obviously not enough bleeding to warrant any concern from the Weasel, every now and then I could feel small rivulets of fluid creeping about my scalp as I continued to slowly leak. It was hot down there too, and as the clock ticked away the countdown to my ending, the icy terror which still gripped me slowly gave way to heated panic.

CHAPTER FORTY-THREE

A bead of sweat slowly grew fat upon my temple until finally it reached critical mass and started a slow and stop-start journey, running past my eye and onto my nose until it finally dripped off the end.

The tickling sensation it caused as it rolled slowly in and out of my field of vision was a form of torture in itself and it soon became all consuming. Frustratingly, as soon as the first droplet left my nose, I felt a replacement forming, but this time setting off on its journey all the quicker for having had its path already wetted by the first.

I decided that enough was enough and quickly wiped away at my nose with a grubby finger. It was bad enough knowing that I would be put out with rubbish as soon as the hour was up and there was no way I was going to spend my final moments being driven crazy by a bead of sweat.

The Weasel looked up.

Something was wrong, but for the life of me, I couldn't work out what. Had he heard something? Was the hour up?

Despite the subsidence of the headache from hell and the settling down of my many other agonies, I was still not thinking all that clearly, until finally, as he got to his feet and stuffed his phone in his pocket, it dawned upon me.

I had moved my hand!

I had moved my hand a good six inches and used it to wipe the sweat from my nose. It was only then, as the realisation reached the slow-moving cogs of my brain, that I realised that I was also able to move my eyeballs and look around the room and had been able to for a while.

If the drilling and the release of pressure from my brain had been as a weight lifted from my shoulders, this new revelation was like having electrical jump leads attached as my foggy thoughts suddenly gave way to sharply focused thinking.

I realised that the Weasel must have only seen my movement in his peripheral vision and he wandered towards me slowly and tentatively, perhaps unsure whether he had actually seen me move.

After a rapid mental assessment of my body state, I knew intuitively that whilst I may have been able to wipe my nose, I could no more sit up than I could run a marathon at that point and that whilst things might be improving fast, the one thing I needed to buy was more time. I lay there inert and gazed at a patch of the table in front of me with deliberately unfocused eyes.

'Wakey wakey, Sunshine' he said, peering into my face and shaking me gently by the shoulder. A fresh droplet of sweat and gore chose that same moment to leave the sanctuary of my scalp and dribbled its way across my face, giving weight to the impression that I was still totally unable to respond. He lifted my right hand and let it drop lifelessly onto the table before sighing heavily and turning back to his chair, pulling out his mobile phone on the way. I could have cried with relief that he hadn't decided to give me another going over with the pliers.

Slowly but surely, I felt my recovery gaining momentum as patches of pins and needles flared up and down my body. But I also knew that I needed to lay as inert as possible for as long as possible and it became something of a challenge to ignore the aches and pains that wracked my body. I had no real way of knowing how long had passed since Griselda and Co had left us down there, but I imagined it to be around twenty minutes.

A small glimmer of hope flickered into being as I considered that, if my guesstimate of time was correct and my rate of recovery increased, there was at least a *possibility* of being able to influence my fate.

With one eye constantly on the Weasel, who was thankfully engrossed by whatever he was doing on his phone, I slowly and carefully tensed each muscle and relaxed it again, seeing what responded and what didn't. I dared not make any actual movements, no matter how small, for fear of alerting the Weasel to my rapidly improving condition.

I started at my head, rolling my eyes before wiggling my ears and then clenching my jaw. I tried to test each muscle methodically, moving from the top of each arm down and through my hands to my fingers, before going back up to my chest, and then my shoulder blades and down to my stomach. I clenched and unclenched every muscle I could without risking any obvious movement until finally, I arrived down at my toes at which point I started from the top of my body once more and repeated the process.

The Weasel looked up a couple of times, which scared the pants off of me, but he obviously didn't see anything which concerned him enough to move off of his chair. Time continued to tick by and I began to think that more than an hour must have passed, but hell, there was no way I was going to complain. I finally reached the point where I thought that I'd have enough strength to stand and maybe to walk, but I was likewise sure that I was still in no fit state to try and fight my way free. I had, after all, had a hole drilled in my head and for all I knew, the moment I sat or stood up, I could easily pass out again. My best, and probably my only hope, I decided, was if the Weasel abandoned his vigil, perhaps to go to the toilet or something, at which point I would at least have an opportunity to test my balance and maybe even to make a run for it.

Les was still sat in the corner leafing backwards and forwards through his comic and grinning inanely, occasionally making small grunts of satisfaction and I felt confident that he posed no threat to me. It seemed as though he would happily carry on sitting there and grinning like the idiot he was, no matter what I did.

Tick, tick, tick, tick.

As the clock marked time and the Weasel stayed rooted to his seat, my panic began to build again as the time ran out. Despite the rapid retreat of my earlier paralysis, I was still pretty sure that I would struggle to fight my way out of a paper bag and if the other three came down the stairs, I would be well and truly fucked; of that, I had no doubt.

My best hope remained in being left alone. If that didn't happen, my next best shot would be to try and take on the Weasel while he was still on his own but going toe to toe with anyone at that time still didn't feel like a realistic prospect for success either. Time was running out and I needed to make a decision before it was too late, but without being able to see the clock, I had no idea how much remained on my side.

And then the door opened, and I knew that I'd blown it.

'How's he doing Doc?' shrieked the all too familiar mongrel tones of Griselda as she stomped down the wooden stairs.

Weasel jumped up and hurried over to me, no doubt trying to create an impression that he had been keeping a much closer vigil than he had done in reality.

'Still alive, but still fucked!' was the depth of his professional diagnosis as he picked up my deliberately limp hand and wiggled it in her direction.

'Hmmmm' she murmured, stepping closer. 'Give him another go with the pliers to see if it makes any difference; if not, we'll have to get rid of him'

I don't know how I managed to not shit myself there and then, or to jump up crying at the mention of the pliers, but blind fear held me paralysed for vital seconds.

'Car coming up the drive' It was Baldy calling down the stairs to Griselda.

'Who is it?'

A moment's pause followed and then, 'looks like the copper's car. Skippy, or whatever the fuck his name is'

A moment's contemplation followed by the mongrel shriek. 'What the fuck does he want?'

'How the fuck should I know?... But it's definitely him'

It seemed as though the word '*fuck*' had the same effect amongst them as watching someone yawn. Once one started, they all had to have a go.

'Tell him to fuck off' yelled the Doc.

'Yeah. Fuck his mother' added Tattoos helpfully, who I was beginning to realise was about as much of an intellectual as Les.

'Shut your fucking faces' yelled Griselda over the top of them, taking charge once more. 'Close the door to the cellar and when he knocks, don't let him in but tell him that you're here alone, but about to leave. There's no one else here as far as he's concerned, Right?'

'OK' said Baldy, and he reached for the door handle.

'But find out what the fuck he wants first' she shrieked before he had a chance to pull the door to, 'find out why he's here'.

Baldy pulled the door closed just as I heard the faint sound of car tyres pulling up in the gravel outside. Moments later I heard the faint thud of a car door followed by three sharp knocks on the front door.

Down in the cellar, nobody moved an inch and we must have looked like a still from a film, a tableau frozen in time, with the only movement being the rise and fall of our chests and a faint rocking motion coming from Les. From the corner of my eye, I saw Griselda looking over at Les, no doubt trying to assess whether or not she could trust him not to make a noise. It struck me then that none of them seemed to contemplate the least possibility that I might be able to call for help and that they must have still been utterly convinced that I remained in a catatonic state.

Weasel stepped silently around the table and put his sweaty palm over my mouth. Huh! Not so 'utterly convinced' after all it seemed.

Upstairs we heard the front door open, followed by the dull murmur of voices, the words and their speakers indistinguishable. Silence again for a long moment, followed by what sounded like a chair being pulled across floorboards and a short exchange of words. Tattoos remained at the bottom of the stairs and I sensed him exchanging looks with Griselda and

Weasel as they tried to work out what was going on above.

Suddenly there was a louder thud followed by a muted 'FUCK' and the sounds of an obvious scuffle going on.

'Go' said Griselda to Tattoos who promptly turned and started to take the wooden stairs two at a time.

'You too Doc', and he finally took his grubby hand away from my face and hurried after Tattoos.

I had no idea what was going on upstairs or whether it had anything to do with me, but I was pretty sure that it was bad news for Griselda and her crew. Which meant good news for me. If only I could just play dead a little longer until an opportunity presented itself to get the hell out of there.

But whilst Griselda might not have been the sharpest of tools in the box, she was possessed of a decisive nature, coupled with animal cunning and an instinct for survival. Satisfied that her three henchmen would be able to deal with whatever the hell it was that was happening upstairs, she once again turned her attention towards me. Having swept up the ball-pein hammer in her right hand, she once again picked up my limp left hand and leaned in close before saying, 'say goodnight little man'.

This time I was under no illusions about what her intentions were and my eyes sprung wide in fright. Her next move would be to bring the hammer down hard upon my head; as hard as she possibly could. And whilst I didn't know how hard she could hit, there was clearly no doubt in her mind that she could do so hard enough to kill me. Judging by the flecks of dried blood on both the pliers and the hammer, I was also inclined to think that I wouldn't have been her first victim. Nor her last if she had her own way.

Adrenaline can be a powerful, but also a strange drug. For some people, a surge of adrenaline is more than their poor minds can cope with and it leaves them literally paralysed with fear. I once read that fainting is an evolutionary throwback to mankind's days as hunter-gatherers, when playing dead could be an effective defence against predators. In modern day America, they call it playing possum and if you look on the internet for videos of possums doing so, you can see just how well it works.

But for most people, a sudden surge of adrenaline activates the 'fight or flight' reflex, which is exactly what happened to me. In that fraction of a moment, I knew that the time for playing possum had well and truly ended. And since I was downstairs, laying on a grubby table after having had a hole drilled into my skull, and there was not only Griselda but also three of her trained apes in between me and freedom, the option of flight was not much of a possibility either.

Which left me with fight.

I'm sure that at that point, Griselda still had no idea that I had regained any of my faculties, and whilst it all happened in less than a heartbeat I still remember the confusion registering on her face as she saw my own expression change from one of terror, to one of blind fury in an equally brief fragment of time.

Snarling with rage I snapped my previously limp wrist from her grasp and threw it behind her neck to pull her in close so that I could clamp my teeth around the fleshy bulldog cheek before me. I still felt the weakness in my body and my grip on the back of her neck, but when you have someone's face clamped between your teeth and you're doing your best to tear a chunk free, they're less than inclined to help by pulling themselves away from you.

As weak as I was throughout the rest of my body, the sudden surge of adrenaline leant strength to my bite and as I tasted the foul metallic tang of her blood entering my mouth, it served only to fuel my crazed bloodlust.

I don't know what she was doing with her hands. Don't know what she was doing with the hammer. For all I know she may have been whacking me good and proper with it, but as the beserker in me took over, I felt nothing other than the need and the desire to rip her apart in any way I could.

I felt her cheek begin to tear away from her face and the warm and fetid air of her piercing scream passing over me as it exited from the hole I had torn in her face. She had pulled me up into a seated position by then and I switched my grip from the back of her neck so that I gripped her head with both of my hands and started to push her away from me as I continued to tear away at her face.

In a sudden movement, a large chunk of her cheek came free and I spat the flesh remaining in my mouth back into her eyes, before hauling her back in and clamping my teeth around her nose, the gristle of the bridge being the only thing stopping me from ripping it free immediately.

I was vaguely aware of her arms flailing about me, whether or not they still held the hammer I couldn't say, and the sound of fighting elsewhere in the cellar. But controlled aggression is a wonderful thing and the switch had been well and truly turned on. Bloodthirsty rage coursed through me, leaving little room to acknowledge anything else.

By then I was standing and I managed to wrap my left leg around Griselda's right and as I snarled and snapped at her nose, which was beginning to break free, I slowly shifted the balance of our body weights until eventually, she fell backwards with my face still clamped firmly onto hers.

She hit the back of her head heavily on the floor, which meant that I lost my bite-hold and jarred my teeth, but it also knocked the wind from her sails, leaving her temporarily dazed. The hammer was still held loosely in her right hand and I snatched it up into my own fist before bringing it down as hard as I could into the side of her head.

But my left hand has always been my weaker side and the blow wasn't delivered with the force I had hoped for. I switched the hammer to my right fist and, blinded by bloodlust and caught up in the sheer ecstasy of violence unleashed, I smashed it down once more, feeling the satisfying crunch of breaking bone beneath.

I guess, with hindsight, that I must have looked very much like Les had done that fateful night when he made such a mess of Campsite Terry's skull. Only worse. I could feel Griselda's blood and snot dripping from my chin and I licked my lips with pleasure as I brought the hammer down again. And again. And again.

It probably didn't last long at all, but whilst I was caught up in the sheer joy of my savage revenge and a thirst for blood, time became meaningless. What felt like an hour may only have been seconds.

Finally, in my weakened state, I wore myself out and stopped, taking in an aware of the rest of my surroundings. Of the splintered wood and the broken body of the Weasel laying lifeless on the floor, who had somehow crashed down from the wooden landing above. His neck twisted to an impossible angle so that he seemed to be looking behind him with the agility of an owl.

Baldy lay at the base of the stairs, trying and failing to raise himself into a seated position as he cradled a broken arm to his chest, the whiteness of the bone jutting clearly against the vivid red of his blood, pumping steadily from the wound in a manner suggesting that he would not be long for this world. Not unless he managed to stem the flow soon. His agonised features a dripping mask of red from another deep wound etched into his brow.

Scattered about the floor were pieces of broken furniture which had not existed before and which could only have come from the room upstairs.

My poor, damaged brain struggled to make sense of the images my eyes were sending it. As I looked in the corner, I saw Les still sitting there and nodding mutely, with a puzzled expression on his face. It seemed that he was just as confused as I was by what had happened.

I wondered briefly whether it was all a part of some horrid dream. If maybe I'd already died, and this was some bizarre hallucination, created by a dying brain in the moments before it finally gave up.

The sound of strange mutterings and panting breaths perforated the fog of my mind and I looked around, not seeing where they came from at first.

And then, as I leaned forward, I saw that they came from the other side of the table where Tattoos was keeping himself busy by murdering Skip Parsons. They both had their backs to me, with Skip sat on the floor and Tattoos kneeling behind him with his colourful arm wrapped around Skip's neck as he slowly but surely choked the life from him.

I watched as Skip flapped his hand about weakly before finally succumbing as his brain was starved of oxygen. And all the while Tattoos seemed to be murmuring sweet nothings into his ear in a foreign language, gently rocking him; as though he were putting a baby to sleep. By that time I'd had my fill of blood and violence and the near orgasmic thrill that I'd experienced only moments before, gave way to nauseating horror at the scene before me.

But really I had no choice. No choice but to pick up that cursed hammer once more and put it to bloody work once last time.

Tattoos was still throttling and crooning and from where I stood Skip looked to be dead already, but I was under no illusions that my turn would be next; particularly after what I had done to his boss. With the hammer still dripping with gore I stumbled quietly towards him, aiming to take him out with one huge blow and end my nightmare once and for all.

I don't think he heard me, but even I noticed the shadow moving across the wall as I hefted the hammer high above my head before starting its downwards arc. In the split second before impact, he turned his head to look up at me and that was probably what saved his life.

As exhausted as I was though, my strength and equilibrium were returning fast and I put everything I had into that blow, which missed the area I was aiming at, but nevertheless crashed into his skull at the edge of his eye-socket throwing him to one side like a rag doll.

I knew how much agony my own injury had been, but his must have been something else altogether. His whole face changed shape as a part of his skull collapsed and his eye had burst open. But he was a natural born brawler and he knew as well as I did, that this was a fight where second place was not an option.

He spun away across the floor, trying to put space between us, and came to his feet in a crouch, keeping the ruined right-hand side of his face away from me, at the same time holding his right hand up as if to comfort it, but not daring to actually touch, knowing the added pain it must cause.

By then, I was dripping with blood and fluids, both my own and that of others, and as a consequence I managed to lose my grip on the hammer as it slid wetly from my grasp during the attack. But I still needed to end this quickly and I stepped in fast aiming to hit his damaged eye with a closed fist. I managed to make contact with his head with my right, but he dodged the left cross I threw at him and countered with two solid punches which sent me spinning backwards.

Troublingly, I realised that he was still in a much better physical state than I was and that despite the obvious damage it had caused, my blow to his face had barely affected him. For my own part, by that time I'd stopped feeling any real pain, just an awareness of the damage he inflicted on me. I wouldn't mind betting that he was in the same state of mind.

He stepped purposely towards me, no doubt aiming to finish me off in one final flurry, but I spun heavily on my left foot and drove the sole of my right hard into the side of his knee, feeling with satisfaction something give way beneath the impact. If he'd been impervious to pain before, he certainly felt that knock and he screamed with pain as his knee gave way beneath him. I made to punch his kneeling form but his reactions were something else, and using both hands, he gripped the backs of my knees and toppled me backwards; transitioning quickly so that he knelt astride me.

Like a bad movie stuck in its own cliché, we took up the same roles as we had earlier that day in the van, and he took a grip on my shirt with his left hand in whilst raising his right fist ready to start pounding.

And once again I wrapped my arm around the outside of his outstretched left in order to lock out the elbow, but he was nothing if not a fast learner and this time, instead of trying to pull away, he leant into me heavily to keep the arm bent and at the same time smashed me across the face with his right elbow and forearm. Three times he smashed me in the face like that and I felt the bones and cartilage moving beneath my skin as I fought to retain consciousness.

He paused for a second to free his entangled left arm from my limp and ineffectual arm-lock before taking my head between his hands and lifting it slightly off of the floor. He waited for my eyes to find focus before smiling back down at me and leaning in to say 'Goodbye little man', which must have been the team motto as they had been exactly the same words which Griselda had uttered to me only minutes before.

He waited another moment for his words to sink in and register; waited until he was sure that I'd realised that this was finally the end, before getting to his feet and raising a huge booted foot, ready to stamp down on my head. I closed my eyes and turned my head to one side, resigning myself to fate, and waited for the boot to fall.

A second later I opened them again, unsure why I wasn't yet dead and curious as to where the scuffling and grunting noises I could now hear were coming from.

And there, like some glorious cross between Columbo and Dirty Harry, was Skip Parsons, hanging off of the back of Tattoos' neck and choking him out with a broken chair leg, whilst Tattoos repeatedly slammed himself backwards into the far wall in an attempt to dislodge him.

I sat up groggily in amongst the scattered debris and the splattered gore, watching mutely as Tattoos' efforts to damage or dislodge Skip gradually subsided into limp and ineffectual flailing, whilst Skip clung on for grim death; all the while spitting obscenities and curses into his ear.

Once again I lost track of time and I watched with detachment as Tattoos' legs finally gave way beneath him and, unable to support his weight, Skip lowered him to the floor, winding up with his own back to the wall and with Tattoos sat in his lap whilst he continued to haul away on the chair leg. As if waking from a dream, my eyes and my brain slowly found focus again until eventually I realised that Tattoos was well and truly past the point of any kind of return, his tongue beginning to loll from one side of his mouth.

'It's done Skip' I stated quietly, 'He's gone'.

But Skip seemed to have passed into a world of his own too and it was obvious that I hadn't been heard.

'Skip' I said a little louder, 'SKIP! He's dead mate. You can let him go'.

I watched Skip slowly return to lucidity and, as my words sank in, he took a measure of the lifeless form in his lap before finally relinquishing his grip on the chair leg and pushing the corpse away from him. He staggered slowly to his feet and limped his way over to me.

'Jesus Christ Owen! You look like something out of a horror movie' he stated in a matter of fact tone.

It was true, I knew. The side of my head felt wet, and I really didn't know whether or not I was still leaking fluids from the hole drilled in my head. I could still taste Griselda's blood in my mouth and as I looked down I saw a morsel of flesh stuck to my thigh which I must have been a part of her face. My clothes looked as though they'd been washed in an abattoir, and looking down at the mess I was in, was not helping to make me feel any better.

In fact, I really had no idea at that time what the extent of my head injury was and whether I would live or die. Truth be told, I was so exhausted then that I really didn't care.

Skip cast his eyes about the room and I followed his gaze to where Baldy lay, the life having bled out of him in those last few minutes, with the broken bone of his arm still jutting out at an impossible angle. To the other side, Griselda was a mangled mess of mauled meat. Barely recognisable as a dead person, let alone identifiable as the ugly face that had spent her life inflicting so much misery on others.

But somehow worse than all of this was the unharmed personage of Les Guscom, still sat in the corner gently rocking himself backwards and forwards, but now with a look of pure terror etched onto his face. He had sat through the entire bloody battle without moving. Probably without even comprehending what had happened. I wondered whether he even knew that Griselda had been his Mother.

'We can't leave him, Owen'

I looked up again and saw Skip still standing there, only now he had his chair leg back in his grip.

'I know' I sighed, 'I'll do it'.

No matter how brain damaged and retarded Les might have been, there was no way we could risk the possibility of him recovering to the point where he might conceivably be able to identify us.

I staggered to my feet and stepped towards him casting about one last time for the discarded hammer. Les looked up at me like a whipped dog and started to jibber, at the same time, backing his chair away from me in terror, one hand outstretched as if to shoo me away. He may have been a shadow of his former brutish self, but he was still a big guy and I decided that there was no way I wanted to risk having a head to head confrontation with him, particularly in my current condition.

Making soothing noises, which must have seemed ridiculous bearing in mind that his mother's blood was literally dripping from me, I placed the hammer back on the floor and carefully picked up the discarded comic and placed it back into his hands, leaving bloody fingerprints in my wake. Like a grateful child, he took the comic from me and I continued to offer words and noises of comfort until finally he settled down again and became engrossed in the pictures before him.

A thick finger traced the pages and he began to chuckle quietly to himself as a broad and idiotic smile spread across his face. The transformation was slow but remarkable. The man I had known as the brutal killer of Campsite Terry had initially been turned into a walking vegetable by my own hand. Moments earlier he had been a shaking and terrified wreck of a human being and yet now he sat there cooing and chuckling to himself with all the innocence of a one-year-old, totally absorbed in the children's comic before him and oblivious to the carnage that he had seen only minutes beforehand.

'I can't do it Skip' I said forlornly. 'I'm sorry mate but I just can't do it'.

It was one thing to be able to kill a man, or a woman for that matter, in the heat of a pitched battle, but killing Les then would have been like killing a helpless child and I just didn't have that level of ruthlessness in me. After a moment's pause, I looked over my shoulder and saw Skip looking at Les with the same sad expression on his face as that which must have been spread across mine.

'I know what you mean Owen. I don't think I can either' another pause followed before he dropped the chair leg to the floor again and turned away saying 'I guess we'll just have to trust to the hope that he won't ever be able to finger us to the cops'.

And looking at Les then, it was hard to believe that he could ever make a recovery sufficient to form a coherent sentence, let alone prove a viable witness.

CHAPTER FORTY-FOUR

We made our way upstairs to the ground floor in silence, stepping over the outstretched legs of Baldy on the way. Looking out of grimy downstairs windows, I was finally able to see that we were in a small farmhouse at the end of a long dirt track, leading across flat fields left fallow and untended. Apart from an open wooden barn off to one side, there were no other buildings in sight and it struck me just how fortunate I had been for Skip to track me down to this remote location.

The farmhouse itself looked to be just on the right side of derelict, as if someone had bought it as a shell and done just enough to make it weatherproof and secure, without wasting any money on cosmetics. Raggedy curtains hung limply next to paint peeled wooden window frames, which suffered in silence behind cheap secondary glazing. The light switches were of a yellowed plastic which probably pre-dated the last World War and a filthy rug with no discernible pattern covered the centre of an otherwise bare and scuffed wooden floor. Ancient furniture clung to walls wearing patches of damp and peeling wallpaper. It seemed that the only thing new or modern in that entire room were the three new locks which studded the front door.

There were two doorways leading out of the room, one of which was open. Beyond it lay an ancient kitchen worktop with a butler sink and an electric kettle and microwave oven rested on a yellow Formica table.

The other doorway was closed shut.

At the other side of the room an open stairway led up to the first floor and after a brief discussion, Skip decided that he would take a look around upstairs whilst I checked downstairs, making sure that there was nothing left lying around which could link either of us to Griselda Guscom and her crew. I was too weary for much in the way of independent thought and at the time I didn't think to question why there would be anything relating to us in the house, and so I turned mutely on the spot and headed straight for the closed door.

The room on the other side was not what I had expected to find. Whilst it was undoubtedly tacky and somewhat shabby, it had obviously had a little time and effort spent on it in order to bring it into the current century. Plastered walls had been painted Magnolia and a plain and cheap fitted carpet covered the floor. In the centre of the room was a king sized double bed with purple bed-sheets and a leather effect headboard, To either side of it, there were bedside cabinets with lamps. and even a digital alarm clock.

But this wasn't a room for sleeping in, it seemed. Not if the three cameras set up on tripods were anything to go by. Arc lighting stood stacked in a corner and electrical cables trailed about the floor. On a table to one side sat a small laptop and a stack of recordable DVDs with permanent marker titles written on them.

I'm not sure what made me do it. Somehow, I knew what I was going to find on those DVDs if I watched them but still I couldn't stop myself. I reached over to switch the laptop on and popped the top DVD into the side before pressing play. I skipped the beginning and moved the cursor of the video bar to somewhere in the middle of the film and sure enough, it was set in the very same room as I was now sat in.

An overweight, balding man knelt naked on the purple bed-sheets, smiling broadly over his shoulder at the camera, stating proudly how much he was going to enjoy 'teaching the little bitch a lesson' as he thrust his 'manhood' back and forth into the rear end of the girl kneeling before him. The cries of pain and her dirty tear stained face were heart-breaking, and yet they seemed only to add to the enjoyment of the fat pervert riding her.

I didn't know who she was, and I didn't know where she had come from, but I did know that she wasn't there of her own volition. And I also knew that she looked to be about ten years old.

I felt my anger swell once more; but there was no useful target for me to vent it on. Part of me wanted the scene to be real, for the fat man to be there then so that I could smash his face in and cut his cock off and tell the poor girl that everything would be OK. That most people weren't like him.

But, of course, they weren't there. I had no way of punishing the man and I had no way of saving the girl. Shit, I still wasn't totally convinced that I had saved myself then.

I leant forward, hoping to turn it off before it became another image to haunt me for the rest of my life, but just as my finger found the off switch, a third party came into view and swept back the hair from the little girls face, presumably so that the cameras would be better placed to film her anguish.

When I say a third party, it wasn't the whole person; it wasn't even a face or the back of a head. It was just an arm. A right forearm. A thick, muscled, right forearm with a watch around the wrist. A white plastic wristwatch.

****

Les was still happily sitting in the corner, tracing lines on his comic with his finger when I went back down into the cellar. He looked up momentarily as I came down and smiled; a sweet, innocent smile of childhood, and then he went straight back to fingering the comic and making happy, but unintelligible noises to it.

I had brought the laptop with me, the sickening video still playing, only now with the sound muted. There's only so much you can stand.

I placed the laptop in his hands and he took it compliantly, still smiling, and immediately started tracing his finger around the screen with no discernible change to his actions or demeanour. I had expected him to become a little animated or excited but it was clear that the scene playing out in the video was about as interesting to him as the comic he'd held previously. None of which mattered to me.

I stepped behind him and in one seamless movement pulled his head back with my left hand whilst opening his throat with the kitchen knife I held in the other. A crimson jet of hot blood fountained outwards, instantly smothering the laptop and its awful display and it seemed that the weight of that gushing spray was enough to force it from Les' hands. I'd plunged the knife in as deep as I could and it must have cut straight through his windpipe as no sounds escaped him, beyond those of the wet slap of his blood hitting the laptop and floor.

He struggled weakly for a moment, on reflex trying to breathe in, but instead ending up with two lungs full of blood. After that I don't know how long it took for his brain to shut down completely, but the whole thing was over in seconds and as I let go my hold on his head, he pitched forward onto the floor, looking for all the world to be as dead as dead can be.

I stood and watched with morbid fascination as the sticky slick of blood bloomed about him on the floor until, with a start, I realised that someone else was standing at the top of the stairs. Looking up my eyes met those of Skip Parsons. I thought that he might be angry or at the very least disapproving, but on closer inspection, I realised that he was standing there with his policeman's telescopic truncheon, his '*asp*', fully extended. The look on his face told me that if I hadn't beaten him to it, Les would not have survived his next encounter with Skip, who had clearly been on his way down there to batter the life out of him.

Only much later did Skip tell me what it was that he had found upstairs and when he did, I was glad that I'd only seen the one video.

CHAPTER FORTY-FIVE

Five weeks later

Despite the biting cold, the sky was a beautiful crisp blue without a cloud in sight as I pulled into the car park of the Rose Café; the satisfying crunch of the car's wheels on the gravel surface replacing the strains of Dire Straits on the radio. I pulled in alongside Skip's filthy BMW wondering whether it was just the dirt that kept it from falling to pieces.

It had been a month since I last heard from Skip Parsons and I had no idea why he'd asked to meet me that morning. Not in any official capacity, I imagined. Not on a Sunday morning. Not in a café.

The last few weeks had been psychologically tough, seemingly in an inverse proportion to my physical wellbeing, but I had questions which needed answering and I was looking forward to having them answered. Whether they would be answered truthfully or not would remain to be seen.

We had left the farmhouse that fateful day as soon as we were sure that the flames had taken hold, confident in the knowledge that it would burn long and hard given the amount of heating oil we'd poured down into the cellar and splashed about everywhere else.

We'd also pulled the van they'd used to kidnap me alongside the building and, after removing my daypack carrying my sports kit, given that a good dousing with oil before setting it aflame.

A part of me hadn't wanted the evidence burned. I wanted the world to know how evil those people were and that their vicious endings had been fully warranted. That they had paid for their crimes in as brutal a fashion as had been possible. Karma on steroids. But Skip had insisted, and even if I had disagreed, which I didn't really, I wouldn't have had the energy to raise any meaningful protest.

In the end, after rinsing away the worst of the gore from my face and arms and changing into the relative cleanliness of the tracksuit bottoms and the T-shirt I'd worn in the gym, he sat me in the passenger seat of his BMW and took care of the 'tidying up' himself.

He didn't take long, not wanting to linger any longer than necessary, but as I sat dumbly in his grubby car with the wind buffeting it, the sight of gale force clouds scudding along the sky warped time itself and it felt as though half a day had passed before he gingerly eased himself back in beside me.

I watched in the rear-view mirror as the flames licked lazily about the van as we drove steadily away up that long and straight farm track. There was no explosion and no sudden rush of flames as there would have been if it had been petrol instead of the heating oil, just a steady growth of orange light and black smoke.

As I sat in his filthy old salon feeling sickened and sorry for myself, Skip did his best to coach me as to what I should expect in the coming days. We had never been to the farmhouse, he told me, no matter what anyone might ask or suggest at any future date. I had never met or spoken to Les Guscom, or Griselda for that matter, although I may have seen them in the pub.

Our cover story would be that Skip had picked me up from the side of the road, he knew a suitably quiet road which we would be detouring past on the way to Harlow Hospital, and that it had appeared to him as though I had been run over. He had cleaned me up as best he could, but it had been obvious that I needed urgent hospital attention.

My part of the story was simple. I had no idea what had happened to me or how I had arrived at the destination where Skip had 'found' me. My answer to the questions which any doctors or nurses might ask would be that I had no recollection of what happened, and given the state of my head, it would not be a difficult story to believe. My story was simple; all I remembered was walking out of the gym, and that the next thing I remembered was a vague image of Skip helping me into his car along the wooded country road. I was to state that I had no idea why I was at that location, nor what had happened. That it was as big a mystery to me as it was to them.

Being the policeman that had 'discovered' me, Skip was fairly confident that he would also be able to take over any investigation into what had happened and who my hit and run driver was, which would obviously then draw a blank.

This was all well and good up to a point, if Skip had taken into account that I was now walking around with a drill hole in my head. But he hadn't known; he'd arrived at the scene of carnage sometime after that nightmarish event, and therefore he couldn't have taken it into account. This did have the effect of necessitating a somewhat more thorough police enquiry, but Skip was still the lead detective and I still pleaded complete amnesia which effectively brought any fresh enquiries to a dead end.

I spent just over a week in Harlow Hospital whilst they ran every imaginable test and scan they could think of before they decided that I hadn't suffered any lasting or permanent damage to my brain or to my body. They told me that the hole in my skull was a small enough diameter to leave as it was. My own body would make its own repairs and it would have no lasting adverse effect.

Skip flitted in and out to keep up the pretence of trying to figure out what had happened and on one of those occasions he tried to give me an update on the farmhouse and the fire, but I cut him off straight away. I didn't want to think about it and I certainly didn't want to talk about it. The sooner I could blank out any vestiges of memory from that day the better.

In the end, my injuries were logged as a suspected hit and run Road Traffic Accident and it was imagined that some unknown person, or persons, had performed some crude emergency first aid at the side of the road, drilling the hole in my head to release the compression.

It was a wholly unconvincing and unsatisfying answer under the circumstances, but given that, as far as the police were concerned, I had no known criminal connections and more to the point no memory of events, it was one that would have to suffice.

I maintained the same story to Steve Bigham and APS and returned to work after taking two weeks out.

CHAPTER FORTY-SIX

My first week back at work was tough. The day I left hospital and returned home, I started having flashbacks. Flashbacks of being kidnapped off the street. Flashbacks of rolling about in the back of a moving van. Flashbacks of having a hole drilled through my skull. Flashbacks of chewing lumps out of Griselda's face and needless to say, flashbacks of plunging a kitchen knife through Les' throat.

For the most part, they came just before I fell asleep. They would come just as I was ready to nod off, jolting me back to being fully awake with an accompanying adrenalin spike that made it impossible to fall asleep again for the next hour or so. And then, when sleep finally did take me, as often as not it was cut short by a plethora of night-time horrors. Not one recurring nightmare but one long recurring sequence of nightmares. Every night the story was slightly different, but every night the cast was the same. Griselda, Les, and me.

Just as it had after I'd witnessed Campsite Terry's murder, the lack of proper sleep soon started to take its toll.

I'd been back at work for a week before Bigham expressed his concern that maybe I'd returned too early from my 'accident'. But the truth was, I simply didn't know what else to do with myself and I shambled on with my daily routine, trying to pretend that nothing was wrong. The bags under my eyes were only slightly smaller than the weight of mental baggage I carried beneath.

I started drinking heavily again, necking a half a bottle of spirits each night in a futile attempt to get a good night's sleep. I knew that it wasn't a good thing to do, that I was in danger of sliding down the same alcoholic slope I had descended previously after David had died, and it wasn't a journey I wanted to make again. But the lack of sleep was debilitating and I didn't have the willpower to stop myself from stepping off of the precipice once more.

Until two nights previously.

Skip had rung me on Friday and asked to meet, saying that there were things we needed to discuss. He'd suggested that Friday evening, but for some reason, I told him I was busy, that I couldn't make it; so we'd chosen Sunday morning, in the Rose Café.

The timing of his call was perfect. I'd just poured myself a large vodka and I took a long and hard look at it before pouring it down the kitchen sink, and the rest of the bottle too. So that was me on Sunday morning. I'd had two nights sober and curiously enough, I'd had two nights of undisturbed sleep. For the first time in the best part of a month, I was feeling rested and alert. Which was just as well because I had questions to ask.

I'd had plenty of time to reflect on the sequence of events that fateful Thursday morning and there were things which simply didn't make sense. Not without coming to some uncomfortable conclusions.

There were two burning questions which needed addressing and they were questions which only Skip could give me the answer to. The only trouble was, I had a nasty feeling that I wouldn't like the answers when I heard them. Whatever, I decided, I needed closure.

****

The Rose Café is a truck stop which sits on a busy, but isolated stretch of road, called Three-Mile Hill on the way South of Chelmsford. It's a single storey brick-built structure with a car park formed from broken tarmac and gravel, big enough to hold a couple of lorries and a dozen cars.

Inside, fixed plastic chairs border chipped Formica tables and aged, curling posters adorn walls badly in need of a lick of paint. None of which detracts from the fact that The Rose Café is Chelmsford's best kept culinary secret. It serves, to my mind at least, probably the best fried -breakfast in the world.

As soon as I entered the warmth of the café my mouth started watering.

Skip Parsons sat in the far corner of the café facing the window and he waved at me as I came in. I nodded back cordially and went straight to the counter where I ordered a mug of steaming tea and a full English breakfast with chips.

As I waited for them to pour my perfectly stewed tea I looked back at Skip gazing out of the window. Whereas I still looked like a victim of a long-term illness after my ordeal and subsequent pathetic attempt at recovery, Skip looked, to all intents and purposes, exactly the same as he ever did. The raincoat he wore must have been new, there had been so much gore on his old one that he'd burnt it in the farmhouse, and yet it still managed to look as though it was ten years old. It wouldn't surprise me if he'd slept in it and certainly, the mess of grey hair atop his head only added to that impression. He conjured up the same old image as he ever had. Like a shit version of Columbo.

And yet despite this shambolic exterior, Skip was the man who had single-handedly come to my rescue and saved me. He had taken on, and killed, three of Griselda's thugs without any qualms and had then gone on to destroy any evidence of our ever having been there

After paying a ridiculously low price, I carried my tea and cutlery over to Skip and sat opposite him, my back to the window.

Unusually for a Sunday morning, there were very few other customers in there, just a solitary figure in a baseball cap hunched over a newspaper in the far corner and a small gathering of what looked to me to be young female gypsies, with that unique blend of beauty and glamour, blended together with an edge of roughness which made you want to avoid crossing them.

Smiling, Skip opened his mouth to offer a greeting, but I held out my hand, palm facing out, to silence him before he could speak.

'Let's get straight to the point' I said, dropping a sugar cube into my tea as I spoke, 'I'm not sure why you've asked to meet me today...'

He opened his mouth to speak again but I silenced him once more with the same hand before he could say a word.

'I'm not sure why you've asked to meet today, but I know why I've come, and it's not just for the pleasure of seeing your ugly mug again.'

He smiled at that and it reminded me then, that whatever the outcome of our little chat, I couldn't help but enjoy his company.

'There are certain questions which need answering, and although I think I already know the answers, I need to hear them from you.'

I paused and glanced about the café, making sure that nobody was taking an interest in our conversation.

'I reckon I can guess what's on your mind Owen but go ahead; ask away' he said.

'How' I said.

'How what Owen?'

'How did they find me? And how did *you* find me?'

I'm sure that these were the questions that Skip had been expecting, but he sighed before answering as though bowing to the inevitable.

'You never met Griselda's husband, Teddy Guscom, did you?'

I shook my head and lifted the steaming mug of tea to my lips.

'Back when I was a copper in Barking, I used to drink in a pub called The Joker which was not far from where I lived at that time. There was nothing special about the pub. It had the usual mix of old timers and young lads and its fair share of bores and rogues; same as any other pub back then. But it was also where Teddy Guscom and his mates used to drink. They weren't villains or anything, at least they weren't as far as I knew, but they were usually a bit lairy and Teddy was always the noisiest out of the bunch. But let's face it, every pub had its fair share of rogues back then.'

It was true. Back in my youth, most of us lads took pride in getting into scrapes or trying to be as outlandish as possible before laughing about it later over a pint or ten. Maybe I'm a bit of a dinosaur, but it seems to me that, for the most part, the current generation are more interested in finding ways to take offence. Either that or concentrating on how their hair looks or what trainers they wear.

I made to interrupt Skip, meaning to ask him to hurry up and get to the point, but he cut me short and told me that the beginning of his story was just as important as its end. He had always considered himself to be something of a raconteur and it seemed that he wasn't going to be denied.

'Every now and then I joined Teddy's little gathering and I always found him good company. They all knew I was a copper of course, but I wasn't a complete arsehole about it, unlike a lot of my fellow officers back then, so I could usually mix in with non-coppers as well as the next bloke. Teddy dealt in second-hand cars and so it was pretty much guaranteed that he would have had some dodgy dealings, every other second-hand car dealer I met back then was involved in one scam or another, but as far as I knew he wasn't up to anything serious.

'Fast forwards to about twelve years ago when I first transferred to Essex Police and had just moved to Chelmsford. I'd lost track of Teddy a few years before and it wasn't until I started drinking in the pubs of Chelmsford that I discovered he'd moved out this way some years before. He also seemed to be doing fairly well for himself.

'I bumped into him in the old Marsham Arms one evening and said hello. I don't think he recognised me at first and seemed a bit suspicious, but as soon as I mentioned The Joker he remembered me straight away.'

'The Joker?' I asked.

'The Joker pub. Where I used to drink in Barking.'

He'd already mentioned it, of course, and I felt strangely embarrassed at not keeping up with the story.

'Teddy seemed to be doing alright for himself then. He was still trading cars and I found out through the grapevine that he also did a bit of money lending and finance here and there as a bit of a side-line. The interest rates would have been eye-watering but if you had no other way of borrowing, Teddy provided a good short-term fix.

'He was still a larger than life character then and a likeable one at that, but the same could not be said about his wife, Griselda. I never met her before when I was in Barking; in fact, I'm not even sure if she was on the scene back then; but the moment I did meet her, in Chelmsford, I just knew that there was something wrong about her.

'She was an ugly bitch even back then, and I'm not just talking about her face either. There was something about her that gave off a bad aura and without really knowing her you immediately sensed that she was a really nasty piece of work. But for some reason, Teddy worshipped her and it wasn't that unusual to see the two of them together in the pub, with Teddy getting pissed and holding court to a few hangers-on whilst Griselda lurked like a bad smell in the background.

'Unfortunately though, whilst Teddy's star seemed to be in the ascendancy, the same could not be said for yours truly. I was still in uniform back then and not on a great wage. At the same time, I was getting royally screwed over by the CSA for half my wages.'

The CSA was the Child Support Agency and had been notorious back in its day for bleeding errant fathers dry without any thought for how much money they left them to live on each month. It was a government department with more than its fair share of blood on its hands in its early days as it drove more than one pour soul to suicide. But the big news to me was that Skip must have had a child somewhere. It wasn't anything I'd ever heard him mention before and I made a mental note to ask him about it. But not just then; he had some other explaining to do first.

'When I first moved to Essex Police from the Met' I hadn't realised how much of a drop in wages I would be taking and it wasn't long before I started to get myself into a bit of bother. Do you remember Sanjay's shop; around the corner from my house?'

I shook my head, still not sure where his story was leading to.

'Sanjay had the shop on the corner, by Moulsham Lodge. It's a crappy Co-op now but back then it was a newsagent, come off-licence, come grocery store. You know the type of place; it sold literally anything and everything and more to the point, Sanjay used to give me credit.

'Sanjay was a smashing bloke with a good sense of humour and you could always have a bit of banter with him. And, if I found myself a bit short towards the end of the month, I could go in there and buy a packet of fags and Sanjay would just add it to my tab. Come payday, I'd go back in and clear it off again. But the real problem was that, what with my drop in wages, and the CSA, and the fags, and the booze, and a shit run of luck with the horses; I was living way beyond my means and it wasn't long before it got to the point where I wasn't clearing off my tab in full when I got paid. Until eventually, we got to the point when Sanjay put a halt on my line of credit. It was only a hundred and fifty quid or so, but it seemed like a mountain at the time. It should have been enough of a wake-up call for me to start tightening my belt and making some serious lifestyle choices, but it didn't.

'Before I knew it, I'd managed to borrow a hundred quid from Teddy Guscom. *And* I know what you're thinking Owen because, believe you me, I agree with you one hundred per cent, but it happened in the pub one night after a few too many drinks, as have most of my bad decisions in life, and I'm sorry to say that I wasn't quite as sensible back then as I am now.'

I wasn't quite sure whether Skip was joking or not with that last line, but he delivered it with a straight face and I chose to let it slide by without comment.

'Two or three days after that, one of the guys from work was having his retirement do in the Endeavour in Springfield. I was supposed to be on patrol but it was back in the days when you could get away with sneaking off duty for an hour or two for that sort of thing and so I called into the pub for a quick pint, just to be sociable.

'One thing led to another and inevitably it was six or seven pints later before I eventually climbed back into the car. I only had about a half hour to go before the end of my shift and I thought it best to take a quick drive around the outskirts of Chelmsford and back through the middle to make sure that there weren't any major incidents going down that I ought to have been aware of.

'Just my luck then that as I approached the Globe, I see a car pull slowly out of the car-park in front of me, wander over onto the wrong side of the road, and then correct itself by veering back and finally crashing headlong into a lamp-post; all at less than fifteen miles per hour. Thankfully it was late evening and there wasn't anyone else about, but needless to say, it was the sort of thing that I couldn't just sit back and ignore. Anyway, when I walk up to the driver's side and look through the window who should I see but Teddy Guscom, looking very much the worse for wear, and sitting next to him, Griselda, grinning up at me in some kind of pathetic attempt at charm. Apparently, they'd had a row and Teddy had insisted on driving, despite the fact that he was barely capable of speech; although Griselda seemed pretty sober at the time.

'Now the thing is, not only did I not particularly want to nick someone who I'd already compromised myself with by illegally borrowing money from them, but I also didn't relish the thought of having to do an hour's worth of paperwork at the end of a night when I myself was feeling more than a little pissed.

Somewhere along the line, something would definitely go wrong with that little scenario.

'But I also didn't want Griselda and Teddy to know that, so I started to give them a hard time and pulled out a notebook to pretend that I was writing it up. Anyway; Griselda starts pleading with me, saying that Teddy wouldn't normally drink and drive but they'd had a row and that no-one's been hurt; so, if I could just let them swap seats, she can drive them home and no-one else needs to know. And I pretend to consider it briefly before dismissing it; as I'm still playing hardball at this time and I want to make them squirm a bit.

'Next thing I know she tells me that they'll write off the hundred quid I owe them. Well, this came as a bit of a shock to me as Griselda hadn't even been there when I borrowed it and I hadn't realised that she'd know about it. But it was obviously more of a family business than I'd realised, and it seemed that Teddy had told her everything. She must have registered the shock on my face and taken it as a sign that I was considering her offer because the next thing she says is that I don't need to worry about paying Sanjay either coz they'll take care of that too.

'You could have knocked me down with a feather then. I was just as surprised to hear that, as I had been that she knew I'd borrowed the hundred, but I guess I must have been blabbing in the pub again when I was pissed.

'It was bad enough that I was starting to suffer from all the drink I'd had earlier that night, but by that time I was starting to feel a bit nauseated by Griselda's whining. So, I decided that enough was enough and I told her to shut up, switch seats with Teddy, and fuck off. I swear that I just meant for them to go. I never meant to accept her offer or to give the impression that I had, but with the benefit of hindsight, that's exactly how it must have seemed.'

Skip's story seemed to have taken something out of him and he sat there staring at his fingernails for a moment or two before continuing.

'I tried to pay Teddy back the hundred quid I'd borrowed a couple of days later, but he wouldn't have it and said that as far as he was concerned, a deal had been done and that he was sticking to it. We were in the pub at the time and it wasn't the sort of thing I wanted to discuss in front of others, so I left it at that, feeling pretty soiled by the whole sordid affair.

'But the worst was yet to come. The next day I went into Sanjay's shop intending to clear my slate but when I went in he just told me to fuck off and never to step foot in his shop again.

'It wasn't hard to guess why. His face was still swollen and blue and one arm was in a sling where Teddy or Griselda's boys must have worked him over. I tried to persuade him that it wasn't my fault and that he should testify against '*whoever*' it was that had beat him up, but he wouldn't speak to me. Didn't even want to look at me. I swear, I've done some dodgy things in my life Owen, but I never, ever, intended for things to work out the way they did. It's something I've had to live with on my conscious for a long time.'

There was another long pause then before he went on, 'not least because Griselda somehow managed to record some of what was said that night and has held it over my head ever since. That night you saw me talking to her in the Butlers Head, she was giving me an ultimatum. Either I gave her a name or she was going to spill the beans about what had happened that night. With Teddy dead and buried a few years back, she didn't really need to worry about incriminating herself because she could blame it all on him. And me, of course.'

Another long pause as Skip sipped at his cold tea.

'I'd known that it was you that tried to kill Les for ages Owen..'

'How?' I sked. I'd been half expecting him to say it, but I still needed to know.

'The surveillance footage for a start'

'But how did you know it was me?' There didn't seem to be any point in my denying it now. Not with everything else that had gone on between us since then.

'Quite a few things really but mostly the car and the crash helmet. The car was identified as a vehicle of interest as no-one seemed to own it and it had been lurking in the vicinity of Les' house for a month or two beforehand. But after the night of the attack, it vanished'

'I burned it' I said.

'I guessed as much. Anyway, unbeknownst to the rest of my colleagues, I'd seen that same car in an Estate Agent's photo on the drive of your house if you recall. I probably wouldn't have noticed it at all but for your terrible acting and suspicious behaviour. Coupled with the fact that I recognised the picture you'd had on your laptop that day, before closing it down so quickly, was enough to make me sure. I knew it was Les Guscom's house and I knew he wasn't selling.

'But the real clincher…' Skip was actually smiling now, obviously feeling a little smug about the fact that he'd worked out that it was me 'was the crash helmet. You could have gone and bought a new one Owen'

'Eh?' I said, dumbly.

'The crash helmet. It was black with a red stripe running through the centre; not exactly an everyday piece of headgear.'

'But how did you know it was mine?'

'Because there's a picture of you holding it under your arm on your kitchen sideboard.'

I felt like a complete idiot. It was true I realised. The picture was of Judy and me on a scooter and it had been taken probably twenty years ago and was now looking a little yellowed. It had been sat there on the sideboard for so long that I no longer even registered that it was there, let alone considered what anyone was wearing in it.

He could have gone on, I'm sure, about all the other little clues I'd inadvertently given out but thought I'd got away with. Like how I knew about Terry's murder or the six-inch nail before he'd ever told me, but there didn't really seem to be any point and so I interrupted him with;

'He killed Campsite Terry you know…'

'Who did? Les?'

'Yeah. I watched him do it in front of me and I was too pissed and too scared to do anything about it. After I'd sobered up and got myself straight, I decided that things needed to change. That I needed to make amends.'

'Ah, I see. Although I'd been sure that it *was* you Owen, I had no real idea what your motive was. I probably should have guessed it was something like that. Anyway, the point is, I had to give Griselda a name and as I was sure that it *was* you that had done the dirty deed I figured that at least if I fingered you it wouldn't be some other poor innocent bastard getting caught up in it.

'But it wasn't supposed to go as far as it did, mate. I was pretty sure that they'd kidnap you of course; they've been doing a lot of that lately; but I had a tracker on their van and I'd been following them from a distance anyway. As soon as I saw them take you, I'd planned on following them to their end destination before calling it in as a concerned citizen. That way some other copper would get the glory of nicking Griselda and her crew red handed and I would have been out of the loop entirely.

'Oh, I knew you'd get a few slaps along the way Owen, but I figured that you were tough enough to take it, and like I said, it seemed fairer that you be the one to get taken than some other complete innocent.'

I felt like I should have hated him but everything that Skip had said was true. One way or another, I had brought it all down upon my own head and for a change, there was no point in trying to blame it on anyone else. There was a time when I would have fallen out with him big time. I'd have probably sworn some kind of lifelong vendetta against him; but it seemed that old age was mellowing me and perhaps I'd changed. That and the fact that he was one of only two real friends I had in the world, made me forgive him instantly.

'So, what went wrong' I asked, with an edge of menace to my question, not willing to let him know that he was off the hook too soon.

But if he noticed it he didn't show.

'Fucking heap of shit car' he said. 'I'd been sitting in it for the previous two hours with the radio on and it must have drained the battery. It's been playing up for a while now and I tried to turn it over as soon as I saw them bundle you into the van and drive off, but there wasn't enough juice. In the end, I had to flag someone down and get a jump start. Good job I had the tracker up and running to see where they'd taken you.'

I didn't really need him to give me any more details; I'd already worked out most of it beforehand.

There was only one real reason why he would have known that I was in trouble down in that cellar and there was only one real reason why he would have known that I was there in the first place. But it had been important for me to hear it from him. If he'd lied or tried to cover up his culpability, I probably would have felt the need to balance the scales again, but the fact that he'd confessed everything somehow made it all OK, and, after a moment or two longer of trying to act grumpy, I told him so.

At that point, my breakfast arrived and at the same time a couple of lads in work clothes sat down at the table next to us which effectively put an end to any further serious discussion. I was happy to let Skip chatter on as I busily shovelled fork-loads of delicious fried food into my face. We both ordered another cup of tea after I'd finished and chatted away for another twenty minutes as though nothing had ever happened, before mutually agreeing that it was time to get up and go.

But once we got outside I found out that Skip wasn't quite finished. I'd been pretty sure that everything that could be said *had* been said, until he asked me to jump into the passenger of his car to discuss something else.

His ageing BMW truly was a great representation of the man that drove it. At fifteen years old, beneath a layer of dirt, the blue paintwork was faded and dull and the interior was testament to how much time he must have spent in it, watching and waiting, as old till receipts and empty drinks cans littered the floor.

'So, tell me Owen' he said after he'd turned the engine over in order to turn on the heaters 'do you have any regrets?'

I'm not sure what I'd thought he wanted to talk about, but it hadn't been that and I looked back at him dumbly for a moment.

'Killing Les' he continued by way of explanation, 'do you regret it? I mean, if you had your time all over again, do you think that you would still kill him?'

It was something I'd spent plenty of time mulling over and despite the horrific consequences and the toll it had taken on me both physically and mentally, the answer I came back to was always the same.

'Yes,' I said, without any hesitation. 'In the first instance, Les killed Terry, and he deserved to die for that. Secondly, you may not know what it was that I saw on the video in that farmhouse, but from the look on your face that day, I'm guessing that you had a pretty good idea, and whilst I don't normally care too much about what consenting adults do to each other, I draw the line at molesting kiddies. As far as I'm concerned, nobody has the right to carry on living after doing what I saw on that laptop.'

We both sat there in Skip's car looking dead ahead out of a misting windscreen, but in the periphery of my vision, I saw Skip nodding slowly in agreement.

'We never talked about what we saw in that house before, Owen, because we never needed to. Well; not before now anyway. When I went upstairs there were two more rooms like the one you saw downstairs. With cameras and lighting set up and little stacks of DVDs. I took a look at a couple of them before deciding to go back down and put an end to that piece of scum once and for all. The only thing was, you beat me to it.

'They'd had kids chained up in that cellar; some of them for long periods of time; boys and girls who'd been kept for the sole purpose of renting them out to highest bidders to be raped. When we left and set fire to the house we didn't just destroy our crime scene, we destroyed theirs too.

'But you might remember that I'd carried a holdall out of the farmhouse that day. Before we left I went through each of Griselda's crew's pockets and took their mobile phones and anything else which might have been useful. I also took away three laptops and all the DVDs I could find. I couldn't turn it over to the police, of course, but I have a friend who used to work for the security services and he knows a thing or two about electronics. Between us, we've managed to piece together quite a lot of the story. We seemed to have stumbled across the link of a long chain which involves professional child snatchers.'

I looked sharply across at Skip in askance.

'I know. It's grim isn't it, but there are actually people out there who make a living out of stealing children and selling them on. Mostly it's Asian and Eastern European kids, but there's also a market for British kids who actually fetch more money. Who knows, maybe the perverts like it better when they can understand their pleas for help. Anyway, at the other end of the chain, there's an organised network of sickos willing to pay, either for the privilege of raping them, or for the footage of their misery.'

'Why now?' I asked.

'Eh?'

'You said that we never needed to talk about what we'd seen in the farmhouse before but now we do. Why do we need to talk about this now?'

'Because from the information we got from the laptops and phone records, I now know who the main players are at the UK end of this sick chain. Being as I can hardly take any of what I have to my colleagues in the police, there seems to be only one course of action left open. These perverts can't be allowed to carry on Owen; I want them dead and I can't think of anyone else better suited to the job of making it happen.

'The only question left then Owen; is are you in, or are you out?'

The End

About the Author

Owen Pitt is the soon to be the best-selling author of Six Inch Nail (it must be true, his mum told him so….) the rollercoaster tale of a vigilante sociopath from Essex.

When he's not writing the best books ever to grace the bookshelves, Owen works as a Financial Controller for a company in Essex.

Born in the 1960s, Owen left school at 16 to become a trainee manager at Presto Supermarket on the Roman Road in Bow.

Since then, Owen has served in both the French Foreign Legion and the British Army, has picked tomatoes in the Negev desert, carried bricks up and down ladders and sold vaccum cleaners to American soldiers in Germany. He's also worked as an Estate Agent, a money broker and a Financial Adviser (and too many other things to bore you with here).

Owen lives with his first wife, his beautiful two daughters and his malodorous dog, Bonzo.

When he's not working or writing, Owen likes to try out new experiences and his past-times which have included, at one time or another, Morris Dancing, Judo, Badminton, playing the guitar and playing rugby (of which he still takes a run out from time to time), but mostly just going up the pub.

Read more at www.owenpitt.co.uk

A message from the Author, Owen (Pitt, not Thomson)

I do hope that you enjoyed reading Six Inch Nail. For my part, writing it has certainly proved to be an epic journey. At once both relaxing and stressful; a pain and a pleasure.

I've started on a sequel to this story which I hope to publish in the coming year, but only if there seems to be a demand for it (otherwise I might as well leave it a cupboard for the grandchildren to laugh at).

So…. If you've enjoyed reading this book, **please, please, please, please**, post a short, written review in as many places as you can find to do so, (there are lots of them, just search under book review sites), even if it's only a few words or a basic star rating.

As an independently published author, it's the only possible way for me to let other people know about my story.

On a final note, thank you, thank you, and thank you again, for all the great reviews which I hope you'll post now (big smiley face).

Owen Pitt
http://www.owenpitt.co.uk/